Cici's
journal

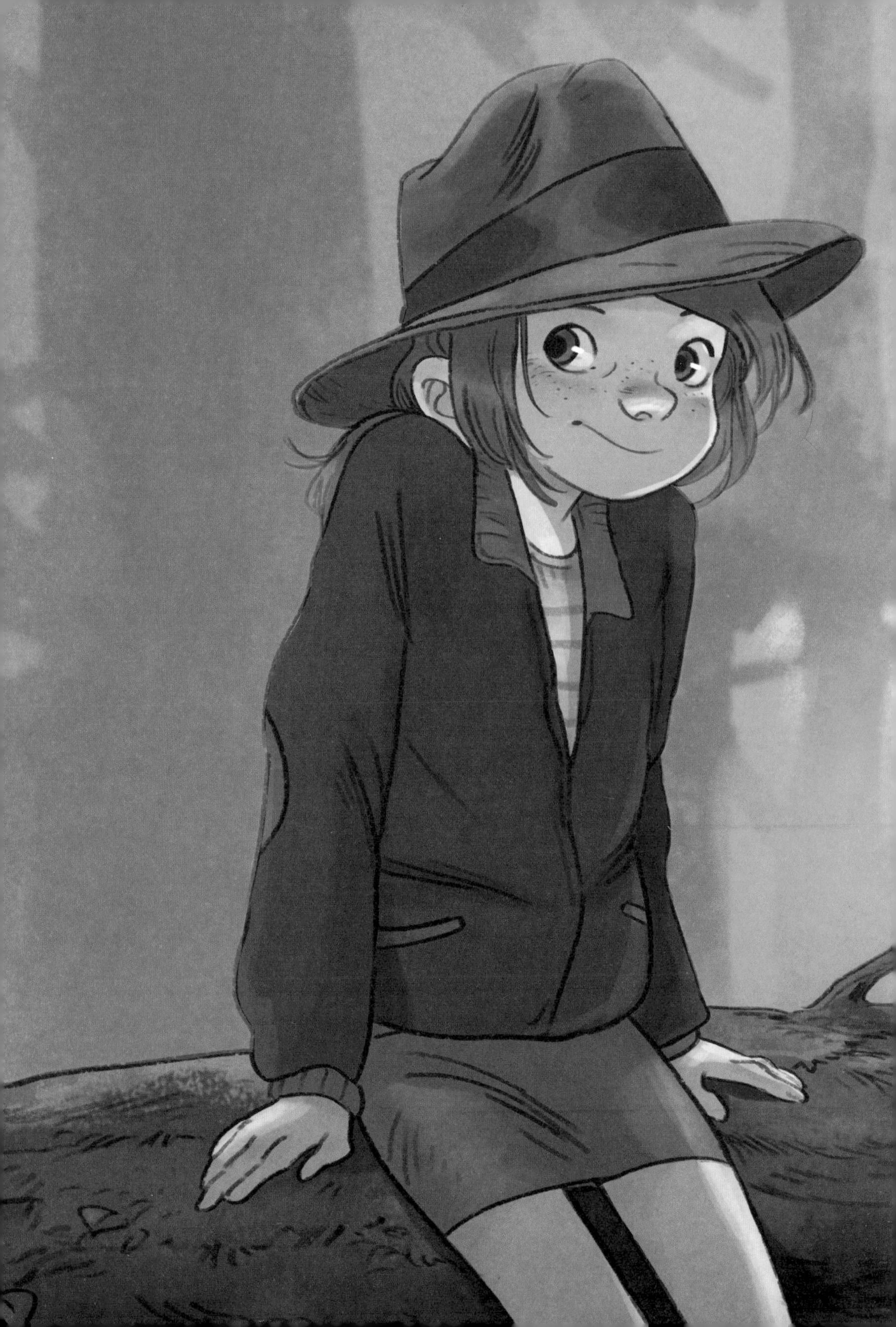

Cici's journal

Joris Chamblain
Aurélie Neyret

:01
First Second
New York

For Part One...

I thank my parents and my friends for their generous and motivating support.

Thank you to Joris for seeing the potential for Cici in my pencil and helping put so much love into it.
Thank you to Barbara and Clotilde for making this adventure possible and coming along with us during this long undertaking. And, finally, thank you to my Nico for his support every day and his help beyond worth.

Aurélie

Life is a road on which we hold each other's hand.
Huge thanks:
—to my parents and my sisters for having accompanied me on my first steps with love, without ever putting the least obstacle in the way of my dreams.
—to Christophe A., who, though he doesn't know it, showed me the way I wanted to take, and to Stéphane B. for having corrected my first steps on the walk, my new path.
—to Nicolas M. for showing me the secret to always walking right. I will never forget. And to Djilali D. for making sure I never stepped off the road. I know what's waiting for me if that happens!
—to Aurélie N., Barbara C., and Clotilde V. for crossing my path and joining me for this part of the journey, this lovely adventure. I hope we'll be together a long way!
—to you, dear reader, for pausing on your route to discover our side path.

—and, finally, thank you, Marjorie C., for joining my path and walking at my side, brightening our way onward.

Joris

For Part Two...

In memory of Aimé, my grandfather.
Thank you to my friends and family for their unstinting support.
Thanks also to Clotilde, Barbara, and Adeline for believing in us and for all their involvement.
Finally, special thanks to Nico, without whom this book would not be what it is, for many reasons.

Aurélie

I dedicate this book:
—to my grandparents, who Cici did not have the chance to know. I hope that wherever you are, they have good bookstores.

—to the little hidden message that slept for fifty years in a treasure chest, before a little boy could discover it...

Joris

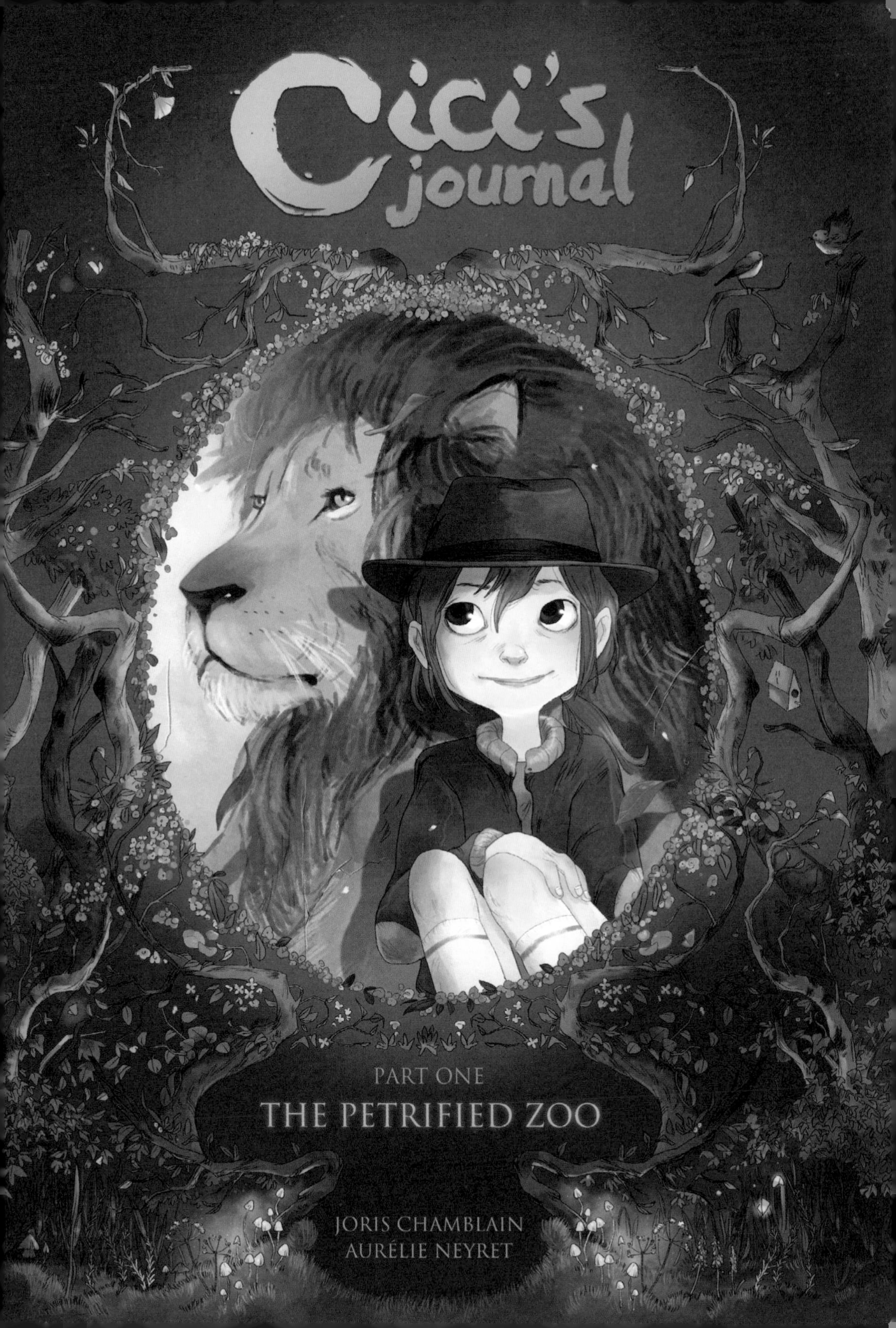
Cici's journal
PART ONE
THE PETRIFIED ZOO
JORIS CHAMBLAIN
AURÉLIE NEYRET

Once upon a time...

When I was little, I promised myself that if I ever had a secret journal, it would start just like that.

I love to read stories, and my favorites all begin with "Once upon a time..."

So Once upon a time ... there was me, Cici!

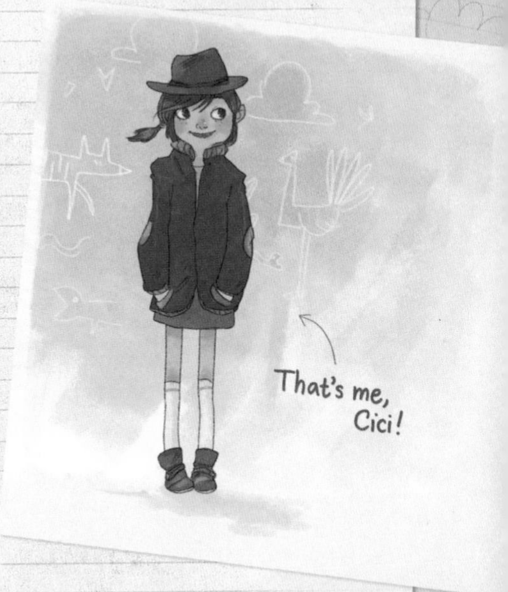
That's me, Cici!

I'm ten and a half years old, and my dream is to become an author. I love to write. And I love to read novels, comics, and science magazines. My mother always tells me that a good vocabulary is the best weapon in life. I didn't used to understand why. Now I do. When you read you discover things and travel places, but you also learn the meanings of words and how to use them. It's very important to understand things, and to pay attention to what we are told.

My trick for telling stories is to observe people, to imagine their lives, their secrets. We all have a secret inside us, something we never talk about. Something that makes us who we are.

So when I meet people I always try to dig out that "thing." I've been doing that since I was little. I don't even know why anymore. I think it helps me understand them better.

Right now, my friends and I are observing someone really mysterious.

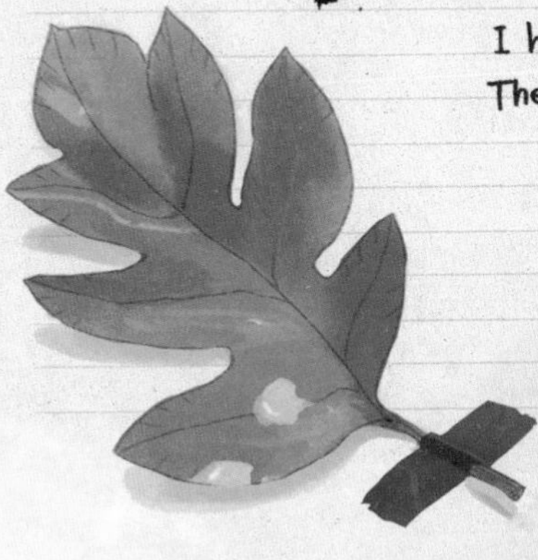

I hope we finally figure out his secret. Then I could tell his whole story. I already have the first line!

It'll start like this:

"Once upon a time..."

Go, Detective Cici!!!

~~Once upon a time,~~
a ~~little~~ girl who ~~was~~

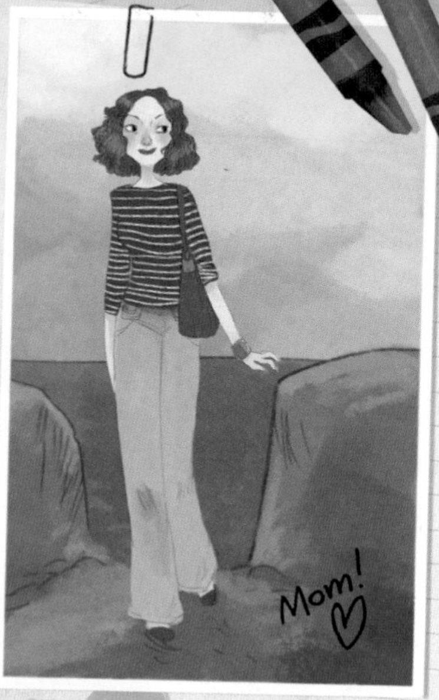
Mom!

Now that I've started my story, I should be a good author and introduce my characters.

And who else could I start with but this lady? My mom!

I live with her in a big house in the country that she inherited from her great uncle, or something like that, I'm not totally sure.

MOM

She bought me this journal. She told me: "If you want to be an author, you have to write! And a personal journal is a good start." That's my mom!

She doesn't love it that I hang out so much with Mrs. Flores, our neighbor. She wants me to play more with girls my own age. But, even so, she doesn't prevent me from believing in my dream to be an author, and this journal is how she's helping me get there!

She isn't up to date on all my little investigations into people's lives. I don't think she'd be so happy about those. Of course, I've never asked her...

We don't always get along, but I love her anyway— she's my mom! One day I'll write a book just for her. In it, I'll finally tell her what I have never really managed to tell her: thanks.

There are all sorts of little words like that. Words that aren't easy to say, that stay stuck at the bottom of my throat.

Does my mom have her own words that refuse to come out?

my friends!

↓ ↓ ♡ ↙

Lena and Erica,

my friends for life.

I always think of them as a pair.
They just belong together. Sometimes I get
a little jealous of how close they are...

We've all known each other since we were really little.
Well, since I moved to town. Lena and Erica have
known each other since they knew how to walk.

Lena is the sweetest ever. She has a sharp eye
and the soul of an artist. Someday she's going to be
a famous photographer. Plus she's going to be an
auntie soon, since her sister is expecting a baby.
Lena can't wait to take tons of pictures of that
baby! In the meantime, she's practicing on her
little brother!

I love how easygoing and open she is. She says what
she thinks, but she never makes fun of people. Sometimes
I wish I were a little more like her...

Erica is the complete opposite of Lena. She complains
constantly, but she has a good heart. She has four big
brothers, so she knows how to defend herself! I don't even
notice her complaining anymore, it's just
part of her. Respect and honesty
are important to her parents
and for their kids too. So Erica
hates it when things don't line up.
Complaining is how she questions
things, to try to shake things up,
to make them better. And I
respect her for that.

Lena, ♡ ☆ Erica,

you're my
best friends!

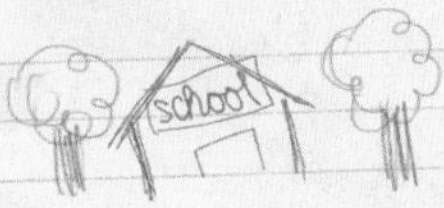
school

I met Mrs. Flores for the first time at school. She was doing a reading. It's really cool, having a famous writer living in our own town. She did some writing exercises with us, and I had a lot of fun.

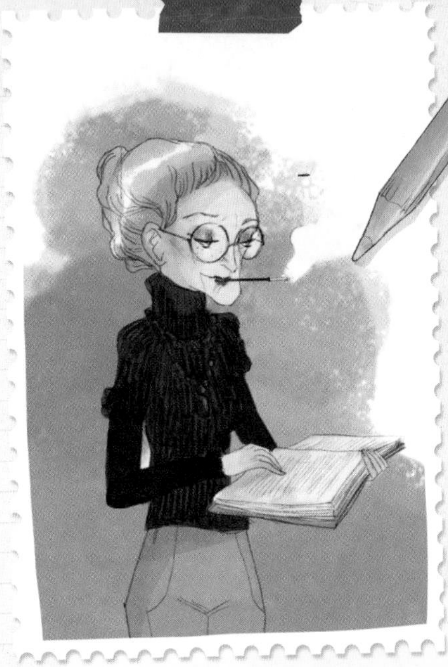

Annabelle Flores

After meeting her that day,
I knew that I wanted to write books too.

We became friends, and now I spend a lot of time with her, learning more about writing and asking lots of questions...even if my mom isn't always happy about that. Sometimes I have to visit her in secret!

But as I write this, I realize I really don't know a lot about her. Mrs. Flores lives in a huge mansion, all alone. Does she have a husband? Kids? I wouldn't dare ask her. I'm not sure how she'd react... She keeps her distance, and she doesn't get a lot of visitors. But she doesn't seem unhappy about it.

On the other hand, she knows a lot of things about me. I think she can read me like an open book! Sometimes it's embarrassing that I can't hide anything from her! Even when I don't say a thing, she understands what I'm feeling.

I wish I could do that. Maybe you get that power when you grow up...

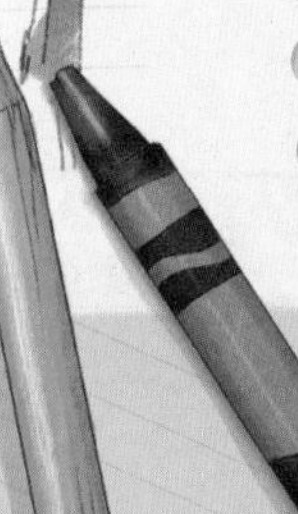
??

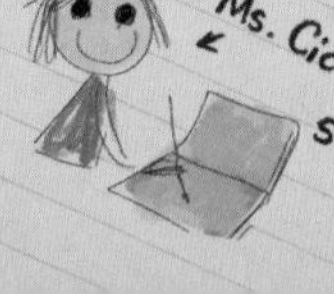
Someday
when I'm
big...
Ms. Cici,
super-amazing writer

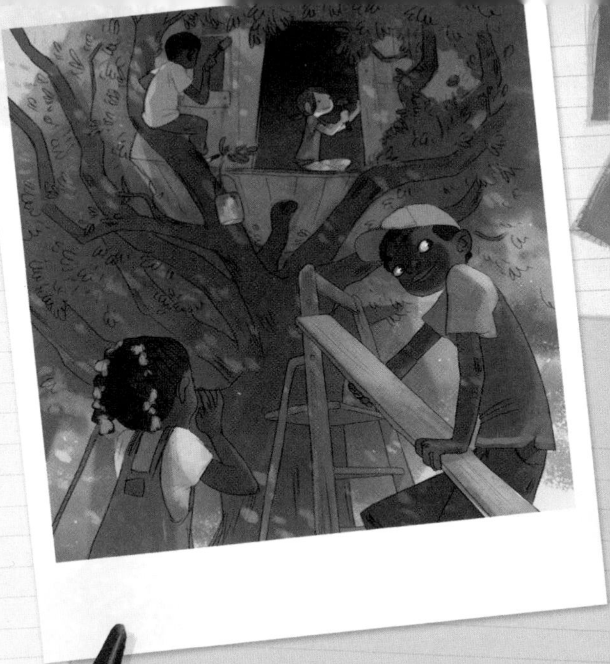

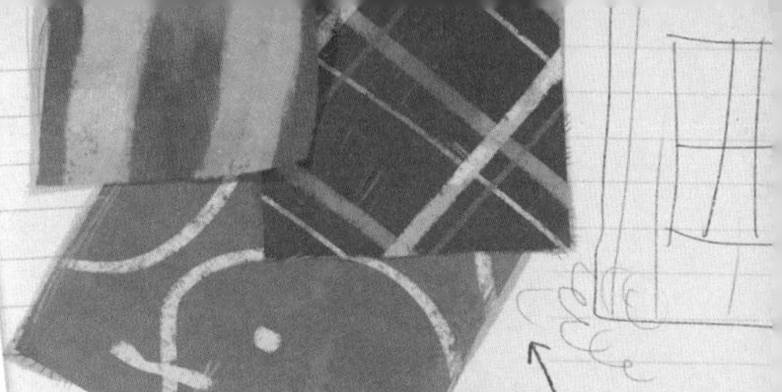

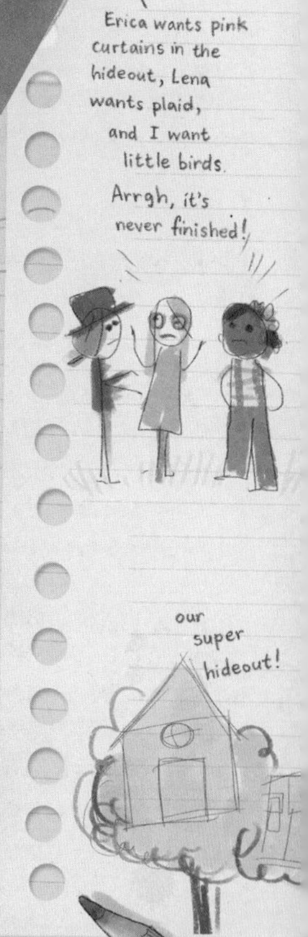
Erica wants pink curtains in the hideout, Lena wants plaid, and I want little birds.
Arrgh, it's never finished!
our super hideout!

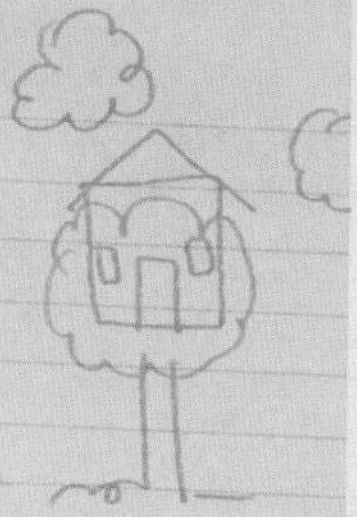

Before a writer starts the plot,
you have to set the scene.

My friends and I have a great spot
for adventures:

our secret hideout!

Erica's brothers helped us build it,
and they found some old furniture
in the trash.

It's kind of goofy.

We just can't agree on the curtains.

But I'm sure we'll figure it out.

We were up in the hideout when we discovered
Mr. Mysterious for the first time.

I have to tell you about this guy!

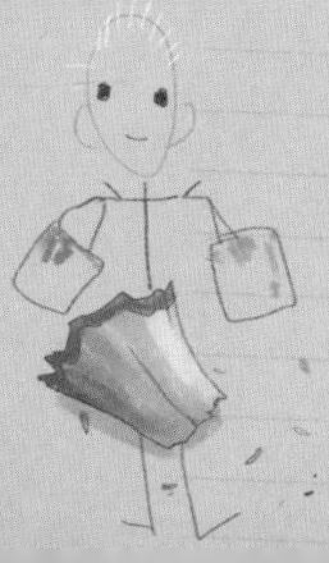

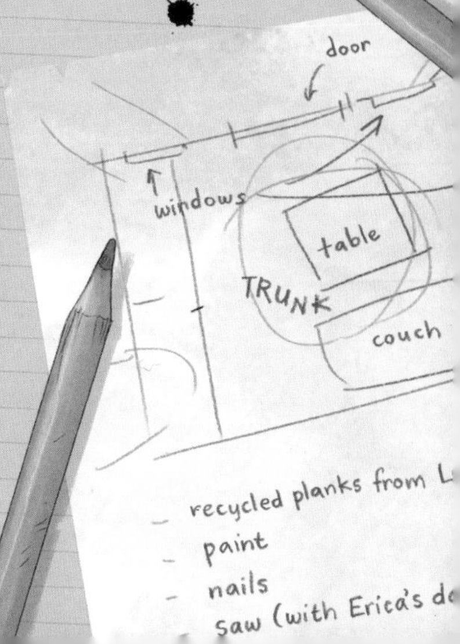
door
windows
table
TRUNK
couch
- recycled planks from L
- paint
- nails
- saw (with Erica's d

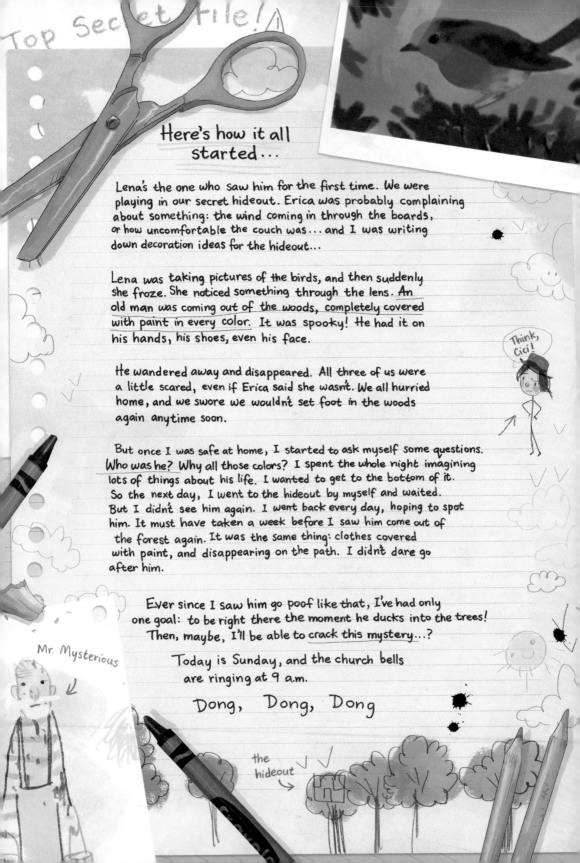

Here's how it all started...

Lena's the one who saw him for the first time. We were playing in our secret hideout. Erica was probably complaining about something: the wind coming in through the boards, or how uncomfortable the couch was... and I was writing down decoration ideas for the hideout...

Lena was taking pictures of the birds, and then suddenly she froze. She noticed something through the lens. An old man was coming out of the woods, completely covered with paint in every color. It was spooky! He had it on his hands, his shoes, even his face.

He wandered away and disappeared. All three of us were a little scared, even if Erica said she wasn't. We all hurried home, and we swore we wouldn't set foot in the woods again anytime soon.

But once I was safe at home, I started to ask myself some questions. Who was he? Why all those colors? I spent the whole night imagining lots of things about his life. I wanted to get to the bottom of it. So the next day, I went to the hideout by myself and waited. But I didn't see him again. I went back every day, hoping to spot him. It must have taken a week before I saw him come out of the forest again. It was the same thing: clothes covered with paint, and disappearing on the path. I didn't dare go after him.

Ever since I saw him go poof like that, I've had only one goal: to be right there the moment he ducks into the trees! Then, maybe, I'll be able to crack this mystery...?

Today is Sunday, and the church bells are ringing at 9 a.m.

Dong, Dong, Dong

Think, Cici!

Mr. Mysterious

the hideout

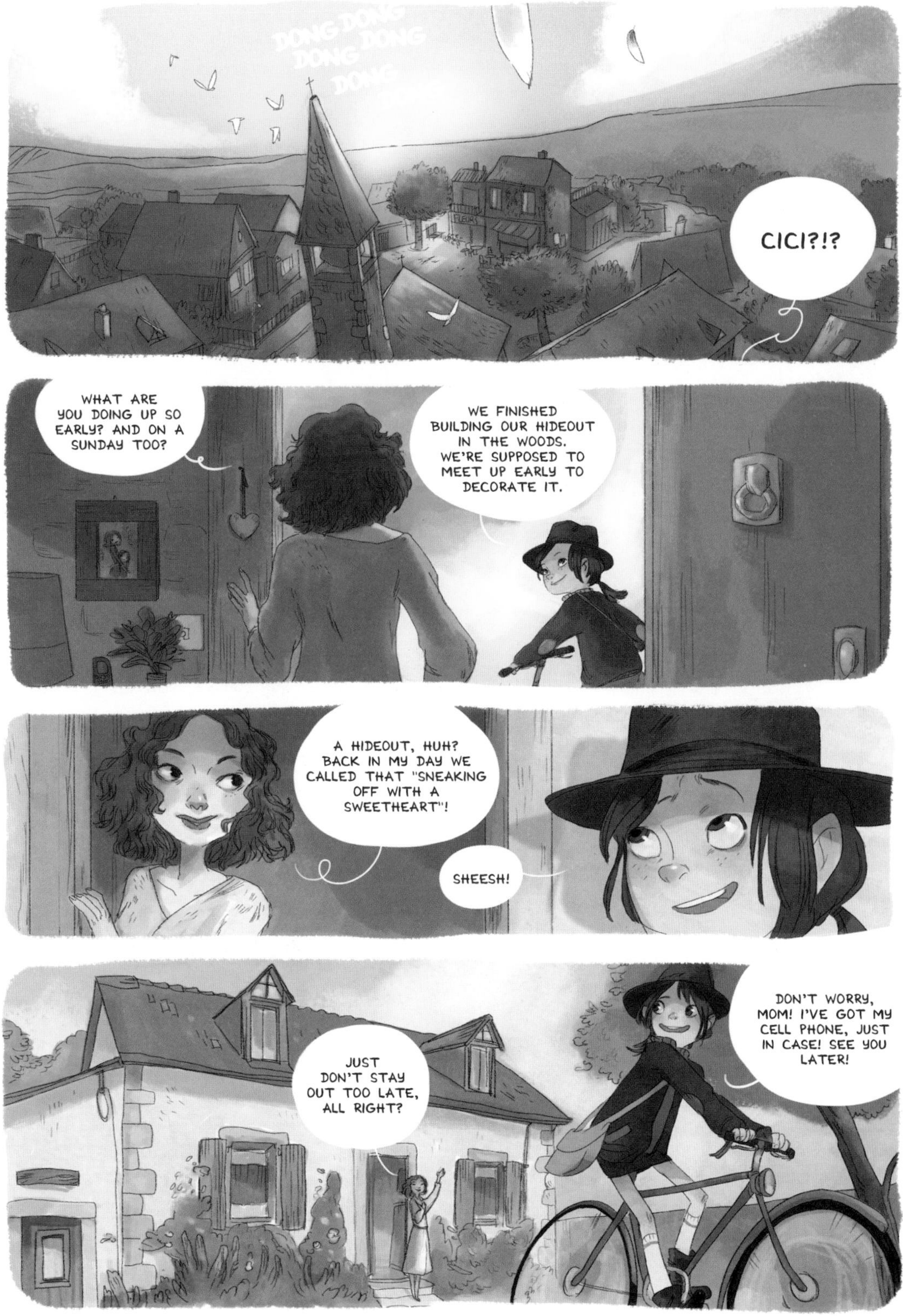
DONG DONG DONG DONG DONG
CICI?!?
WHAT ARE YOU DOING UP SO EARLY? AND ON A SUNDAY TOO?
WE FINISHED BUILDING OUR HIDEOUT IN THE WOODS. WE'RE SUPPOSED TO MEET UP EARLY TO DECORATE IT.
A HIDEOUT, HUH? BACK IN MY DAY WE CALLED THAT "SNEAKING OFF WITH A SWEETHEART"!
SHEESH!
JUST DON'T STAY OUT TOO LATE, ALL RIGHT?
DON'T WORRY, MOM! I'VE GOT MY CELL PHONE, JUST IN CASE! SEE YOU LATER!

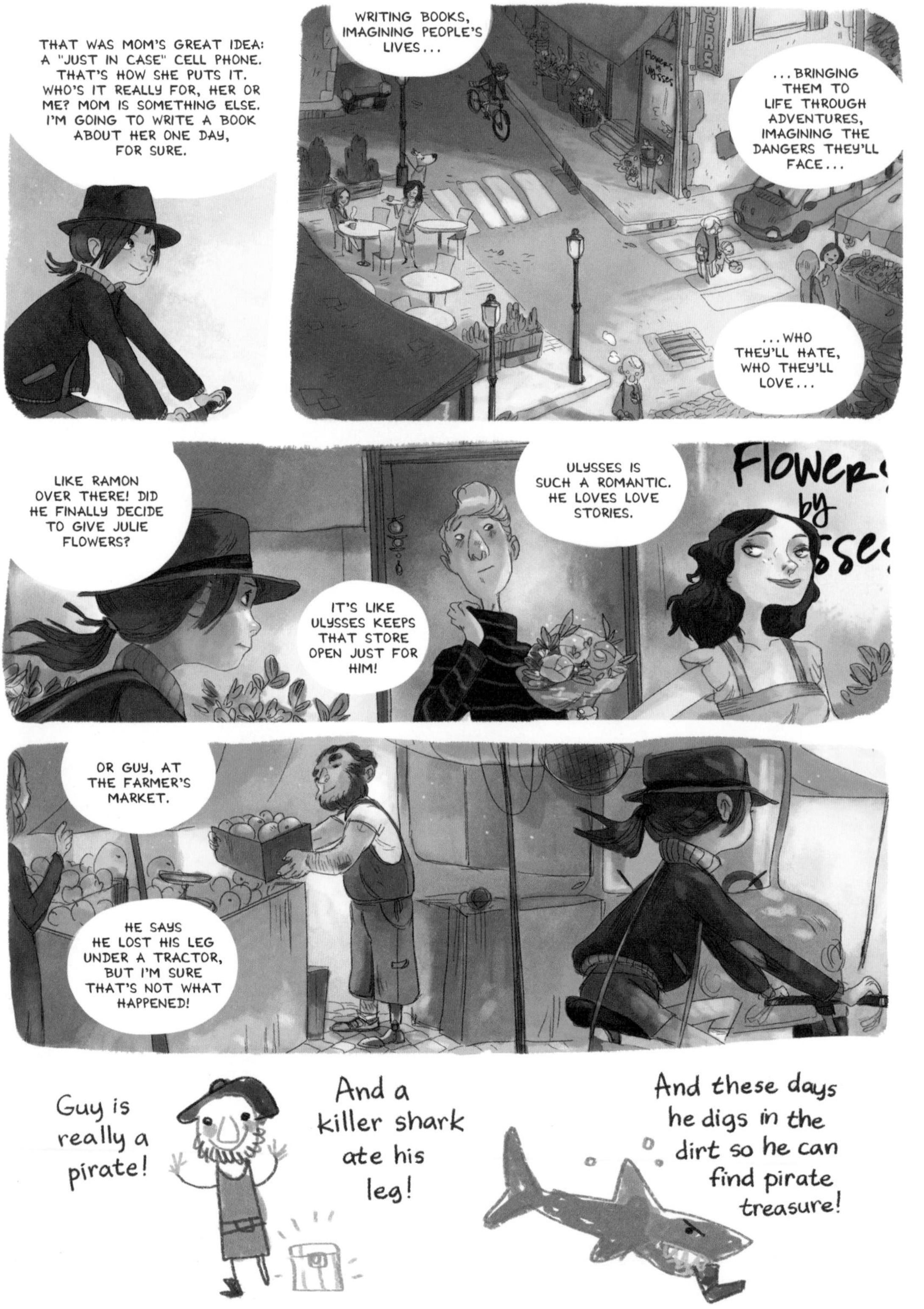
THAT WAS MOM'S GREAT IDEA: A "JUST IN CASE" CELL PHONE. THAT'S HOW SHE PUTS IT. WHO'S IT REALLY FOR, HER OR ME? MOM IS SOMETHING ELSE. I'M GOING TO WRITE A BOOK ABOUT HER ONE DAY, FOR SURE.
WRITING BOOKS, IMAGINING PEOPLE'S LIVES...
...BRINGING THEM TO LIFE THROUGH ADVENTURES, IMAGINING THE DANGERS THEY'LL FACE...
...WHO THEY'LL HATE, WHO THEY'LL LOVE...
LIKE RAMON OVER THERE! DID HE FINALLY DECIDE TO GIVE JULIE FLOWERS?
IT'S LIKE ULYSSES KEEPS THAT STORE OPEN JUST FOR HIM!
ULYSSES IS SUCH A ROMANTIC. HE LOVES LOVE STORIES.
OR GUY, AT THE FARMER'S MARKET.
HE SAYS HE LOST HIS LEG UNDER A TRACTOR, BUT I'M SURE THAT'S NOT WHAT HAPPENED!
Guy is really a pirate!
And a killer shark ate his leg!
And these days he digs in the dirt so he can find pirate treasure!

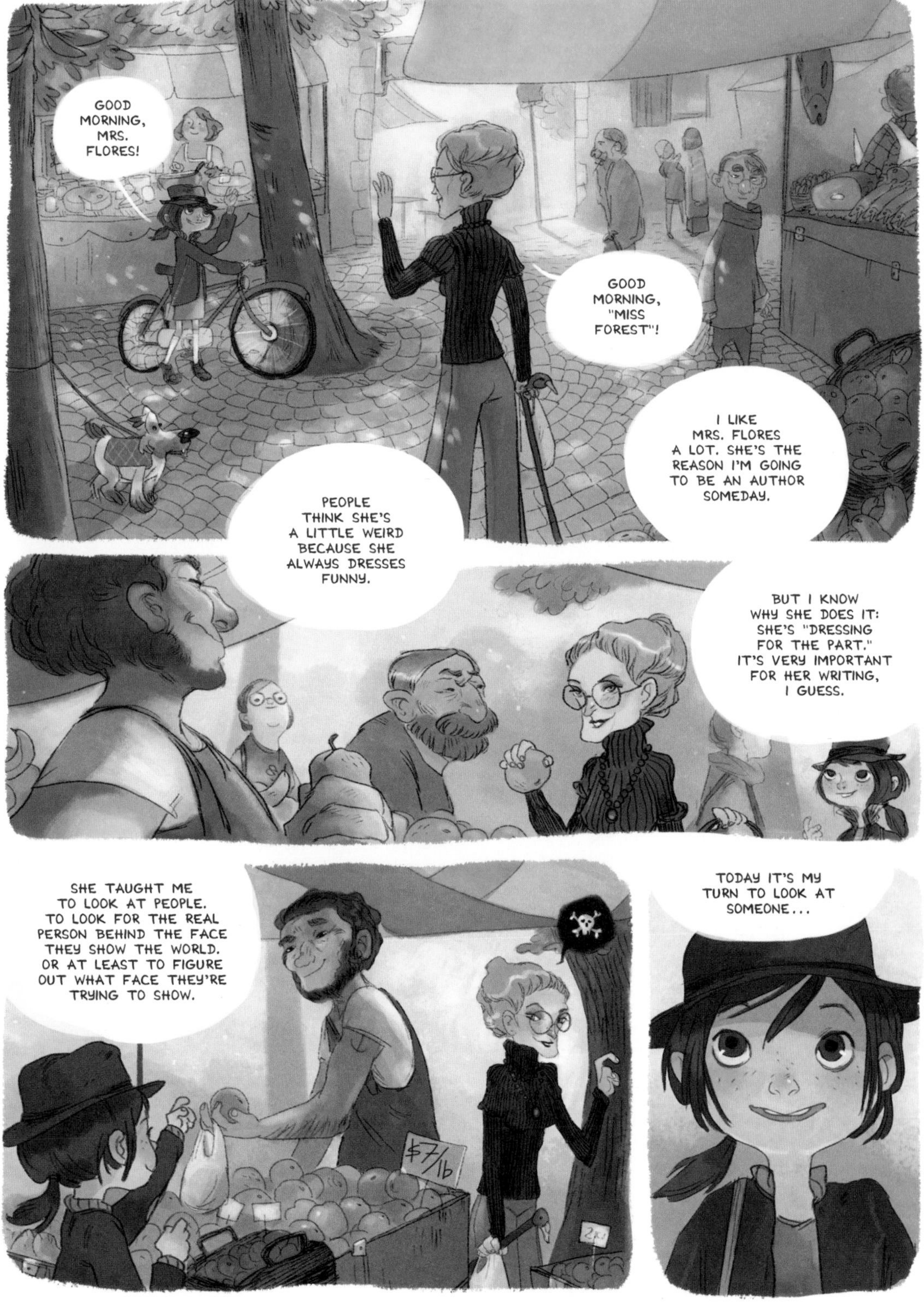
GOOD MORNING, MRS. FLORES!
GOOD MORNING, "MISS FOREST"!
I LIKE MRS. FLORES A LOT. SHE'S THE REASON I'M GOING TO BE AN AUTHOR SOMEDAY.
PEOPLE THINK SHE'S A LITTLE WEIRD BECAUSE SHE ALWAYS DRESSES FUNNY.
BUT I KNOW WHY SHE DOES IT: SHE'S "DRESSING FOR THE PART." IT'S VERY IMPORTANT FOR HER WRITING, I GUESS.
SHE TAUGHT ME TO LOOK AT PEOPLE. TO LOOK FOR THE REAL PERSON BEHIND THE FACE THEY SHOW THE WORLD. OR AT LEAST TO FIGURE OUT WHAT FACE THEY'RE TRYING TO SHOW.
$7/lb
TODAY IT'S MY TURN TO LOOK AT SOMEONE...

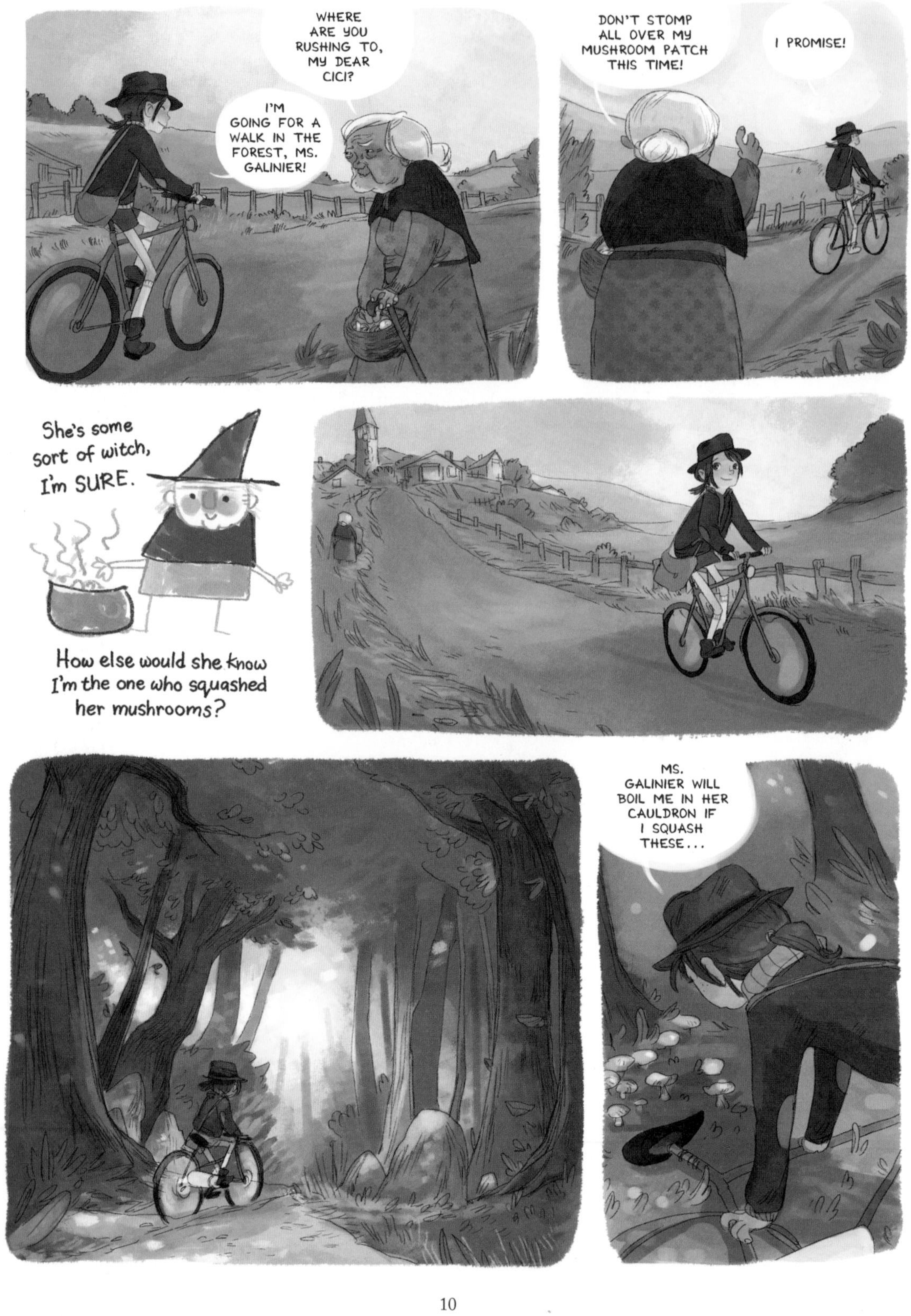
WHERE ARE YOU RUSHING TO, MY DEAR CICI?
I'M GOING FOR A WALK IN THE FOREST, MS. GALINIER!
DON'T STOMP ALL OVER MY MUSHROOM PATCH THIS TIME!
I PROMISE!
She's some sort of witch, I'm SURE.
How else would she know I'm the one who squashed her mushrooms?
MS. GALINIER WILL BOIL ME IN HER CAULDRON IF I SQUASH THESE...

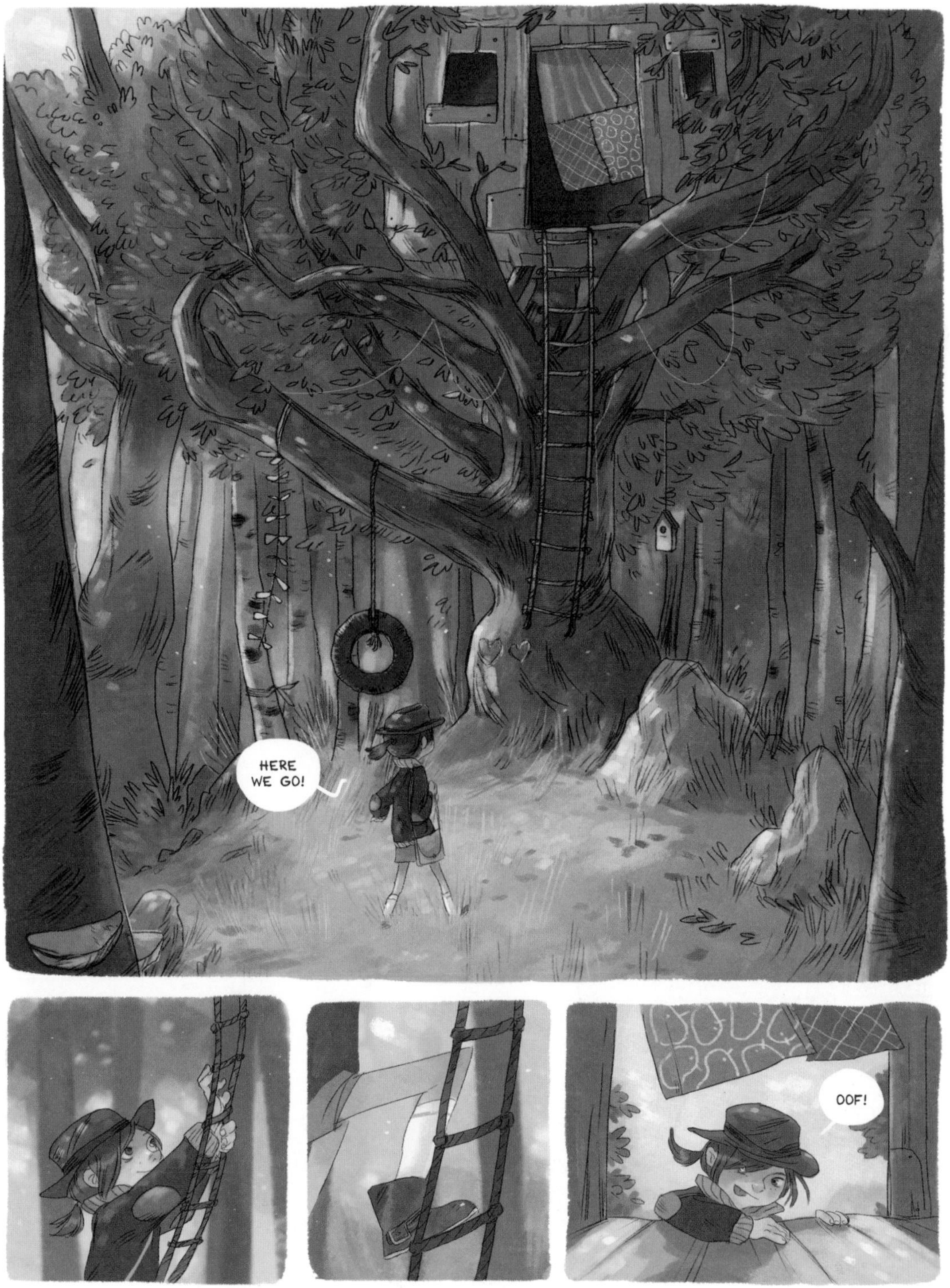
HERE WE GO!
OOF!

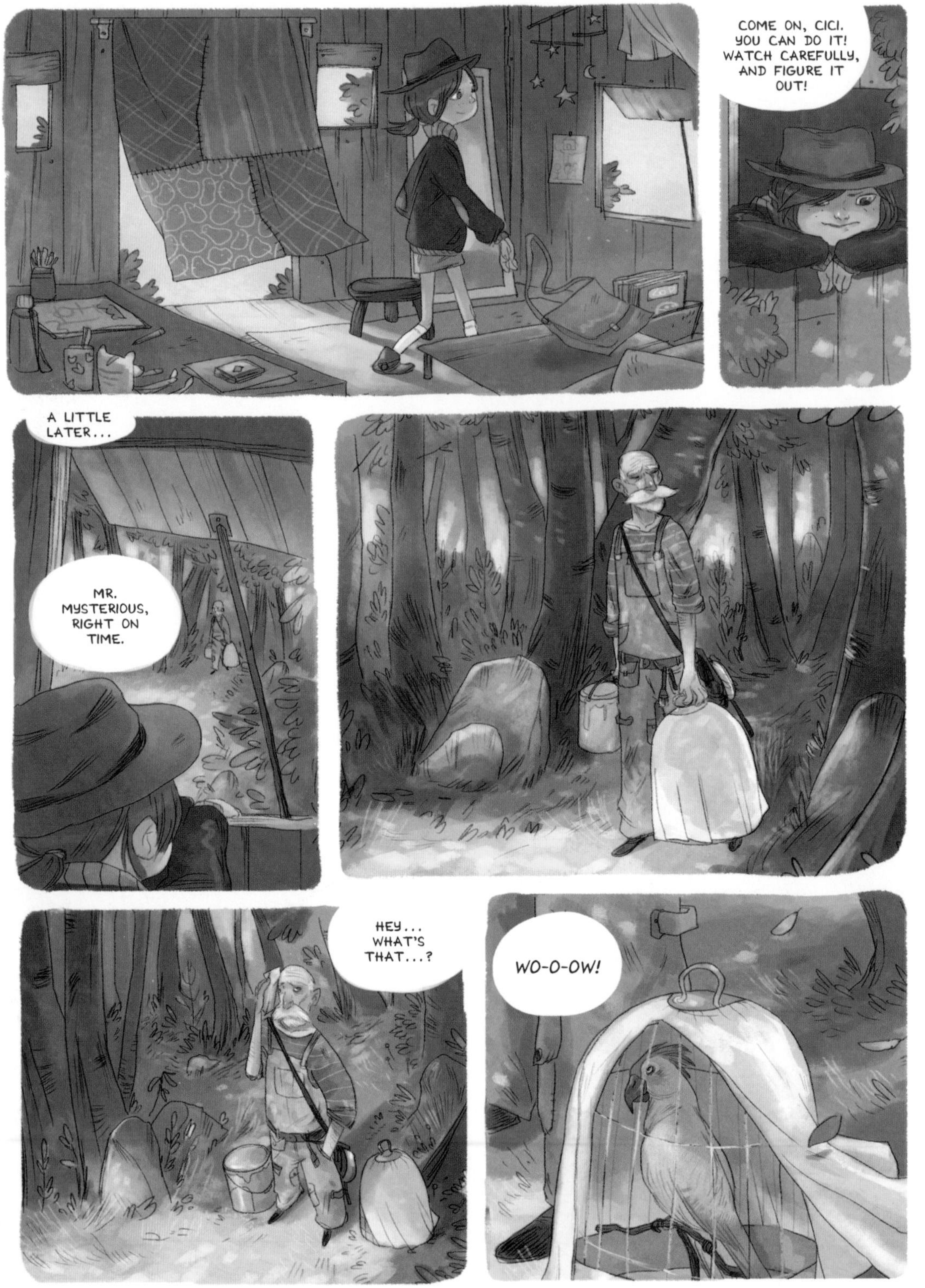
COME ON, CICI. YOU CAN DO IT! WATCH CAREFULLY, AND FIGURE IT OUT!
A LITTLE LATER...
MR. MYSTERIOUS, RIGHT ON TIME.
HEY... WHAT'S THAT...?
WO-O-OW!

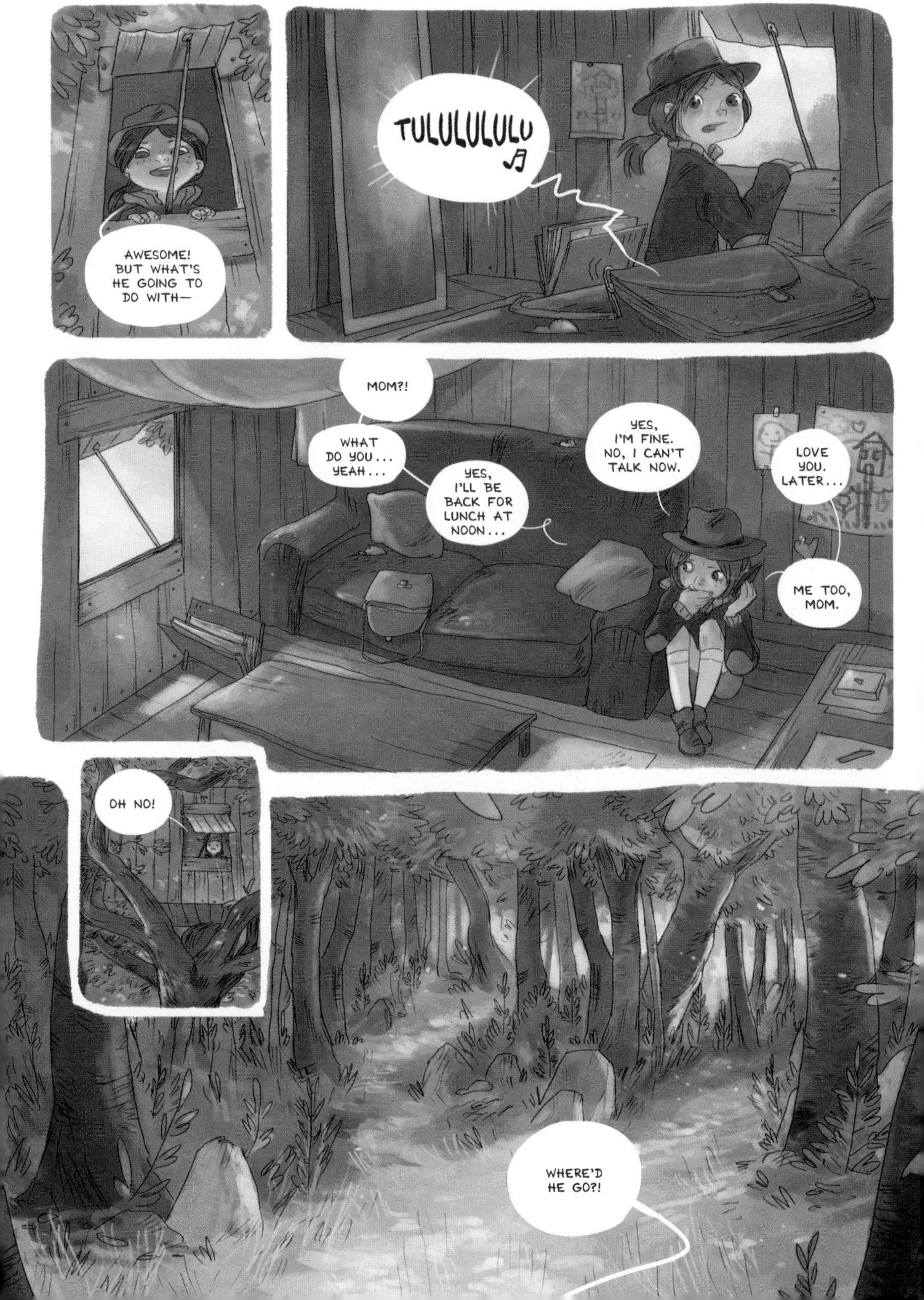
AWESOME! BUT WHAT'S HE GOING TO DO WITH—
TULULULULU
MOM?!
WHAT DO YOU... YEAH...
YES, I'LL BE BACK FOR LUNCH AT NOON...
YES, I'M FINE. NO, I CAN'T TALK NOW.
LOVE YOU. LATER...
ME TOO, MOM.
OH NO!
WHERE'D HE GO?!

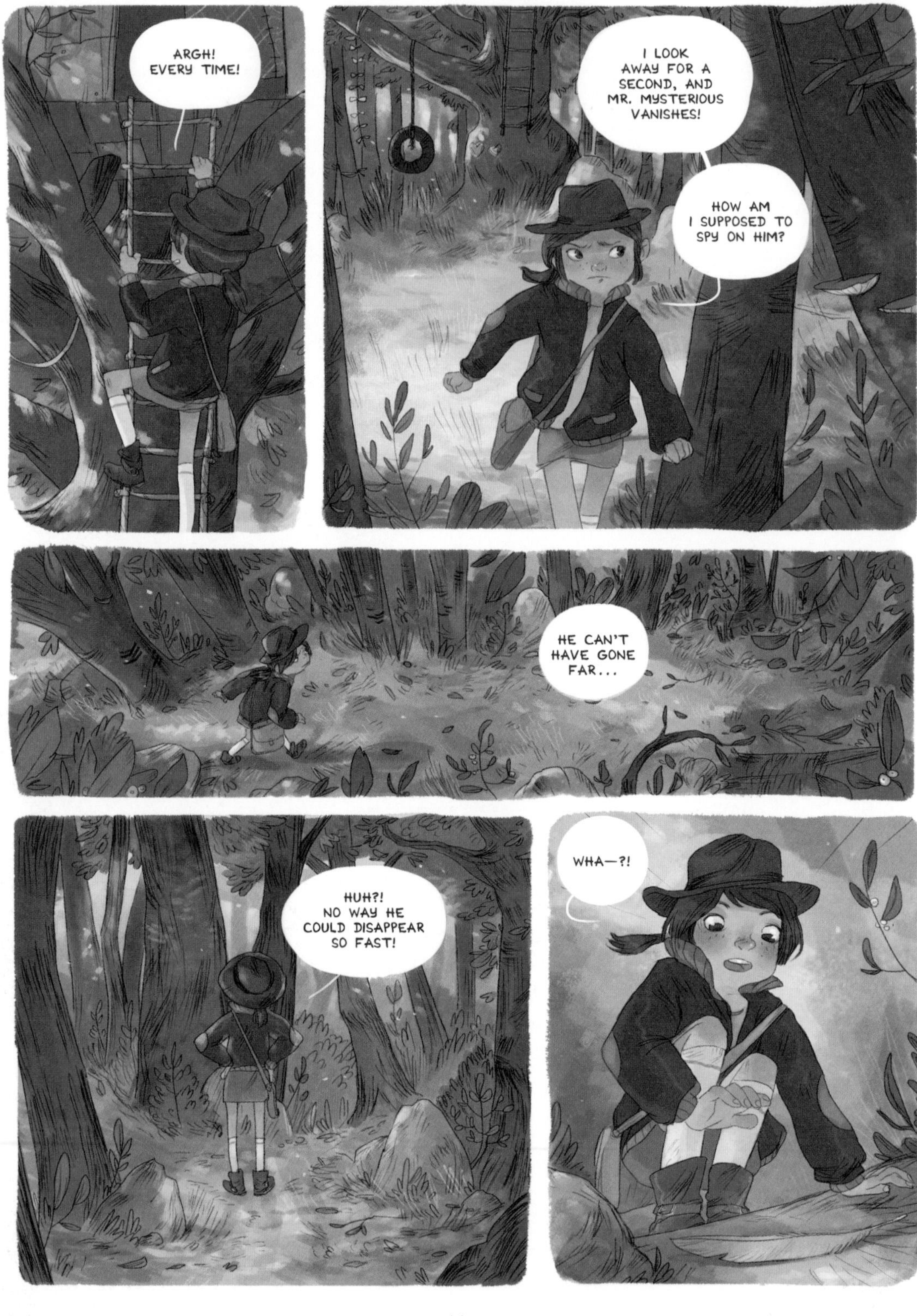
ARGH! EVERY TIME!
I LOOK AWAY FOR A SECOND, AND MR. MYSTERIOUS VANISHES!
HOW AM I SUPPOSED TO SPY ON HIM?
HE CAN'T HAVE GONE FAR...
HUH?! NO WAY HE COULD DISAPPEAR SO FAST!
WHA—?!

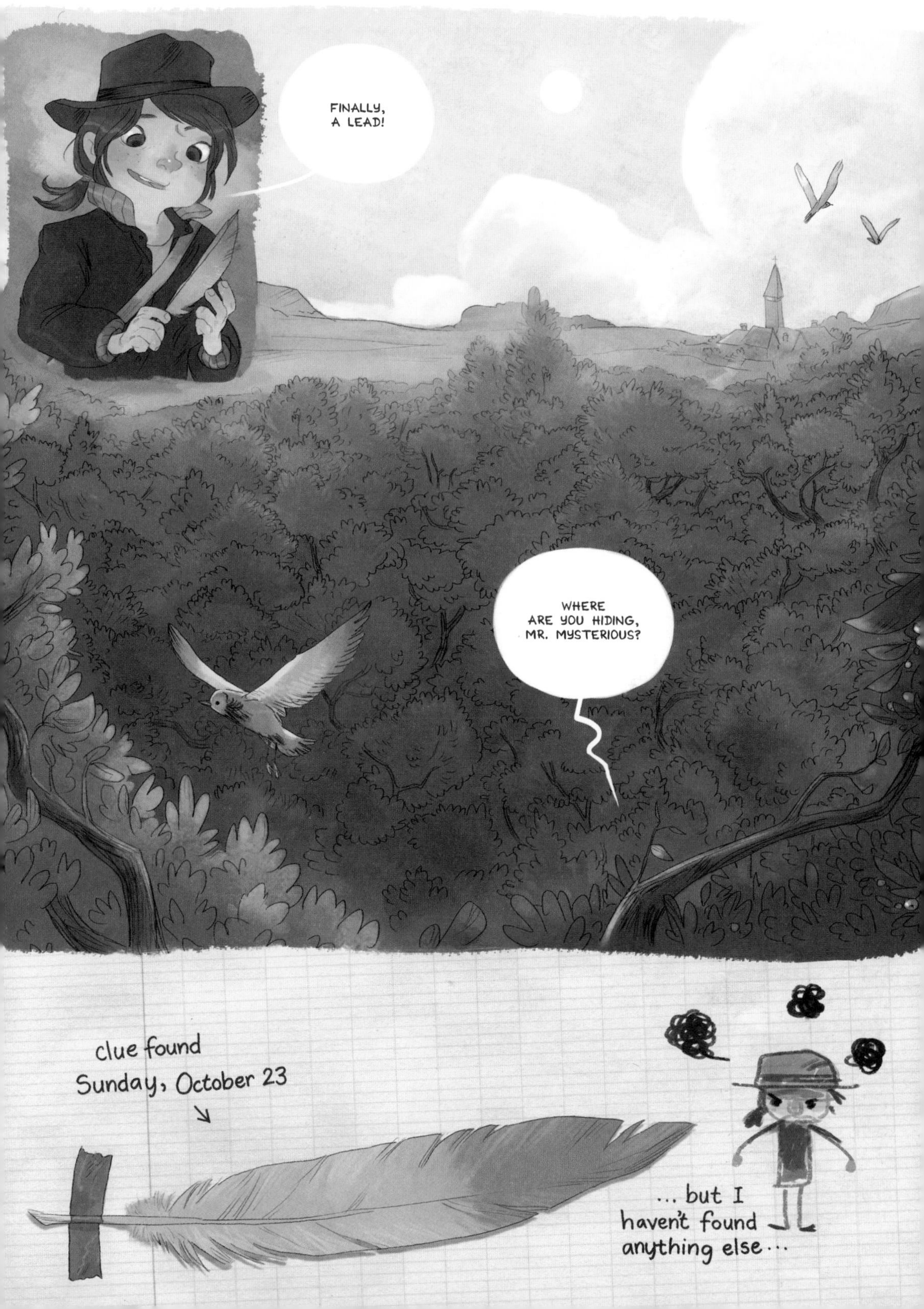
FINALLY, A LEAD!
WHERE ARE YOU HIDING, MR. MYSTERIOUS?
clue found
Sunday, October 23
... but I haven't found anything else...

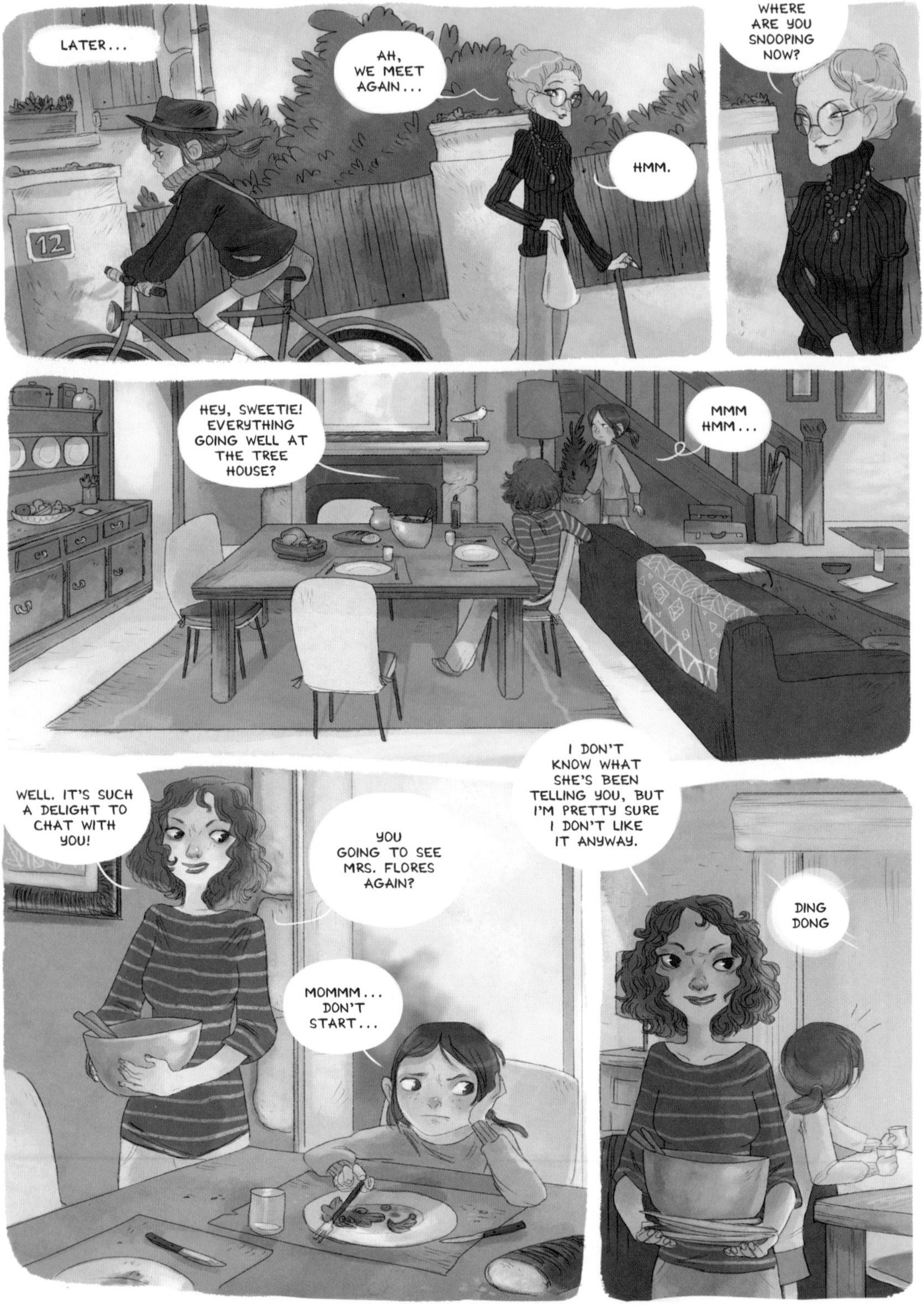
LATER...
AH, WE MEET AGAIN...
HMM.
WHERE ARE YOU SNOOPING NOW?
HEY, SWEETIE! EVERYTHING GOING WELL AT THE TREE HOUSE?
MMM HMM...
WELL. IT'S SUCH A DELIGHT TO CHAT WITH YOU!
YOU GOING TO SEE MRS. FLORES AGAIN?
MOMMM... DON'T START...
I DON'T KNOW WHAT SHE'S BEEN TELLING YOU, BUT I'M PRETTY SURE I DON'T LIKE IT ANYWAY.
DING DONG

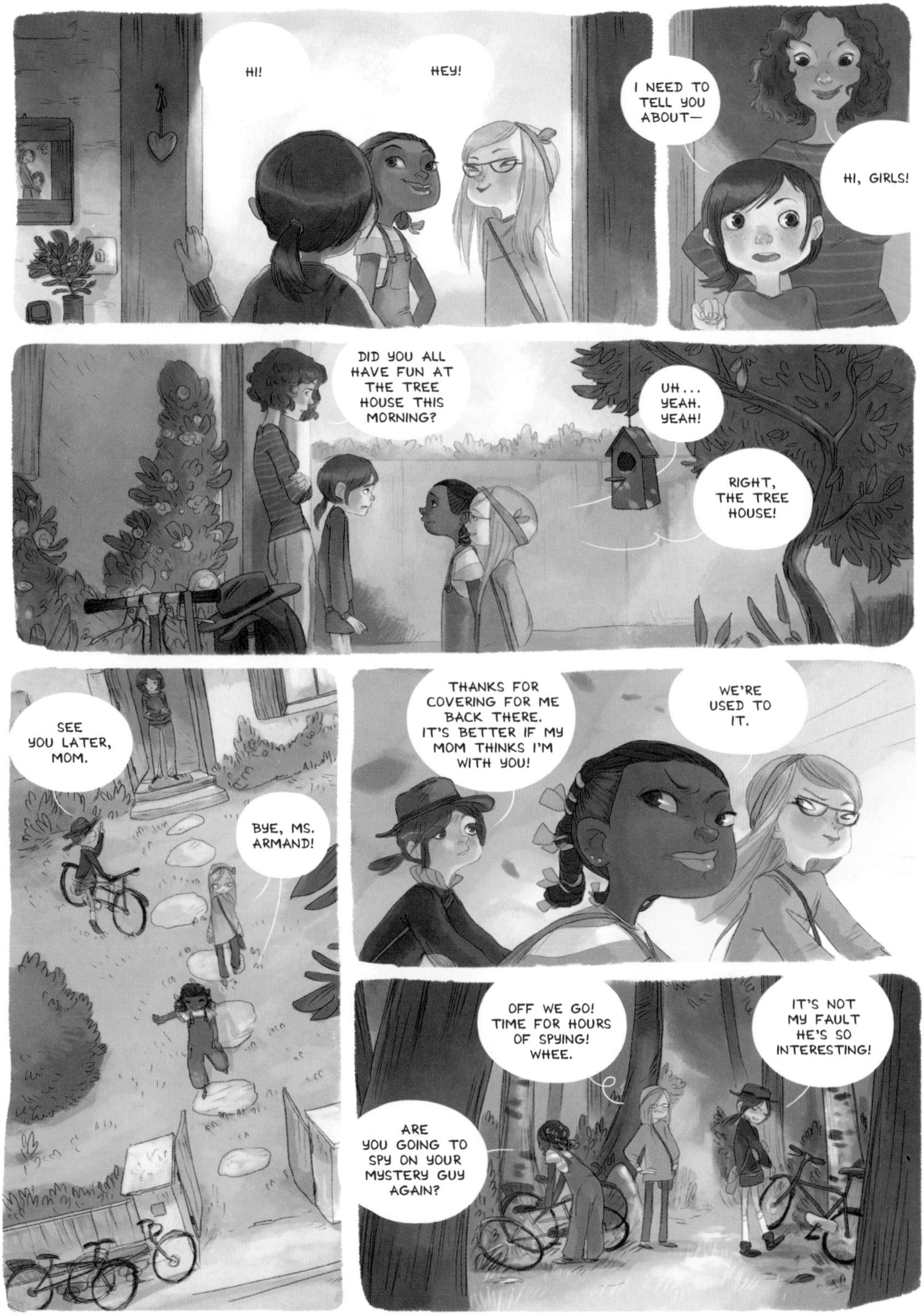
HI!
HEY!
I NEED TO TELL YOU ABOUT—
HI, GIRLS!
DID YOU ALL HAVE FUN AT THE TREE HOUSE THIS MORNING?
UH... YEAH. YEAH!
RIGHT, THE TREE HOUSE!
SEE YOU LATER, MOM.
BYE, MS. ARMAND!
THANKS FOR COVERING FOR ME BACK THERE. IT'S BETTER IF MY MOM THINKS I'M WITH YOU!
WE'RE USED TO IT.
ARE YOU GOING TO SPY ON YOUR MYSTERY GUY AGAIN?
OFF WE GO! TIME FOR HOURS OF SPYING! WHEE.
IT'S NOT MY FAULT HE'S SO INTERESTING!

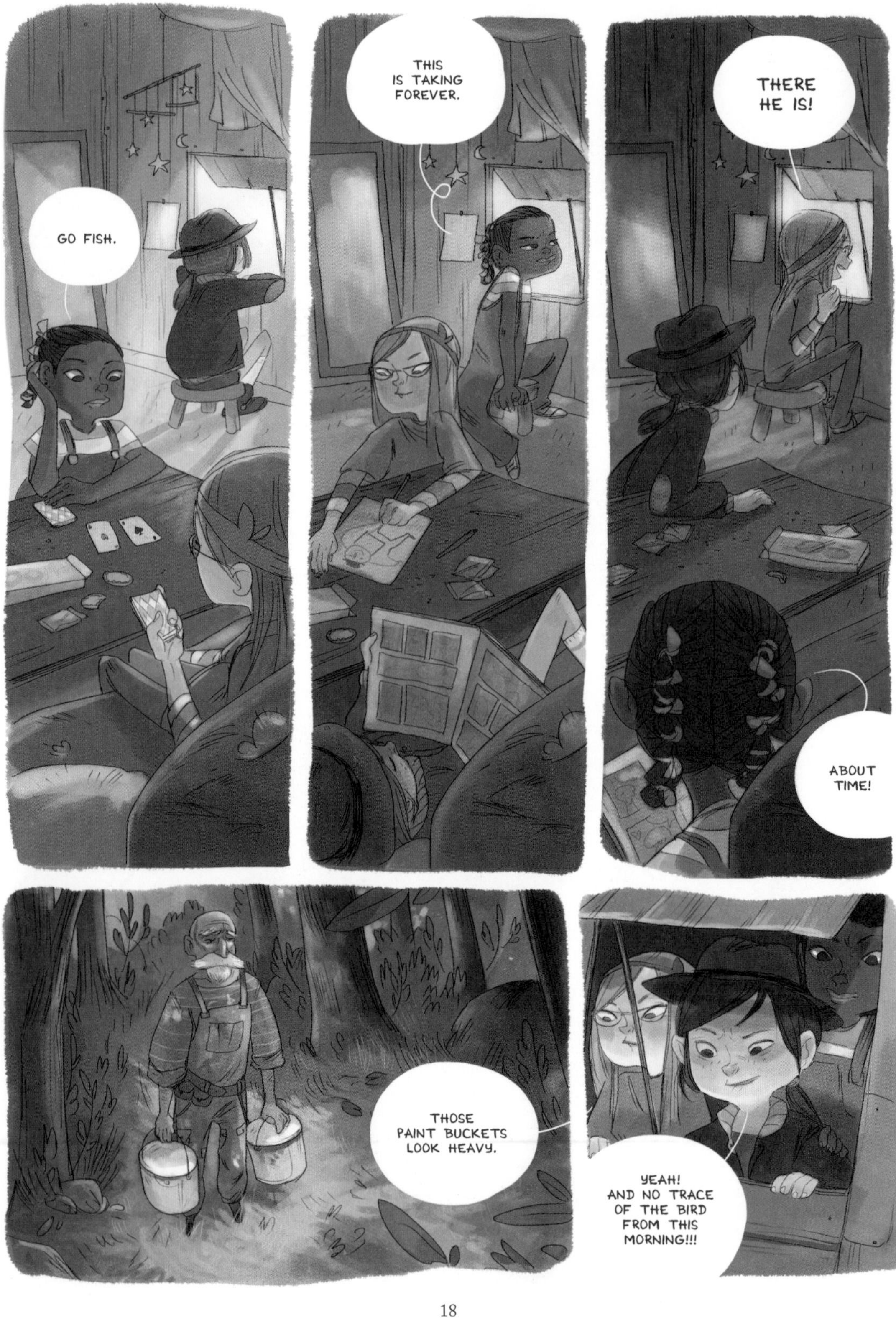
GO FISH.
THIS IS TAKING FOREVER.
THERE HE IS!
ABOUT TIME!
THOSE PAINT BUCKETS LOOK HEAVY.
YEAH! AND NO TRACE OF THE BIRD FROM THIS MORNING!!!

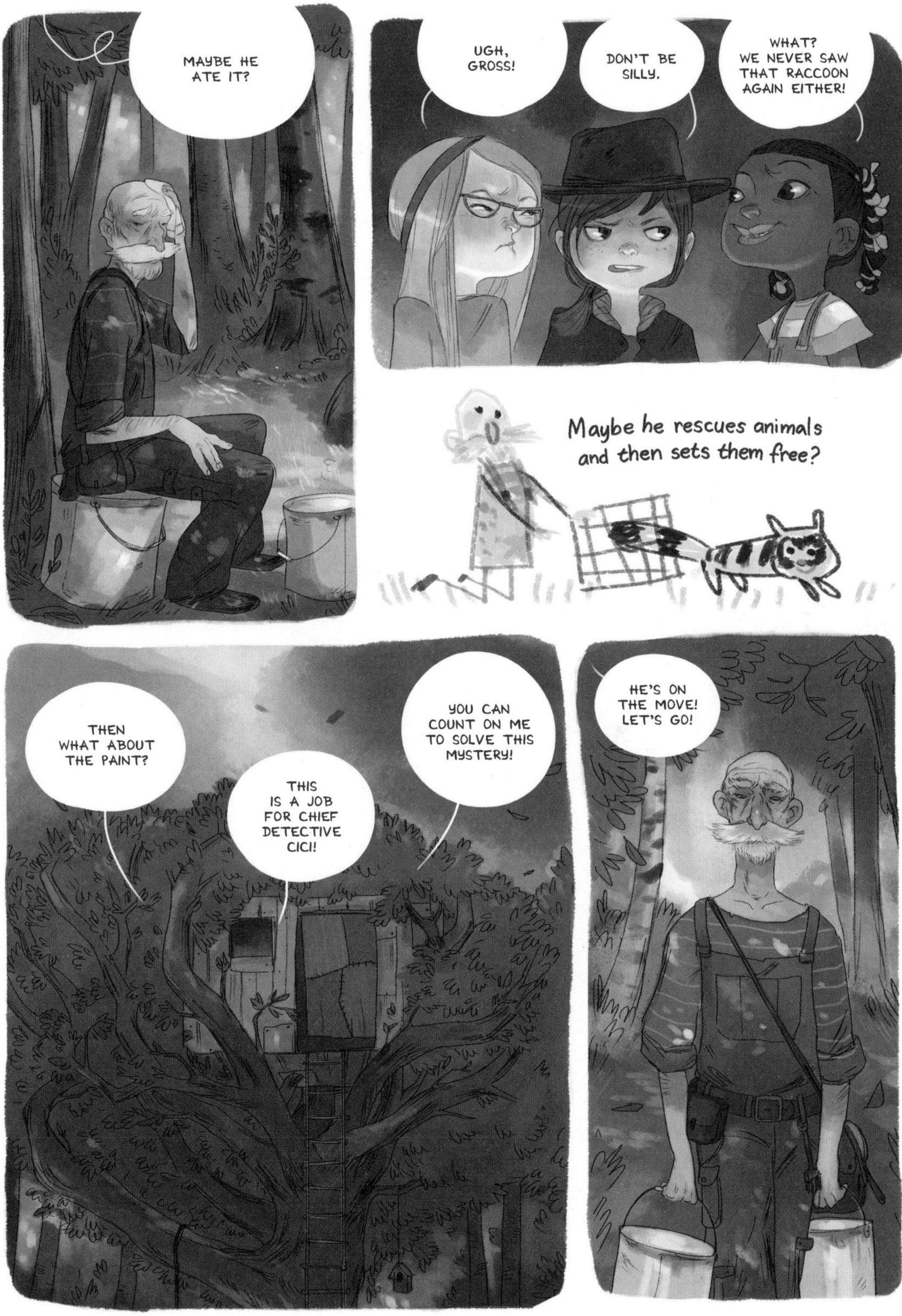
MAYBE HE ATE IT?
UGH, GROSS!
DON'T BE SILLY.
WHAT? WE NEVER SAW THAT RACCOON AGAIN EITHER!
Maybe he rescues animals and then sets them free?
THEN WHAT ABOUT THE PAINT?
THIS IS A JOB FOR CHIEF DETECTIVE CICI!
YOU CAN COUNT ON ME TO SOLVE THIS MYSTERY!
HE'S ON THE MOVE! LET'S GO!

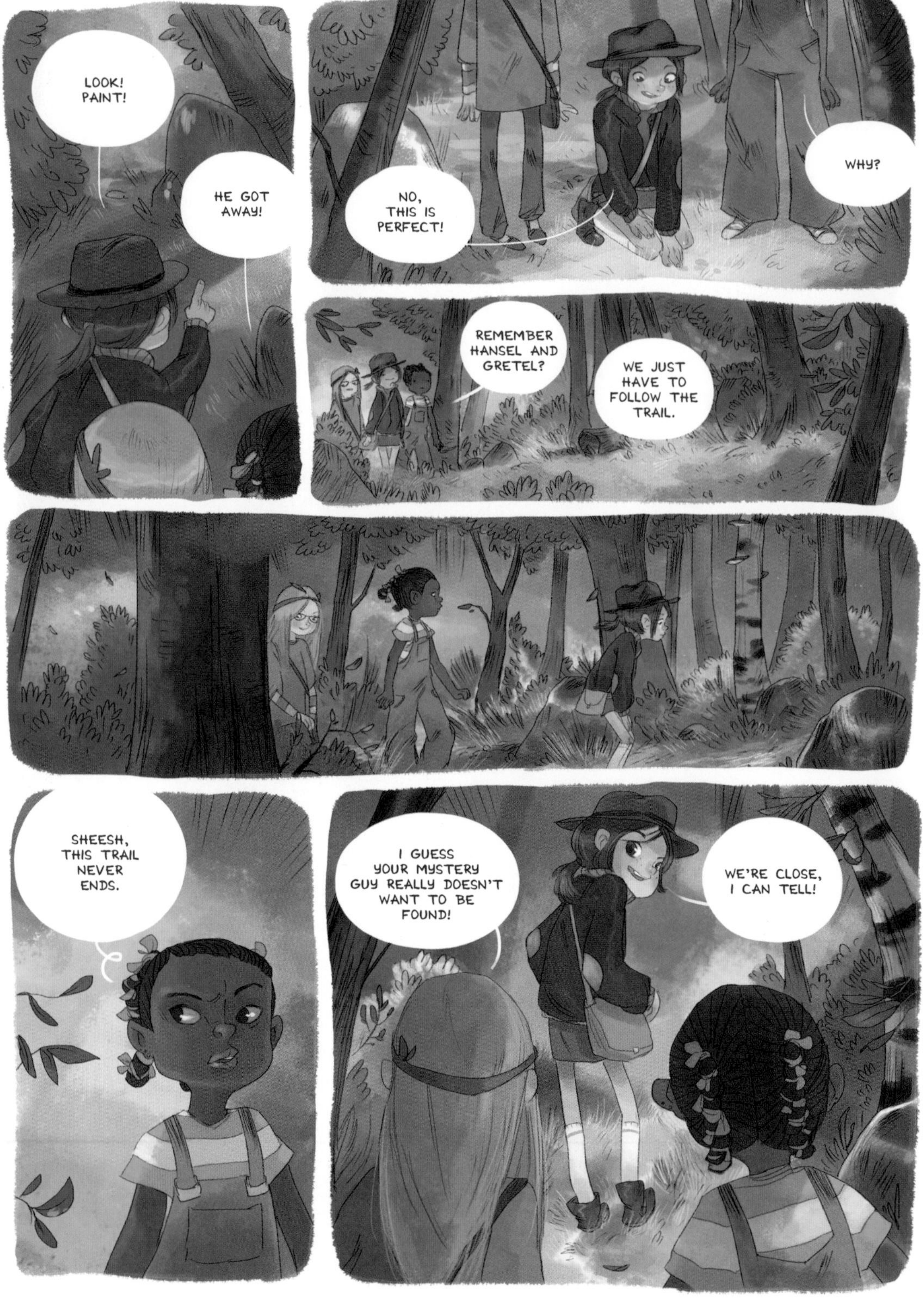
LOOK! PAINT!
HE GOT AWAY!
NO, THIS IS PERFECT!
WHY?
REMEMBER HANSEL AND GRETEL?
WE JUST HAVE TO FOLLOW THE TRAIL.
SHEESH, THIS TRAIL NEVER ENDS.
I GUESS YOUR MYSTERY GUY REALLY DOESN'T WANT TO BE FOUND!
WE'RE CLOSE, I CAN TELL!

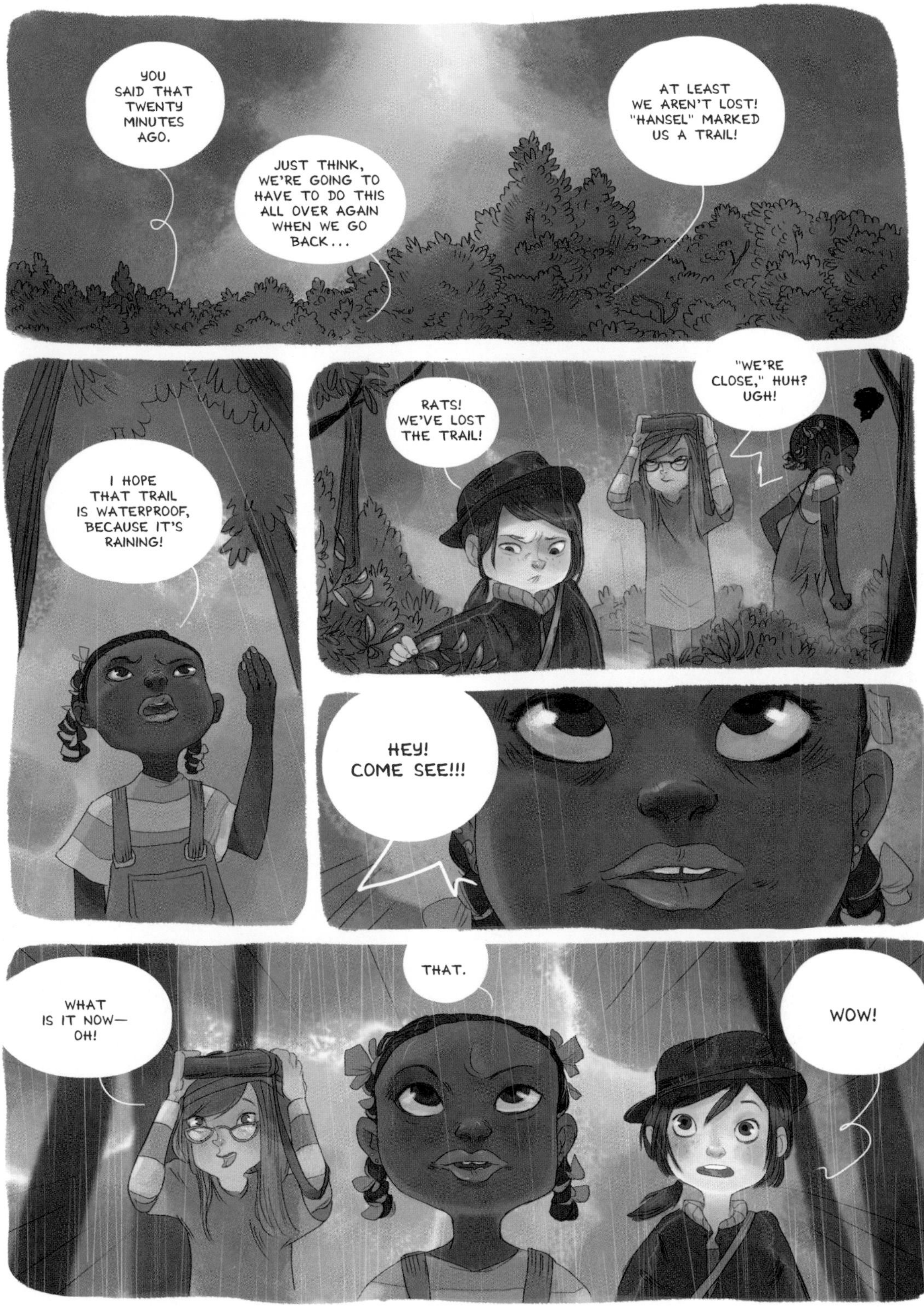

YOU SAID THAT TWENTY MINUTES AGO.
JUST THINK, WE'RE GOING TO HAVE TO DO THIS ALL OVER AGAIN WHEN WE GO BACK...
AT LEAST WE AREN'T LOST! "HANSEL" MARKED US A TRAIL!
I HOPE THAT TRAIL IS WATERPROOF, BECAUSE IT'S RAINING!
RATS! WE'VE LOST THE TRAIL!
"WE'RE CLOSE," HUH? UGH!
HEY! COME SEE!!!
WHAT IS IT NOW— OH!
THAT.
WOW!

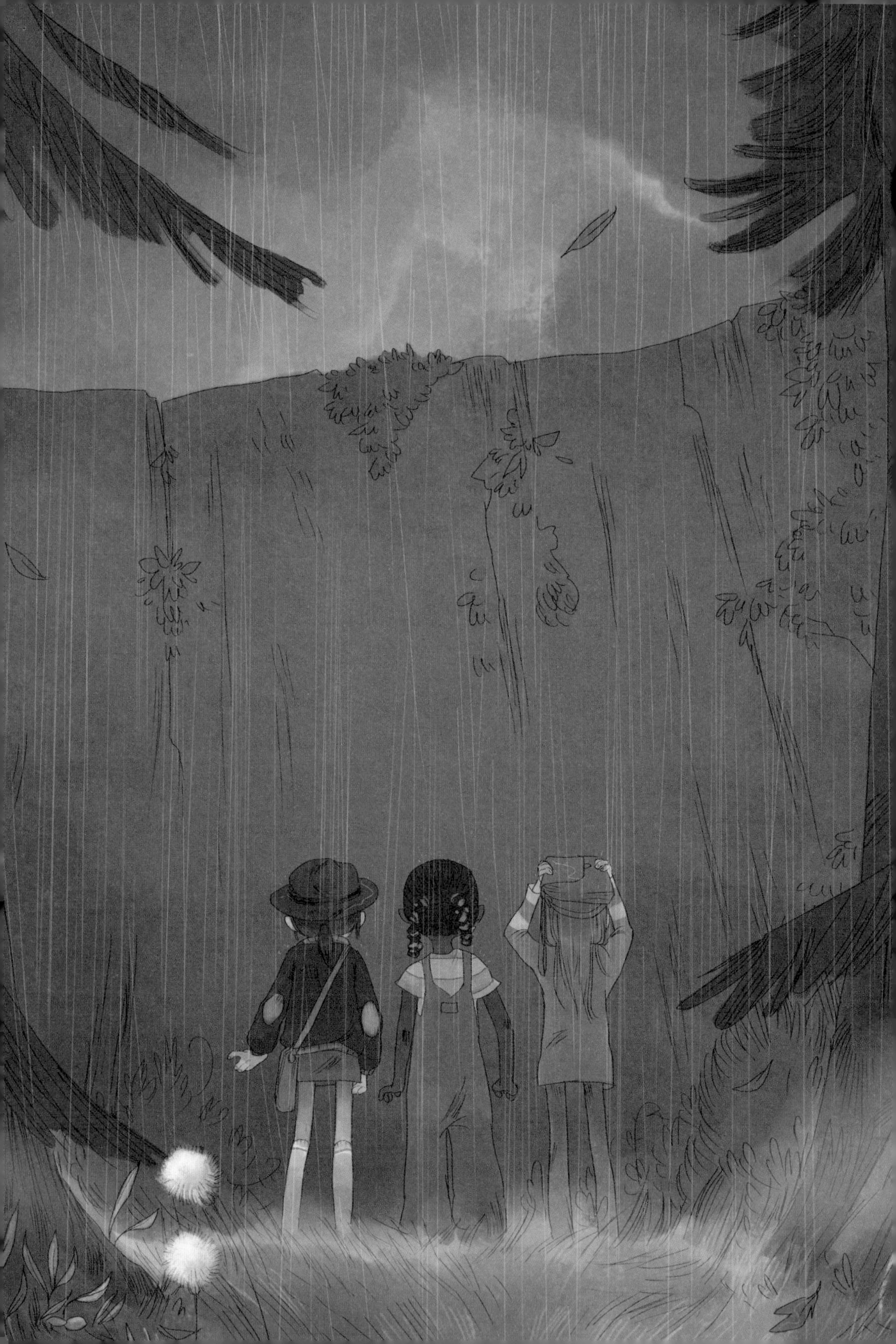

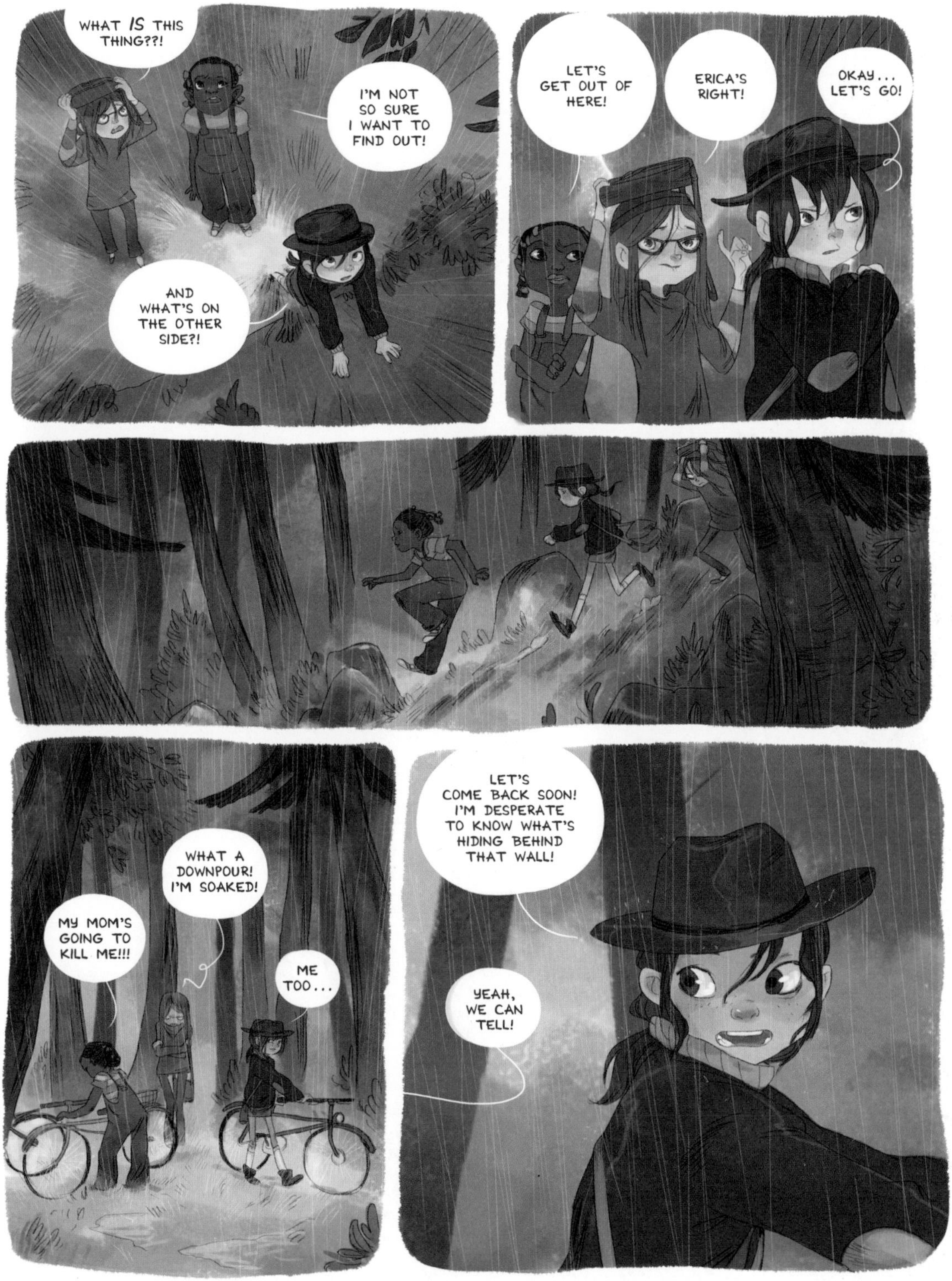
WHAT IS THIS THING??!
I'M NOT SO SURE I WANT TO FIND OUT!
AND WHAT'S ON THE OTHER SIDE?!
LET'S GET OUT OF HERE!
ERICA'S RIGHT!
OKAY... LET'S GO!
WHAT A DOWNPOUR! I'M SOAKED!
MY MOM'S GOING TO KILL ME!!!
ME TOO...
LET'S COME BACK SOON! I'M DESPERATE TO KNOW WHAT'S HIDING BEHIND THAT WALL!
YEAH, WE CAN TELL!

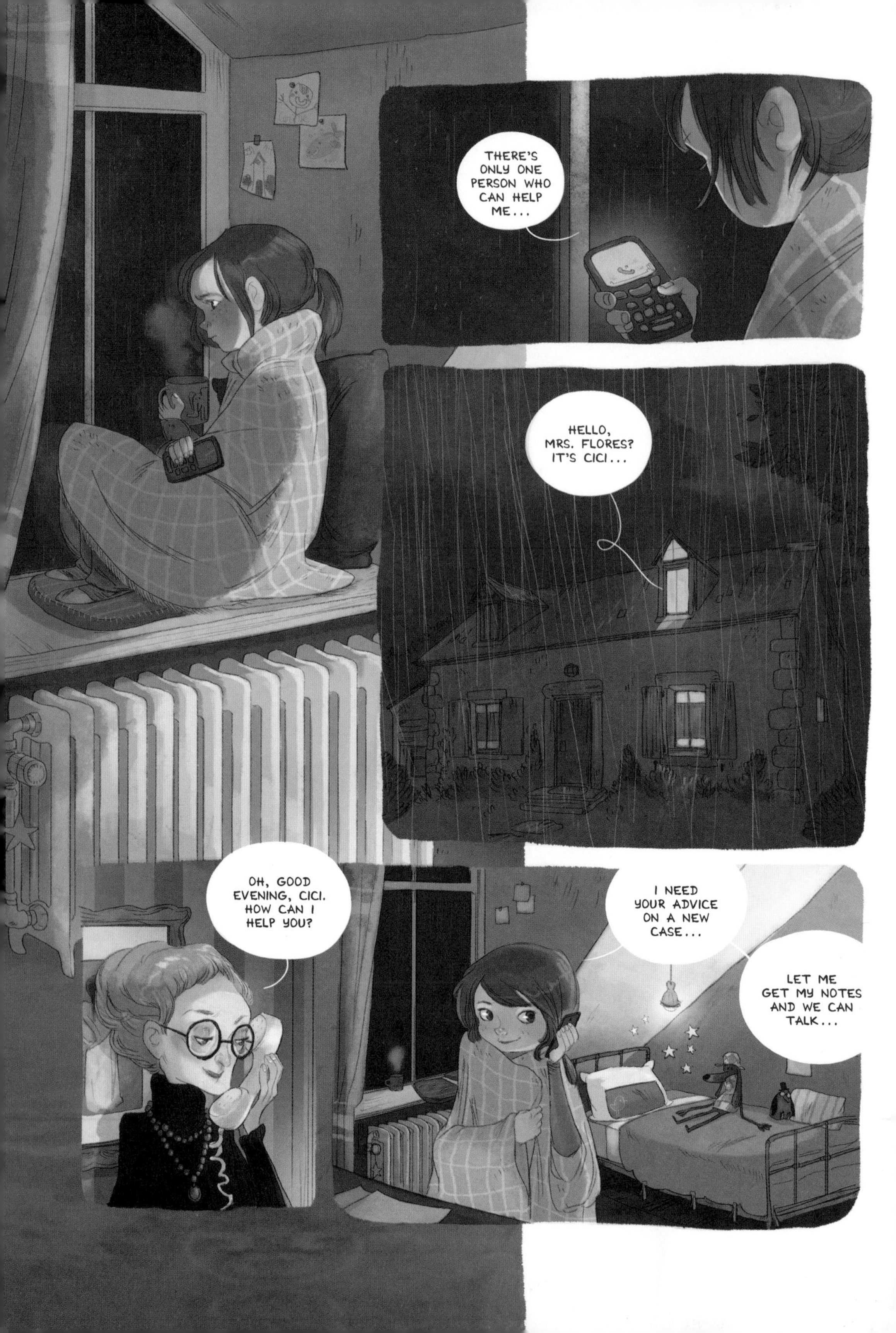
THERE'S ONLY ONE PERSON WHO CAN HELP ME...
HELLO, MRS. FLORES? IT'S CICI...
OH, GOOD EVENING, CICI. HOW CAN I HELP YOU?
I NEED YOUR ADVICE ON A NEW CASE...
LET ME GET MY NOTES AND WE CAN TALK...

Clues:

- cage?
- paint (all colors)
  → a lot of colors for repainting a building... arrrggh!

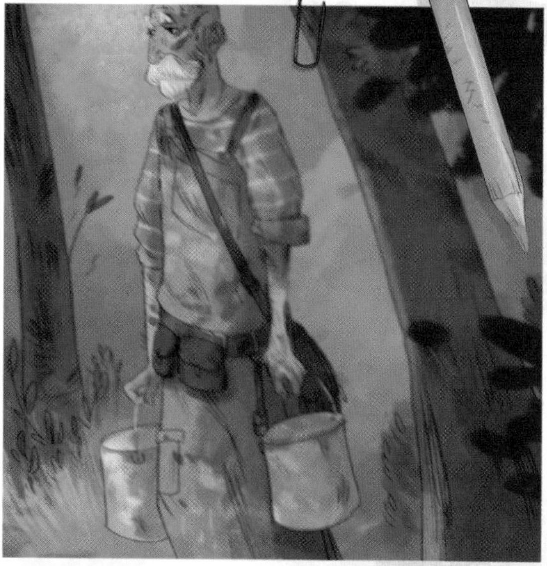

photo taken by Lena!

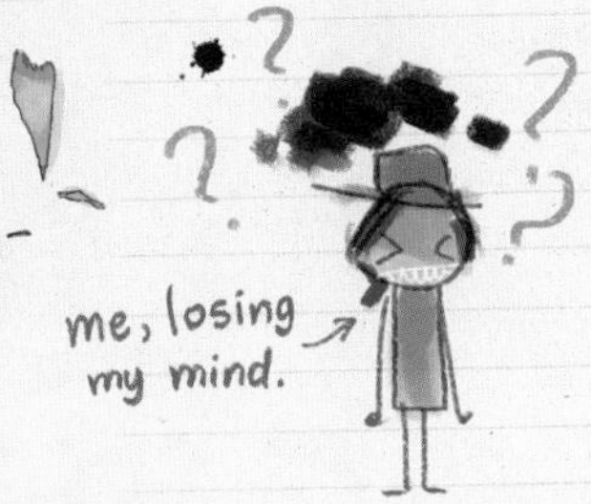

me, losing my mind.

Mr. Mysterious!

The first time Lena saw him she took his picture by accident! She who never takes a blurry photo! But she gave this one to me, which is good, because it's full of clues!

My friends and I have a lot of questions about Mr. Mysterious! We each have a different theory:

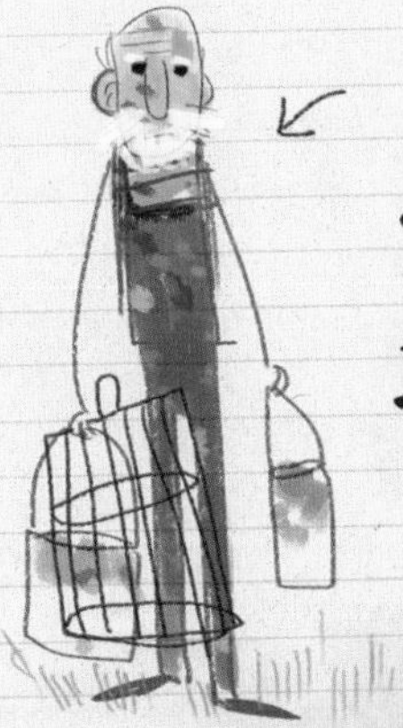

Erica's theory:

He eats the animals. He chooses a new one each week.

- Problem: What would he do if he wanted to eat a giraffe?

Lena's theory:

He frees the animals in the woods.

- Problem: Why carry a parrot the whole way and then open the cage?
- Problem #2: If he wanted to free a giraffe, how would he do it?

My theory:

He's painting a castle (or a haunted house!) from top to bottom.

- Problem: Why haven't we ever seen it in the woods?

Mr. M ... into the ... the animals

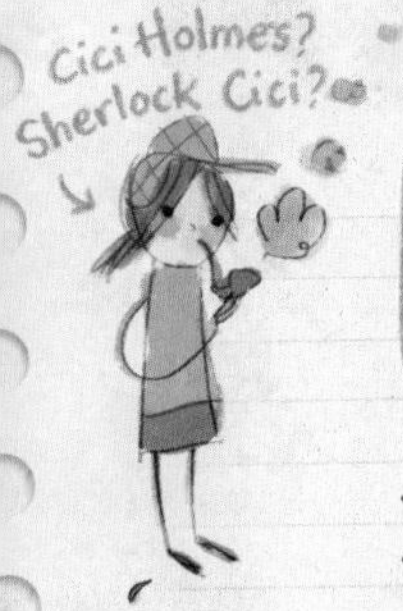
Cici Holmes?
Sherlock Cici?

To conduct a proper investigation, one must gather the facts (like Sherlock Holmes).

- Mr. Mysterious is only seen in the woods on the weekend.
- Gets there around 10 a.m., leaves around 7 p.m.
- We found a wall that cuts the woods in half... Is there a link to Mr. Mysterious?

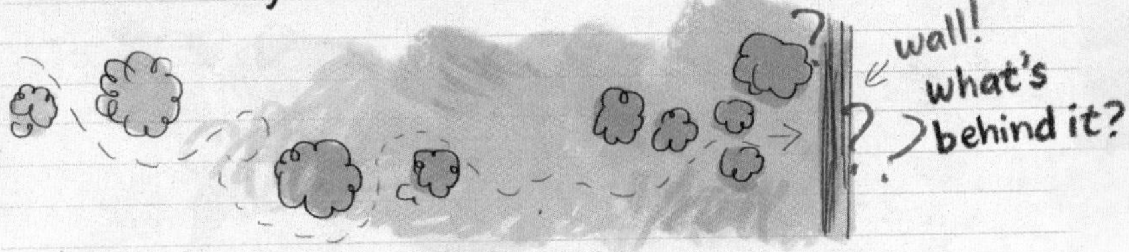
wall!
what's behind it?

Next, one must conduct interviews. Back to town!

- The baker, like most of the people I interrogated, doesn't know what I'm talking about.
- The retired policeman says the photo is too blurry to figure out what he's doing.
- Ms. Galinier doesn't know and doesn't care who he is as long as he doesn't step on her mushrooms.
- Guy the pirate farmer has never seen this sailor on board his ship.
- I didn't interrogate Mom. If I tried, she'd find out about my investigation, and she'd definitely stop me from spying on Mr. Mysterious!

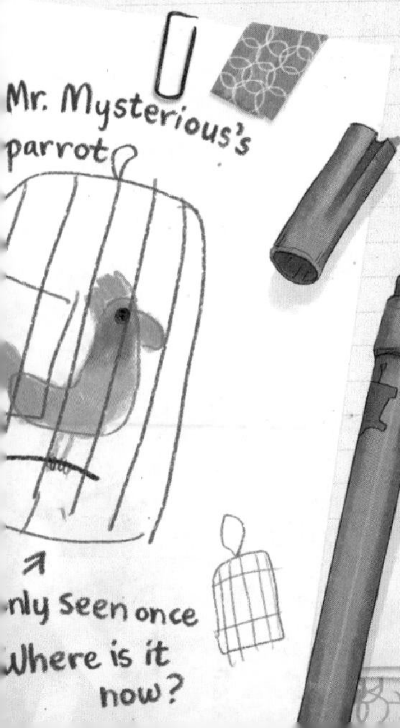
Mr. Mysterious's parrot
nly seen once
Where is it now?

Mrs. Flores's advice:

A good detective searches for clues. You have to find something unusual or unexpected. An unusual detail that's out of place. In short: a lead.

The parrot! It must have come from a pet shop. There's one at the mall. The investigation will start there.

First goal: convince my mother to take me, without revealing why.

eureka! but it's good that

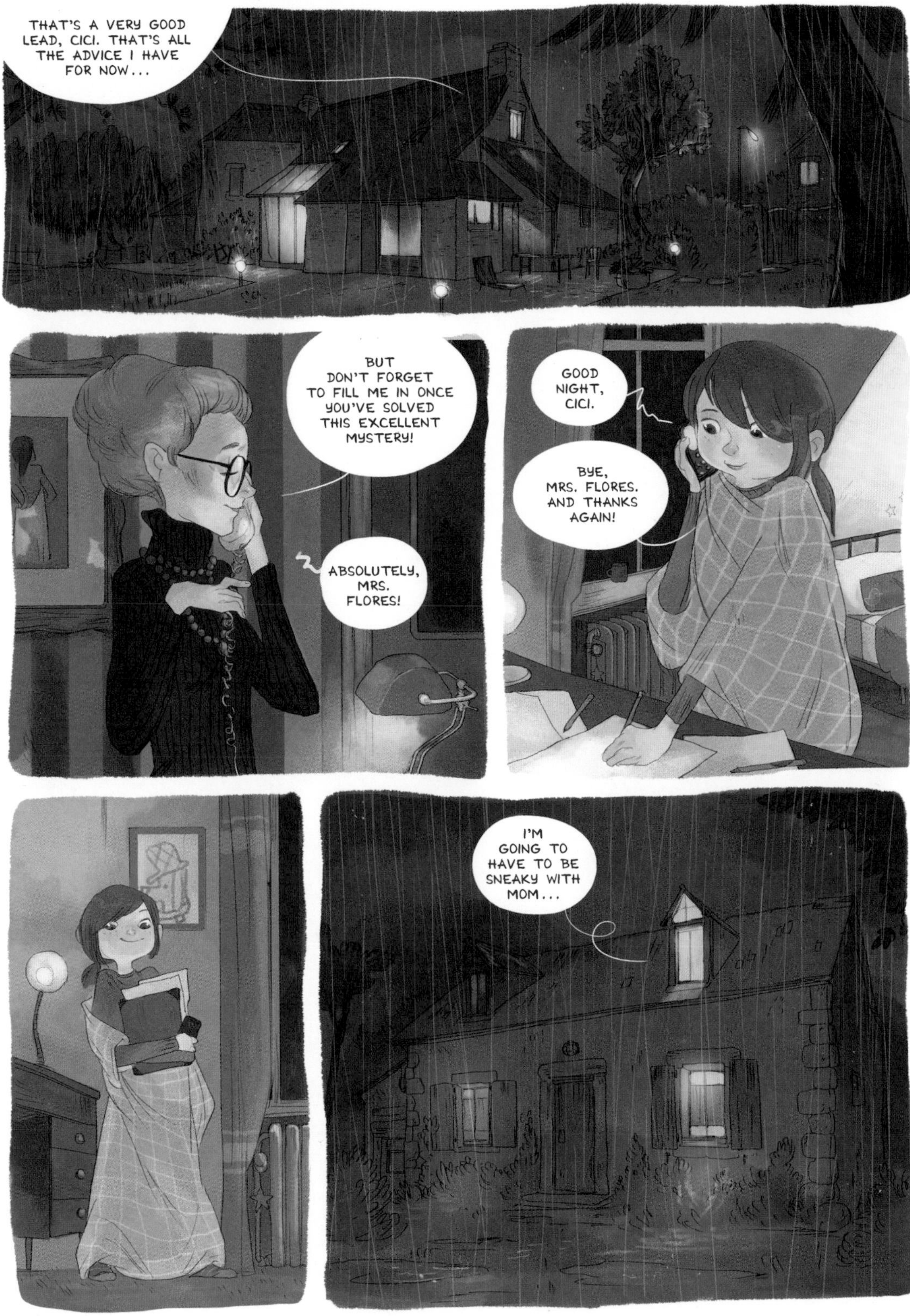
THAT'S A VERY GOOD LEAD, CICI. THAT'S ALL THE ADVICE I HAVE FOR NOW...
BUT DON'T FORGET TO FILL ME IN ONCE YOU'VE SOLVED THIS EXCELLENT MYSTERY!
ABSOLUTELY, MRS. FLORES!
GOOD NIGHT, CICI.
BYE, MRS. FLORES. AND THANKS AGAIN!
I'M GOING TO HAVE TO BE SNEAKY WITH MOM...

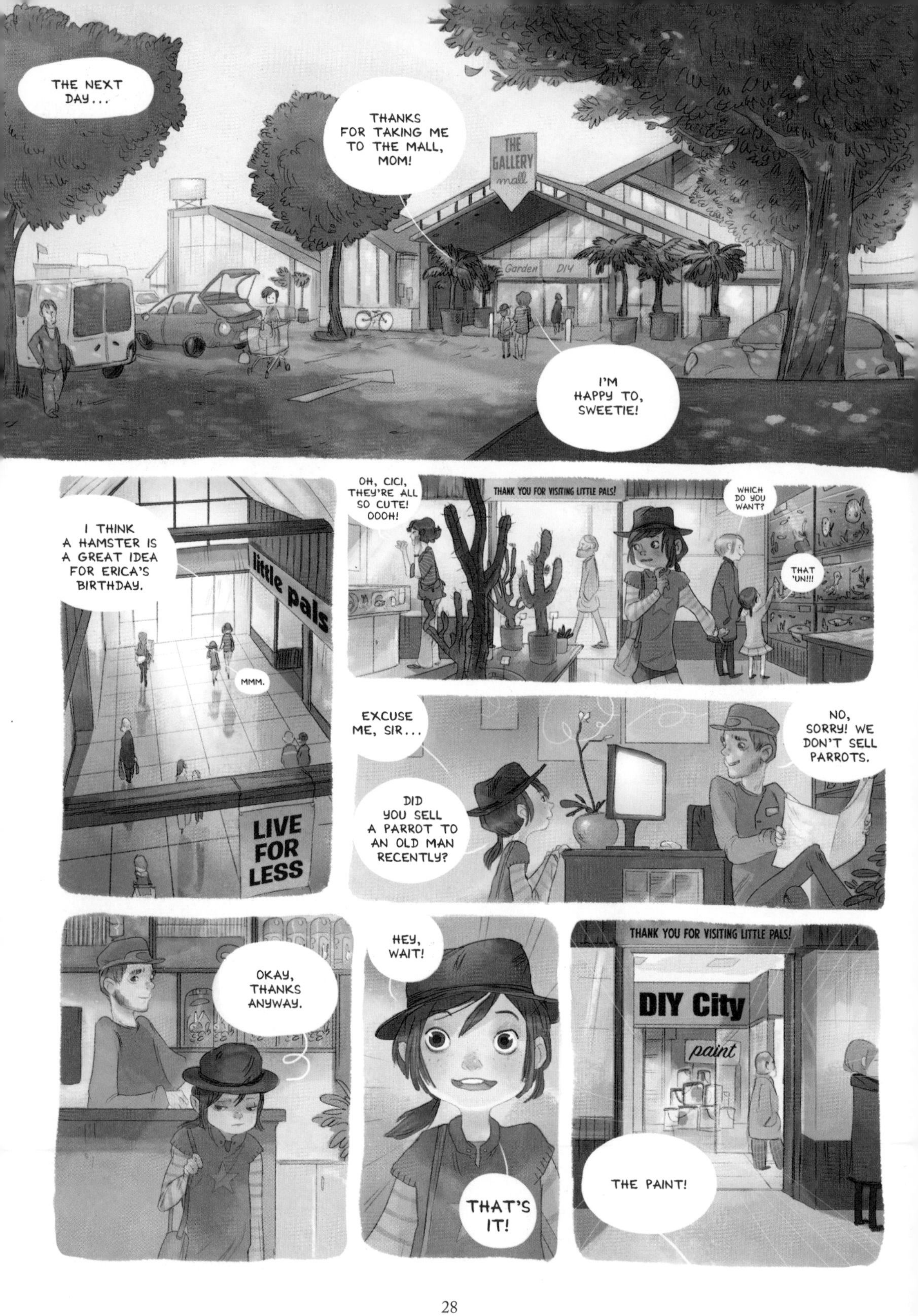
THE NEXT DAY...
THANKS FOR TAKING ME TO THE MALL, MOM!
THE GALLERY mall
Garden
DIY
I'M HAPPY TO, SWEETIE!
I THINK A HAMSTER IS A GREAT IDEA FOR ERICA'S BIRTHDAY.
little pals
MMM.
LIVE FOR LESS
OH, CICI, THEY'RE ALL SO CUTE! OOOH!
THANK YOU FOR VISITING LITTLE PALS!
WHICH DO YOU WANT?
THAT 'UN!!!
EXCUSE ME, SIR...
DID YOU SELL A PARROT TO AN OLD MAN RECENTLY?
NO, SORRY! WE DON'T SELL PARROTS.
OKAY, THANKS ANYWAY.
HEY, WAIT!
THAT'S IT!
THANK YOU FOR VISITING LITTLE PALS!
DIY City
paint
THE PAINT!

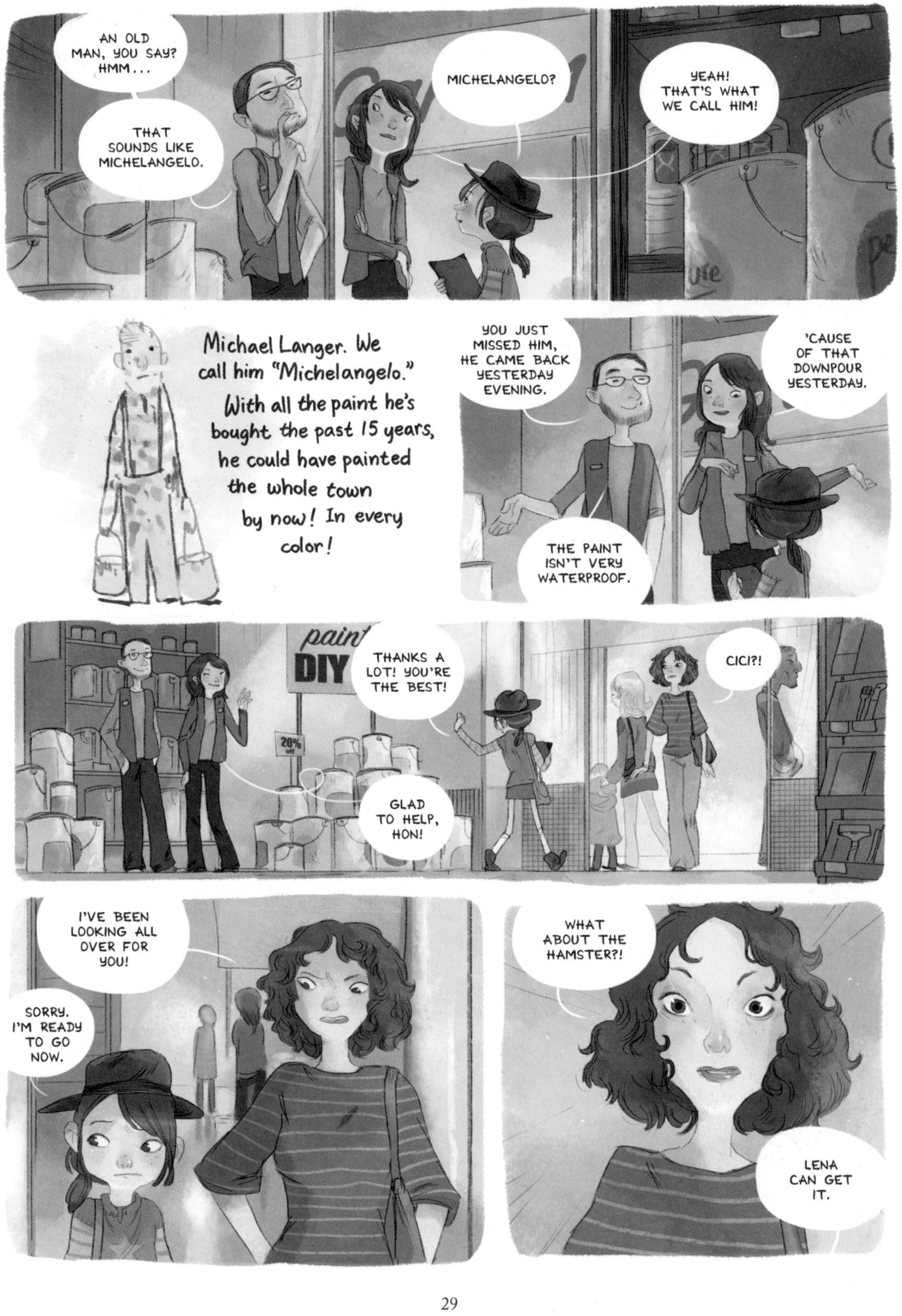

AN OLD MAN, YOU SAY? HMM...
THAT SOUNDS LIKE MICHELANGELO.
MICHELANGELO?
YEAH! THAT'S WHAT WE CALL HIM!
Michael Langer. We call him "Michelangelo." With all the paint he's bought the past 15 years, he could have painted the whole town by now! In every color!
YOU JUST MISSED HIM, HE CAME BACK YESTERDAY EVENING.
'CAUSE OF THAT DOWNPOUR YESTERDAY.
THE PAINT ISN'T VERY WATERPROOF.
paint
DIY
20% off
THANKS A LOT! YOU'RE THE BEST!
GLAD TO HELP, HON!
CICI?!
I'VE BEEN LOOKING ALL OVER FOR YOU!
SORRY. I'M READY TO GO NOW.
WHAT ABOUT THE HAMSTER?!
LENA CAN GET IT.

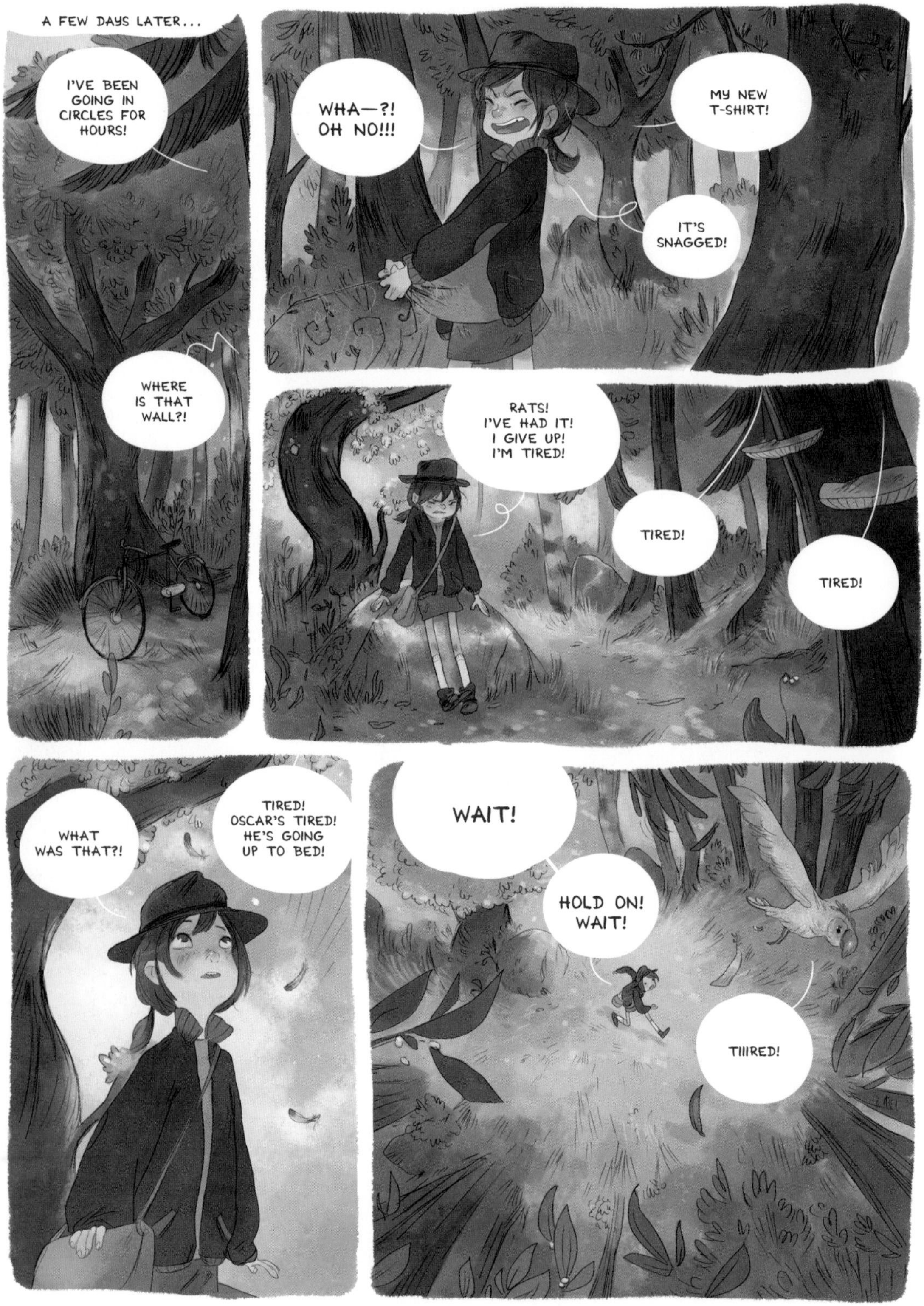
A FEW DAYS LATER...
I'VE BEEN GOING IN CIRCLES FOR HOURS!
WHERE IS THAT WALL?!
WHA—?! OH NO!!!
MY NEW T-SHIRT!
IT'S SNAGGED!
RATS! I'VE HAD IT! I GIVE UP! I'M TIRED!
TIRED!
TIRED!
WHAT WAS THAT?!
TIRED! OSCAR'S TIRED! HE'S GOING UP TO BED!
WAIT!
HOLD ON! WAIT!
TIIIRED!

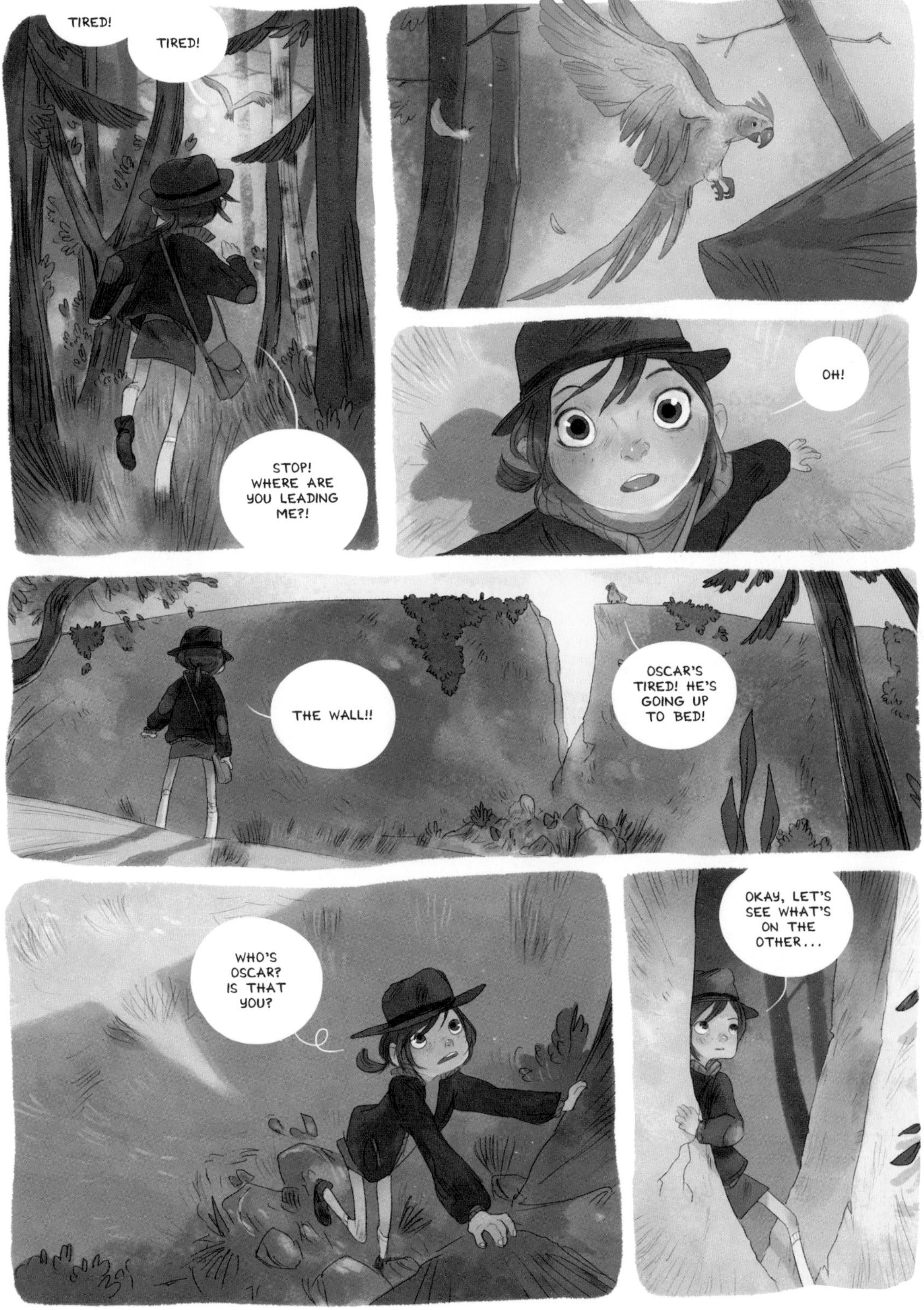
TIRED!
TIRED!
STOP! WHERE ARE YOU LEADING ME?!
OH!
THE WALL!!
OSCAR'S TIRED! HE'S GOING UP TO BED!
WHO'S OSCAR? IS THAT YOU?
OKAY, LET'S SEE WHAT'S ON THE OTHER...

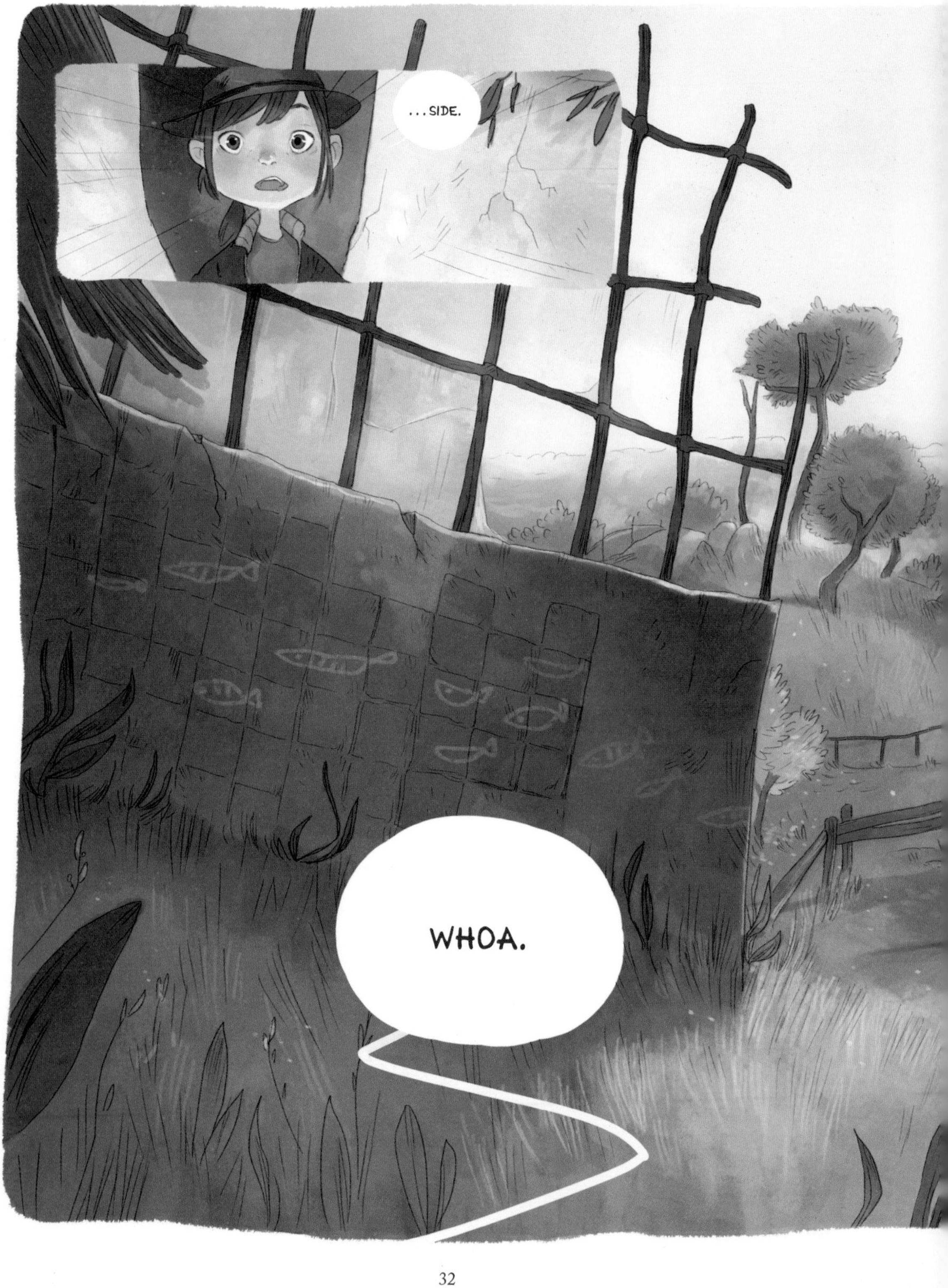
...SIDE.
WHOA.

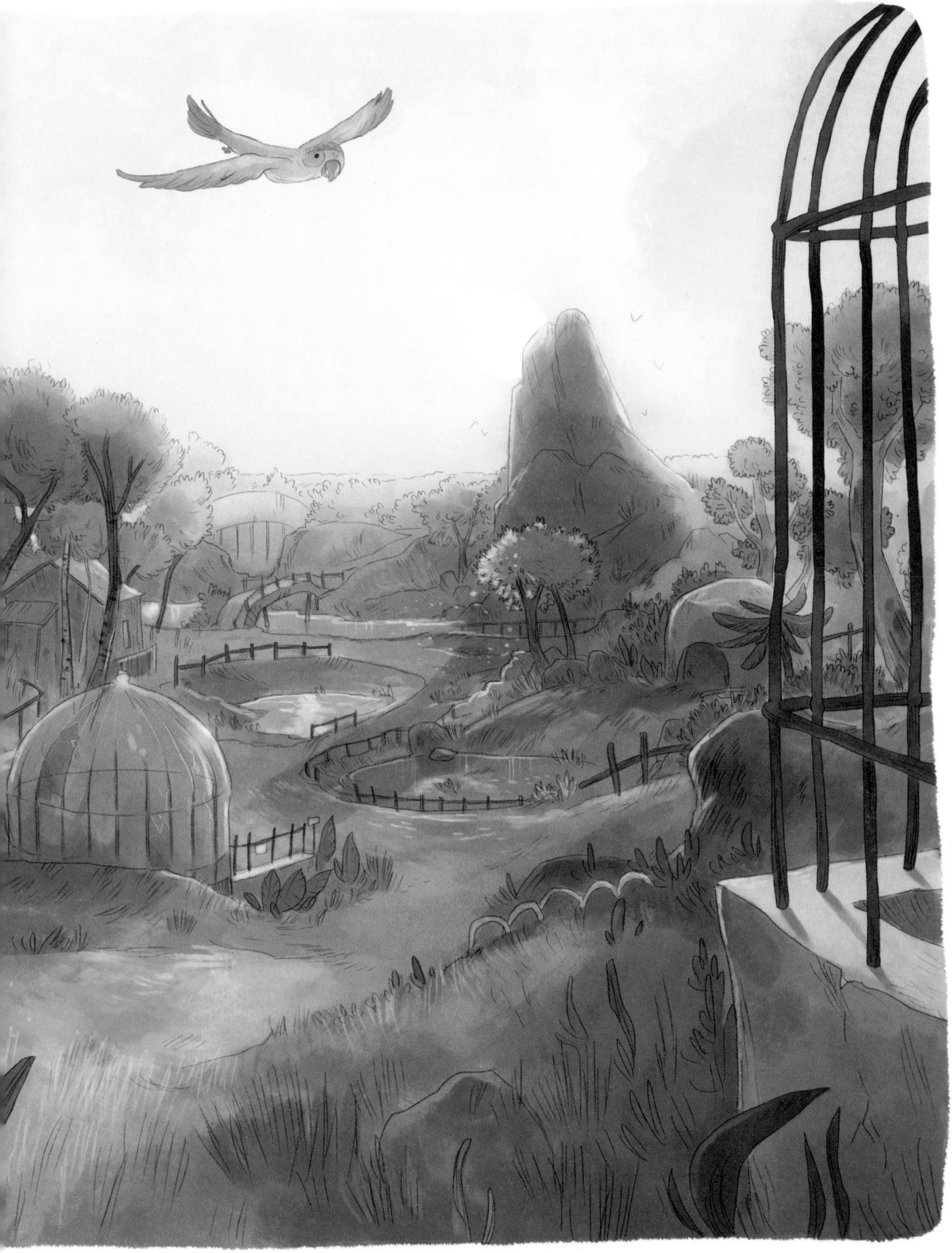

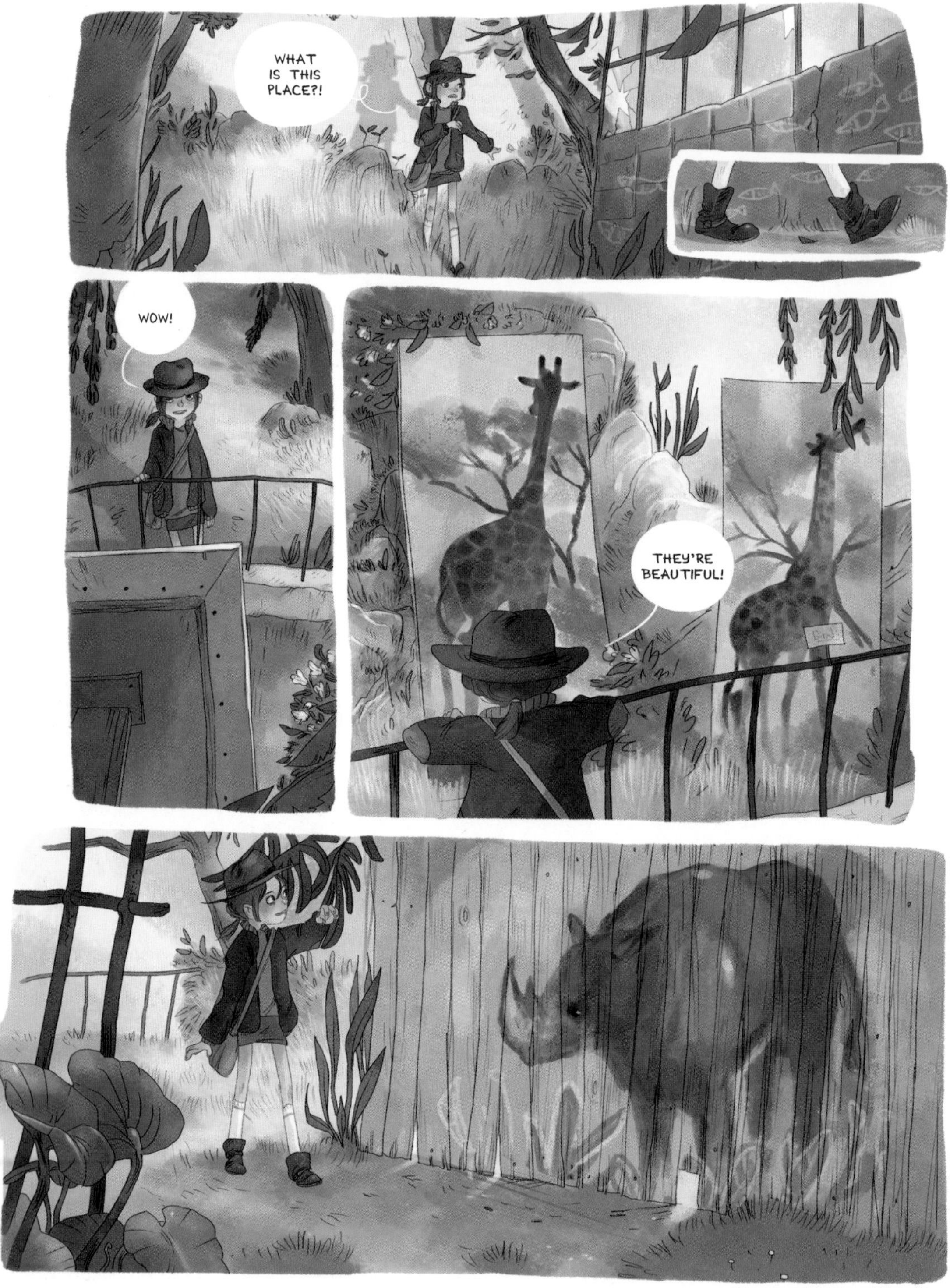
WHAT IS THIS PLACE?!
WOW!
THEY'RE BEAUTIFUL!

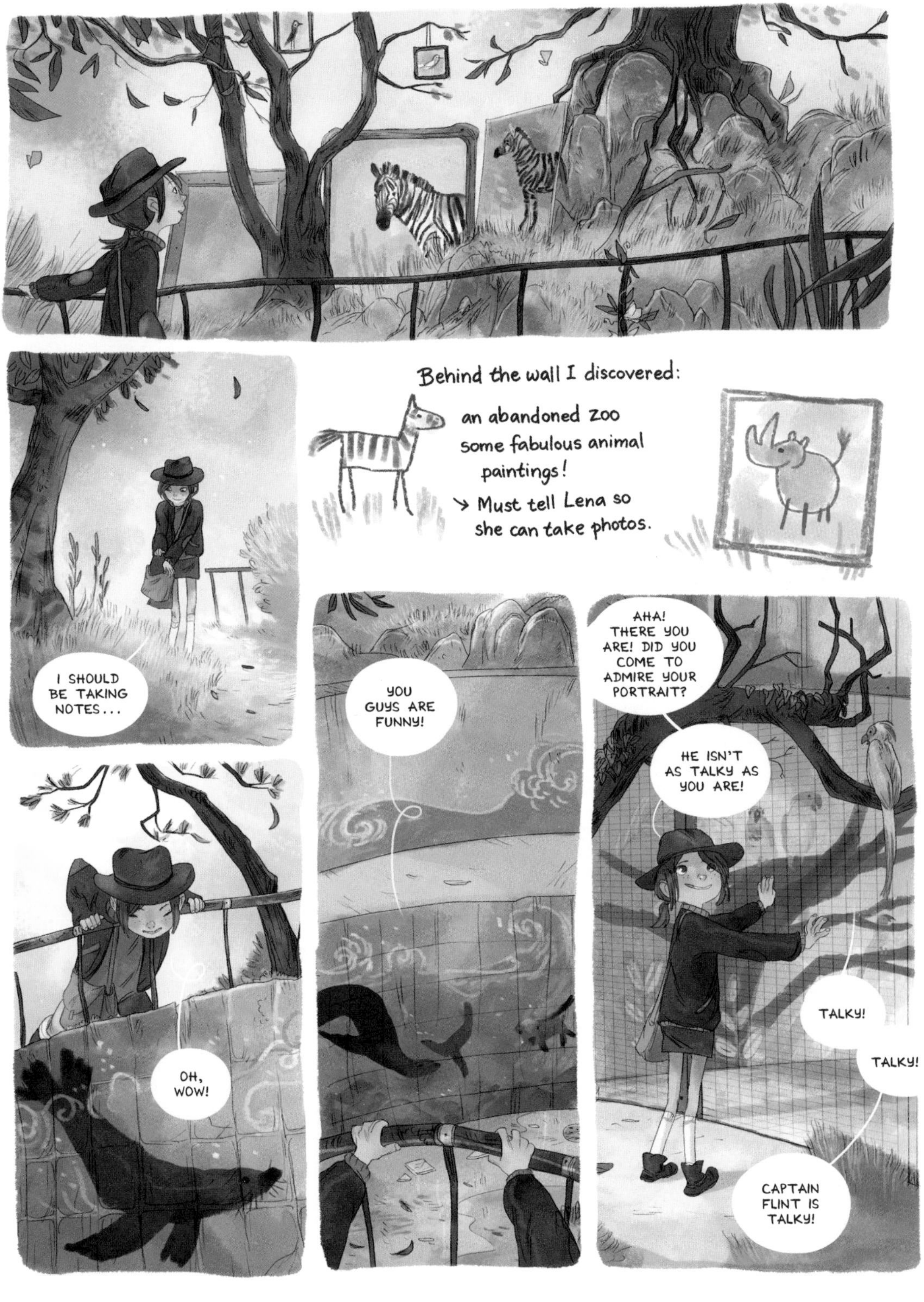
I SHOULD BE TAKING NOTES...
Behind the wall I discovered:
an abandoned zoo
some fabulous animal paintings!
→ Must tell Lena so she can take photos.
OH, WOW!
YOU GUYS ARE FUNNY!
AHA! THERE YOU ARE! DID YOU COME TO ADMIRE YOUR PORTRAIT?
HE ISN'T AS TALKY AS YOU ARE!
TALKY!
TALKY!
CAPTAIN FLINT IS TALKY!

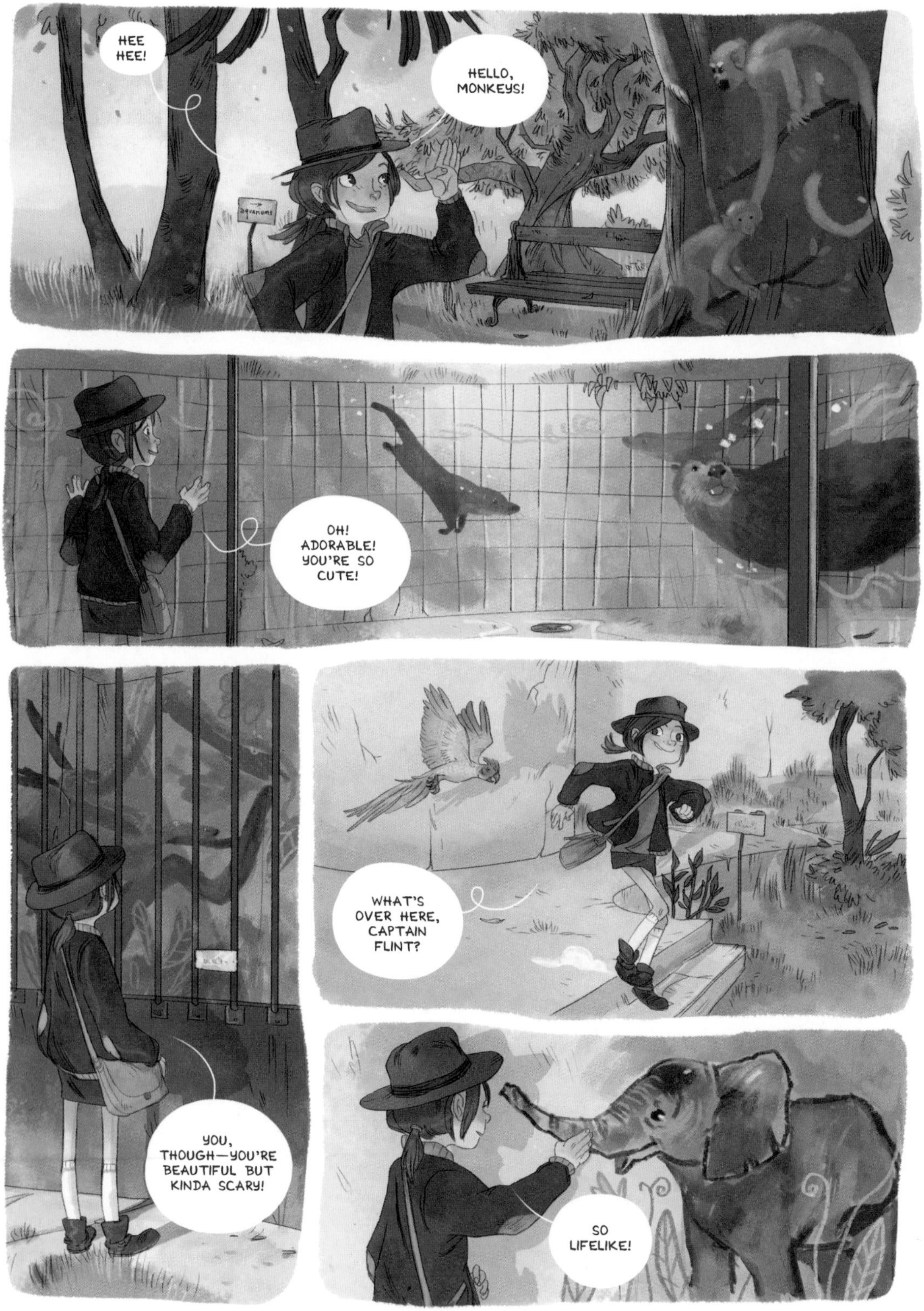
HEE HEE!
HELLO, MONKEYS!
OH! ADORABLE! YOU'RE SO CUTE!
YOU, THOUGH—YOU'RE BEAUTIFUL BUT KINDA SCARY!
WHAT'S OVER HERE, CAPTAIN FLINT?
SO LIFELIKE!

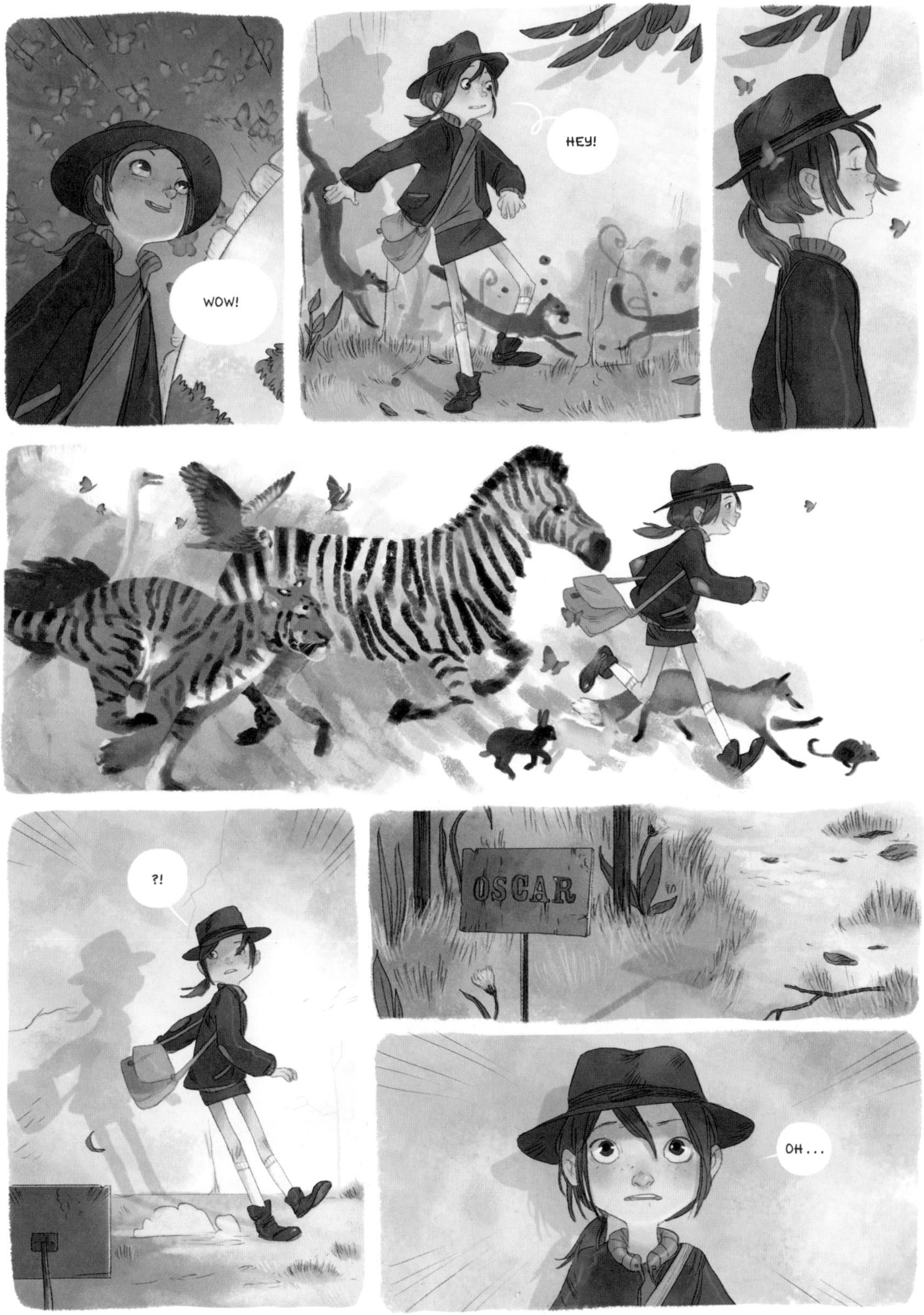
WOW!
HEY!
?!
OSCAR
OH...

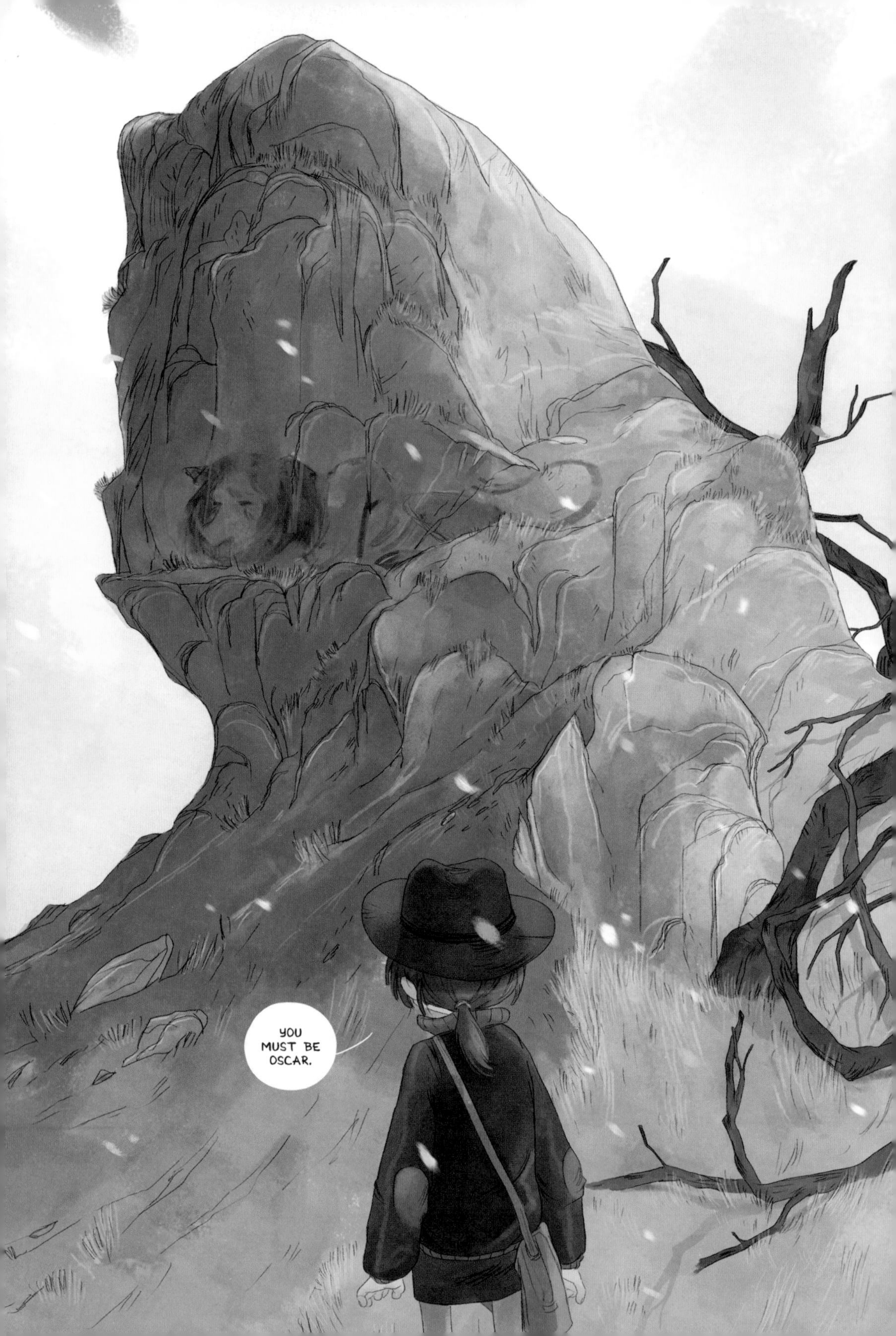
YOU MUST BE OSCAR.

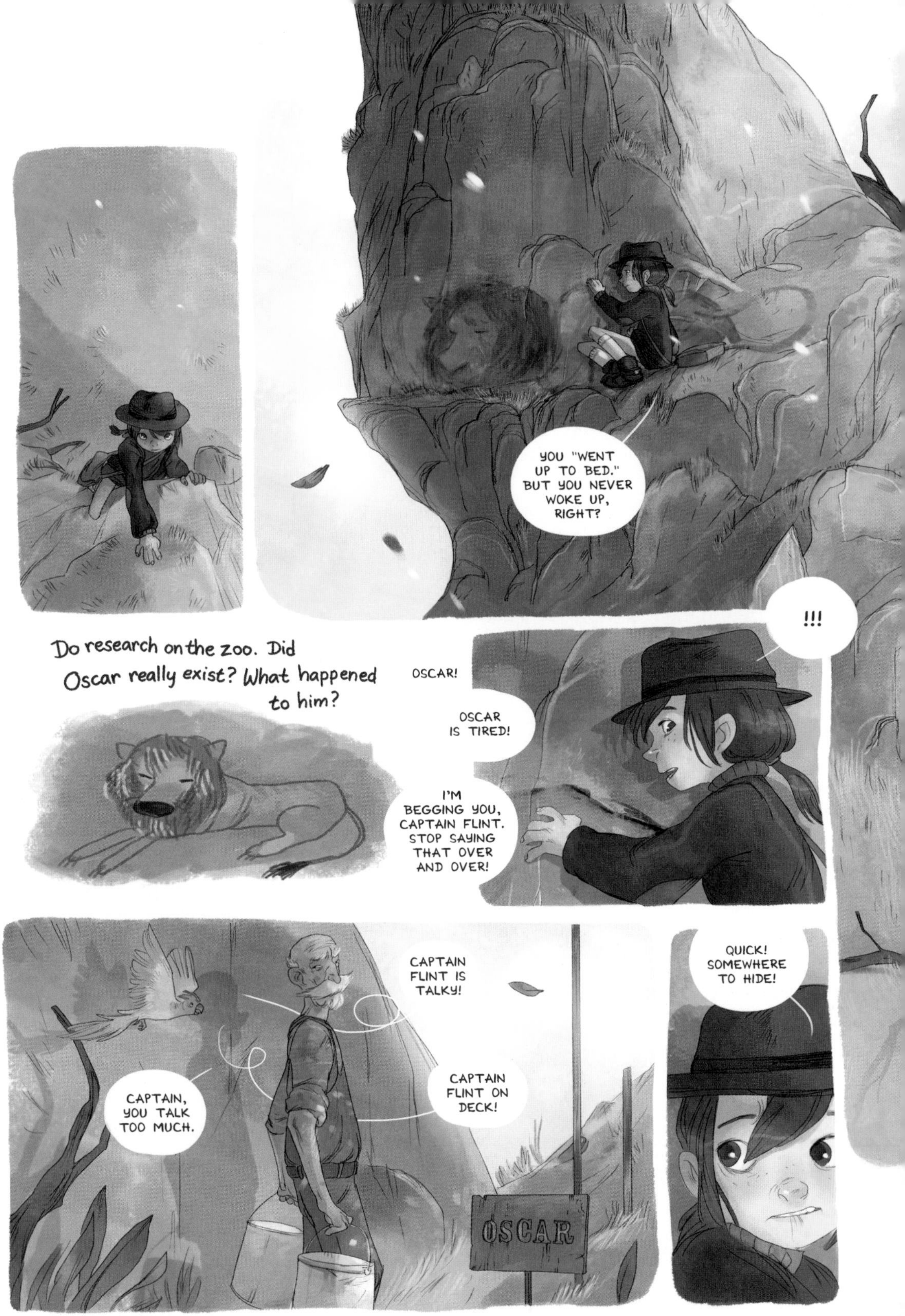
YOU "WENT UP TO BED." BUT YOU NEVER WOKE UP, RIGHT?
Do research on the zoo. Did Oscar really exist? What happened to him?
!!!
OSCAR!
OSCAR IS TIRED!
I'M BEGGING YOU, CAPTAIN FLINT. STOP SAYING THAT OVER AND OVER!
CAPTAIN FLINT IS TALKY!
CAPTAIN FLINT ON DECK!
CAPTAIN, YOU TALK TOO MUCH.
OSCAR
QUICK! SOMEWHERE TO HIDE!

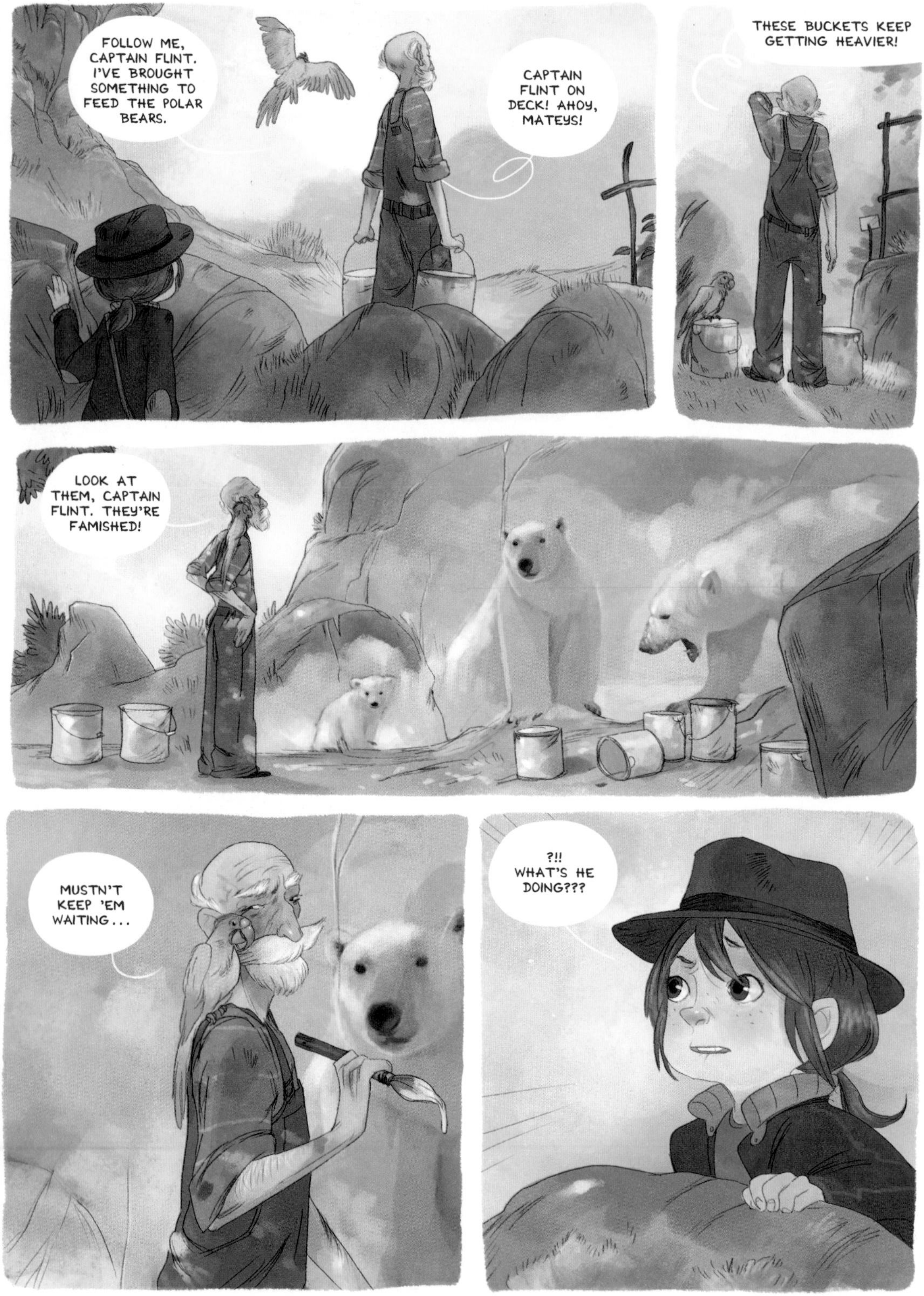
FOLLOW ME, CAPTAIN FLINT. I'VE BROUGHT SOMETHING TO FEED THE POLAR BEARS.
CAPTAIN FLINT ON DECK! AHOY, MATEYS!
THESE BUCKETS KEEP GETTING HEAVIER!
LOOK AT THEM, CAPTAIN FLINT. THEY'RE FAMISHED!
MUSTN'T KEEP 'EM WAITING...
?!! WHAT'S HE DOING???

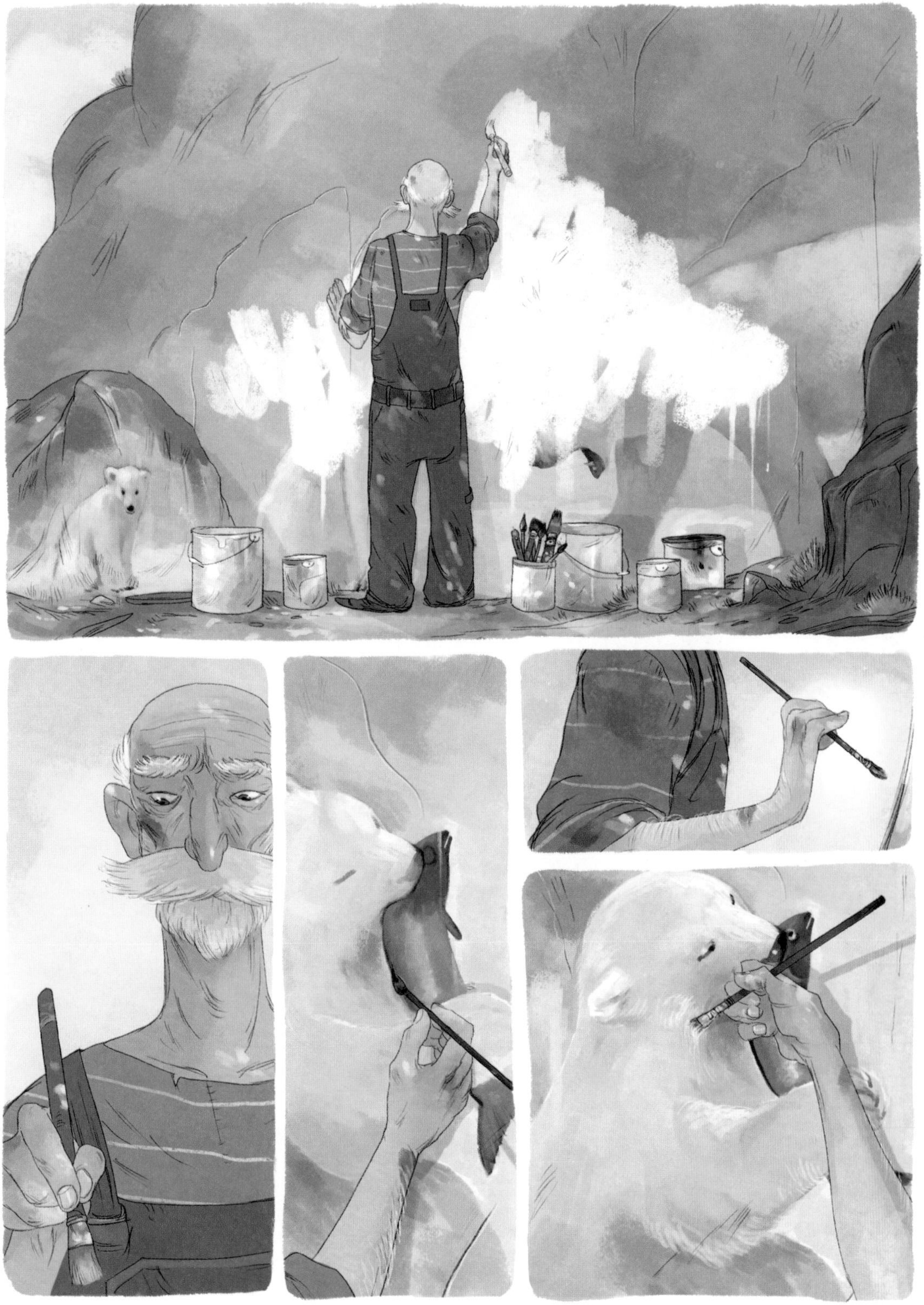

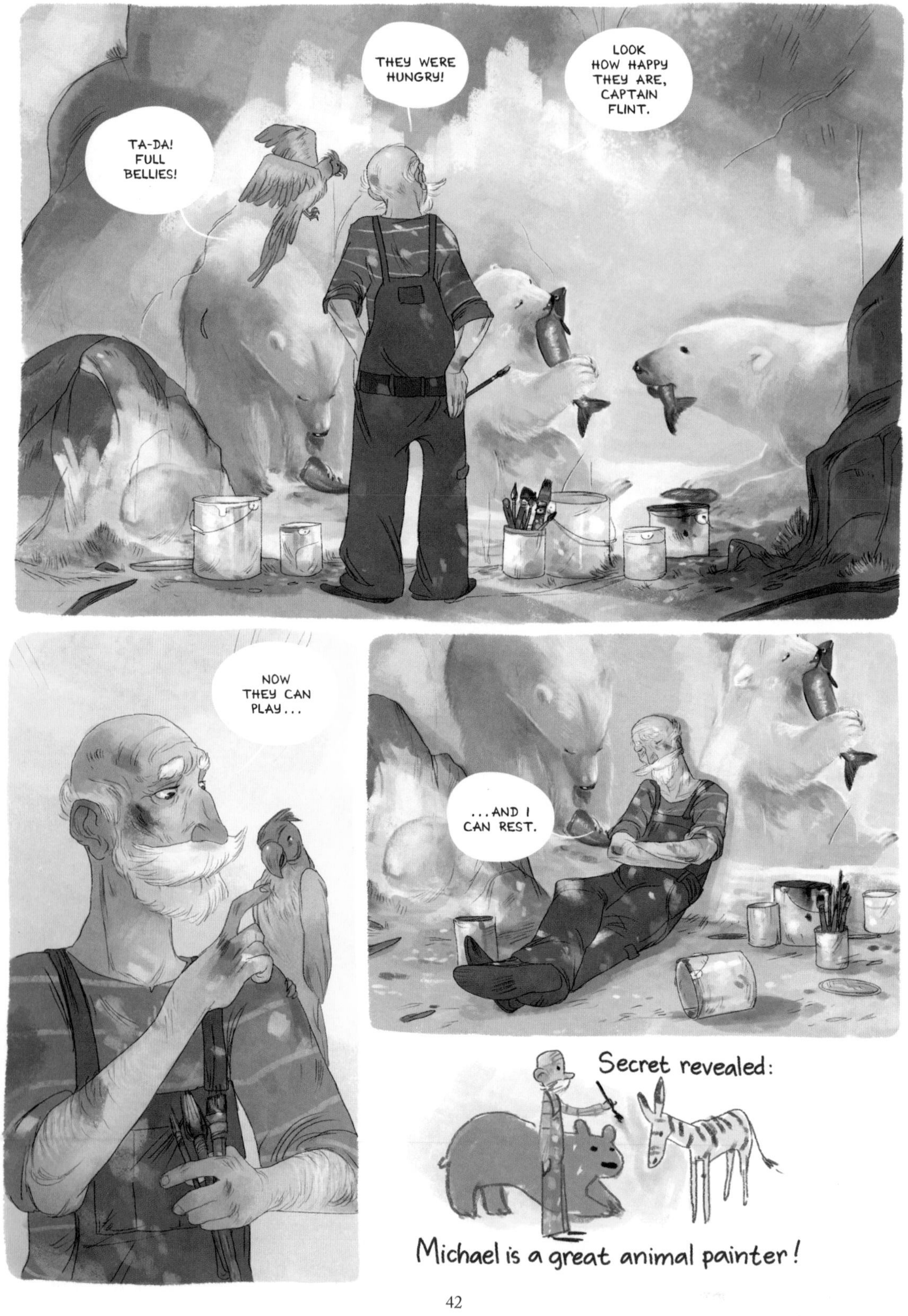
TA-DA! FULL BELLIES!
THEY WERE HUNGRY!
LOOK HOW HAPPY THEY ARE, CAPTAIN FLINT.
NOW THEY CAN PLAY...
...AND I CAN REST.
Secret revealed:
Michael is a great animal painter!

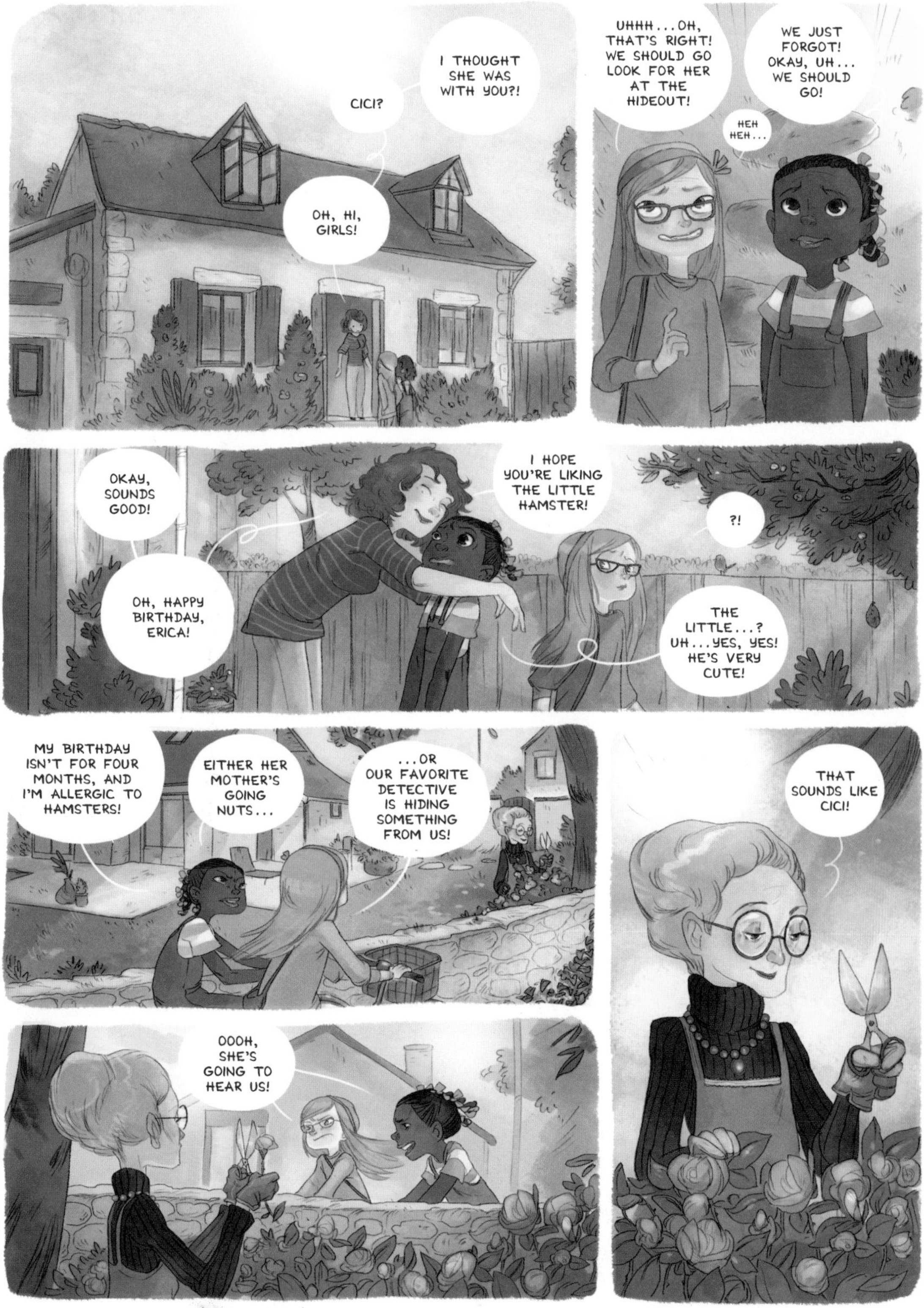
CICI?
I THOUGHT SHE WAS WITH YOU?!
OH, HI, GIRLS!
UHHH...OH, THAT'S RIGHT! WE SHOULD GO LOOK FOR HER AT THE HIDEOUT!
HEH HEH...
WE JUST FORGOT! OKAY, UH... WE SHOULD GO!
OKAY, SOUNDS GOOD!
OH, HAPPY BIRTHDAY, ERICA!
I HOPE YOU'RE LIKING THE LITTLE HAMSTER!
?!
THE LITTLE...? UH...YES, YES! HE'S VERY CUTE!
MY BIRTHDAY ISN'T FOR FOUR MONTHS, AND I'M ALLERGIC TO HAMSTERS!
EITHER HER MOTHER'S GOING NUTS...
...OR OUR FAVORITE DETECTIVE IS HIDING SOMETHING FROM US!
OOOH, SHE'S GOING TO HEAR US!
THAT SOUNDS LIKE CICI!

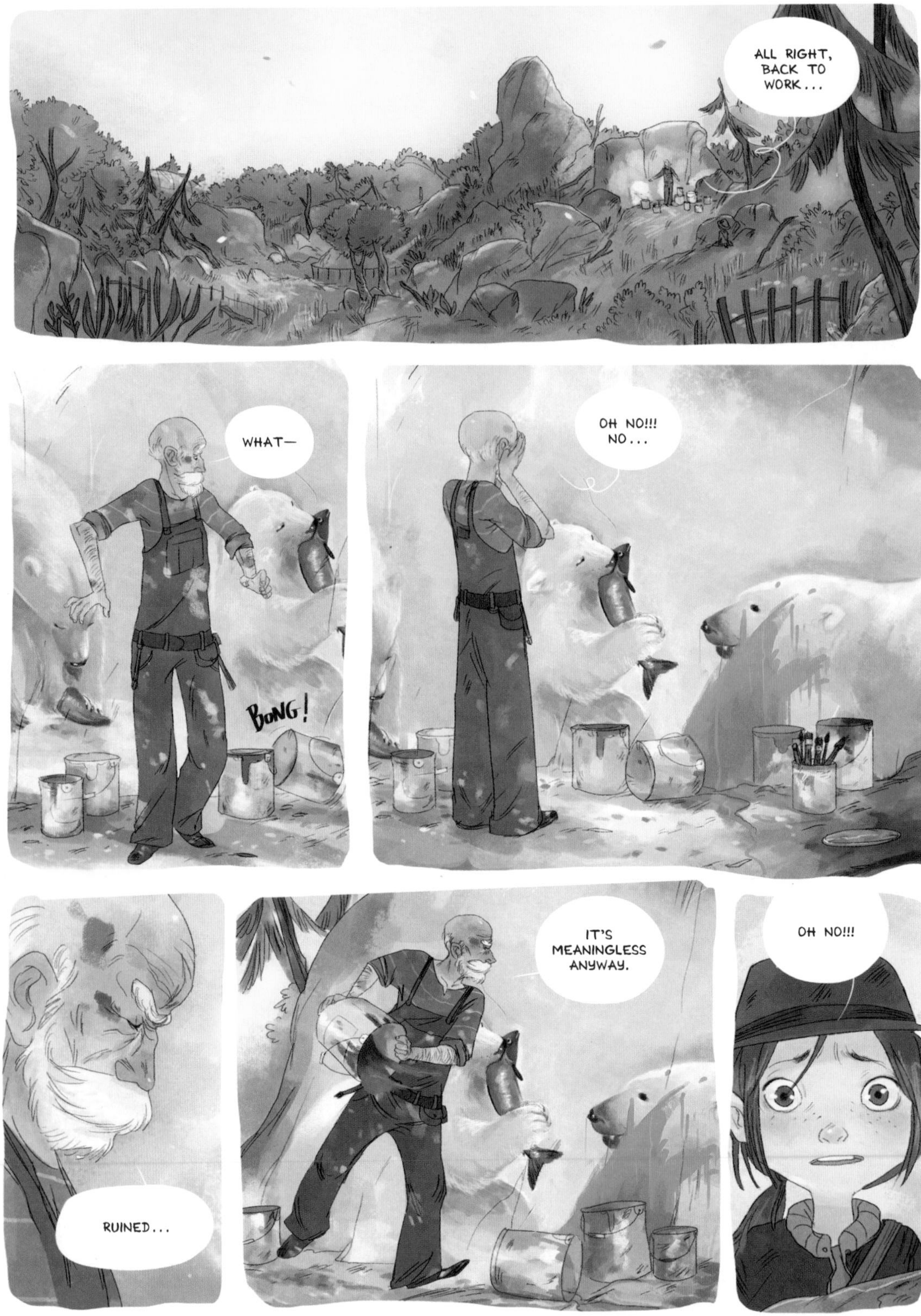
ALL RIGHT, BACK TO WORK...
WHAT—
BONG!
OH NO!!! NO...
RUINED...
IT'S MEANINGLESS ANYWAY.
OH NO!!!

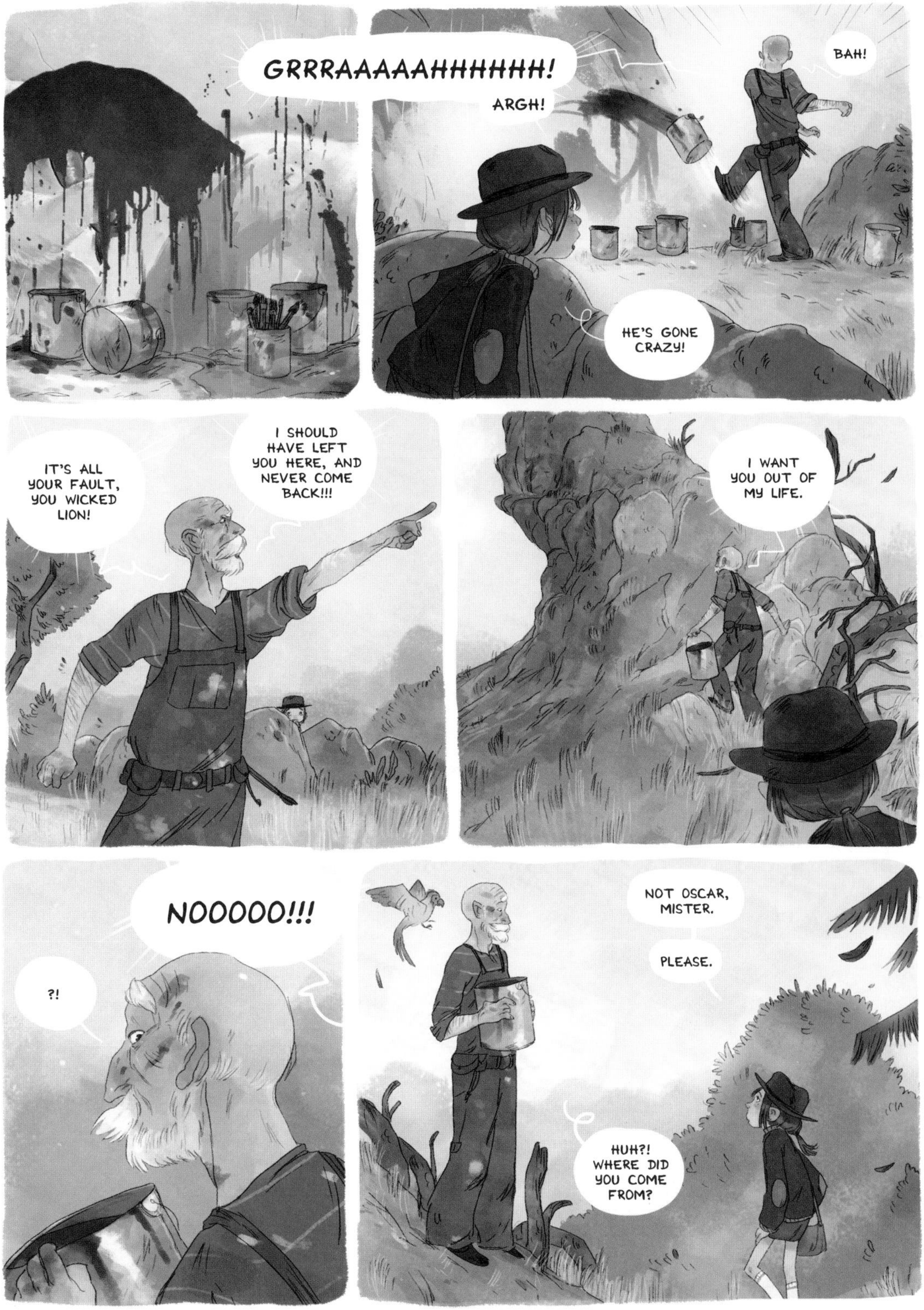
GRRRAAAAAHHHHHH!
ARGH!
BAH!
HE'S GONE CRAZY!
IT'S ALL YOUR FAULT, YOU WICKED LION!
I SHOULD HAVE LEFT YOU HERE, AND NEVER COME BACK!!!
I WANT YOU OUT OF MY LIFE.
NOOOOO!!!
?!
NOT OSCAR, MISTER.
PLEASE.
HUH?! WHERE DID YOU COME FROM?

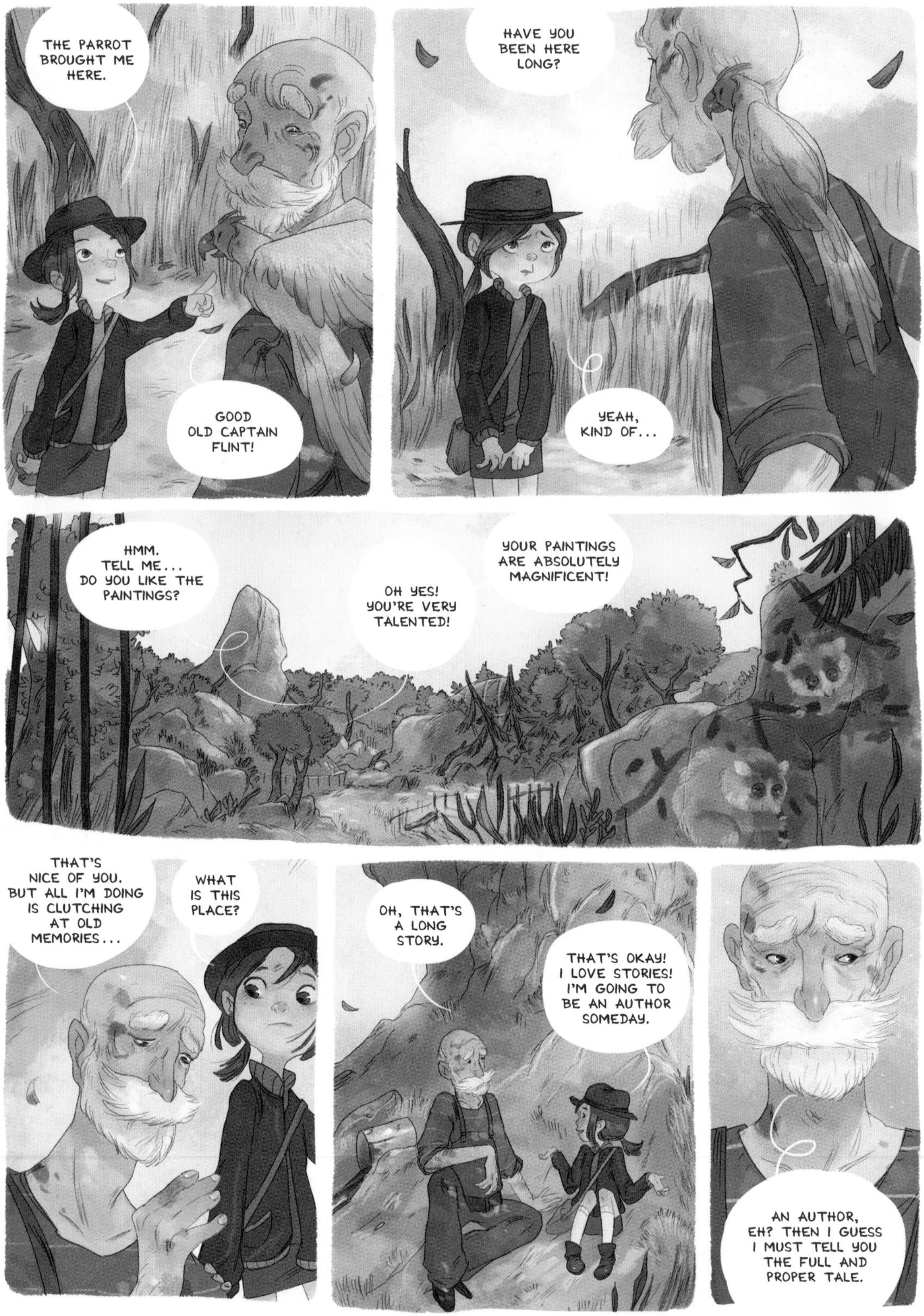
THE PARROT BROUGHT ME HERE.
GOOD OLD CAPTAIN FLINT!
HAVE YOU BEEN HERE LONG?
YEAH, KIND OF...
HMM. TELL ME... DO YOU LIKE THE PAINTINGS?
OH YES! YOU'RE VERY TALENTED!
YOUR PAINTINGS ARE ABSOLUTELY MAGNIFICENT!
THAT'S NICE OF YOU. BUT ALL I'M DOING IS CLUTCHING AT OLD MEMORIES...
WHAT IS THIS PLACE?
OH, THAT'S A LONG STORY.
THAT'S OKAY! I LOVE STORIES! I'M GOING TO BE AN AUTHOR SOMEDAY.
AN AUTHOR, EH? THEN I GUESS I MUST TELL YOU THE FULL AND PROPER TALE.

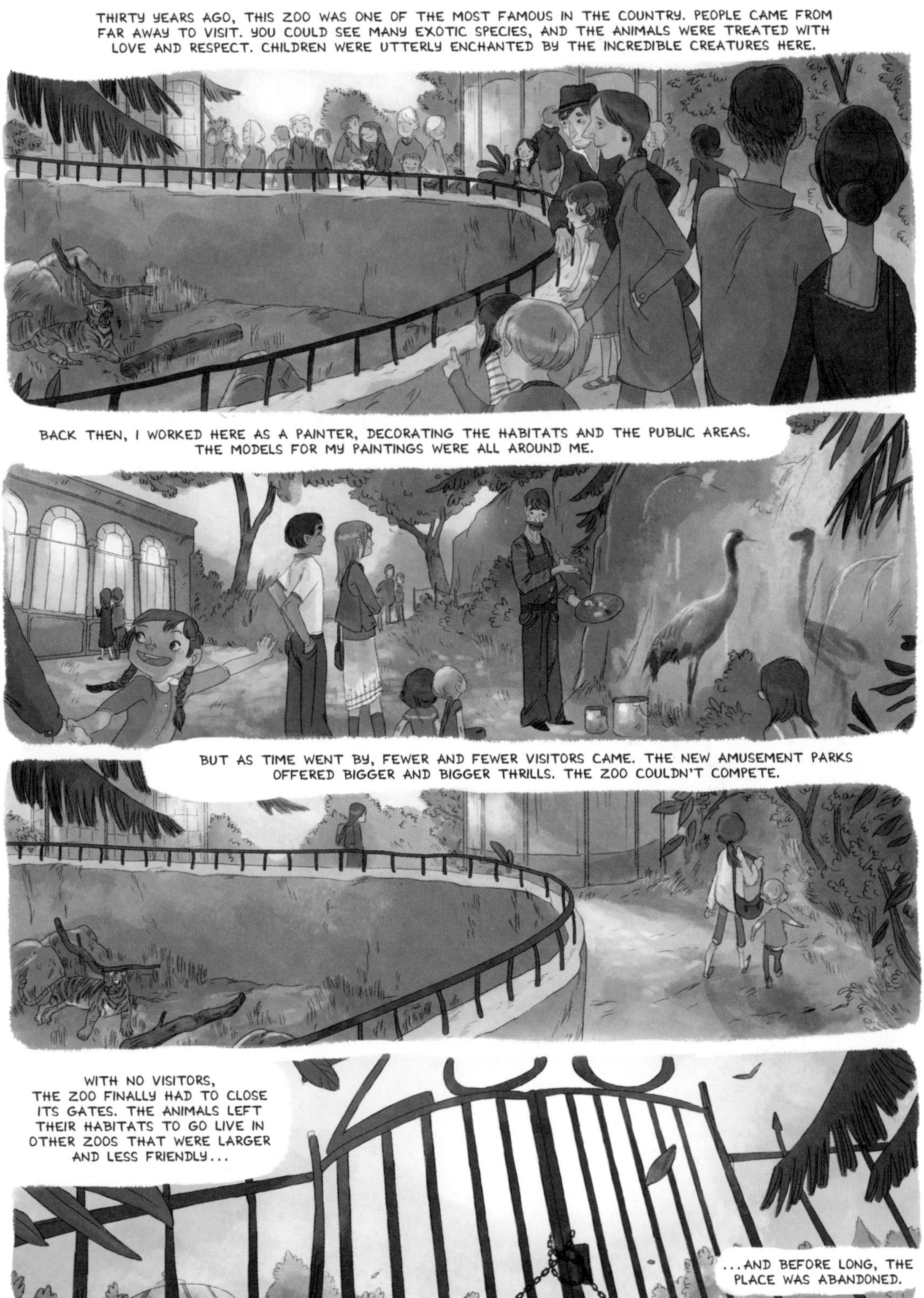
THIRTY YEARS AGO, THIS ZOO WAS ONE OF THE MOST FAMOUS IN THE COUNTRY. PEOPLE CAME FROM FAR AWAY TO VISIT. YOU COULD SEE MANY EXOTIC SPECIES, AND THE ANIMALS WERE TREATED WITH LOVE AND RESPECT. CHILDREN WERE UTTERLY ENCHANTED BY THE INCREDIBLE CREATURES HERE.
BACK THEN, I WORKED HERE AS A PAINTER, DECORATING THE HABITATS AND THE PUBLIC AREAS. THE MODELS FOR MY PAINTINGS WERE ALL AROUND ME.
BUT AS TIME WENT BY, FEWER AND FEWER VISITORS CAME. THE NEW AMUSEMENT PARKS OFFERED BIGGER AND BIGGER THRILLS. THE ZOO COULDN'T COMPETE.
WITH NO VISITORS, THE ZOO FINALLY HAD TO CLOSE ITS GATES. THE ANIMALS LEFT THEIR HABITATS TO GO LIVE IN OTHER ZOOS THAT WERE LARGER AND LESS FRIENDLY...
...AND BEFORE LONG, THE PLACE WAS ABANDONED.

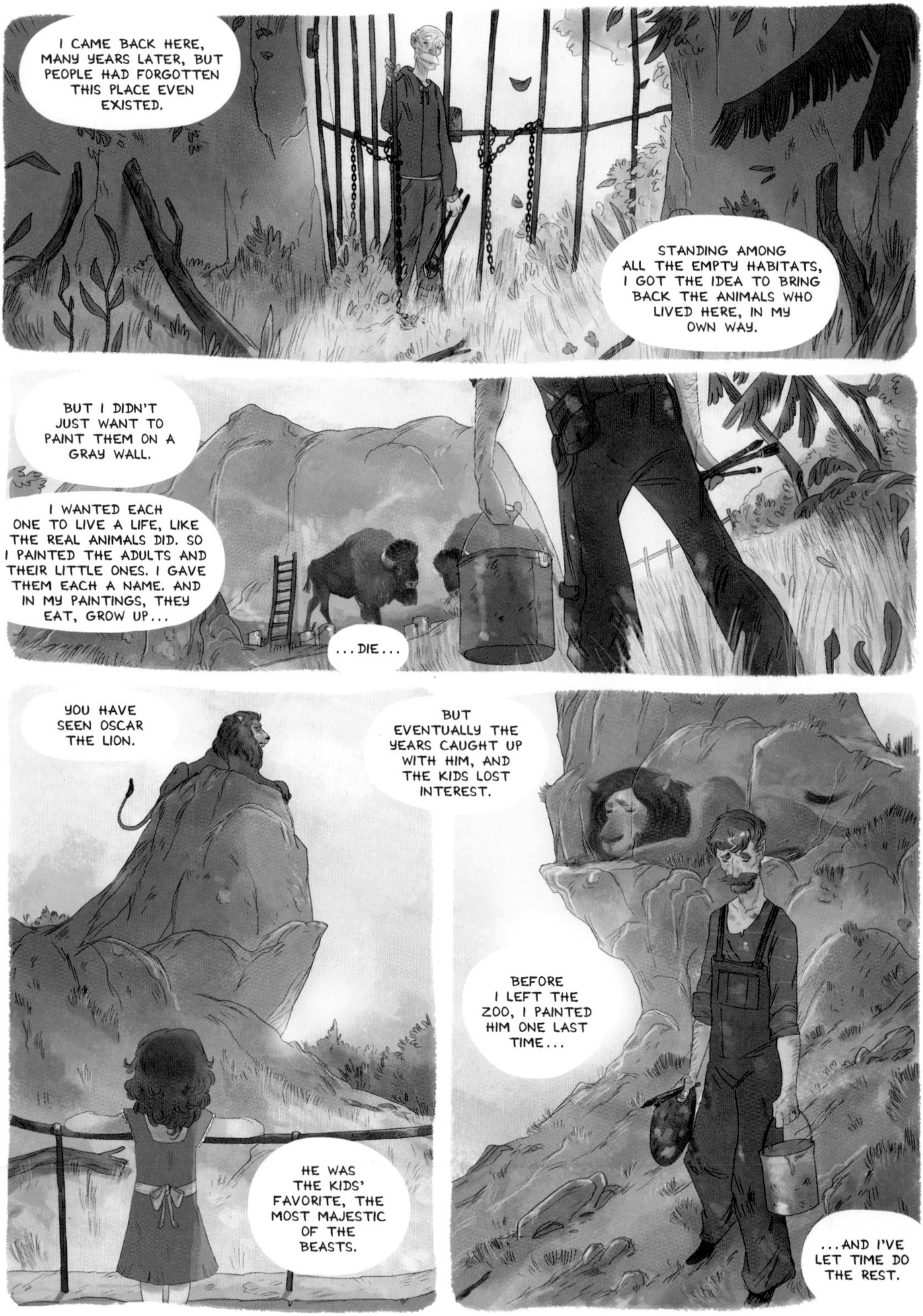
I CAME BACK HERE, MANY YEARS LATER, BUT PEOPLE HAD FORGOTTEN THIS PLACE EVEN EXISTED.
STANDING AMONG ALL THE EMPTY HABITATS, I GOT THE IDEA TO BRING BACK THE ANIMALS WHO LIVED HERE, IN MY OWN WAY.
BUT I DIDN'T JUST WANT TO PAINT THEM ON A GRAY WALL.
I WANTED EACH ONE TO LIVE A LIFE, LIKE THE REAL ANIMALS DID. SO I PAINTED THE ADULTS AND THEIR LITTLE ONES. I GAVE THEM EACH A NAME. AND IN MY PAINTINGS, THEY EAT, GROW UP...
...DIE...
YOU HAVE SEEN OSCAR THE LION.
HE WAS THE KIDS' FAVORITE, THE MOST MAJESTIC OF THE BEASTS.
BUT EVENTUALLY THE YEARS CAUGHT UP WITH HIM, AND THE KIDS LOST INTEREST.
BEFORE I LEFT THE ZOO, I PAINTED HIM ONE LAST TIME...
...AND I'VE LET TIME DO THE REST.

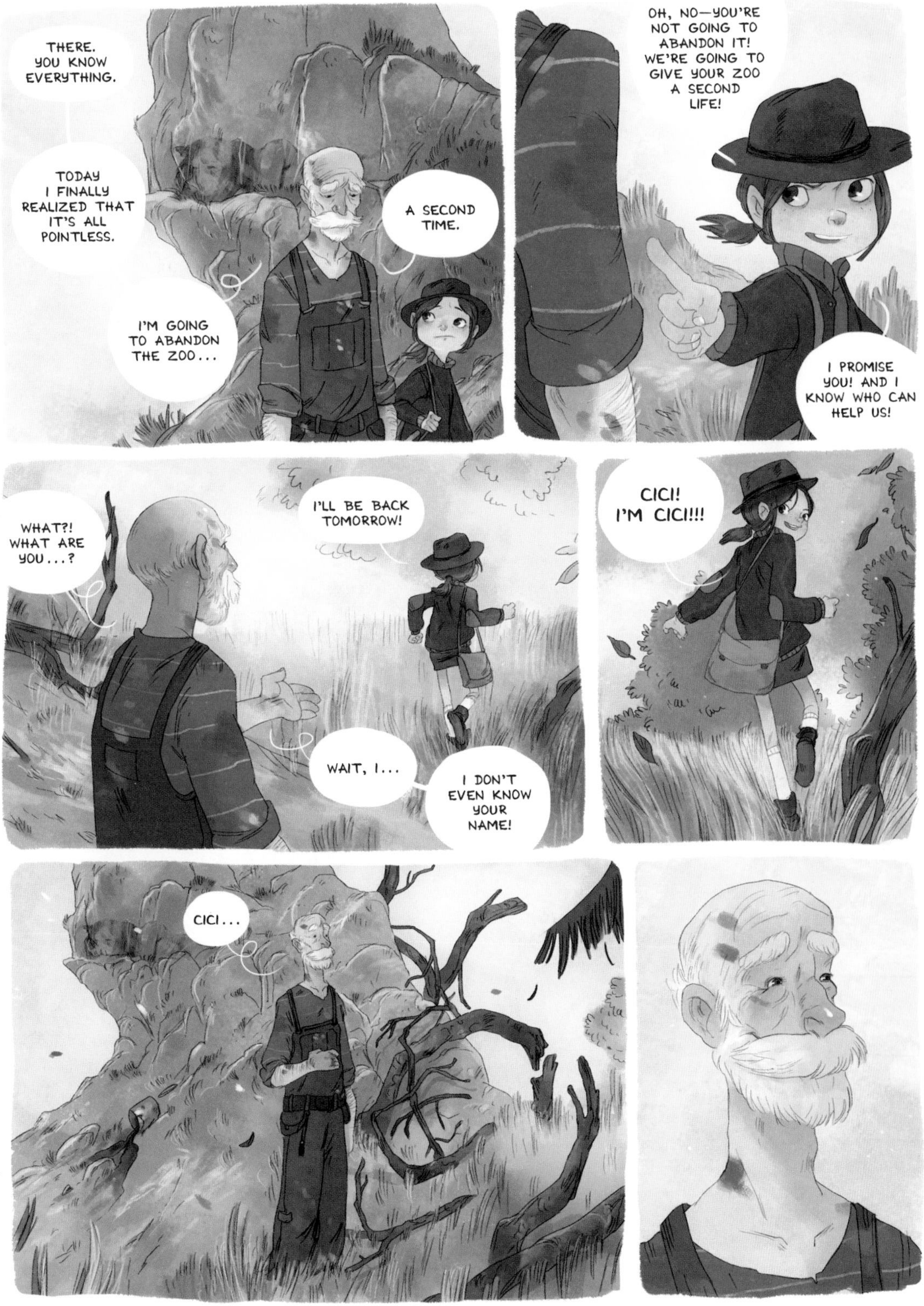
THERE. YOU KNOW EVERYTHING.
TODAY I FINALLY REALIZED THAT IT'S ALL POINTLESS.
A SECOND TIME.
I'M GOING TO ABANDON THE ZOO...
OH, NO—YOU'RE NOT GOING TO ABANDON IT! WE'RE GOING TO GIVE YOUR ZOO A SECOND LIFE!
I PROMISE YOU! AND I KNOW WHO CAN HELP US!
WHAT?! WHAT ARE YOU...?
I'LL BE BACK TOMORROW!
WAIT, I...
I DON'T EVEN KNOW YOUR NAME!
CICI! I'M CICI!!!
CICI...

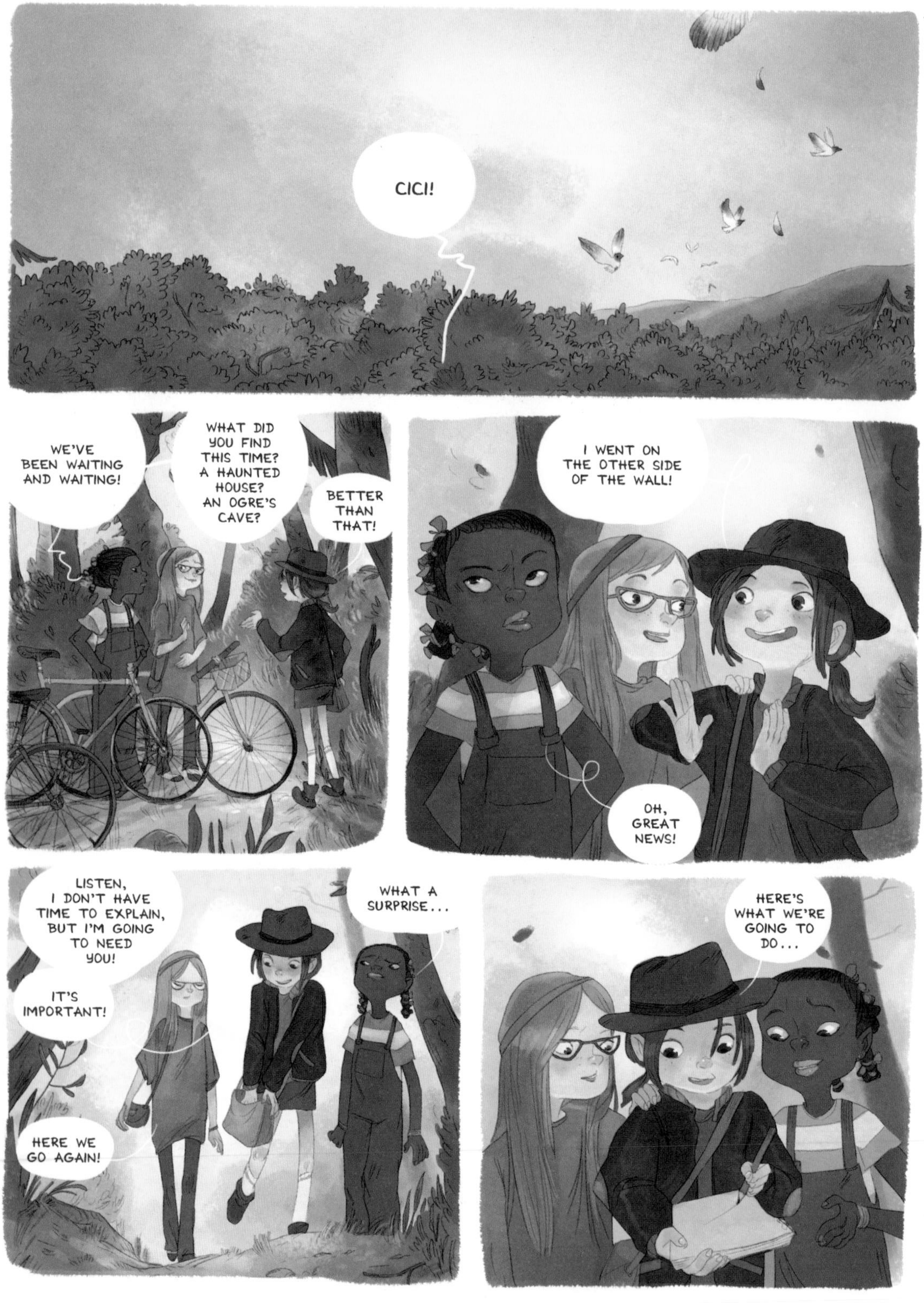
CICI!
WE'VE BEEN WAITING AND WAITING!
WHAT DID YOU FIND THIS TIME? A HAUNTED HOUSE? AN OGRE'S CAVE?
BETTER THAN THAT!
I WENT ON THE OTHER SIDE OF THE WALL!
OH, GREAT NEWS!
LISTEN, I DON'T HAVE TIME TO EXPLAIN, BUT I'M GOING TO NEED YOU!
IT'S IMPORTANT!
HERE WE GO AGAIN!
WHAT A SURPRISE...
HERE'S WHAT WE'RE GOING TO DO...

Lena took great photos of us working in the zoo. She gave me some as souvenirs!

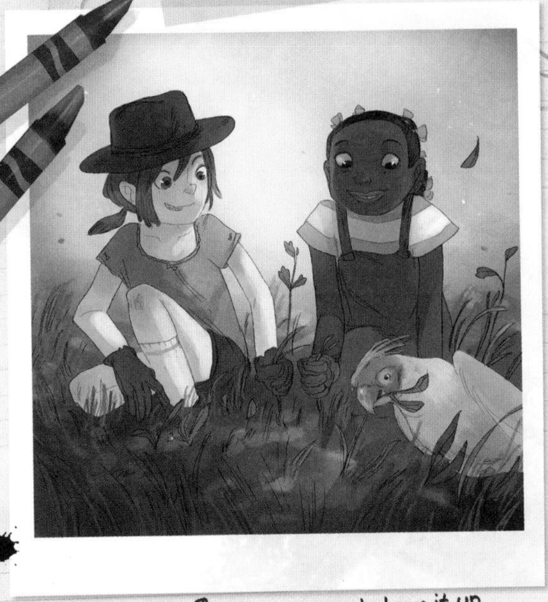

We all helped clean it up. Even Captain Flint!

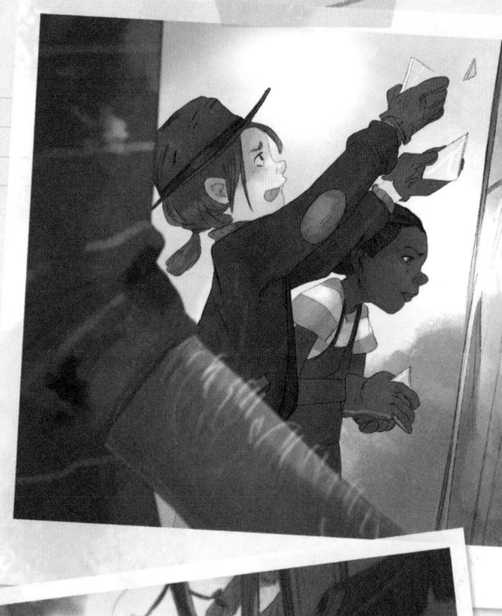

The broken glass was very fragile. And very dangerous. Luckily, Michael had lots of work gloves to lend us.

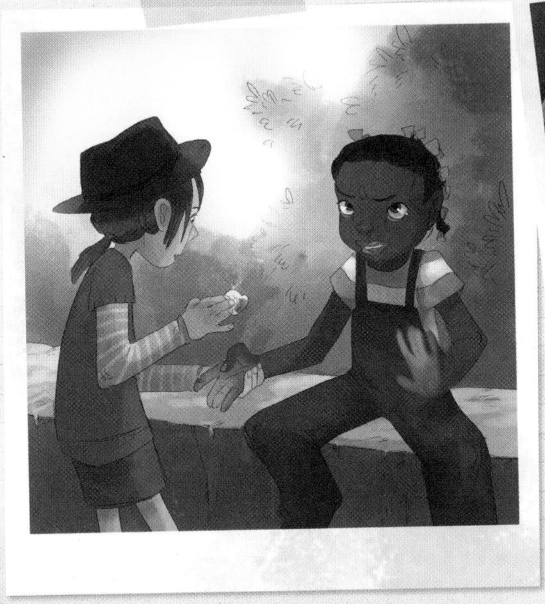

But even so, we had some casualties... For once, Erica had a good reason to complain!

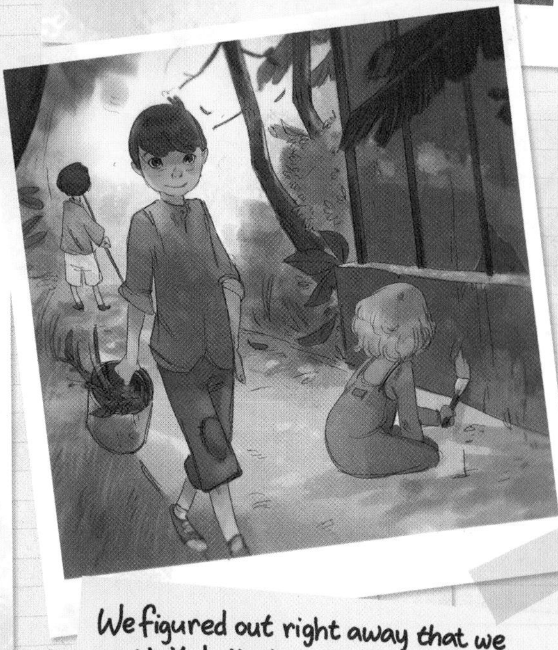

We figured out right away that we couldn't do it alone. So we quietly began to get our friends to come help.

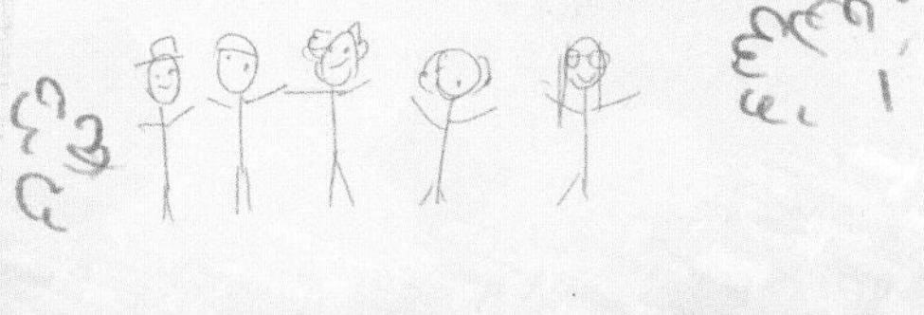

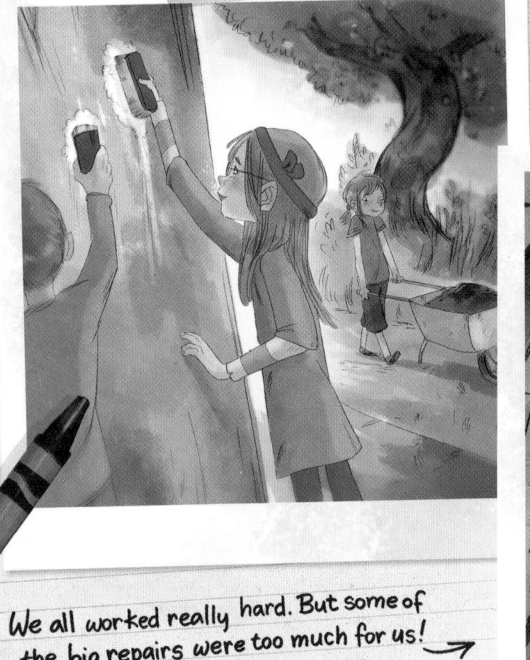

I took that one, so Lena could be in a few photos. Now you can see that she worked hard too!

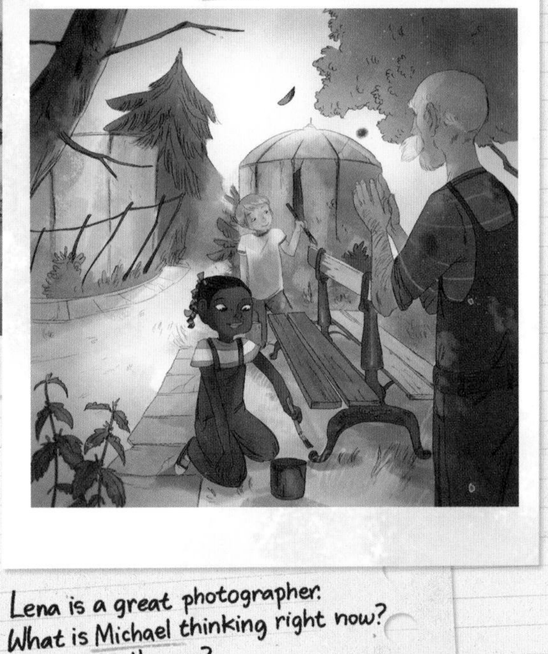

We all worked really hard. But some of the big repairs were too much for us!

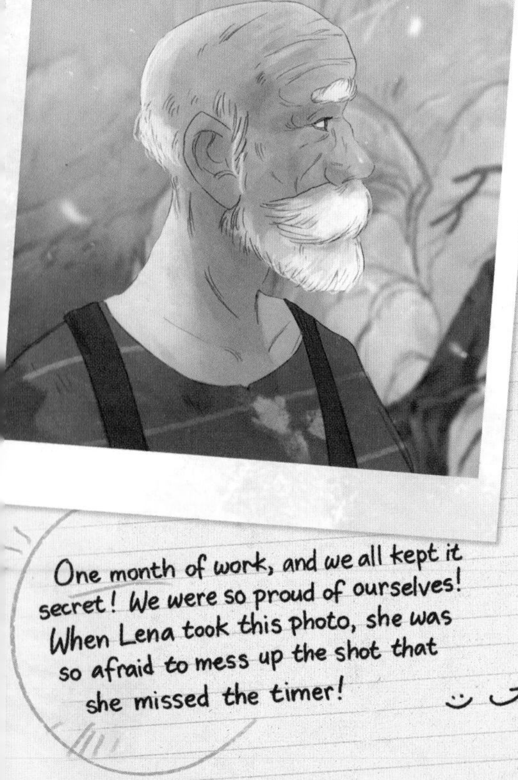

Lena is a great photographer. What is Michael thinking right now? Is he sad? Happy?...

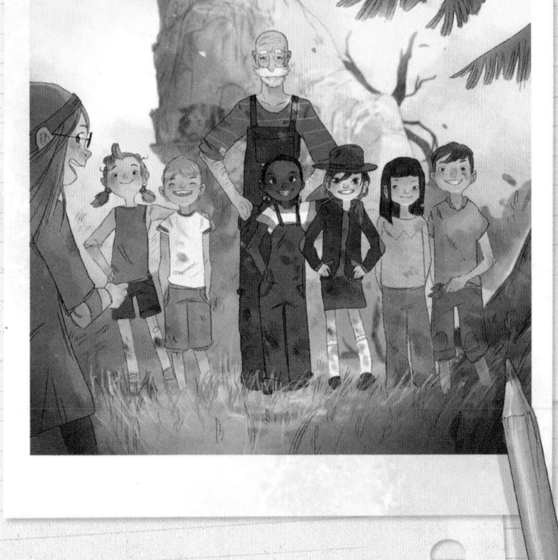

One month of work, and we all kept it secret! We were so proud of ourselves! When Lena took this photo, she was so afraid to mess up the shot that she missed the timer!

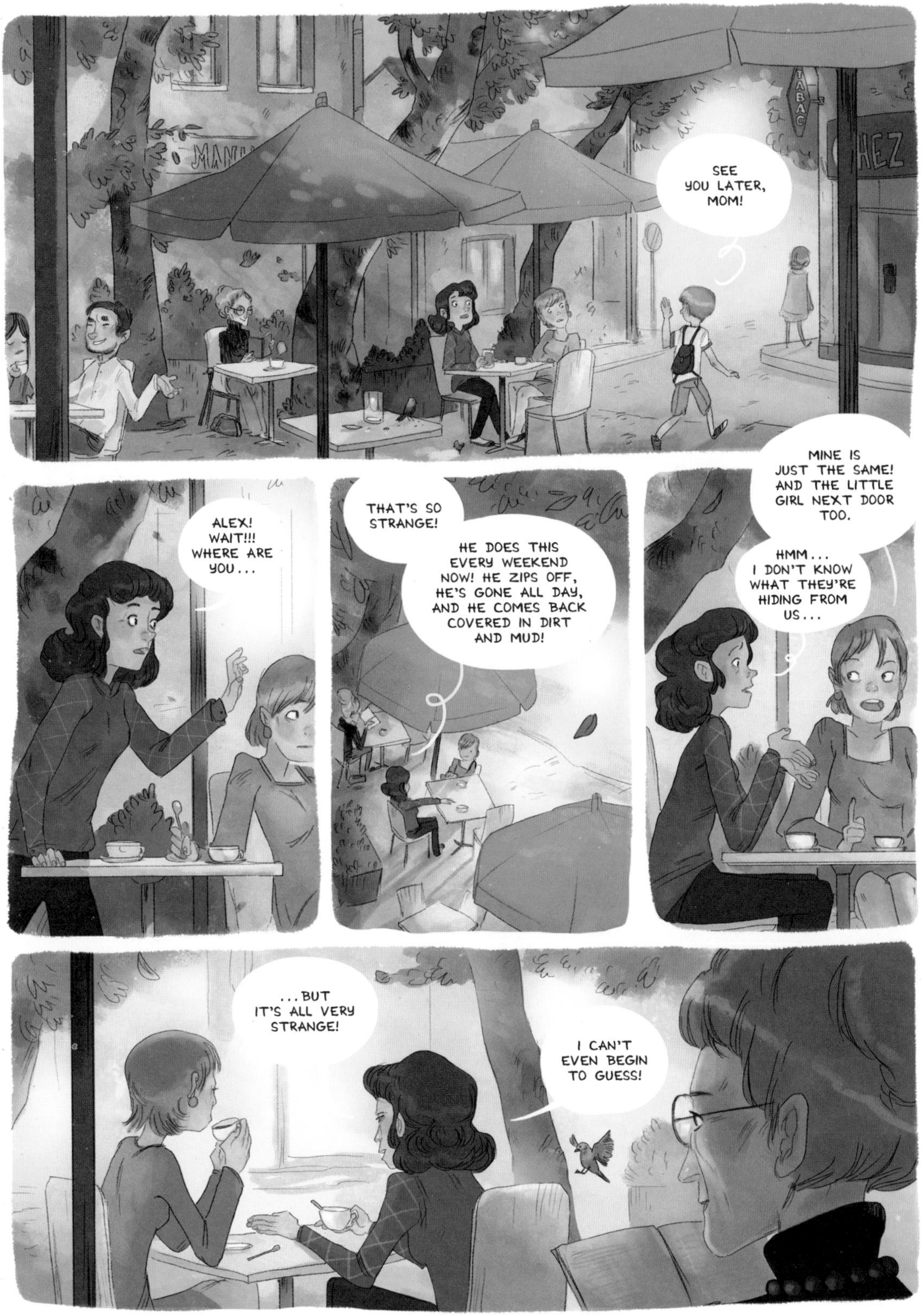
MANU
TABAC
HEZ
SEE YOU LATER, MOM!
ALEX! WAIT!!! WHERE ARE YOU...
THAT'S SO STRANGE!
HE DOES THIS EVERY WEEKEND NOW! HE ZIPS OFF, HE'S GONE ALL DAY, AND HE COMES BACK COVERED IN DIRT AND MUD!
MINE IS JUST THE SAME! AND THE LITTLE GIRL NEXT DOOR TOO.
HMM... I DON'T KNOW WHAT THEY'RE HIDING FROM US...
...BUT IT'S ALL VERY STRANGE!
I CAN'T EVEN BEGIN TO GUESS!

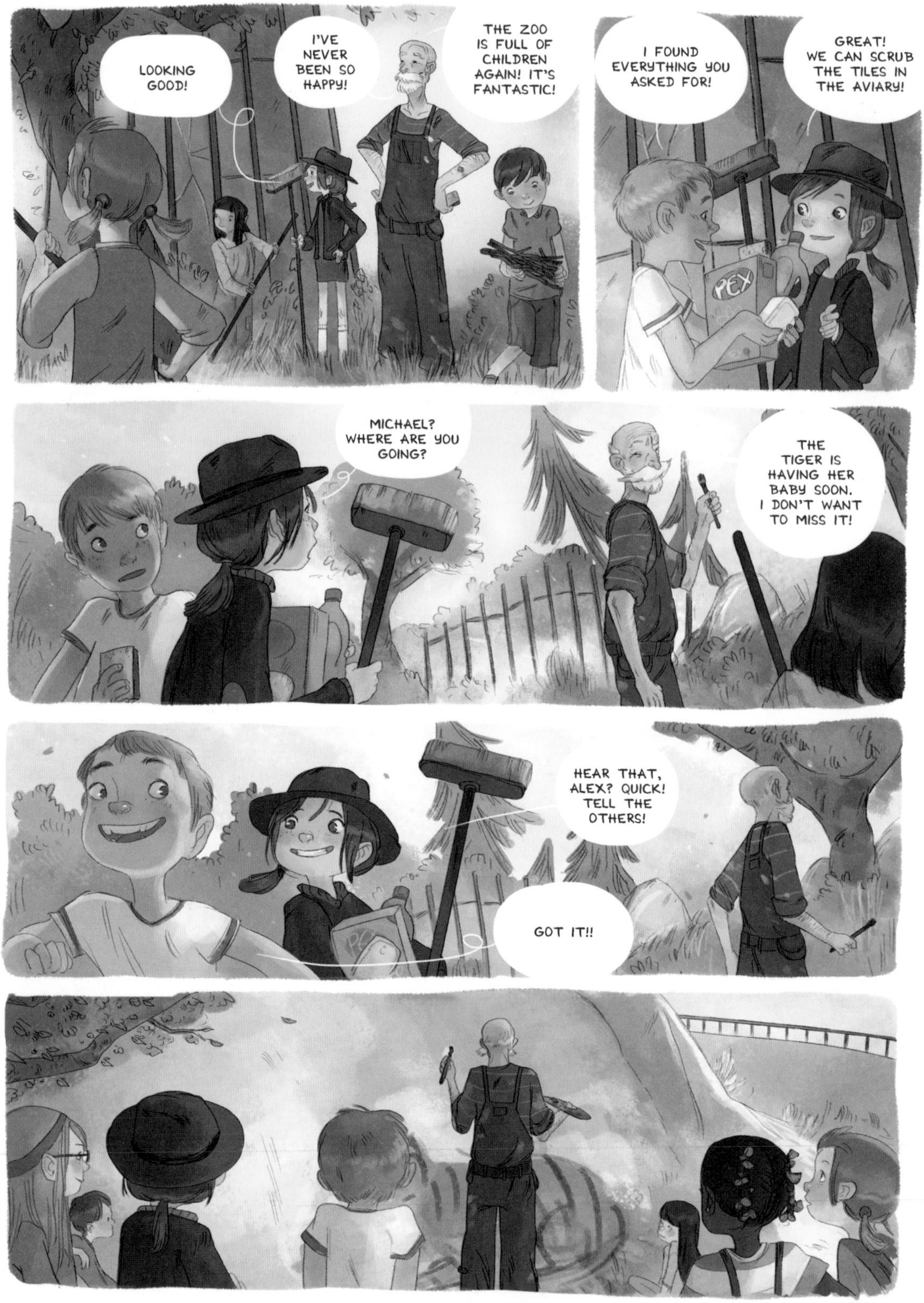
LOOKING GOOD!
I'VE NEVER BEEN SO HAPPY!
THE ZOO IS FULL OF CHILDREN AGAIN! IT'S FANTASTIC!
I FOUND EVERYTHING YOU ASKED FOR!
GREAT! WE CAN SCRUB THE TILES IN THE AVIARY!
PEX
MICHAEL? WHERE ARE YOU GOING?
THE TIGER IS HAVING HER BABY SOON. I DON'T WANT TO MISS IT!
HEAR THAT, ALEX? QUICK! TELL THE OTHERS!
GOT IT!!

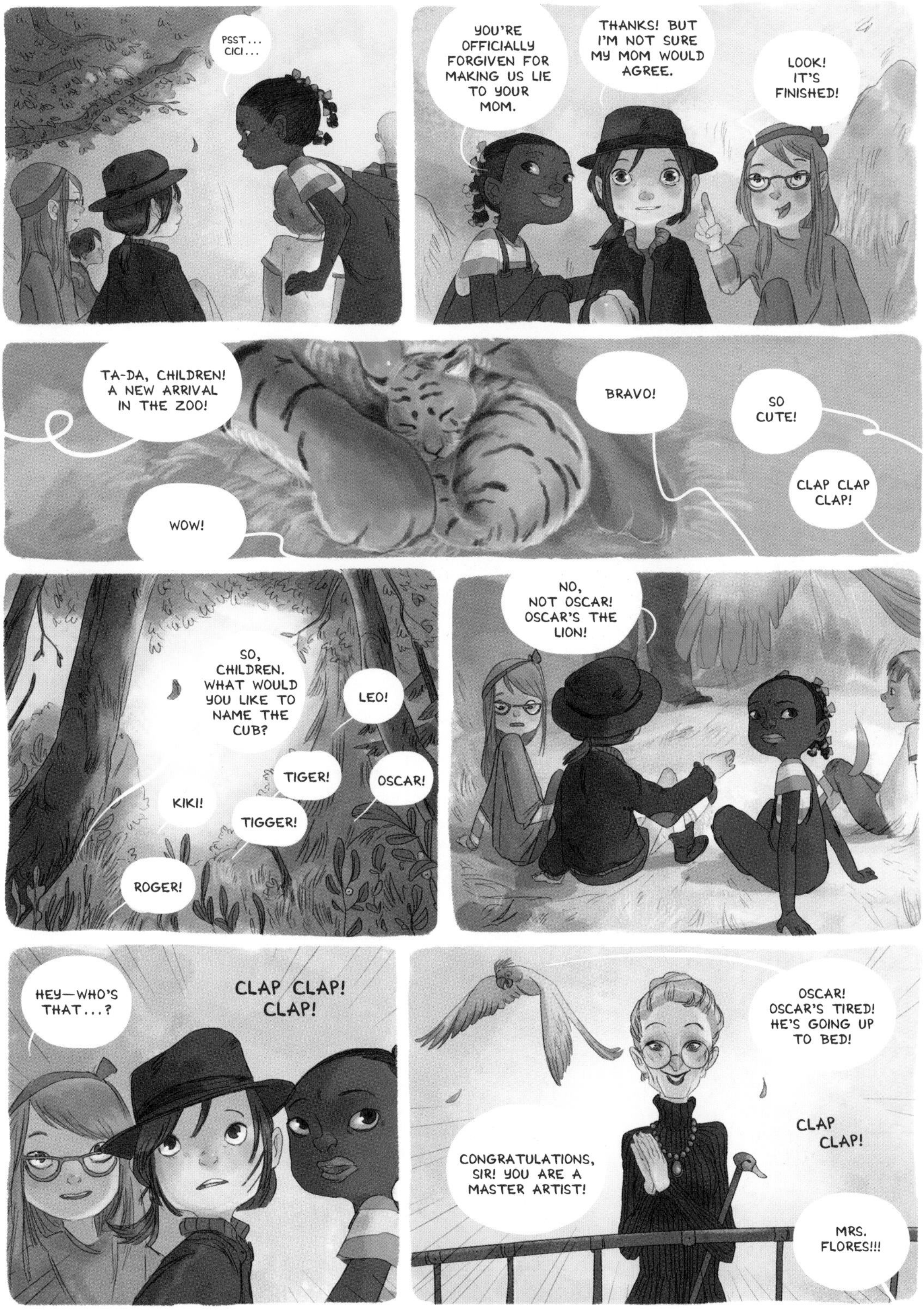
PSST... CICI...
YOU'RE OFFICIALLY FORGIVEN FOR MAKING US LIE TO YOUR MOM.
THANKS! BUT I'M NOT SURE MY MOM WOULD AGREE.
LOOK! IT'S FINISHED!
TA-DA, CHILDREN! A NEW ARRIVAL IN THE ZOO!
WOW!
BRAVO!
SO CUTE!
CLAP CLAP CLAP!
SO, CHILDREN. WHAT WOULD YOU LIKE TO NAME THE CUB?
LEO!
TIGER!
OSCAR!
KIKI!
TIGGER!
ROGER!
NO, NOT OSCAR! OSCAR'S THE LION!
HEY—WHO'S THAT...?
CLAP CLAP! CLAP!
OSCAR! OSCAR'S TIRED! HE'S GOING UP TO BED!
CONGRATULATIONS, SIR! YOU ARE A MASTER ARTIST!
CLAP CLAP!
MRS. FLORES!!!

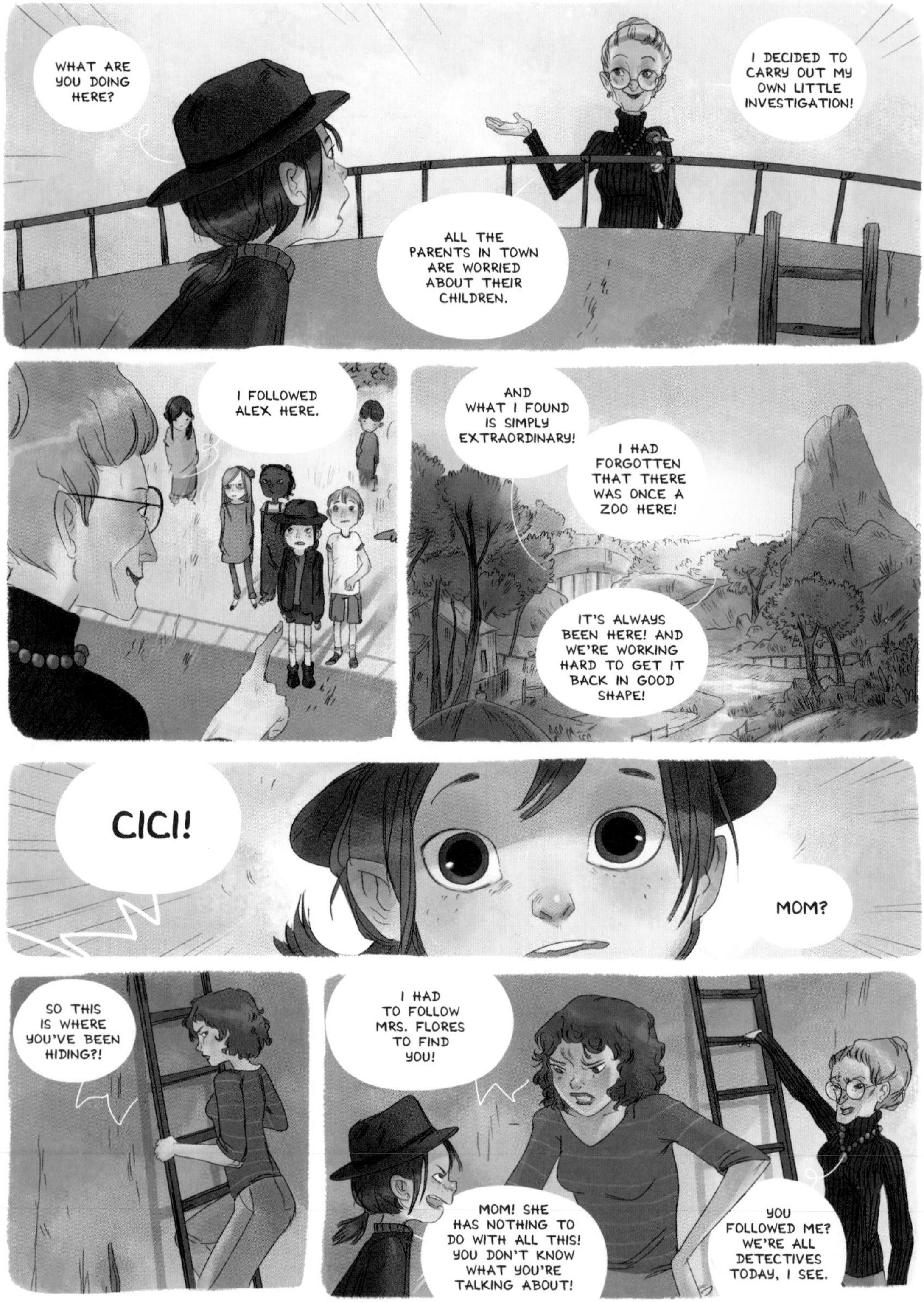
WHAT ARE YOU DOING HERE?
I DECIDED TO CARRY OUT MY OWN LITTLE INVESTIGATION!
ALL THE PARENTS IN TOWN ARE WORRIED ABOUT THEIR CHILDREN.
I FOLLOWED ALEX HERE.
AND WHAT I FOUND IS SIMPLY EXTRAORDINARY!
I HAD FORGOTTEN THAT THERE WAS ONCE A ZOO HERE!
IT'S ALWAYS BEEN HERE! AND WE'RE WORKING HARD TO GET IT BACK IN GOOD SHAPE!
CICI!
MOM?
SO THIS IS WHERE YOU'VE BEEN HIDING?!
I HAD TO FOLLOW MRS. FLORES TO FIND YOU!
MOM! SHE HAS NOTHING TO DO WITH ALL THIS! YOU DON'T KNOW WHAT YOU'RE TALKING ABOUT!
YOU FOLLOWED ME? WE'RE ALL DETECTIVES TODAY, I SEE.

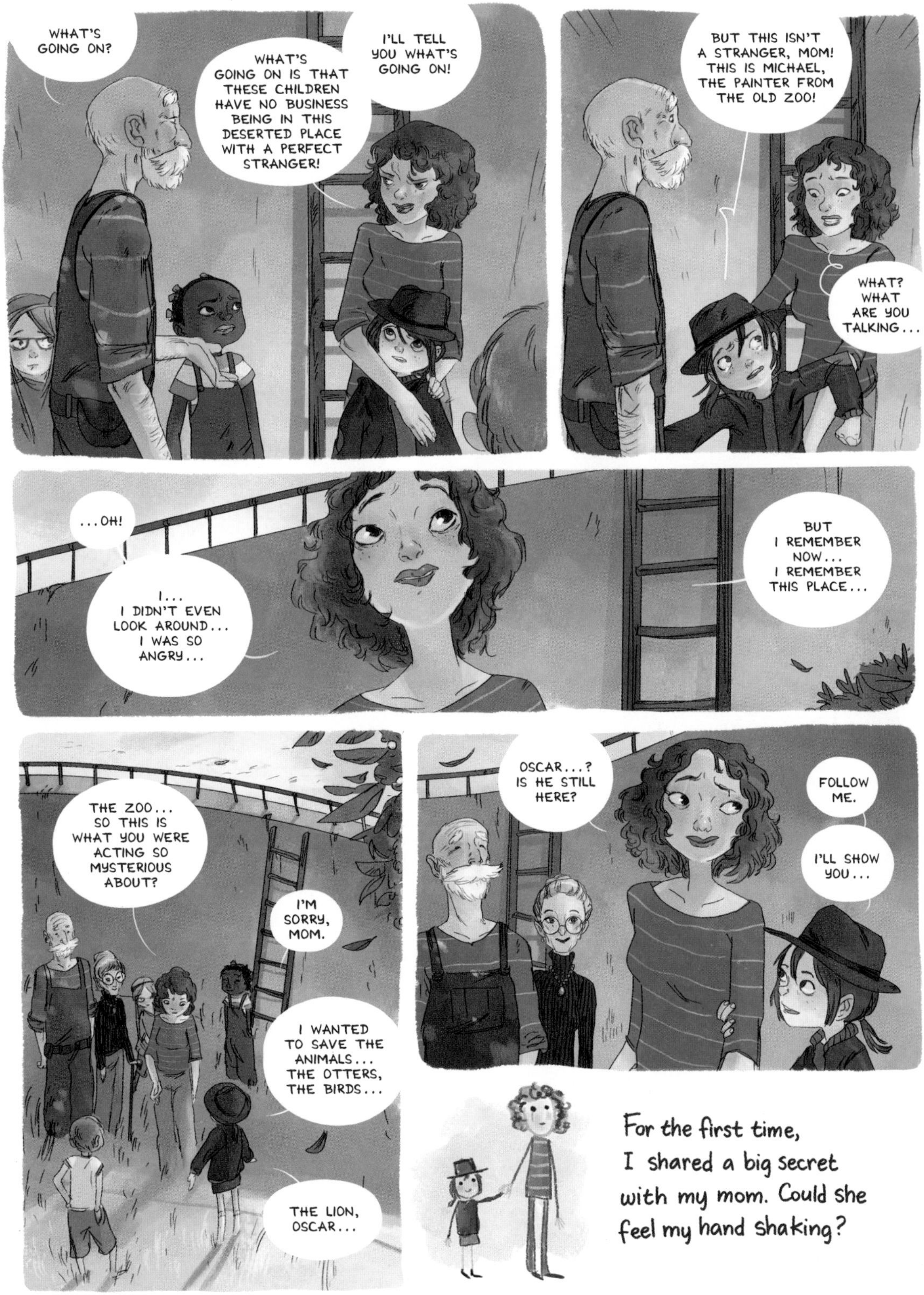
WHAT'S GOING ON?
WHAT'S GOING ON IS THAT THESE CHILDREN HAVE NO BUSINESS BEING IN THIS DESERTED PLACE WITH A PERFECT STRANGER!
I'LL TELL YOU WHAT'S GOING ON!
BUT THIS ISN'T A STRANGER, MOM! THIS IS MICHAEL, THE PAINTER FROM THE OLD ZOO!
WHAT? WHAT ARE YOU TALKING...
...OH!
I... I DIDN'T EVEN LOOK AROUND... I WAS SO ANGRY...
BUT I REMEMBER NOW... I REMEMBER THIS PLACE...
THE ZOO... SO THIS IS WHAT YOU WERE ACTING SO MYSTERIOUS ABOUT?
I'M SORRY, MOM.
I WANTED TO SAVE THE ANIMALS... THE OTTERS, THE BIRDS...
THE LION, OSCAR...
OSCAR...? IS HE STILL HERE?
FOLLOW ME.
I'LL SHOW YOU...
For the first time, I shared a big secret with my mom. Could she feel my hand shaking?

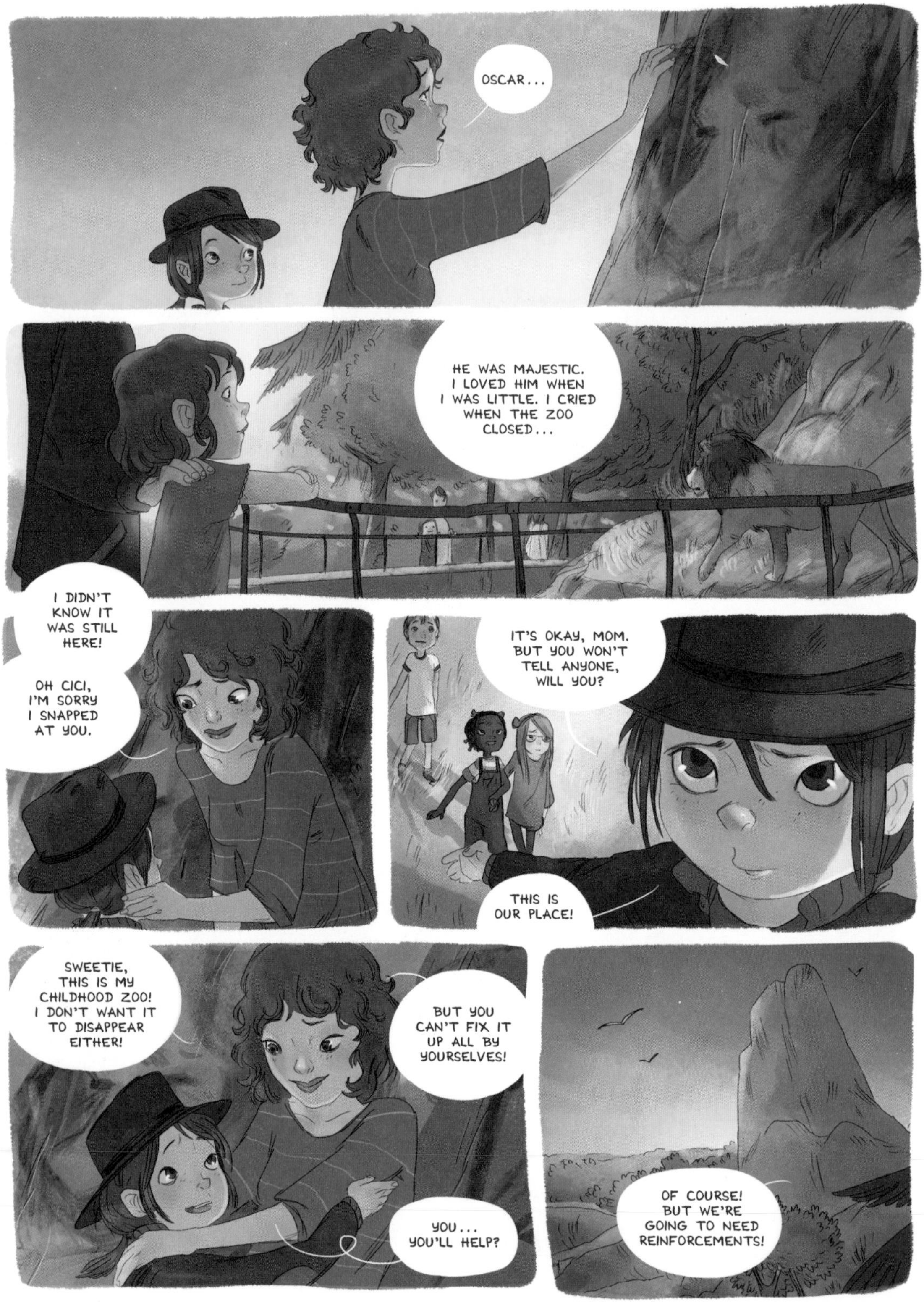
OSCAR...
HE WAS MAJESTIC. I LOVED HIM WHEN I WAS LITTLE. I CRIED WHEN THE ZOO CLOSED...
I DIDN'T KNOW IT WAS STILL HERE!
OH CICI, I'M SORRY I SNAPPED AT YOU.
IT'S OKAY, MOM. BUT YOU WON'T TELL ANYONE, WILL YOU?
THIS IS OUR PLACE!
SWEETIE, THIS IS MY CHILDHOOD ZOO! I DON'T WANT IT TO DISAPPEAR EITHER!
BUT YOU CAN'T FIX IT UP ALL BY YOURSELVES!
YOU... YOU'LL HELP?
OF COURSE! BUT WE'RE GOING TO NEED REINFORCEMENTS!

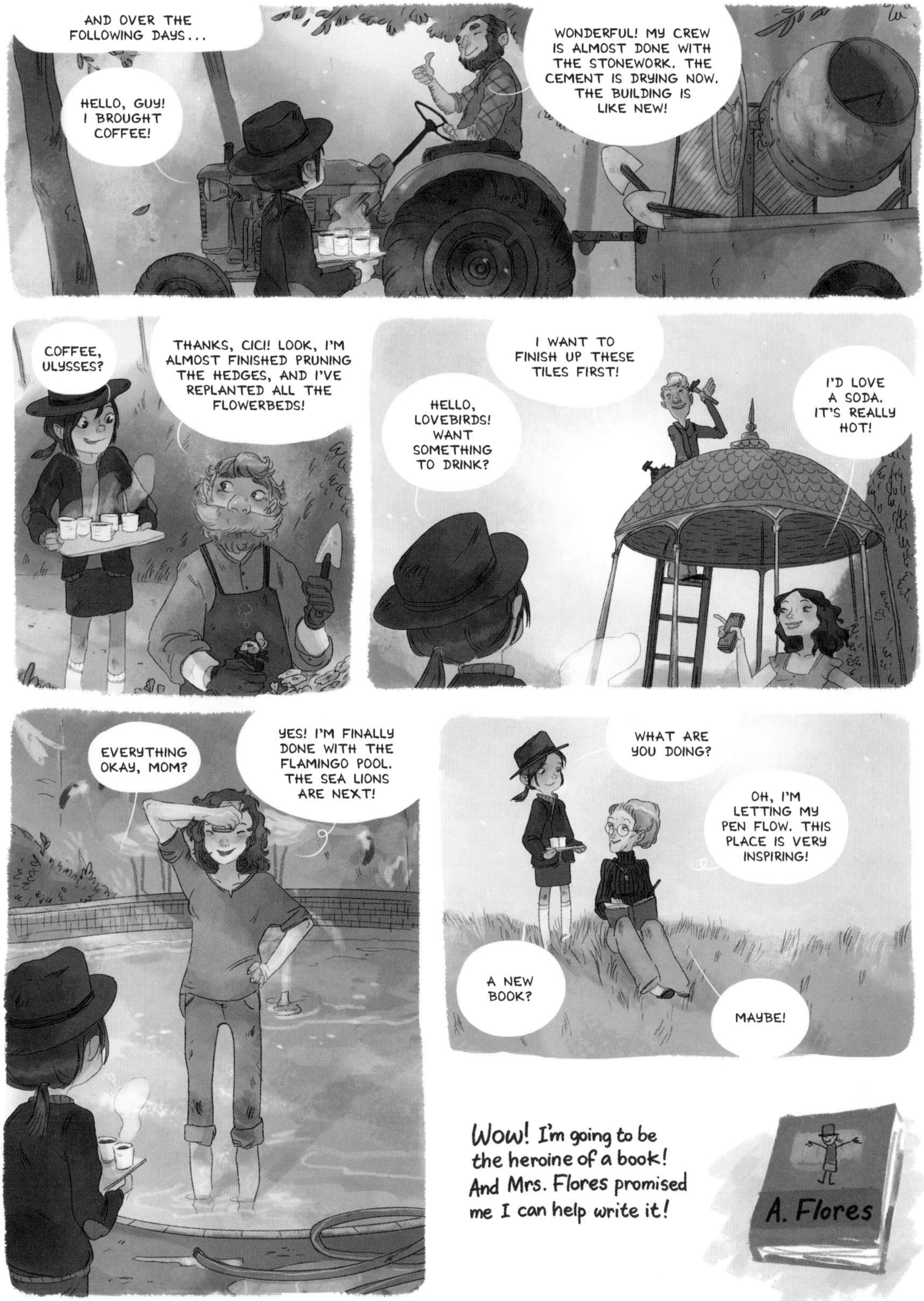
AND OVER THE FOLLOWING DAYS...
HELLO, GUY! I BROUGHT COFFEE!
WONDERFUL! MY CREW IS ALMOST DONE WITH THE STONEWORK. THE CEMENT IS DRYING NOW. THE BUILDING IS LIKE NEW!
COFFEE, ULYSSES?
THANKS, CICI! LOOK, I'M ALMOST FINISHED PRUNING THE HEDGES, AND I'VE REPLANTED ALL THE FLOWERBEDS!
HELLO, LOVEBIRDS! WANT SOMETHING TO DRINK?
I WANT TO FINISH UP THESE TILES FIRST!
I'D LOVE A SODA. IT'S REALLY HOT!
EVERYTHING OKAY, MOM?
YES! I'M FINALLY DONE WITH THE FLAMINGO POOL. THE SEA LIONS ARE NEXT!
WHAT ARE YOU DOING?
OH, I'M LETTING MY PEN FLOW. THIS PLACE IS VERY INSPIRING!
A NEW BOOK?
MAYBE!
Wow! I'm going to be the heroine of a book! And Mrs. Flores promised me I can help write it!
A. Flores

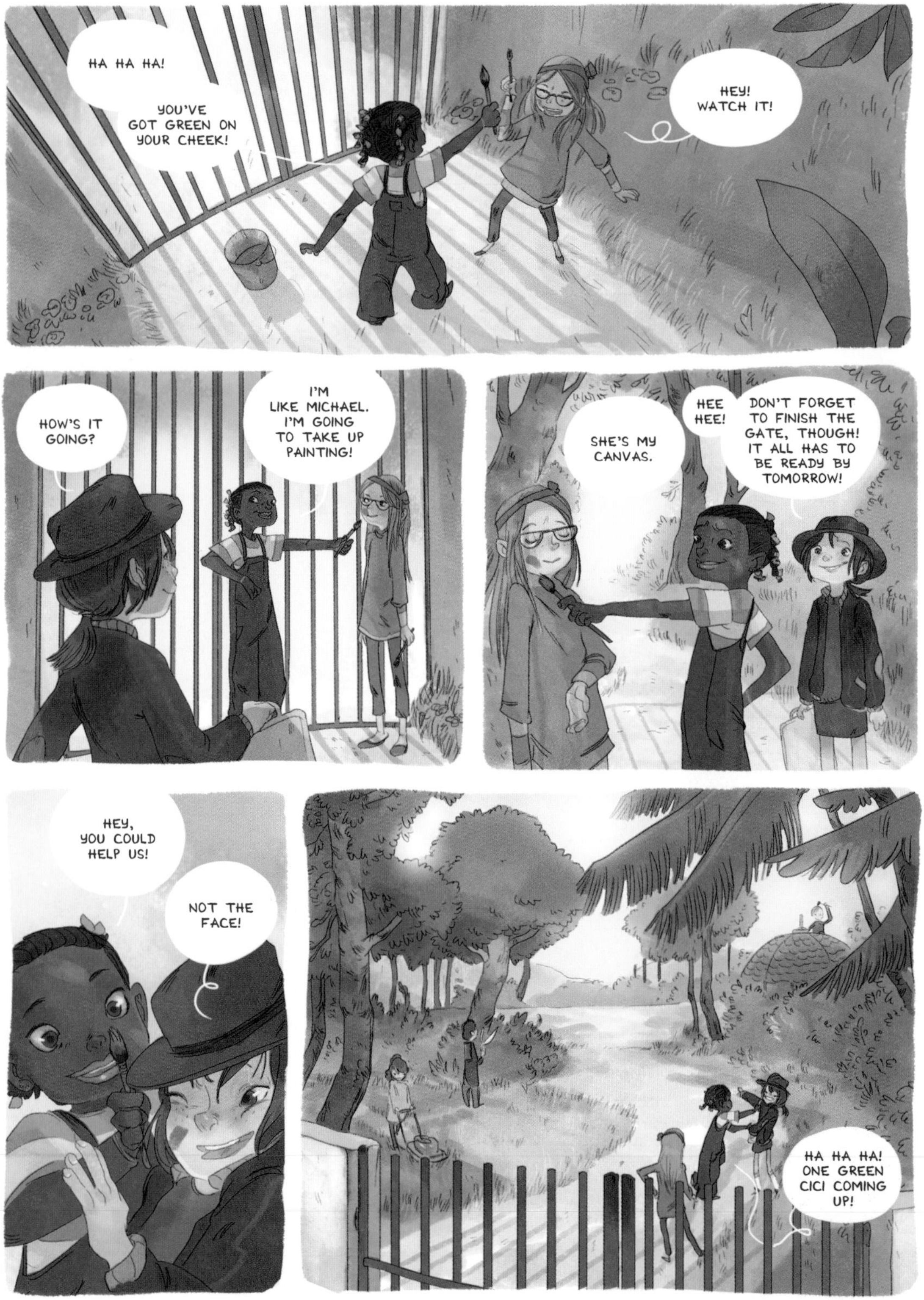
HA HA HA!
YOU'VE GOT GREEN ON YOUR CHEEK!
HEY! WATCH IT!
HOW'S IT GOING?
I'M LIKE MICHAEL. I'M GOING TO TAKE UP PAINTING!
SHE'S MY CANVAS.
HEE HEE!
DON'T FORGET TO FINISH THE GATE, THOUGH! IT ALL HAS TO BE READY BY TOMORROW!
HEY, YOU COULD HELP US!
NOT THE FACE!
HA HA HA! ONE GREEN CICI COMING UP!

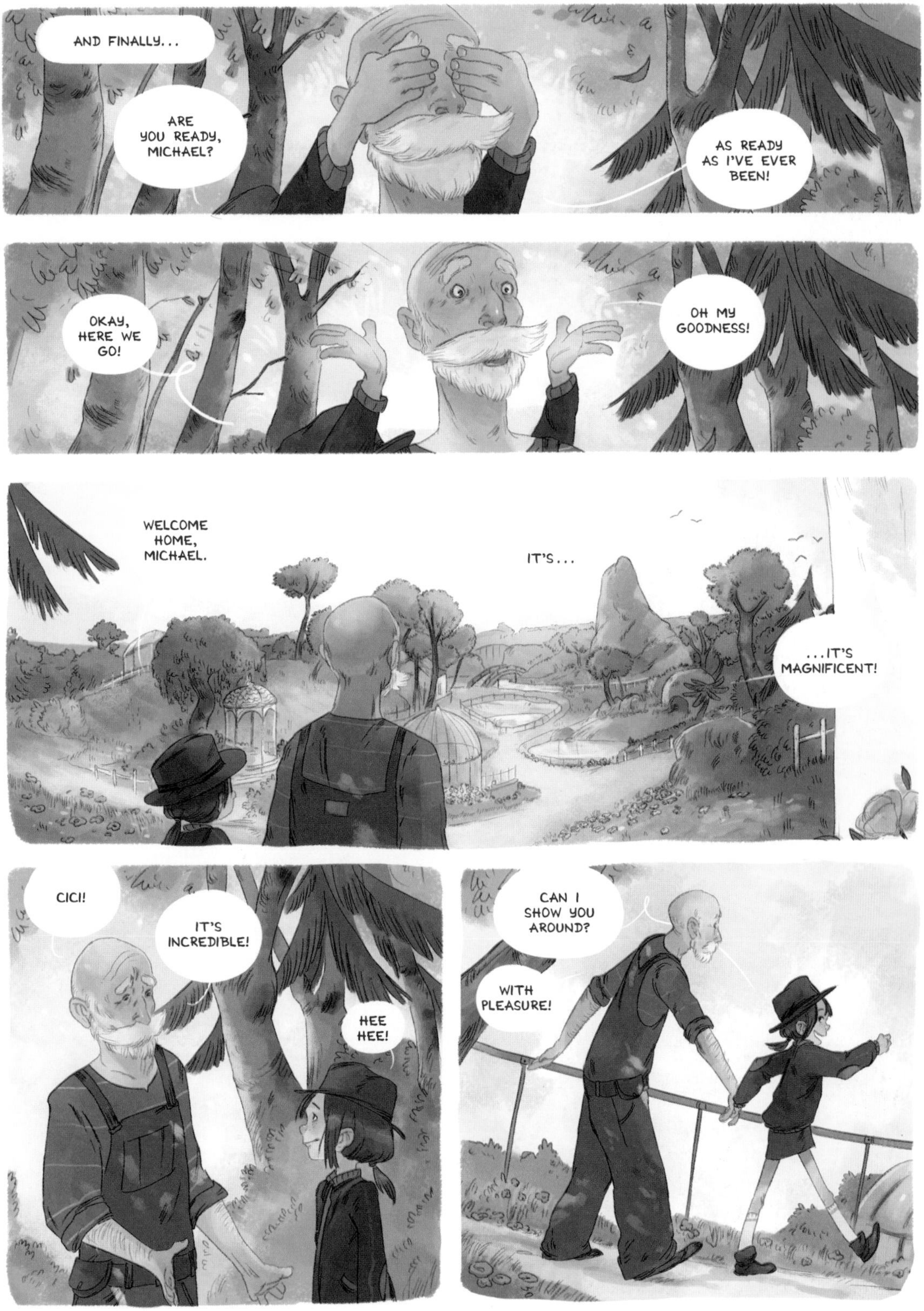
AND FINALLY...
ARE YOU READY, MICHAEL?
AS READY AS I'VE EVER BEEN!
OKAY, HERE WE GO!
OH MY GOODNESS!
WELCOME HOME, MICHAEL.
IT'S...
...IT'S MAGNIFICENT!
CICI!
IT'S INCREDIBLE!
HEE HEE!
CAN I SHOW YOU AROUND?
WITH PLEASURE!

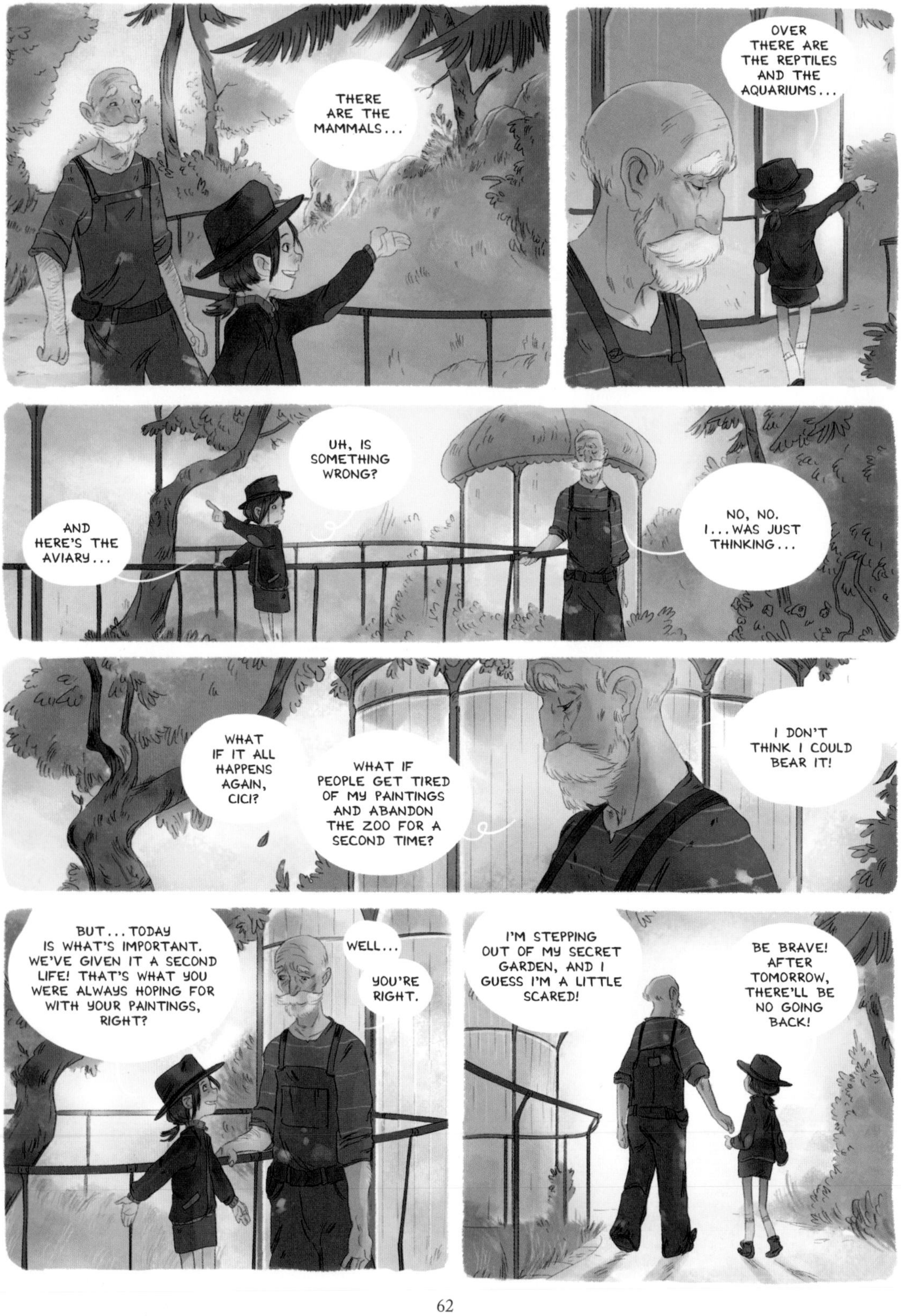
THERE ARE THE MAMMALS...
OVER THERE ARE THE REPTILES AND THE AQUARIUMS...
AND HERE'S THE AVIARY...
UH, IS SOMETHING WRONG?
NO, NO. I...WAS JUST THINKING...
WHAT IF IT ALL HAPPENS AGAIN, CICI?
WHAT IF PEOPLE GET TIRED OF MY PAINTINGS AND ABANDON THE ZOO FOR A SECOND TIME?
I DON'T THINK I COULD BEAR IT!
BUT...TODAY IS WHAT'S IMPORTANT. WE'VE GIVEN IT A SECOND LIFE! THAT'S WHAT YOU WERE ALWAYS HOPING FOR WITH YOUR PAINTINGS, RIGHT?
WELL...
YOU'RE RIGHT.
I'M STEPPING OUT OF MY SECRET GARDEN, AND I GUESS I'M A LITTLE SCARED!
BE BRAVE! AFTER TOMORROW, THERE'LL BE NO GOING BACK!

The zoo has only been open a little while, but I've already collected a lot of newspaper articles!

News in Brief

Two weeks ago, a zoo in a small provincial town reopened its gates, twenty-five years after closing them. But it features a whole new kind of animal exhibit. Here, there are no animals in cages. No roars or squawks—only the sounds of visitors' footsteps and the laughter of children.

In this museum-like zoo, immense canvases await the curious. There are more and more each week: amazingly realistic animal frescoes, the work of one man, Michael Langer. The one-time official painter for this zoo, he's deeply passionate about animals. The crowds flocking to this zoo come not only for his talent but also for the style that he has developed. For Michael never stops with just one animal scene.

He constantly retouches every scene, making them evolve to suit his wishes and to reflect the passage of time.

As you can imagine, a fabulous journey awaits visitors here, caught up in these astonishingly rich works. The zoo is a veritable hymn to the beauty of nature, an ode of respect to life of all stripes.

An exhibit to see, and see again, for both young and old.

A.N.

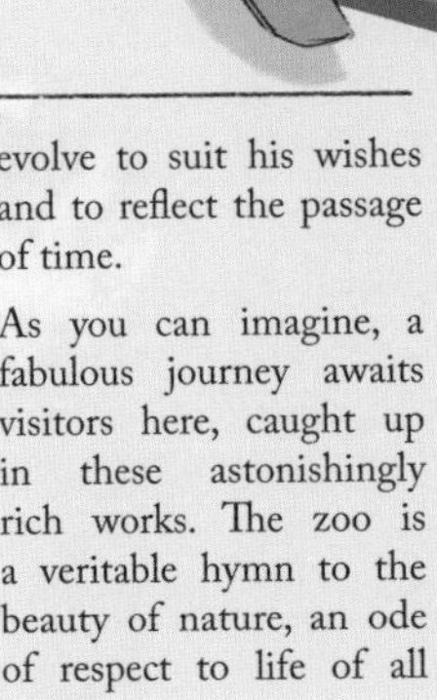

Birth at the Zoo!

After several weeks, under the careful paintbrush of zookeeper Michael Langer, "Bonbon," an African elephant, has been born. The birth follows the disappearance of a mother bear too elderly to make it through the coming winter. Another big event: those who once roamed the zoo's paths as children no doubt remember Oscar, the majestic lion. He had vanished for twenty-five years, but today he has returned, more magnificent than ever. And the artist promises us that he has many wonderful years ahead of him!

C.V.

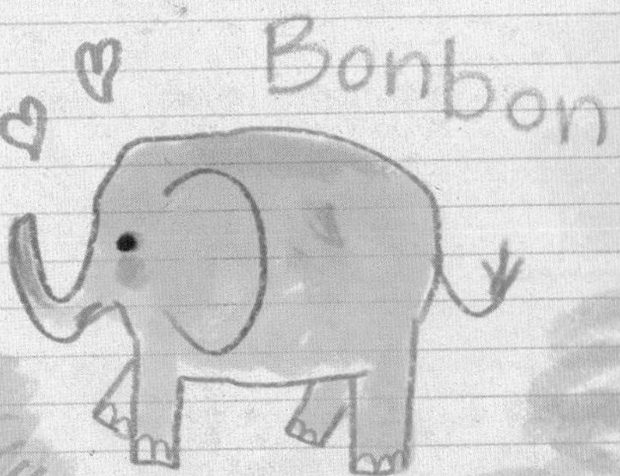
Bonbon

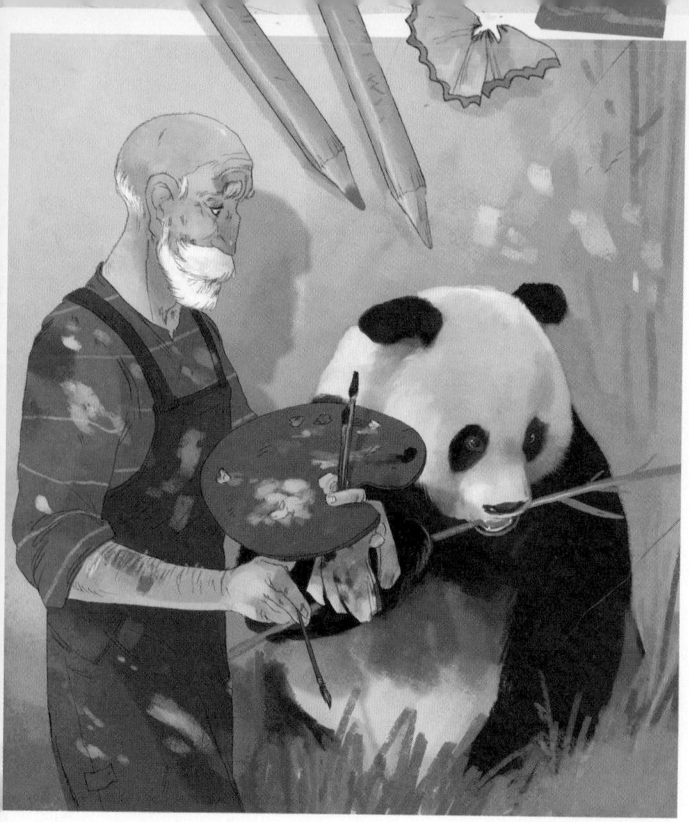

Michael Langer: Portrait of an Extraordinary Painter of Extraordinary Paintings

Michael Langer started painting at a very young age. A nature lover, he drew colorful animals with the precision of a naturalist. He soon mastered fur and plumage. With his canvases under his arm, he met the director of a rural zoo, who offered him a job: Michael would decorate the pathways of the zoo with animal frescoes. Ten years later, the zoo closed, and Michael found himself unemployed again. But his passion for painting had not disappeared, and his steps led him back to the heart of the abandoned zoo, where he made the decision to continue to keep its occupants alive with a startling idea—he would make the scenes evolve over time. We asked him how he came up with this idea. His response: "When I first began to paint, I was never satisfied with my work. I'm a perfectionist. So, naturally, I'd retouch my paintings constantly. Eventually, I gave a name to each animal and grew attached to them. Little by little, touch-up after touch-up, it amused me to change their poses, their behavior, to paint meals for them, to show them over every stage of their lives. It just happened naturally, almost in spite of myself."

An extraordinary exhibit, for fans of animals and art.

J.C.

It's been a few months since the zoo reopened with an exhibit of a whole new kind. It's also become a place for artists to meet.

For thirty-five years, Michael Langer, creator of the 230 images on display, took the time to retouch each painting to "make them live." Today, he admits he no longer has the energy to keep up such a colossal job. But the reopening of the zoo has allowed him to meet many talented artists, and nine more painters are already on board to ensure the ongoing evolution of the works.

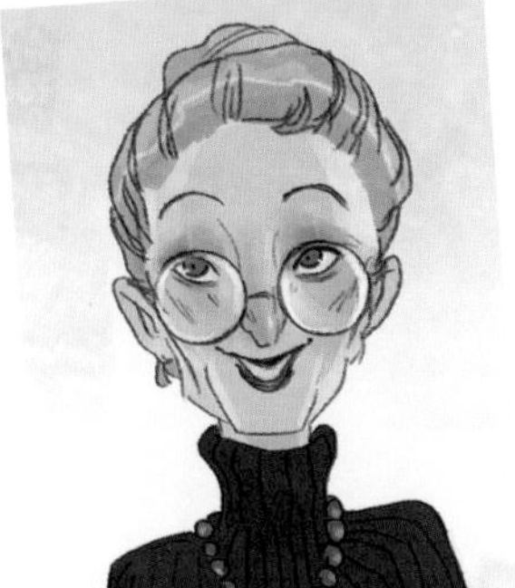

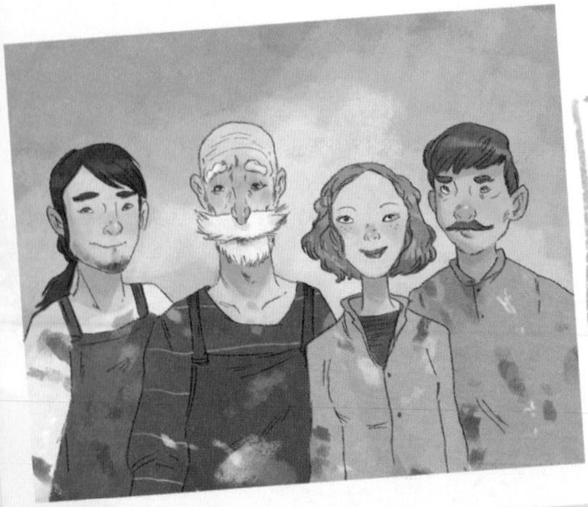

But his work hasn't inspired only artists. Annabelle Flores, a renowned author, released her nineteenth novel, *The Petrified Zoo*, on the occasion of the zoo's anniversary. In it we follow the incredible but true story of a little girl and a painter. It's bound to be a big hit.

B.C.

that's me!!!

Since the grand opening, Michael hasn't had a moment to himself. I don't know if he's even happy. I hope he is, anyway...

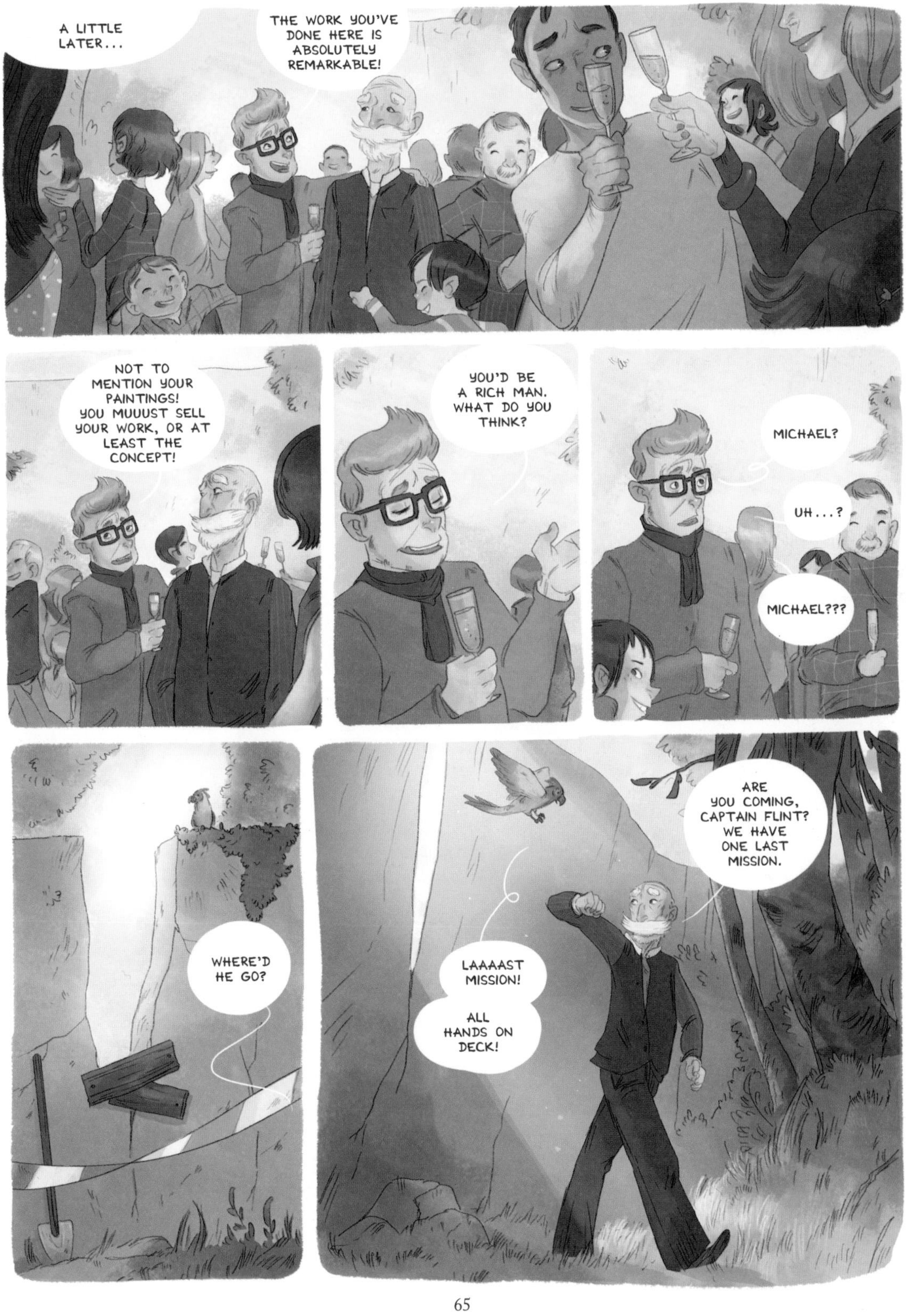
A LITTLE LATER...
THE WORK YOU'VE DONE HERE IS ABSOLUTELY REMARKABLE!
NOT TO MENTION YOUR PAINTINGS! YOU MUUUST SELL YOUR WORK, OR AT LEAST THE CONCEPT!
YOU'D BE A RICH MAN. WHAT DO YOU THINK?
MICHAEL?
UH...?
MICHAEL???
WHERE'D HE GO?
ARE YOU COMING, CAPTAIN FLINT? WE HAVE ONE LAST MISSION.
LAAAAST MISSION!
ALL HANDS ON DECK!

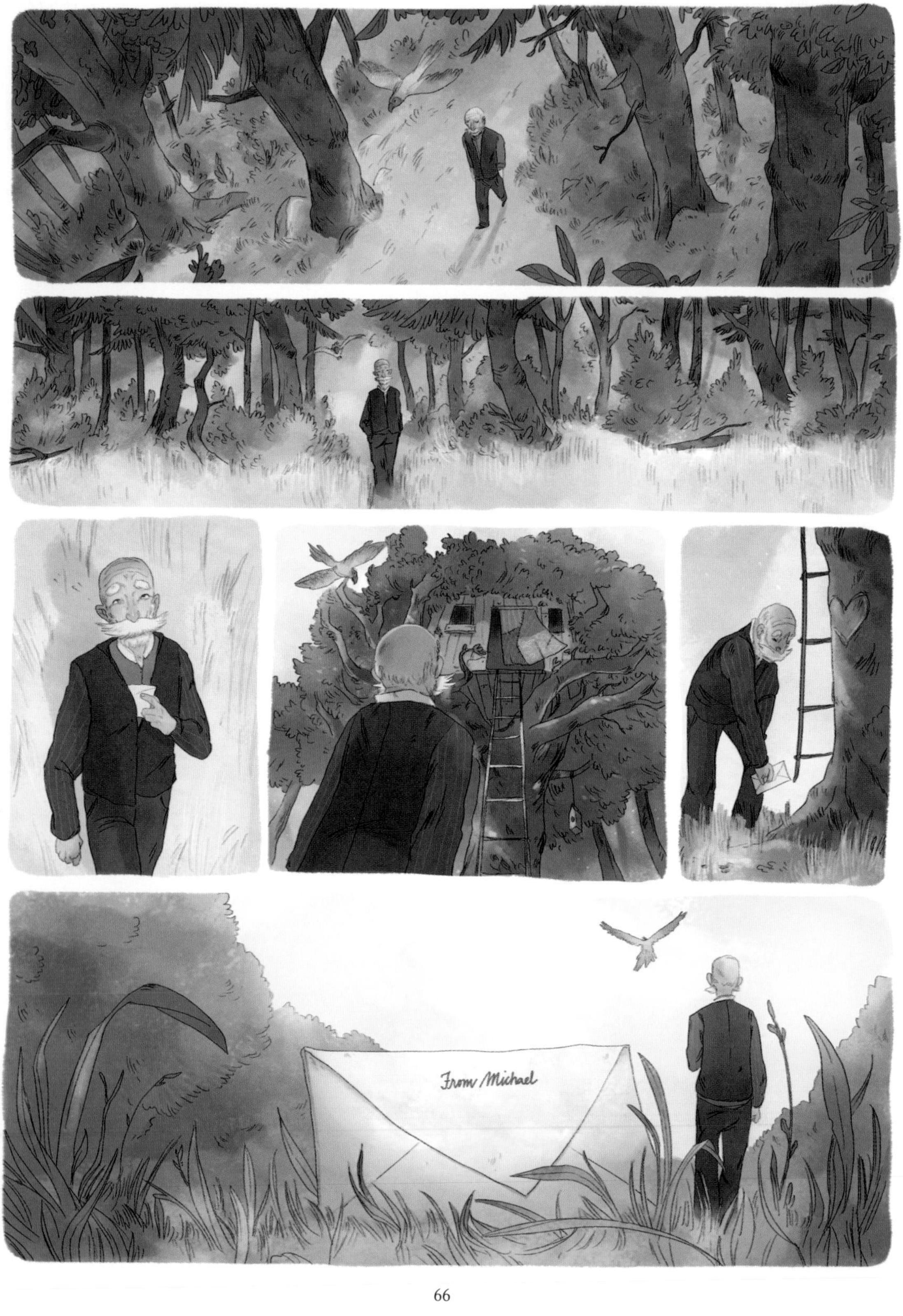
From Michael

My dear Cici,

It's been so many months now since we've seen each other, and I hate that. Like me, you've been very busy, partly because of the recent events that brought us together. Because the zoo's been such a success, I'm not as free as before! But I don't regret anything. And I know that our hearts will be united forever.

Looking back, I realized that I'd forgotten something important that has to do with you. Something I'd rather tell you in person. (And I'll do so when we see each other again. I need to tell you right away, now that I've noticed I forgot!)

Thank you. Thank you for spying on me from up in your hideout, for looking for me in the woods, for having found my secret garden, and, above all, thank you for loving it, and for giving it new life.

A lot of people have been talking to me about the wealth my paintings could bring me. I could become a rich man. But the thing those people don't understand is that I'm already rich. I'm rich from all the wonderful friends I've made during the past months, rich with the laughter of kids who came to help renovate the zoo, rich with the heart of the whole town. And I owe all this wealth to you. Just as the townspeople have done for the zoo, you've made me live again.

That's my wealth. That's your gift. Thank you, Cici. For everything.

One last thing. If you have the chance, stop by and see me at the zoo. There's a new painting I'm hoping to show you. A painting that, unlike the others, will never change.

Good-bye, Cici. May you help others the way you helped me, and drive away their sadness...

With affection, Michael

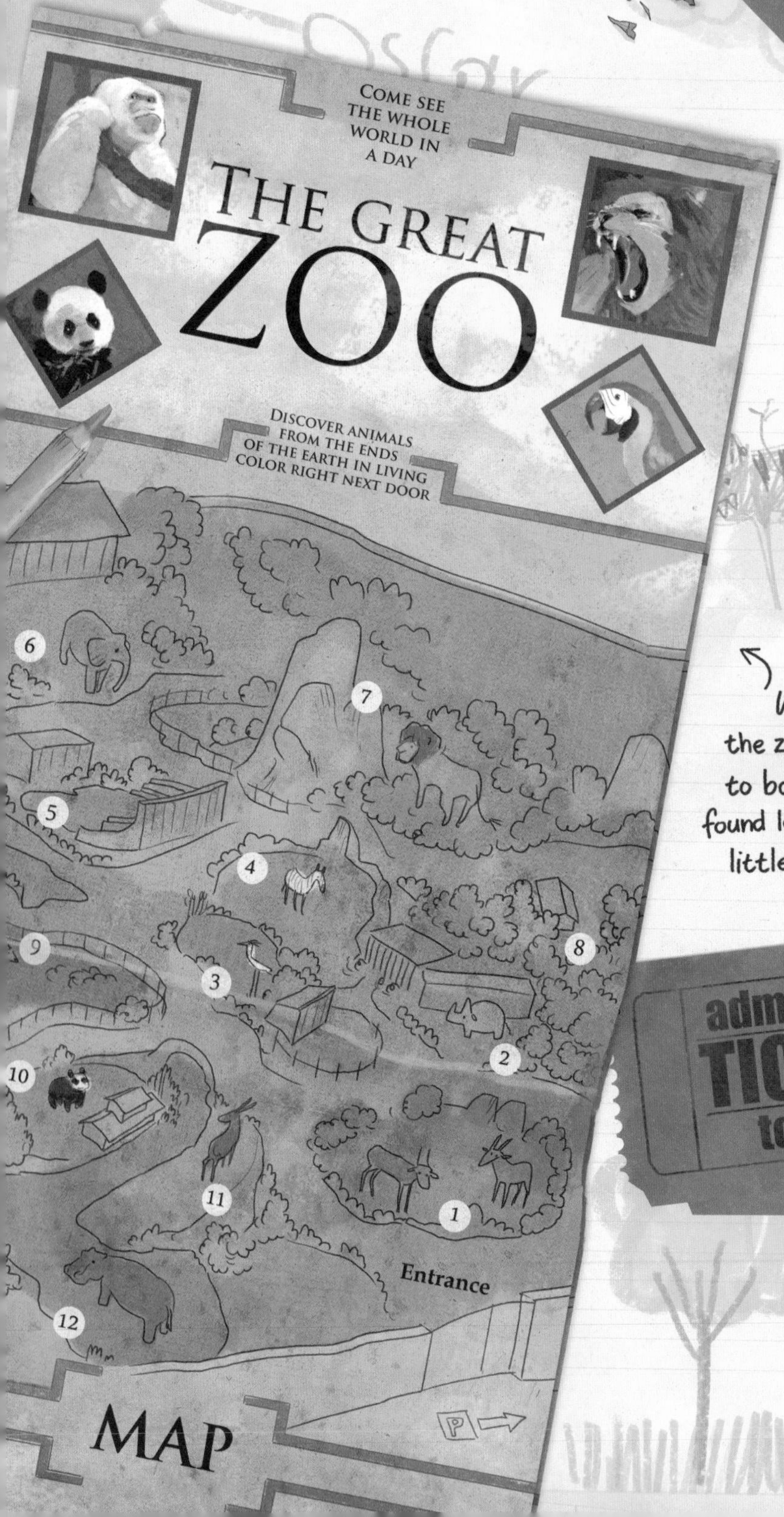
Come see the whole world in a day
The Great Zoo
Discover animals from the ends of the earth in living color right next door
6
7
5
4
9
8
3
2
10
11
1
Entrance
12
MAP

While cleaning up the zoo from top to bottom, we found lots of little souvenirs.

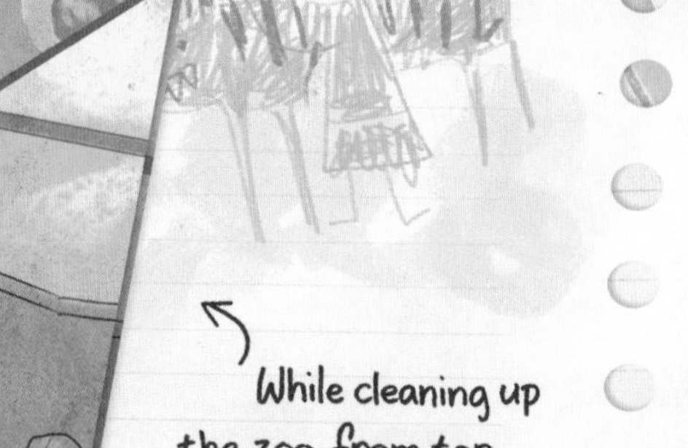
admit one
TICKET
to zoo

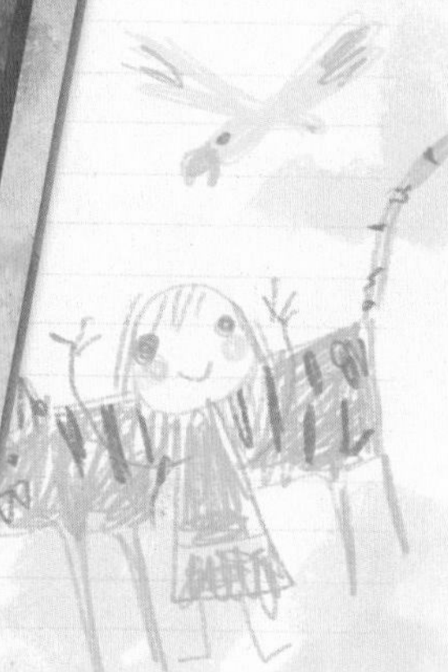

Doing research on the Internet, I came across a site called "Friends of Oscar." The story is so moving, I really wanted it to be part of my journal. I've pasted in the article.

Oscar in his enclosure at the zoo.

When he was just a cub, Oscar was the indirect victim of poachers. Facing certain death, he was saved by a veterinarian who brought him to a zoo in a small town.

Although far from his home, he nonetheless spent happy days there and had a good life. When the zoo closed, a number of people were moved to offer Oscar one last trip back to his roots. This was the birth of the "Friends of Oscar" association, which, twenty-five years later, continues to work for the well-being of animals.

Oscar passed away under the African sun on a nature reserve after a long life.

"Mr. Mysterious." That's what the girls and I called him the the first time we saw him.

From now on he's Michael the fabulous painter! I'm glad to be able to tell his story in this journal.

He was the first real mystery I solved (even though there were already some little ones before him—I'll have to write about those someday). The story of an old painter, passionate about his art, who "painted ghosts in color." Those are his words. But he did so much more than that. He gave the zoo something it was missing for a long time: a soul.

I hope I see you again soon, Michael!

And so, that's the end of this chapter. I'm very proud
of it, but a little sad too. It's time to sum up the
whole adventure!

My friends and I are super happy to have helped Michael.
Lena took great photos, and Erica had a thousand chances
to complain while we worked! I know they don't really like
the way I write them into my stories, but I'm happy that
it all turned out well. I'd be mad at myself if I lost my
friends over that.

Mom's figured out a bit about my investigations.
I think she didn't really appreciate my little fibs, but she
still hasn't said anything. I'm not feeling very comfortable
about it. I get the feeling she doesn't know whether to praise me
for helping Michael, or to scold me for lying to her. I'd really
like to go talk to her... but it's so hard!

Mrs. Flores asked me to help with writing her new book. That was
so nice! She even paid me a little for it! She explained to me
about "author royalties," but I didn't understand all of it.

So here it is. I've finally gone back to the zoo, like Michael
asked me to. I got all teary-eyed seeing him again. And I
just bawled when he showed me the famous new painting.
I took a picture, and I'll keep it with me the rest of my life.

He told me: "This painting is the story of a meeting.
                If it had a title, this is what it would be..."

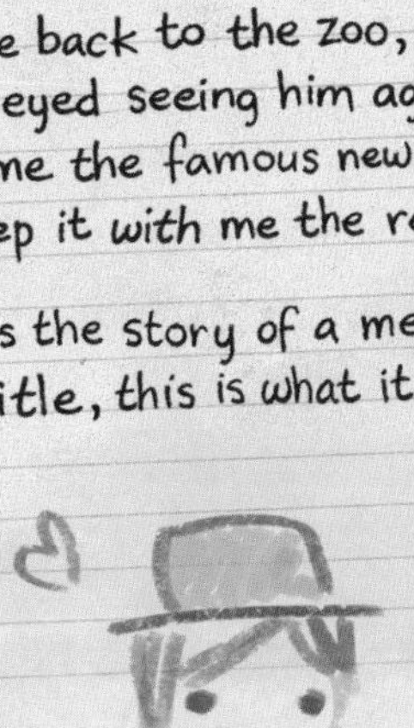

turn →

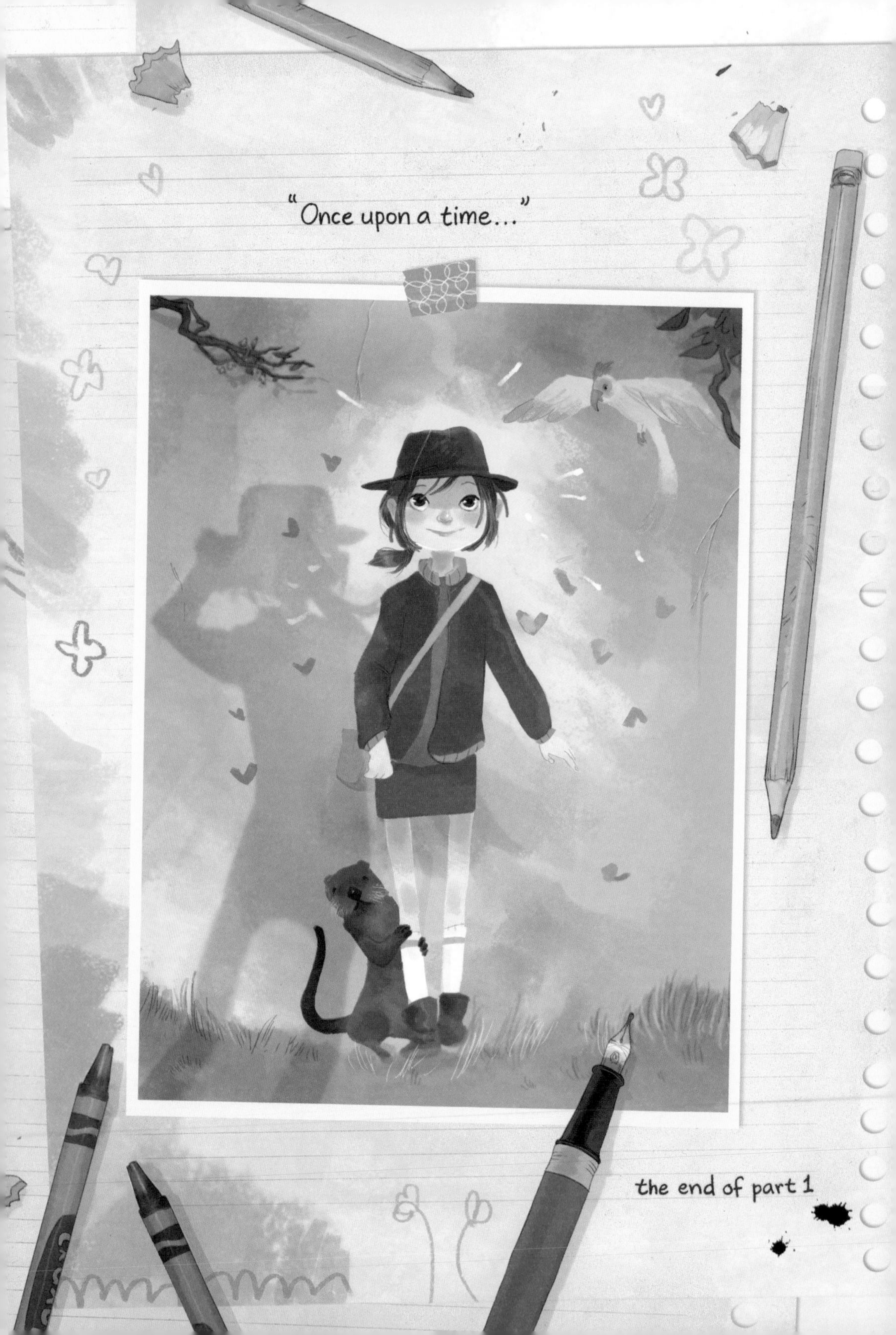
"Once upon a time..."
the end of part 1

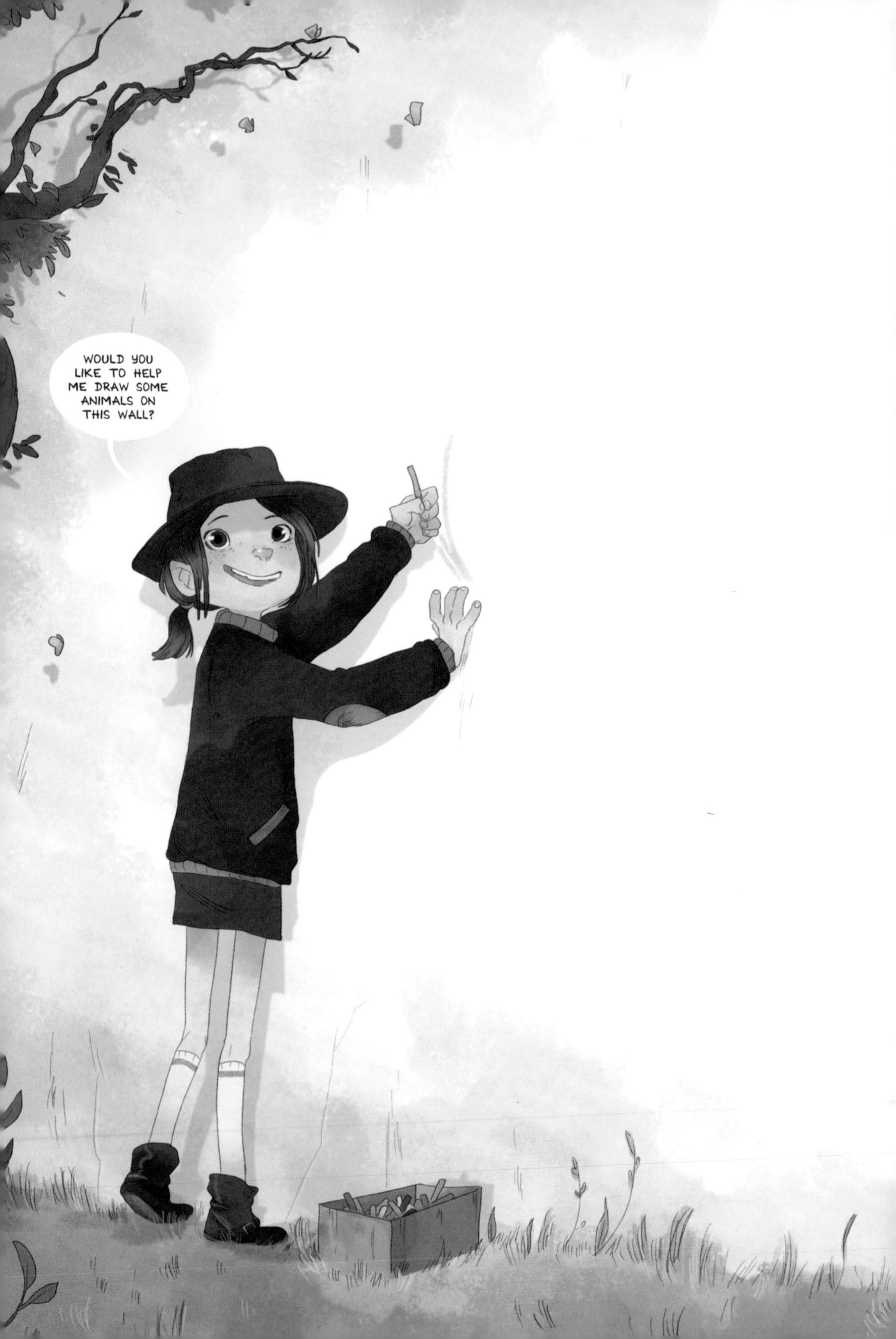
WOULD YOU LIKE TO HELP ME DRAW SOME ANIMALS ON THIS WALL?

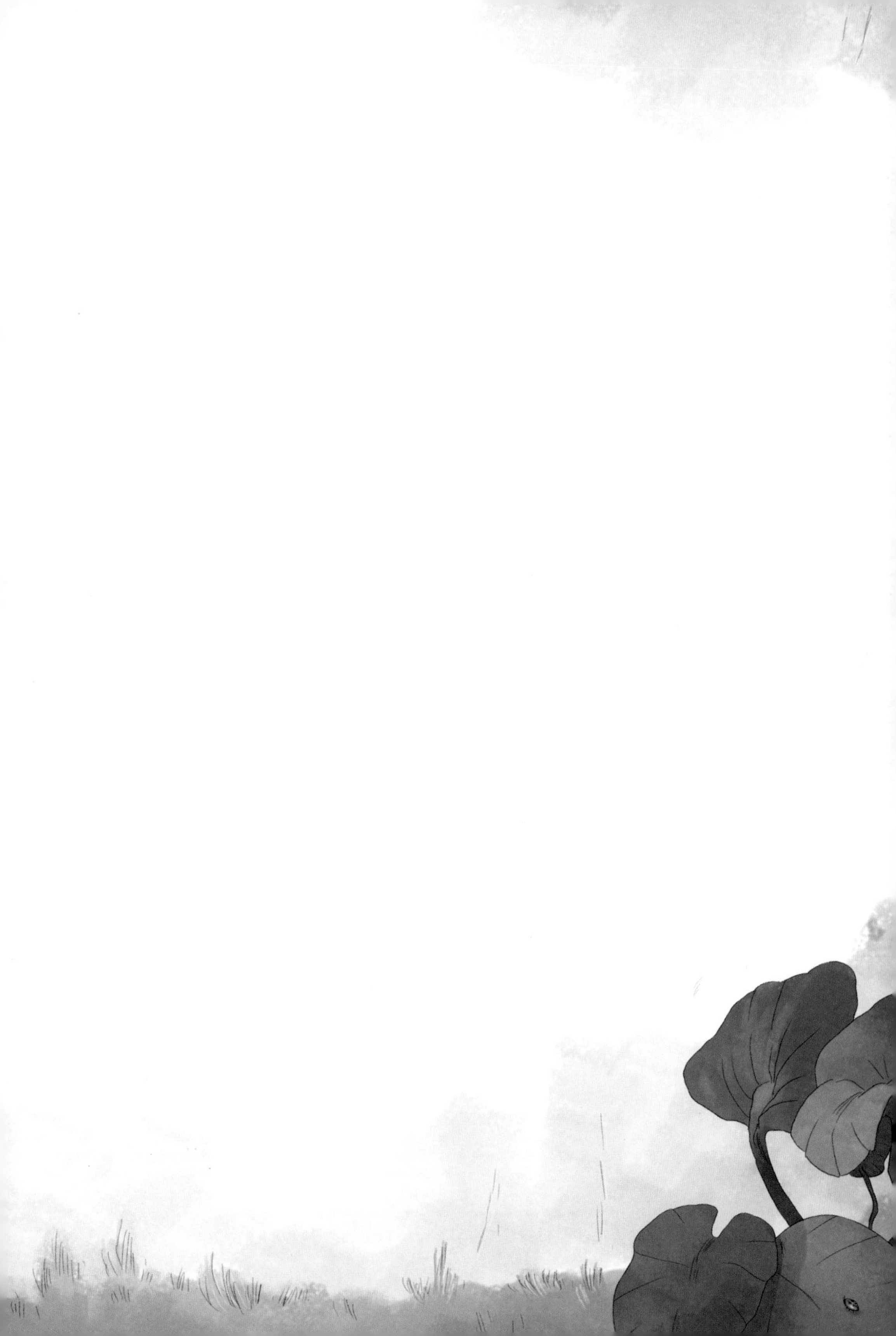

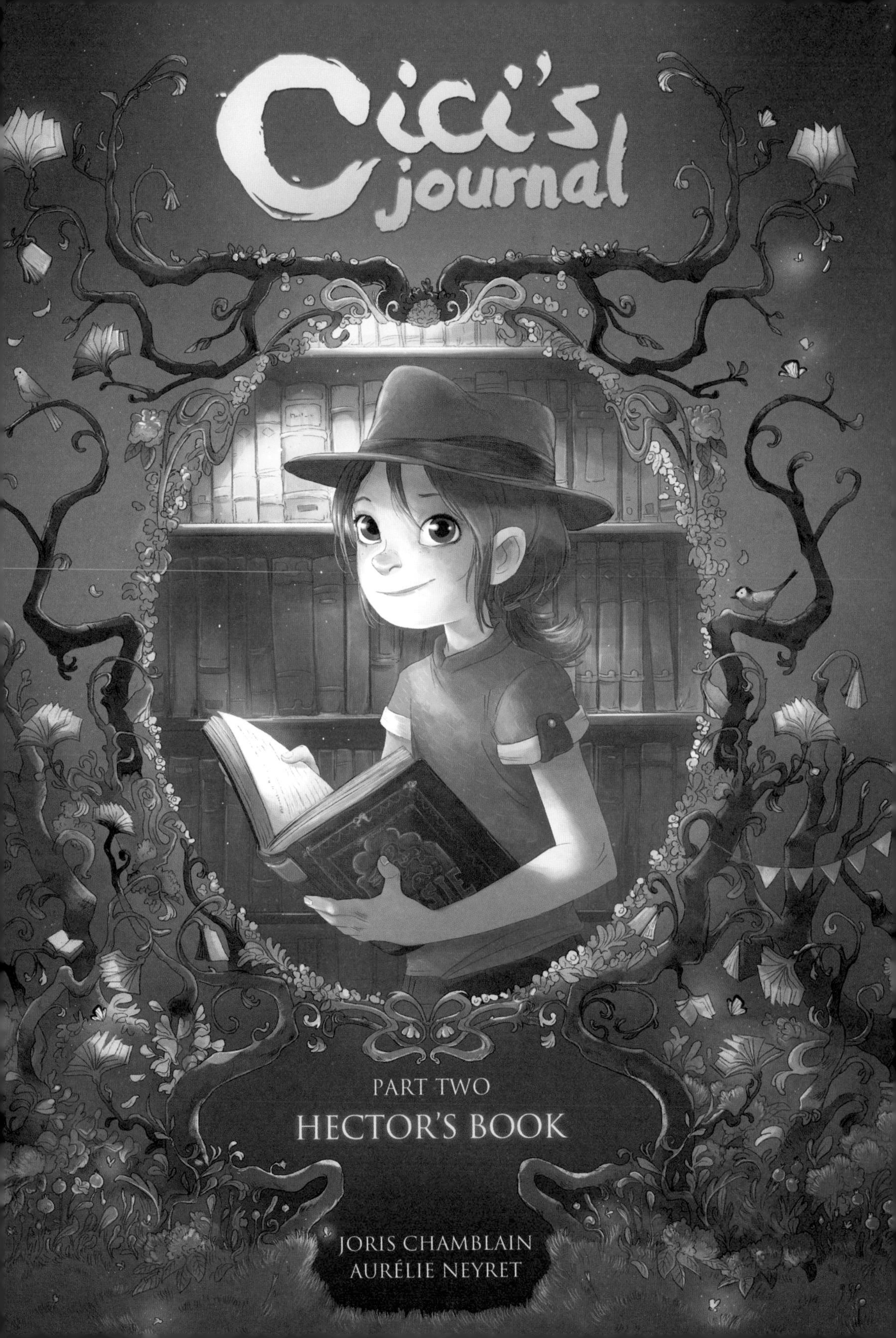
Cici's journal
PART TWO
HECTOR'S BOOK
JORIS CHAMBLAIN
AURÉLIE NEYRET

Vacation time!!!

School ended two days ago. We put on a great
show for the end of the year! I'll have lots of good
memories from this school. I'm going to miss it—next
year is middle school! It's a little scary. I hope my friends
and I will be in the same class. I wouldn't want to
end up all alone.

Lena is an auntie!
She went to her big sister's
house with her parents and
her little brother to help
with the baby. His name is
Cory and he's so cute! I
can't wait to see all the pictures
Lena's going to take of him.

Erica's gone off to
camp for the whole
month of July. A whole
month to grumble about all
the activities she'll be doing.
Living the dream! When she
gets back, she'll have a new
bedroom. Her mom told me.

I'm going to be spending the whole summer at home with Mom.
The mood around here isn't so great after the fibbing about the
zoo. But this new journal will keep me busy while I'm waiting for the
girls to get back.

July is going to be so long without them!

It's been one week since Lena and Erica left.
I hope they got my letters.

Day 9: Going to the pool with my mom this afternoon. But does my bathing suit still fit? Swimming will do me good... not having to think about anything...

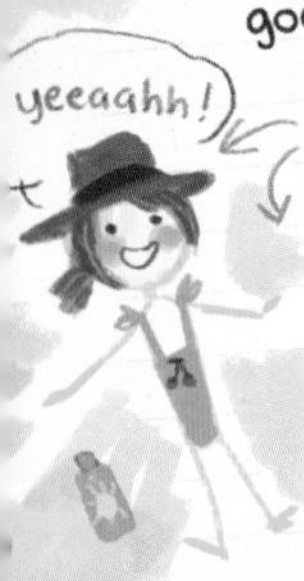
yeeaahh!

For the pool!

- ☑ bathing suit
- ☑ towel
- ☑ sunscreen
- ☑ goggles
- ☑ magazine
- ☑ bottle of water
- ☑ cookies (that won't end up in the bottom of the bag this time...)

nommm!

Day 10: The afternoon at the pool was awesome. I crossed paths with all sorts of mysterious people. Maybe I should start doing Mrs. Flores's writing exercises again. But I don't know if I kept all that stuff. I'm going to look in the attic. It's been a long time since I went up there. I must have been 6 or 7 the last time. We had just done a big cleanout of my room, and Mom and me carried up some stuff to put into storage. My toys, some pictures...

When I came back down, I looked like this!

I found my jacket and hat up there! They were my great-uncle's!

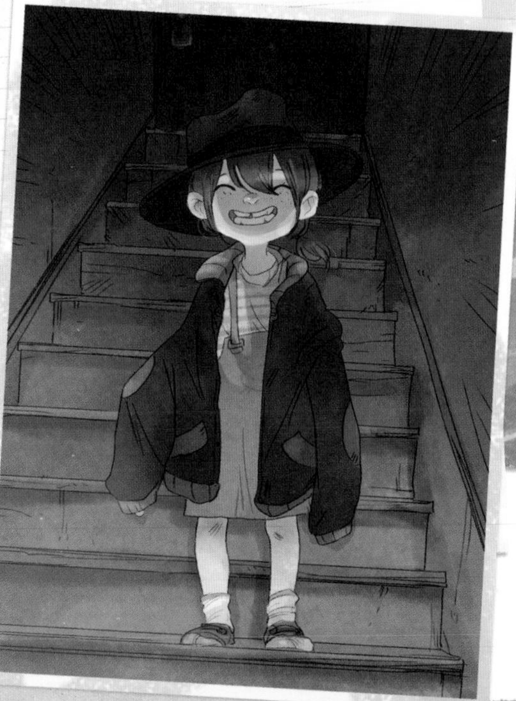

What's happened to that other Cici I left up in the attic, after all this time?

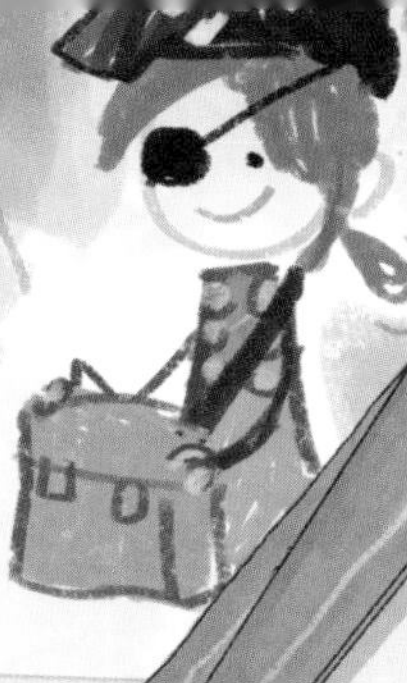
hidden treasure!

Day 11. I found my toy box, like a pirate digging up treasure!

I almost wanted to cry, seeing my dolls again, my stuffed animals... I'm glad they weren't thrown away. Touching them again felt like little shivers going up my fingertips. My fingers remembered them too.

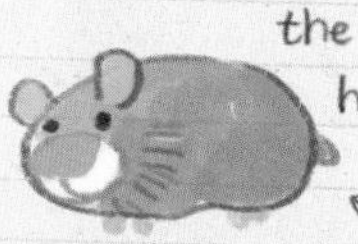
Albert, the stuffed hamster!

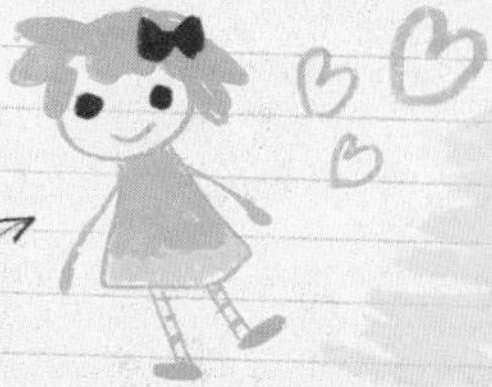
my baby doll Cherie!

And my photo box! Now I know how archaeologists feel when they dig up traces of some ancient civilization. My whole childhood is in that box. I can put it all back together, like a big puzzle.

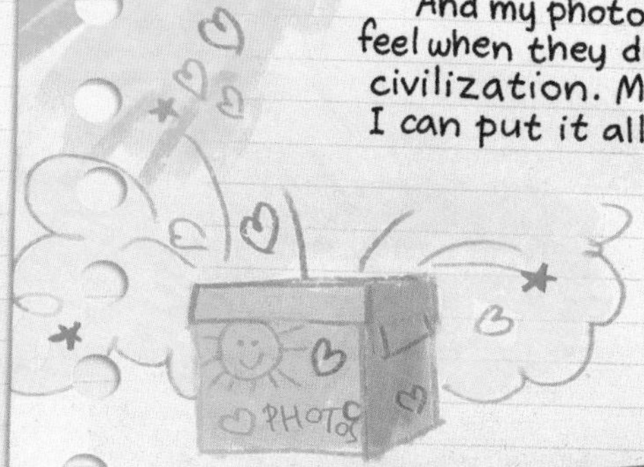
PHOTOS

I found this inside!

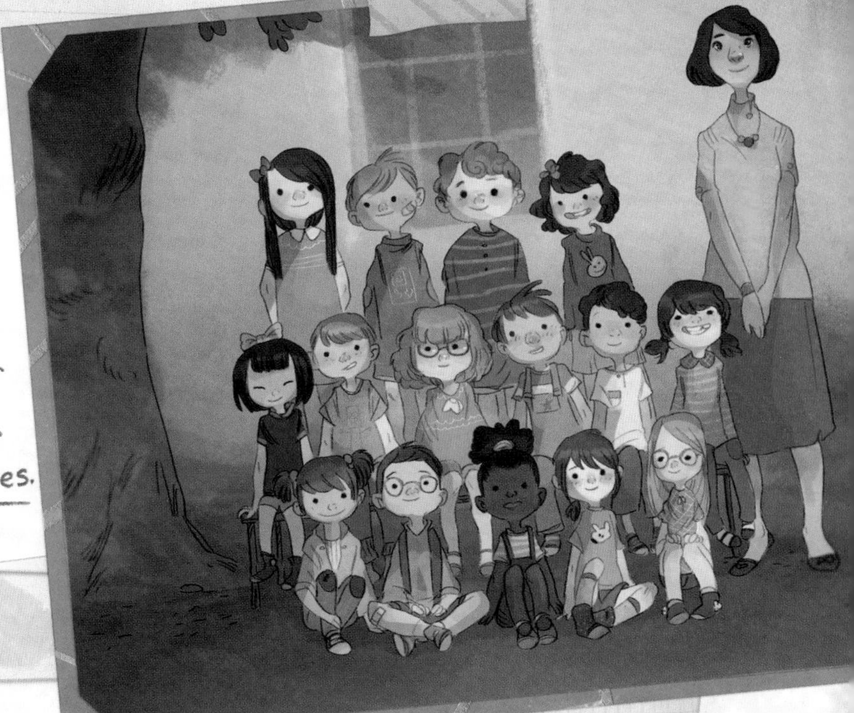

I was 4 years old when we moved to town. ~~Right after Dad~~ It was good there were so few kids in my class, and that the teacher was very nice. That's the year I met Mrs. Flores.

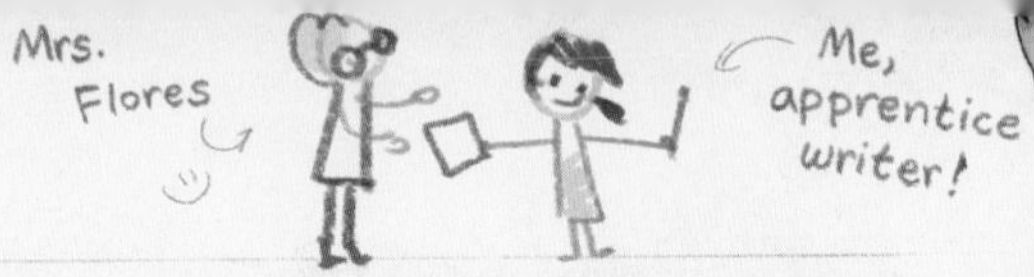
Mrs. Flores
Me, apprentice writer!

One day when I was sick, Mrs. Flores came to the house to see how I was doing. She said I should try writing to pass the time, since I couldn't leave my room. She had me watch people from the window, draw them, and imagine their lives. I still have a bunch of these little cards!

Jerome
34 years old

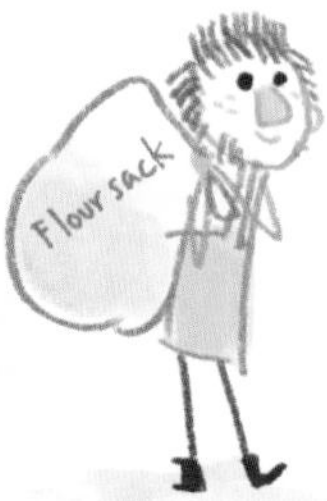
Flour sack

- Baker
- Used to be a secret agent. Good at hiding messages in the best hiding places. His job as a baker is a cover. He's spying on bad guys...

Linda
29 years old

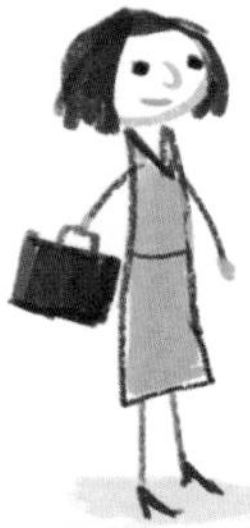

- Head of a big charity organization
- At work all the time, she doesn't have time to take care of herself, but she takes care of others. She has a kind heart and dreams of traveling.

After I made these cards, the second part of the exercise was to make the characters meet and imagine them having an adventure. It was very funny! Then Mrs. Flores read them over and corrected the mistakes, and I copied them out neatly.

Every morning, before she goes to the office, Linda buys a pastry at the bakery. It reminds her of her childhood, when her grandmother made her breakfast.

Jerome loves when it's the right time of year to make King Cake, because he can hide a lucky charm in each cake. It's a little like his old job, except that what he's hiding this time makes people happier. This particular morning, he was all worked up, because he knew she was coming and she would choose the most golden croissant, the one with a little bit of glaze on top. He put it at the front of the case to catch her eye.

It wasn't Three Kings Day. It wasn't a cake. But in this special croissant that he made just for her, a treasure was hidden. A message. A question.

Linda left the bakery, not knowing that this croissant would change her life forever. And that forever after, it would be Jerome who made her breakfast.

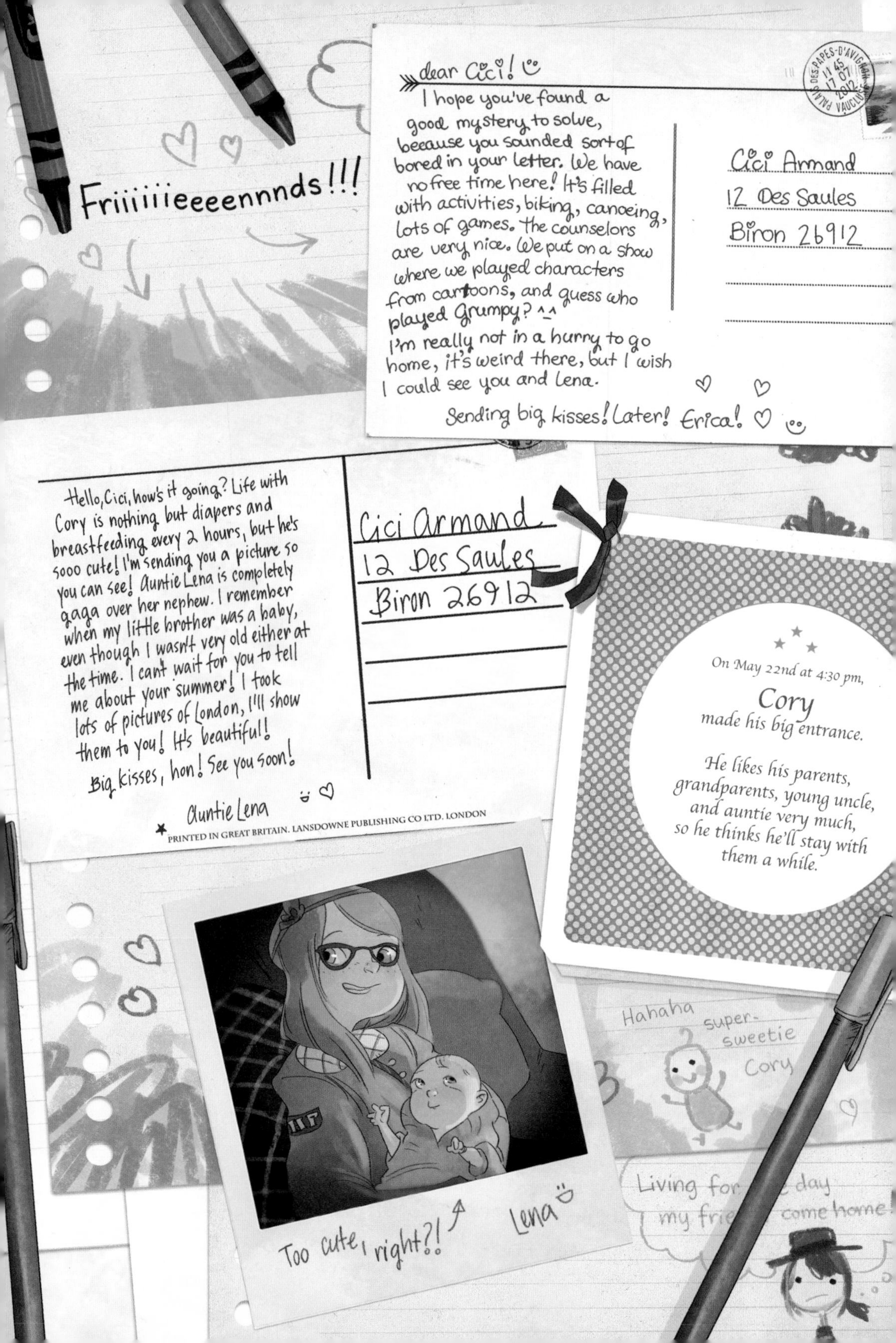
Friiiiiieeeennnds!!!
dear Cici! ☺
I hope you've found a good mystery to solve, because you sounded sort of bored in your letter. We have no free time here! It's filled with activities, biking, canoeing, lots of games. The counselors are very nice. We put on a show where we played characters from cartoons, and guess who played Grumpy? ^^
I'm really not in a hurry to go home, it's weird there, but I wish I could see you and Lena.
Sending big kisses! Later! Erica!
PALAIS DES PAPES-D'AVIGNON 11 45 17 07 2012 VAUCLUSE
Cici Armand
12 Des Saules
Biron 26912
Hello, Cici, how's it going? Life with Cory is nothing but diapers and breastfeeding every 2 hours, but he's sooo cute! I'm sending you a picture so you can see! Auntie Lena is completely gaga over her nephew. I remember when my little brother was a baby, even though I wasn't very old either at the time. I can't wait for you to tell me about your summer! I took lots of pictures of London, I'll show them to you! It's beautiful!
Big kisses, hon! See you soon!
Auntie Lena
Cici Armand
12 Des Saules
Biron 26912
PRINTED IN GREAT BRITAIN. LANSDOWNE PUBLISHING CO LTD. LONDON
On May 22nd at 4:30 pm,
Cory
made his big entrance.
He likes his parents, grandparents, young uncle, and auntie very much, so he thinks he'll stay with them a while.
Too cute, right?!
Lena
Hahaha
super-sweetie
Cory
Living for
day
my frie
come home!

Day 16 of vacation. Mom's vacation is over, so I'm home alone. I can go out, but it's no fun without my friends. Going to the pool this afternoon, I noticed something I also saw last week. I should check it out some more. It happens every Tuesday...

Day 25 of vacation. A little note came from Mrs. Flores this morning, with a gift!!!

My dear Cici,

I hope that your vacation is going well and that you'll have plenty of things to tell me about when I get back. A change in scenery has done me a lot of good, and my new book as well. Speaking of books, I'm sending you a little something that I owe you from a while back.

I hope you like the story.

Affectionately,

Annabelle

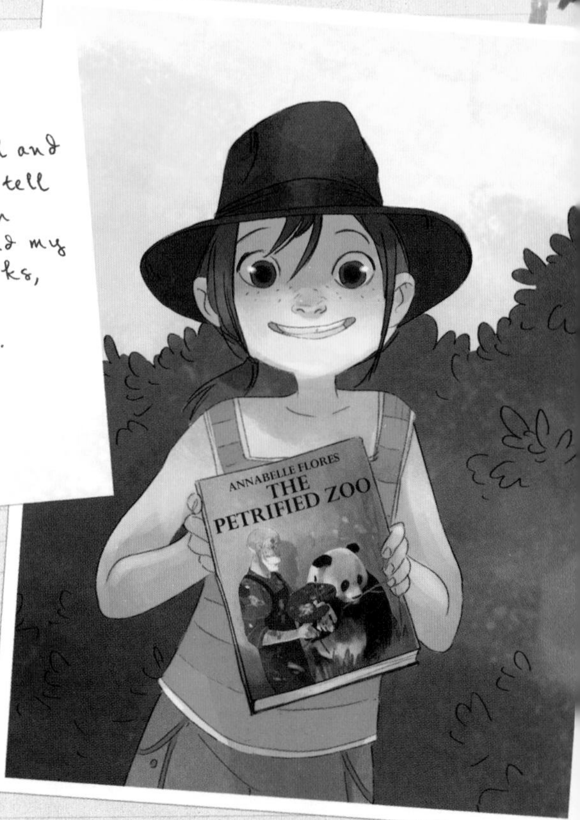
ANNABELLE FLORES
THE PETRIFIED ZOO

Wow! →
Mrs. Flores's book about Michael's story and a little bit about me!

Day 29 of vacation. At last, July is coming to an end, and the girls are coming back tonight! I can't wait to see them again! Also, I have a new mystery to solve, but I won't be able to do it without their help.

Tomorrow, we meet at the café to start the investigation!

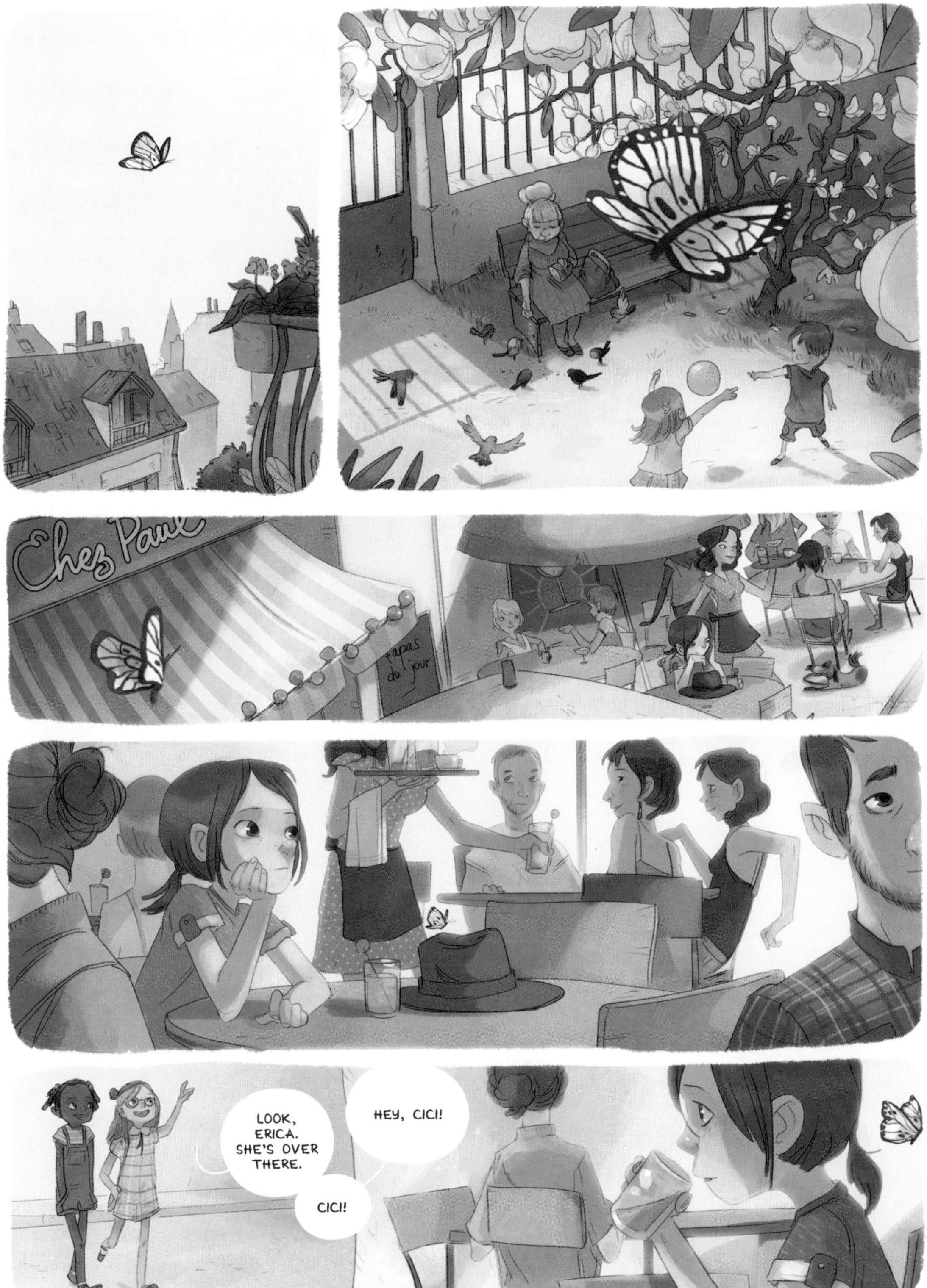
Chez Paul
tapas du jour
LOOK, ERICA. SHE'S OVER THERE.
HEY, CICI!
CICI!

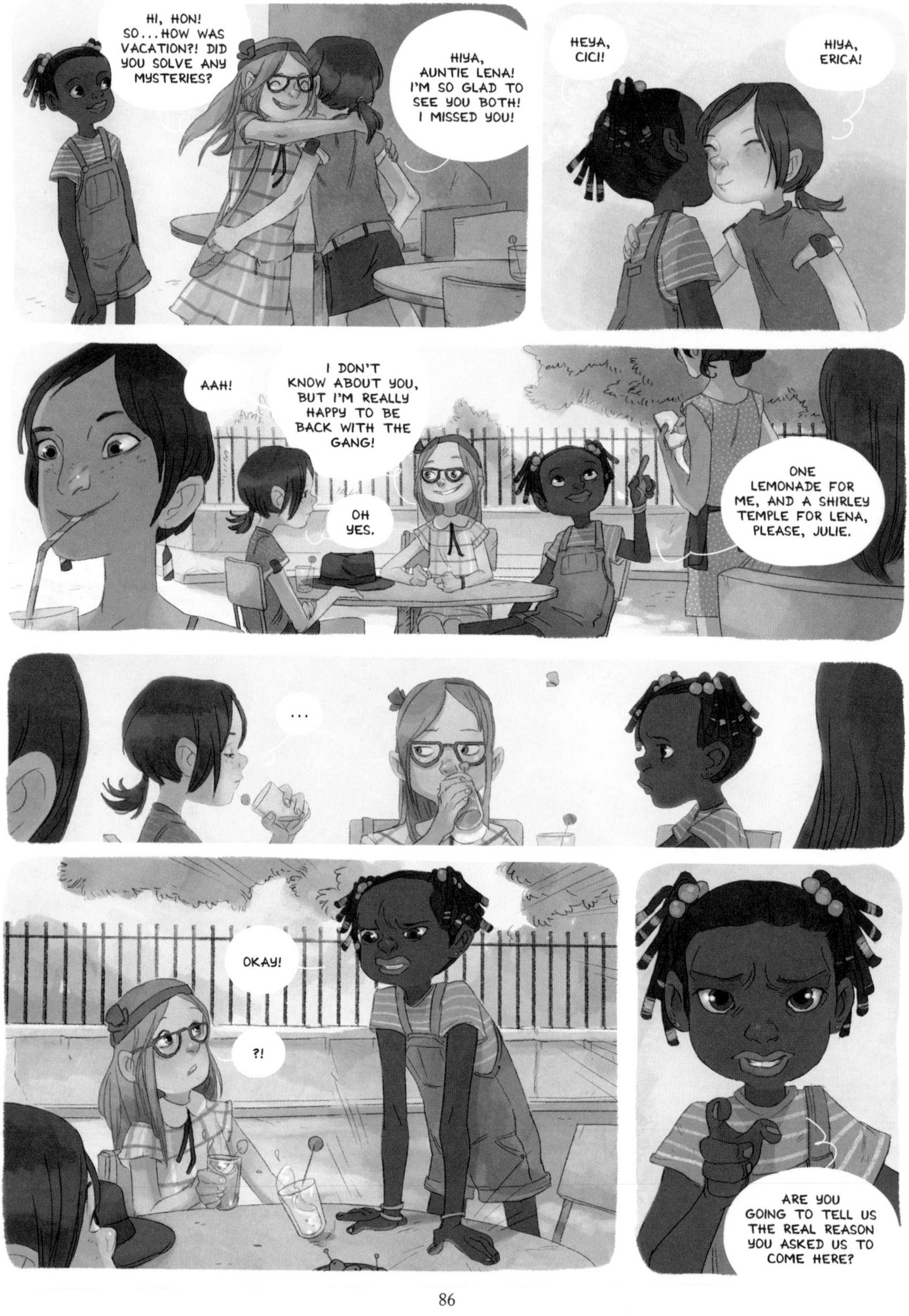
HI, HON! SO...HOW WAS VACATION?! DID YOU SOLVE ANY MYSTERIES?
HIYA, AUNTIE LENA! I'M SO GLAD TO SEE YOU BOTH! I MISSED YOU!
HEYA, CICI!
HIYA, ERICA!
AAH!
I DON'T KNOW ABOUT YOU, BUT I'M REALLY HAPPY TO BE BACK WITH THE GANG!
OH YES.
ONE LEMONADE FOR ME, AND A SHIRLEY TEMPLE FOR LENA, PLEASE, JULIE.
...
OKAY!
?!
ARE YOU GOING TO TELL US THE REAL REASON YOU ASKED US TO COME HERE?

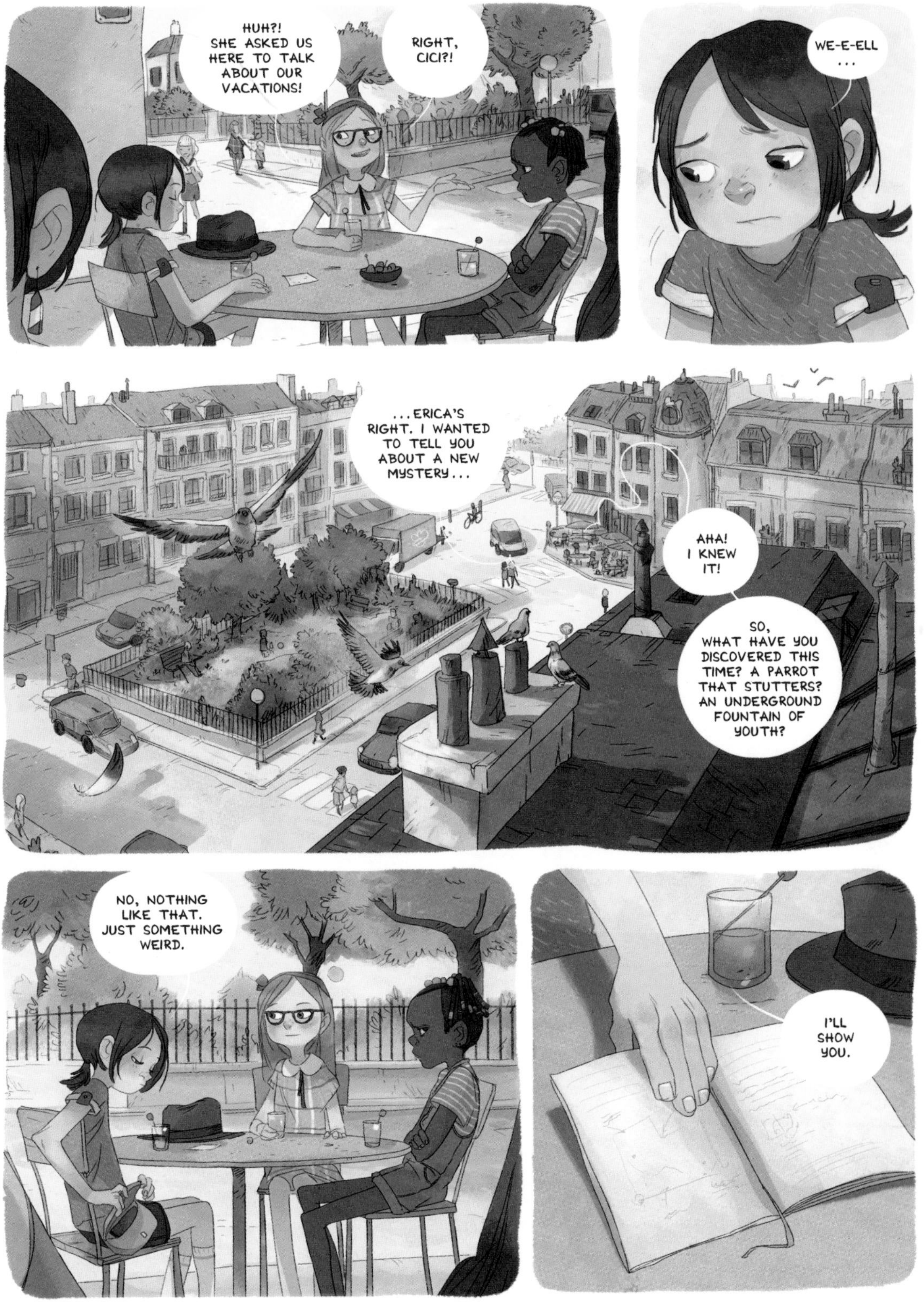
HUH?! SHE ASKED US HERE TO TALK ABOUT OUR VACATIONS!
RIGHT, CICI?!
WE-E-ELL ...
...ERICA'S RIGHT. I WANTED TO TELL YOU ABOUT A NEW MYSTERY...
AHA! I KNEW IT!
SO, WHAT HAVE YOU DISCOVERED THIS TIME? A PARROT THAT STUTTERS? AN UNDERGROUND FOUNTAIN OF YOUTH?
NO, NOTHING LIKE THAT. JUST SOMETHING WEIRD.
I'LL SHOW YOU.

- Saw her on the 10th, around 3 p.m. She left home, Mom and I went to the pool. This time I didn't pay any more attention than that.

- Saw her on the 17th, around 3 p.m. She left home, at exactly the same time as the week before. And with the same thing in her hands. I waited all afternoon to see what time she would come back. I staked out her front door from a bunch of different spots.

Her house

the café

the bench

Ulysses the florist

← bus stop

- 3:05 to 4:30 p.m.: The café. I don't think I've ever drunk so many sodas!

- 4:35 to 5 p.m.: Ulysses the florist. I am SO interested in the flower display in the window—so I can peek outside! A bus passes, but she isn't on it.

- 5:05 to 5:25 p.m.: On the bench in the square watching pigeons.

- 5:30 to 5:40 p.m.: In front of the bus stop, sitting on the little wall. That thing hurts your bottom after a while. Another bus passes, but still nothing.

- 5:45 to 6 p.m.: I'm just hanging around. I really don't know what else to do. I should get a book.

- 6:05 p.m.: The bus comes, she gets out!!

Question: Does she take the bus every day, or only on Tuesday? I'll have to hang out there every day at 3 p.m. to find out.

- Wednesday: Nothing
- Thursday: Nothing
- Friday: Nothing. Imagine if Mom knew what I'm doing with my afternoons!
- Saturday: Mom and I went for a walk. I wasn't able to watch the house.
- Sunday: Mom wanted to go back to the pool. We passed the house at 3 p.m., but no sign.
- Monday: Still nothing. But I'll have a better chance tomorrow.

- Saw her on the 24th, at 3 p.m. Returned at 6:05 p.m. (This time, I had something to read.)
  Next appointment: Next Tuesday at 3 p.m.!!!

Hmph! Another case for Detective Cici

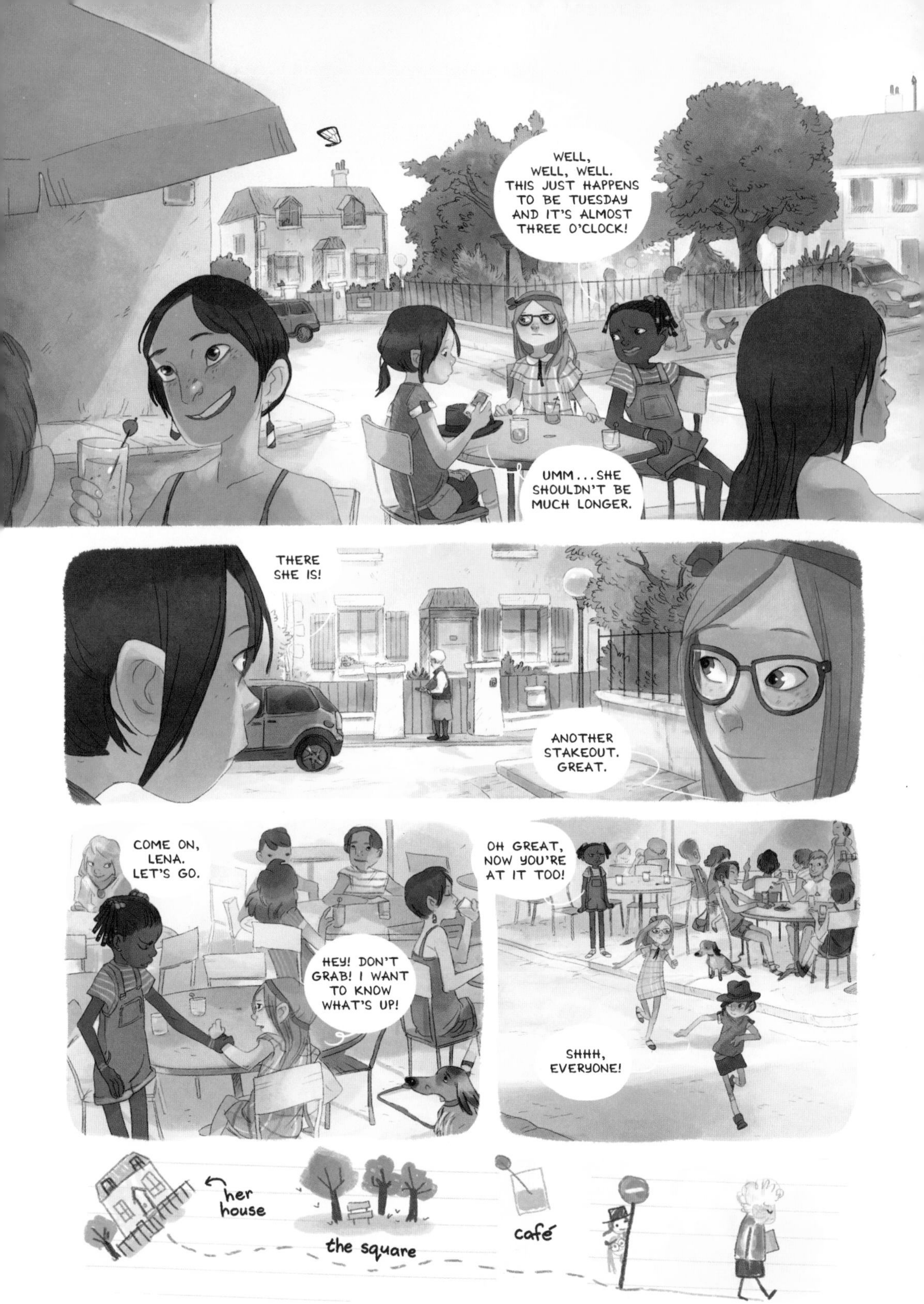
WELL, WELL, WELL. THIS JUST HAPPENS TO BE TUESDAY AND IT'S ALMOST THREE O'CLOCK!
UMM...SHE SHOULDN'T BE MUCH LONGER.
THERE SHE IS!
ANOTHER STAKEOUT. GREAT.
COME ON, LENA. LET'S GO.
HEY! DON'T GRAB! I WANT TO KNOW WHAT'S UP!
OH GREAT, NOW YOU'RE AT IT TOO!
SHHH, EVERYONE!
her house
the square
café

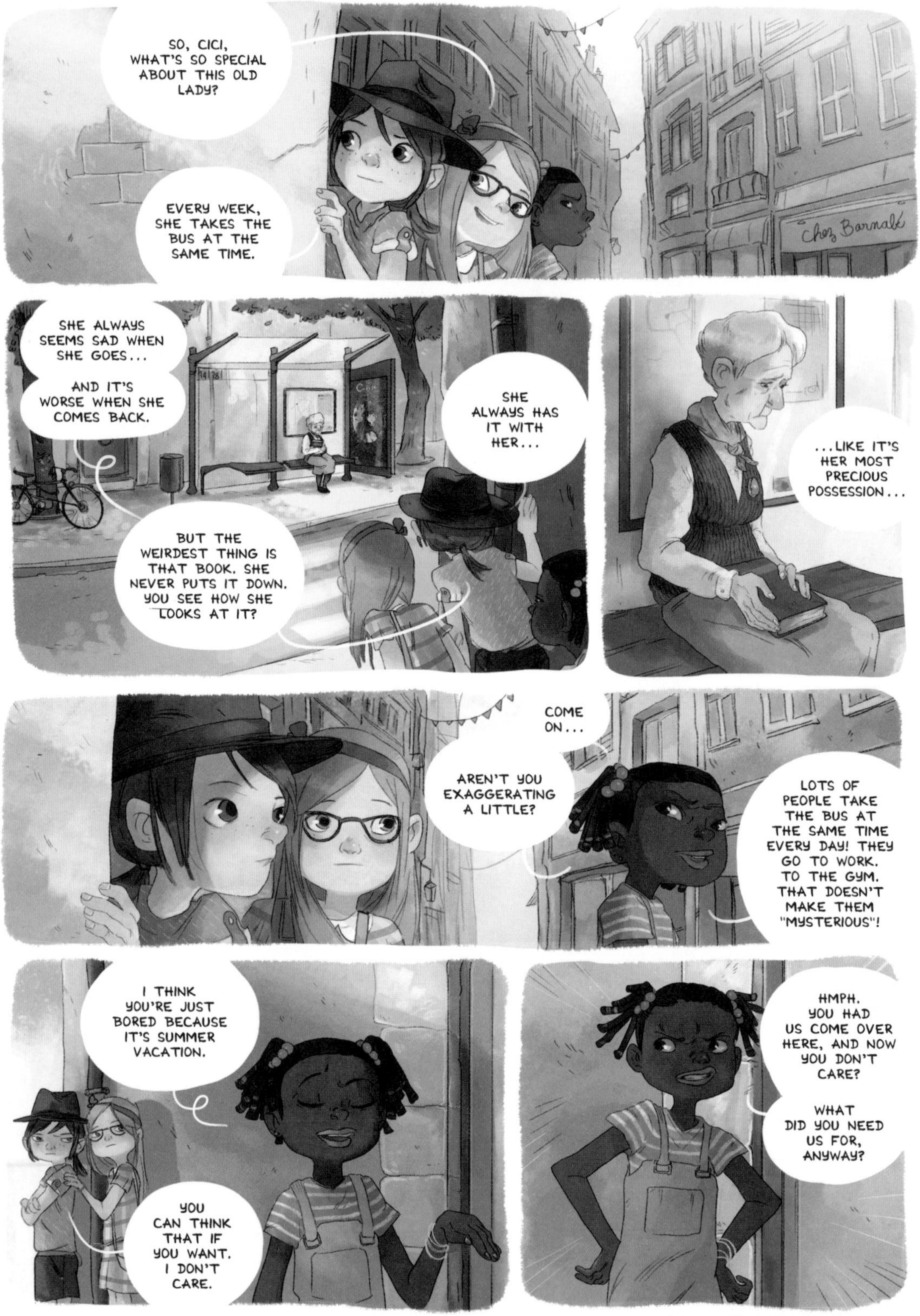
SO, CICI, WHAT'S SO SPECIAL ABOUT THIS OLD LADY?
EVERY WEEK, SHE TAKES THE BUS AT THE SAME TIME.
Chez Barnabé
SHE ALWAYS SEEMS SAD WHEN SHE GOES...
AND IT'S WORSE WHEN SHE COMES BACK.
BUT THE WEIRDEST THING IS THAT BOOK. SHE NEVER PUTS IT DOWN. YOU SEE HOW SHE LOOKS AT IT?
SHE ALWAYS HAS IT WITH HER...
...LIKE IT'S HER MOST PRECIOUS POSSESSION...
COME ON...
AREN'T YOU EXAGGERATING A LITTLE?
LOTS OF PEOPLE TAKE THE BUS AT THE SAME TIME EVERY DAY! THEY GO TO WORK. TO THE GYM. THAT DOESN'T MAKE THEM "MYSTERIOUS"!
I THINK YOU'RE JUST BORED BECAUSE IT'S SUMMER VACATION.
YOU CAN THINK THAT IF YOU WANT. I DON'T CARE.
HMPH. YOU HAD US COME OVER HERE, AND NOW YOU DON'T CARE?
WHAT DID YOU NEED US FOR, ANYWAY?

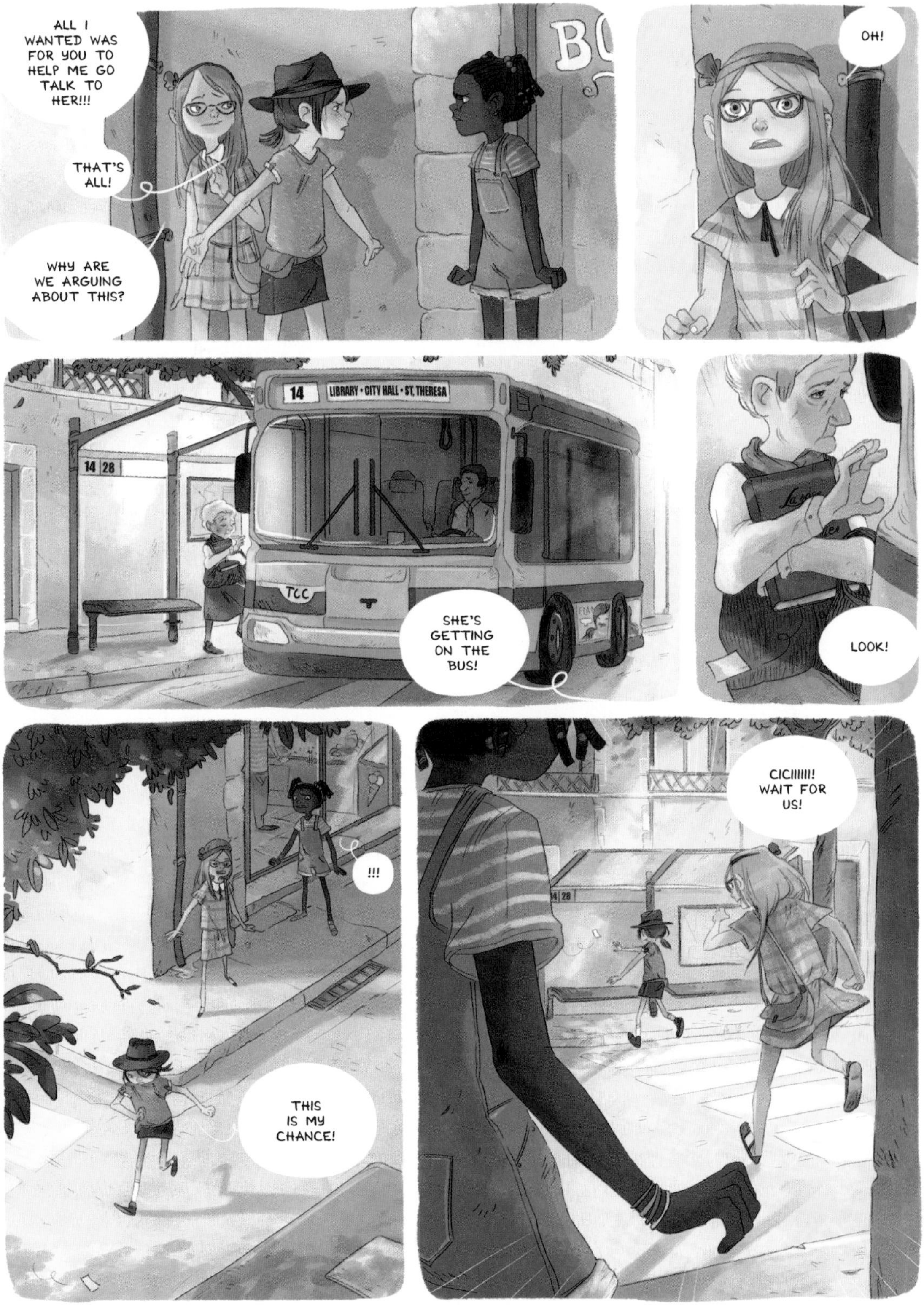
ALL I WANTED WAS FOR YOU TO HELP ME GO TALK TO HER!!!
THAT'S ALL!
WHY ARE WE ARGUING ABOUT THIS?
OH!
14
LIBRARY • CITY HALL • ST. THERESA
14 28
TCC
SHE'S GETTING ON THE BUS!
LOOK!
!!!
THIS IS MY CHANCE!
CICIIIIII! WAIT FOR US!

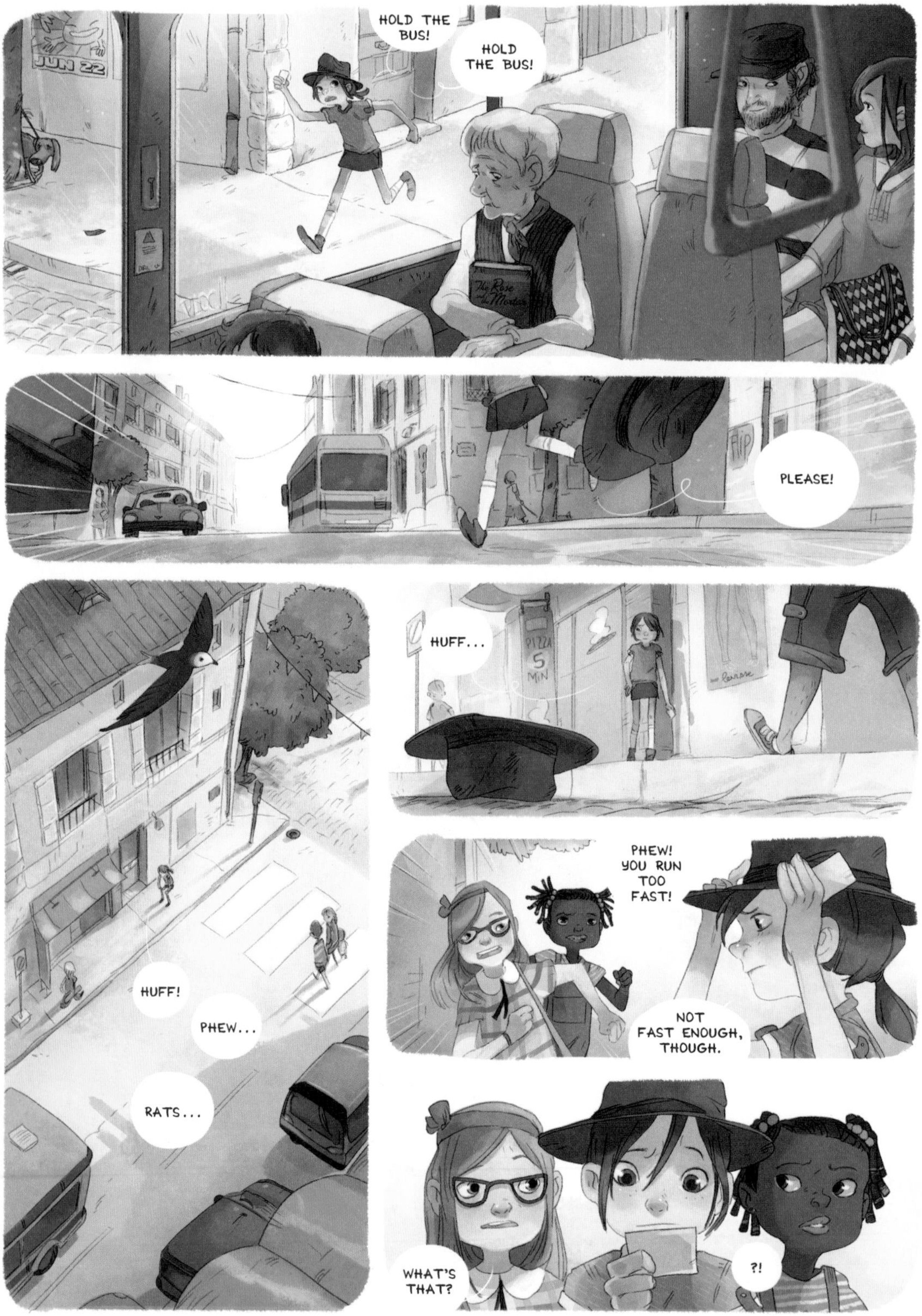
JUN 22
HOLD THE BUS!
HOLD THE BUS!
PLEASE!
HUFF...
PIZZA 5 MIN
HUFF!
PHEW...
RATS...
PHEW! YOU RUN TOO FAST!
NOT FAST ENOUGH, THOUGH.
WHAT'S THAT?
?!

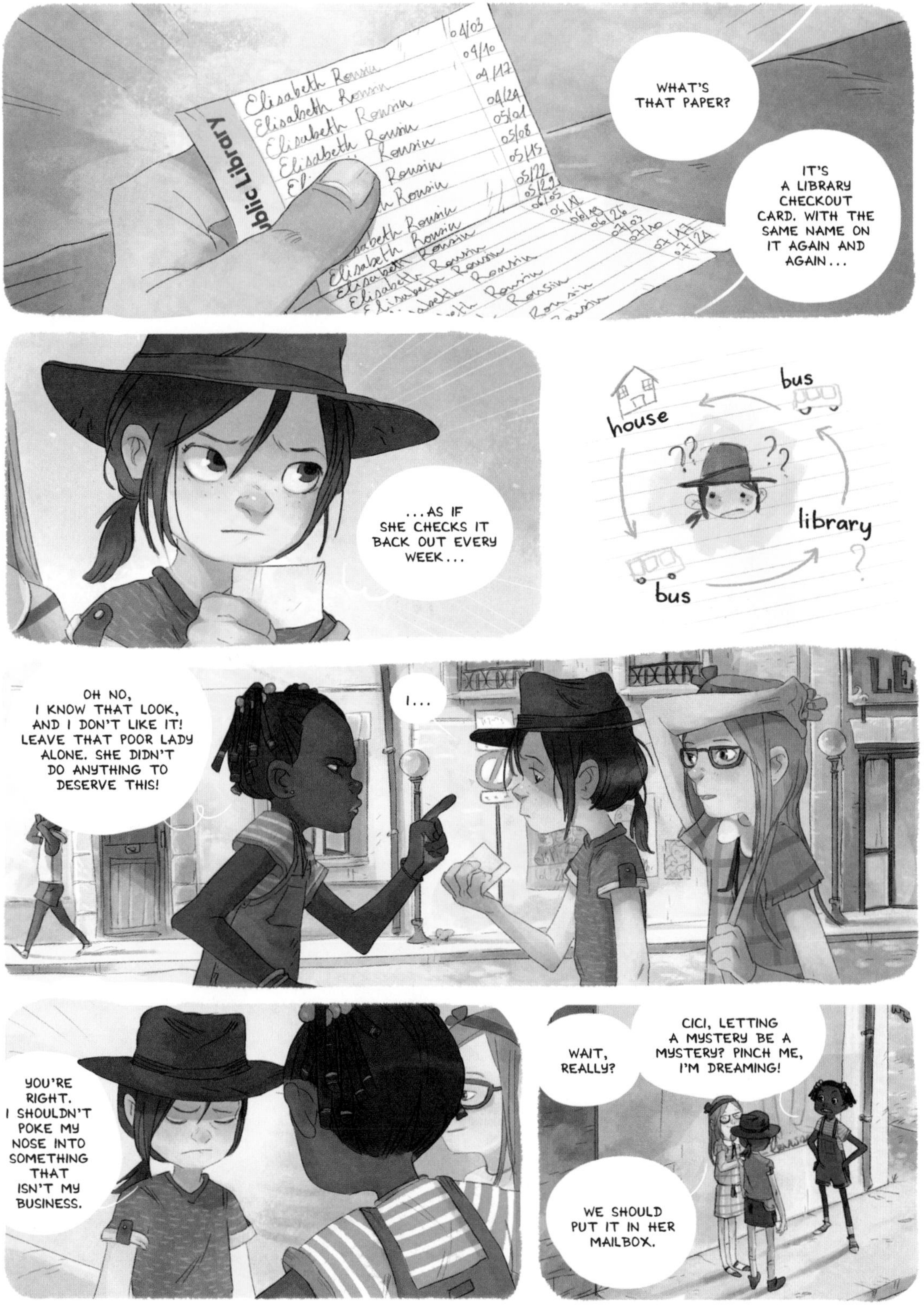
WHAT'S THAT PAPER?
IT'S A LIBRARY CHECKOUT CARD. WITH THE SAME NAME ON IT AGAIN AND AGAIN...
...AS IF SHE CHECKS IT BACK OUT EVERY WEEK...
bus
house
library
bus
OH NO, I KNOW THAT LOOK, AND I DON'T LIKE IT! LEAVE THAT POOR LADY ALONE. SHE DIDN'T DO ANYTHING TO DESERVE THIS!
I...
YOU'RE RIGHT. I SHOULDN'T POKE MY NOSE INTO SOMETHING THAT ISN'T MY BUSINESS.
WAIT, REALLY?
CICI, LETTING A MYSTERY BE A MYSTERY? PINCH ME, I'M DREAMING!
WE SHOULD PUT IT IN HER MAILBOX.

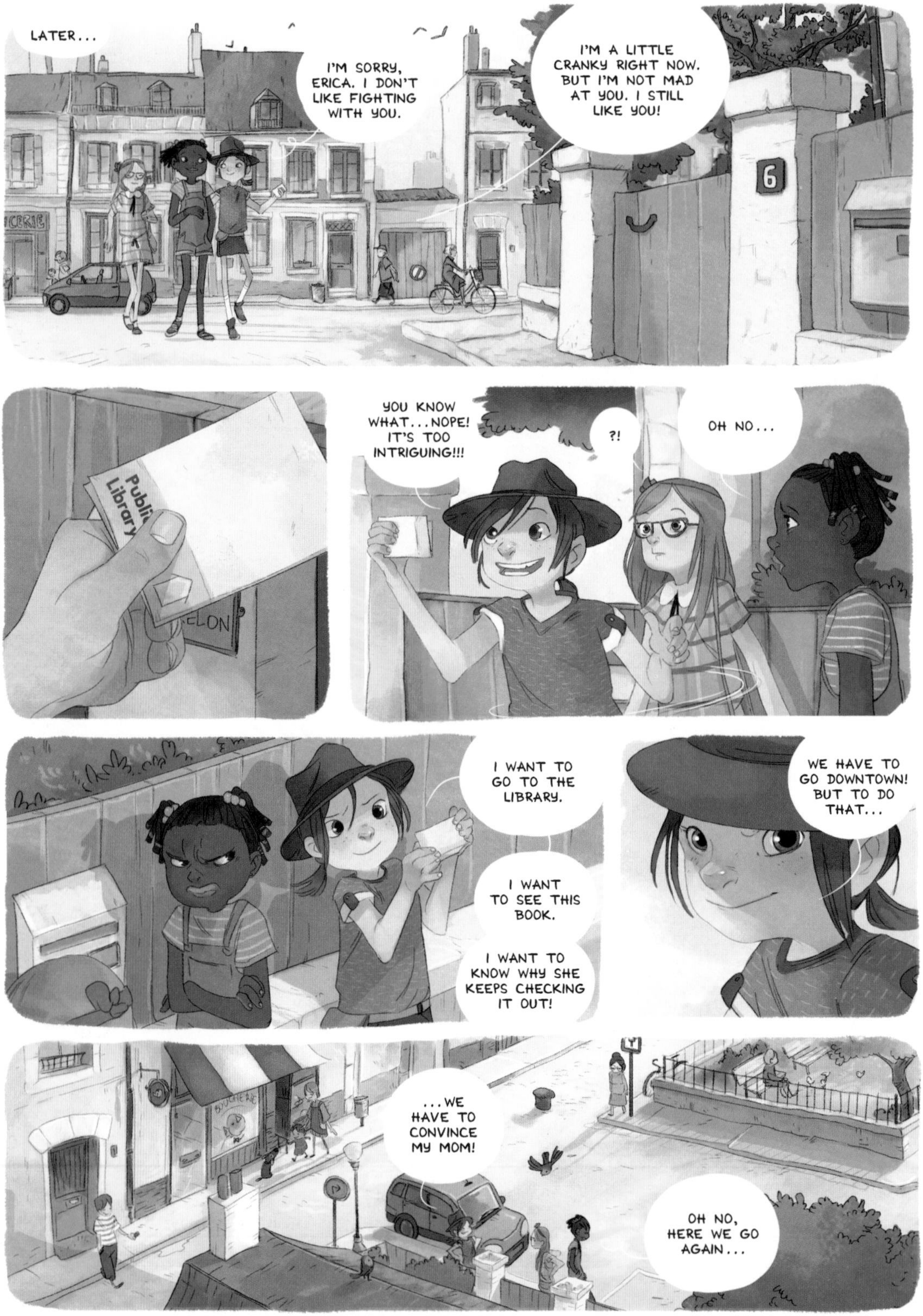
LATER...
I'M SORRY, ERICA. I DON'T LIKE FIGHTING WITH YOU.
I'M A LITTLE CRANKY RIGHT NOW. BUT I'M NOT MAD AT YOU. I STILL LIKE YOU!
6
Public Library
YOU KNOW WHAT...NOPE! IT'S TOO INTRIGUING!!!
?!
OH NO...
I WANT TO GO TO THE LIBRARY.
I WANT TO SEE THIS BOOK.
I WANT TO KNOW WHY SHE KEEPS CHECKING IT OUT!
WE HAVE TO GO DOWNTOWN! BUT TO DO THAT...
...WE HAVE TO CONVINCE MY MOM!
OH NO, HERE WE GO AGAIN...

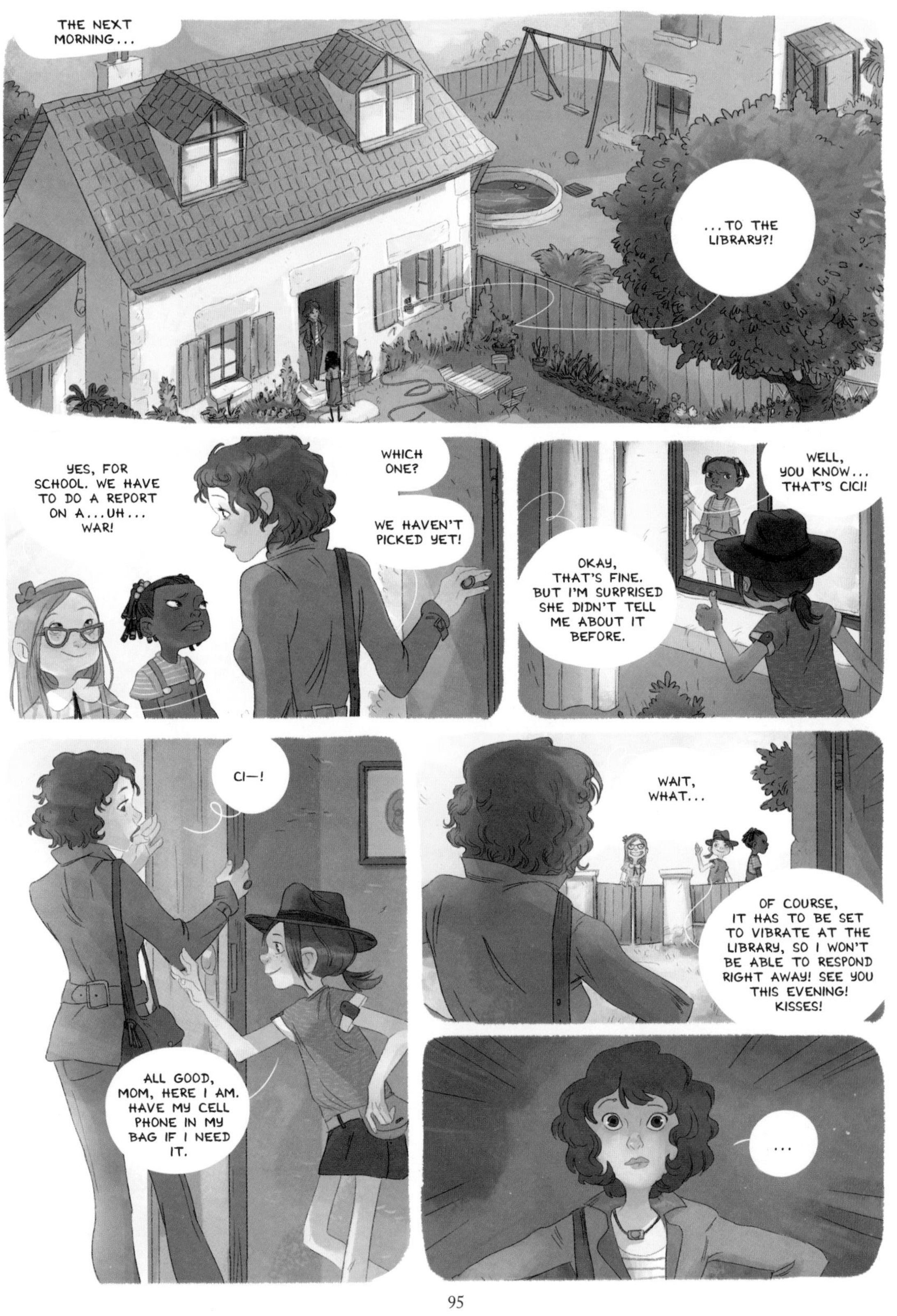
THE NEXT MORNING...
...TO THE LIBRARY?!
YES, FOR SCHOOL. WE HAVE TO DO A REPORT ON A...UH... WAR!
WHICH ONE?
WE HAVEN'T PICKED YET!
OKAY, THAT'S FINE. BUT I'M SURPRISED SHE DIDN'T TELL ME ABOUT IT BEFORE.
WELL, YOU KNOW... THAT'S CICI!
CI—!
ALL GOOD, MOM, HERE I AM. HAVE MY CELL PHONE IN MY BAG IF I NEED IT.
WAIT, WHAT...
OF COURSE, IT HAS TO BE SET TO VIBRATE AT THE LIBRARY, SO I WON'T BE ABLE TO RESPOND RIGHT AWAY! SEE YOU THIS EVENING! KISSES!
...

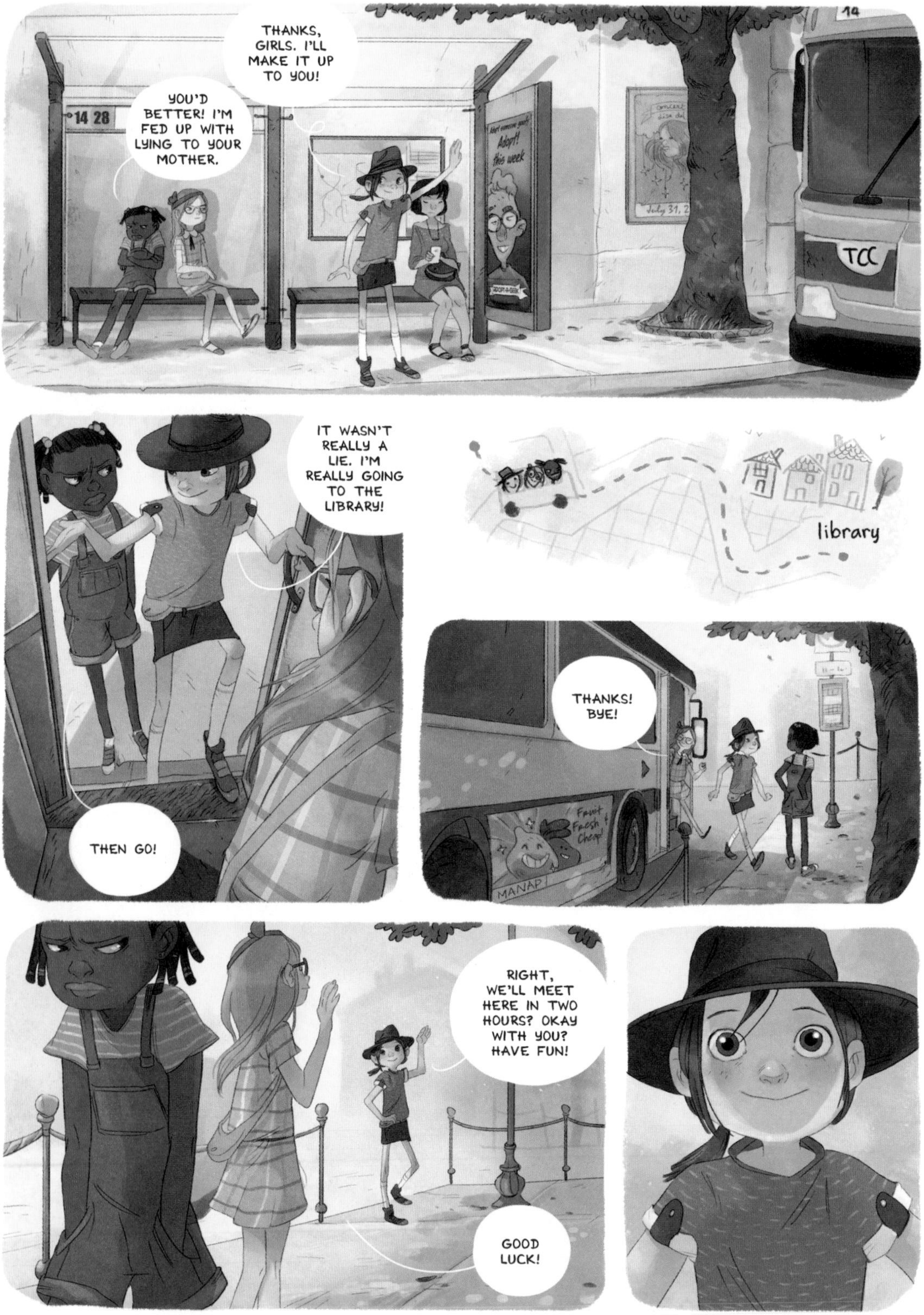
14 28
YOU'D BETTER! I'M FED UP WITH LYING TO YOUR MOTHER.
THANKS, GIRLS. I'LL MAKE IT UP TO YOU!
TCC
IT WASN'T REALLY A LIE. I'M REALLY GOING TO THE LIBRARY!
THEN GO!
library
THANKS! BYE!
MANAP
RIGHT, WE'LL MEET HERE IN TWO HOURS? OKAY WITH YOU? HAVE FUN!
GOOD LUCK!

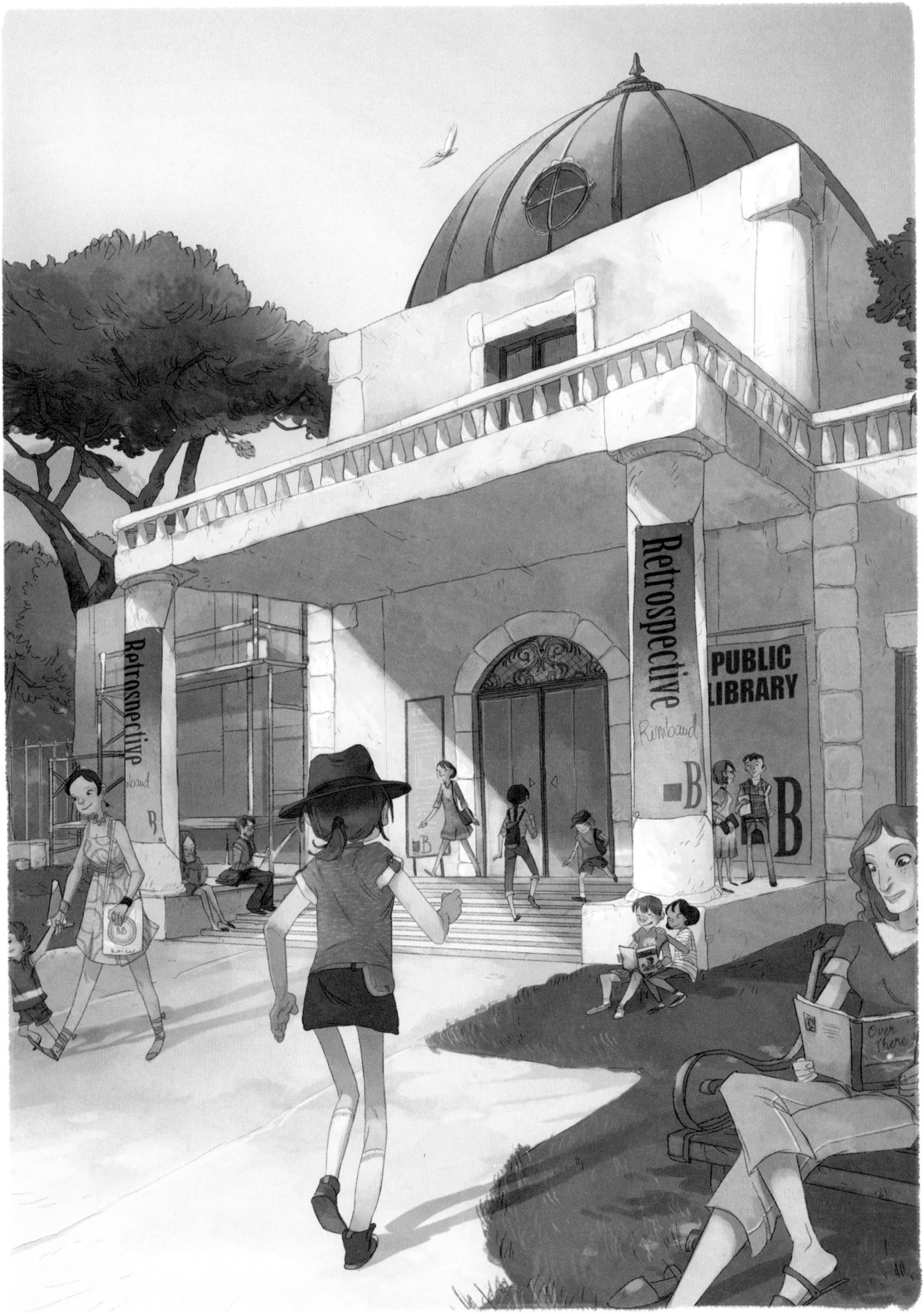
Retrospective
Retrospective
Rimbaud
B
PUBLIC
LIBRARY
B
Over There

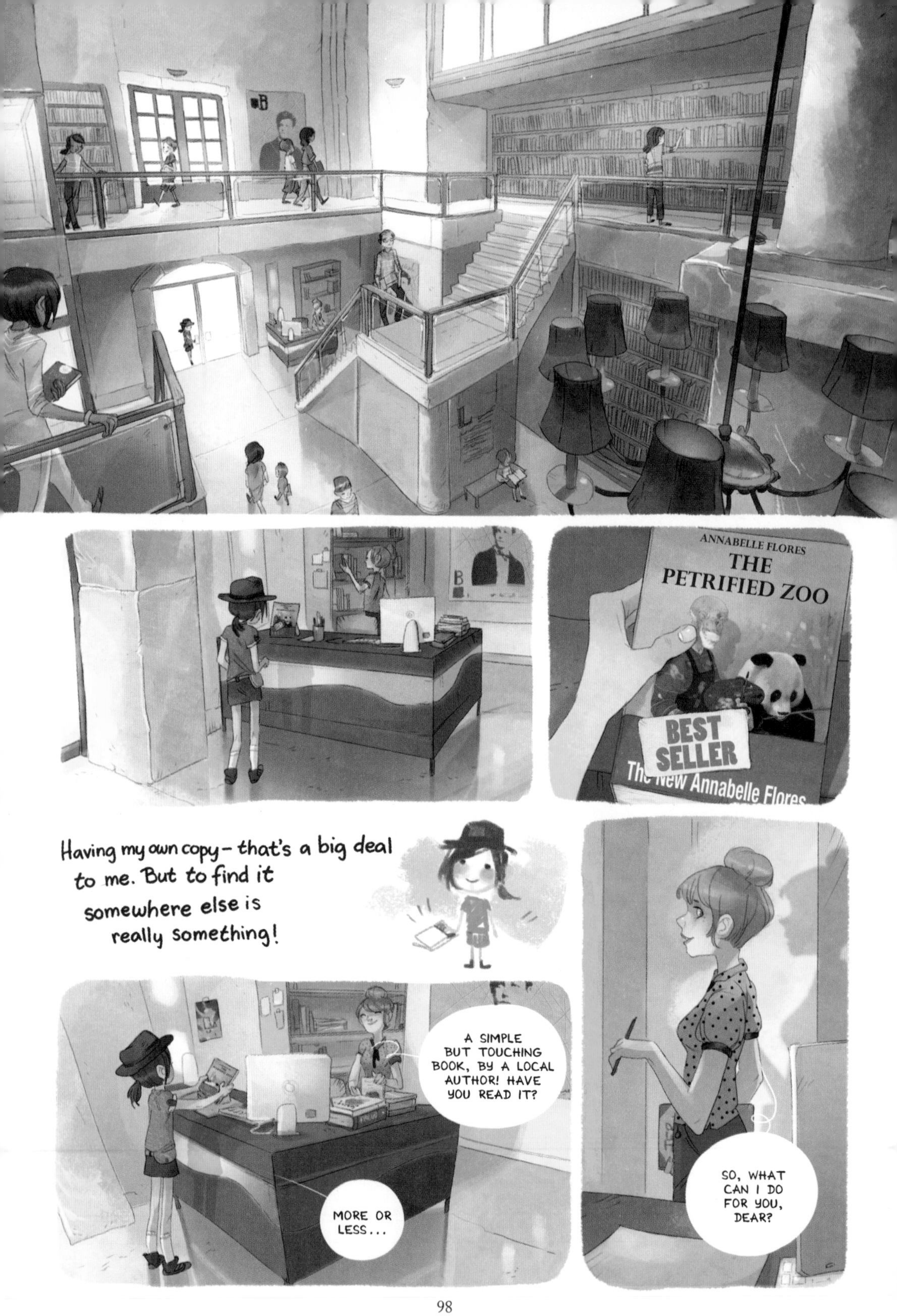
ANNABELLE FLORES
THE PETRIFIED ZOO
BEST SELLER
The New Annabelle Flores
Having my own copy – that's a big deal to me. But to find it somewhere else is really something!
A SIMPLE BUT TOUCHING BOOK, BY A LOCAL AUTHOR! HAVE YOU READ IT?
MORE OR LESS...
SO, WHAT CAN I DO FOR YOU, DEAR?

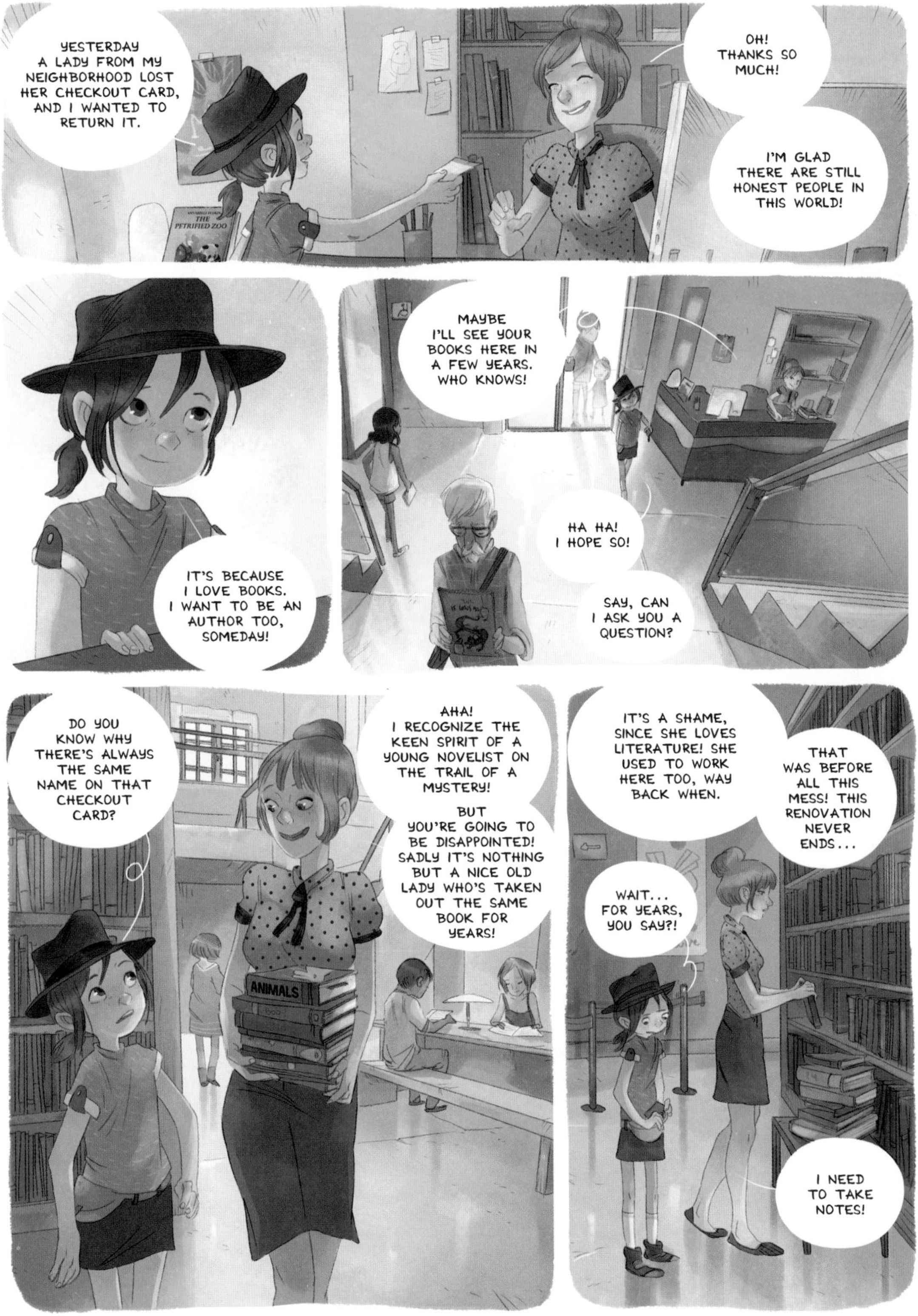
YESTERDAY A LADY FROM MY NEIGHBORHOOD LOST HER CHECKOUT CARD, AND I WANTED TO RETURN IT.
THE PETRIFIED ZOO
OH! THANKS SO MUCH!
I'M GLAD THERE ARE STILL HONEST PEOPLE IN THIS WORLD!
IT'S BECAUSE I LOVE BOOKS. I WANT TO BE AN AUTHOR TOO, SOMEDAY!
MAYBE I'LL SEE YOUR BOOKS HERE IN A FEW YEARS. WHO KNOWS!
HA HA! I HOPE SO!
SAY, CAN I ASK YOU A QUESTION?
DO YOU KNOW WHY THERE'S ALWAYS THE SAME NAME ON THAT CHECKOUT CARD?
AHA! I RECOGNIZE THE KEEN SPIRIT OF A YOUNG NOVELIST ON THE TRAIL OF A MYSTERY!
BUT YOU'RE GOING TO BE DISAPPOINTED! SADLY IT'S NOTHING BUT A NICE OLD LADY WHO'S TAKEN OUT THE SAME BOOK FOR YEARS!
ANIMALS
IT'S A SHAME, SINCE SHE LOVES LITERATURE! SHE USED TO WORK HERE TOO, WAY BACK WHEN.
THAT WAS BEFORE ALL THIS MESS! THIS RENOVATION NEVER ENDS...
WAIT... FOR YEARS, YOU SAY?!
I NEED TO TAKE NOTES!

The "Elisabeth Mystery"

Quick notes on the ritual of Elisabeth Ronsin, our new Mrs. Mysterious

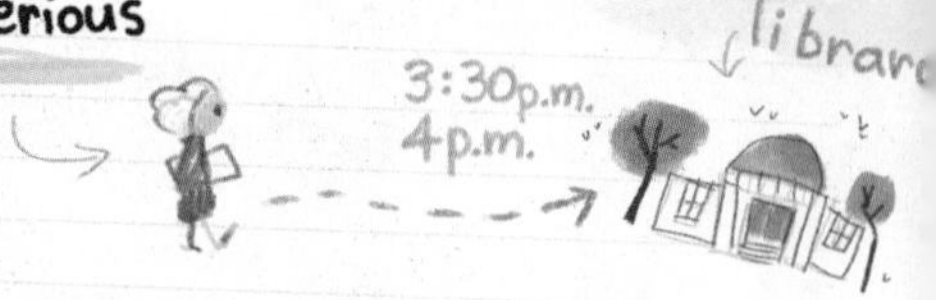

library
3:30p.m.
4p.m.

- She comes on Tuesdays from 3:30 to 4 p.m., turns in the book she borrowed for the week, then flips through some other books for about twenty minutes.

- During this time, the librarian consults her registry to see if anyone else wants to borrow that book. But since it's always with Ms. Ronsin, everyone's forgotten it exists. So the librarian puts it back on the stack of books to return to the shelf.

every week!

- Ms. Ronsin goes to the counter, takes back the book, and checks it out again for another week. She always returns the book on time.

for 15 or 20 years!

- She's done this for about twenty years. The old librarian told the new one, when she started there, that it had already been 5 years!

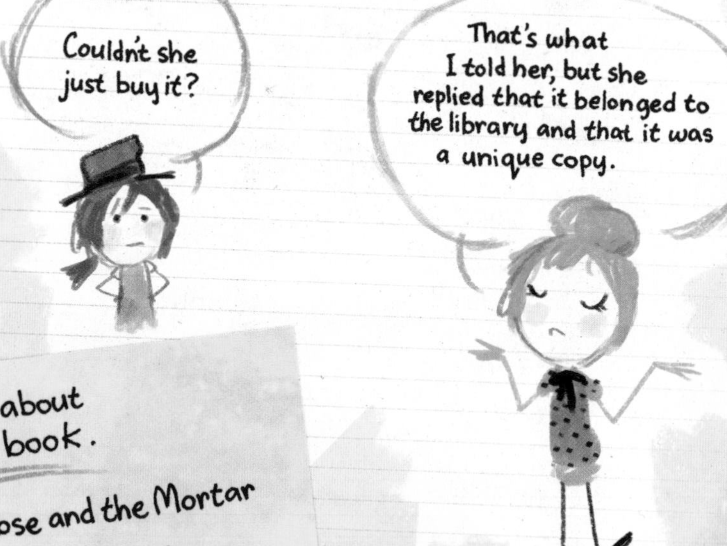

Couldn't she just buy it?
That's what I told her, but she replied that it belonged to the library and that it was a unique copy.

Details about the book.

Title: The Rose and the Mortar

Author: Hector Bertelon

Publisher: self-published.

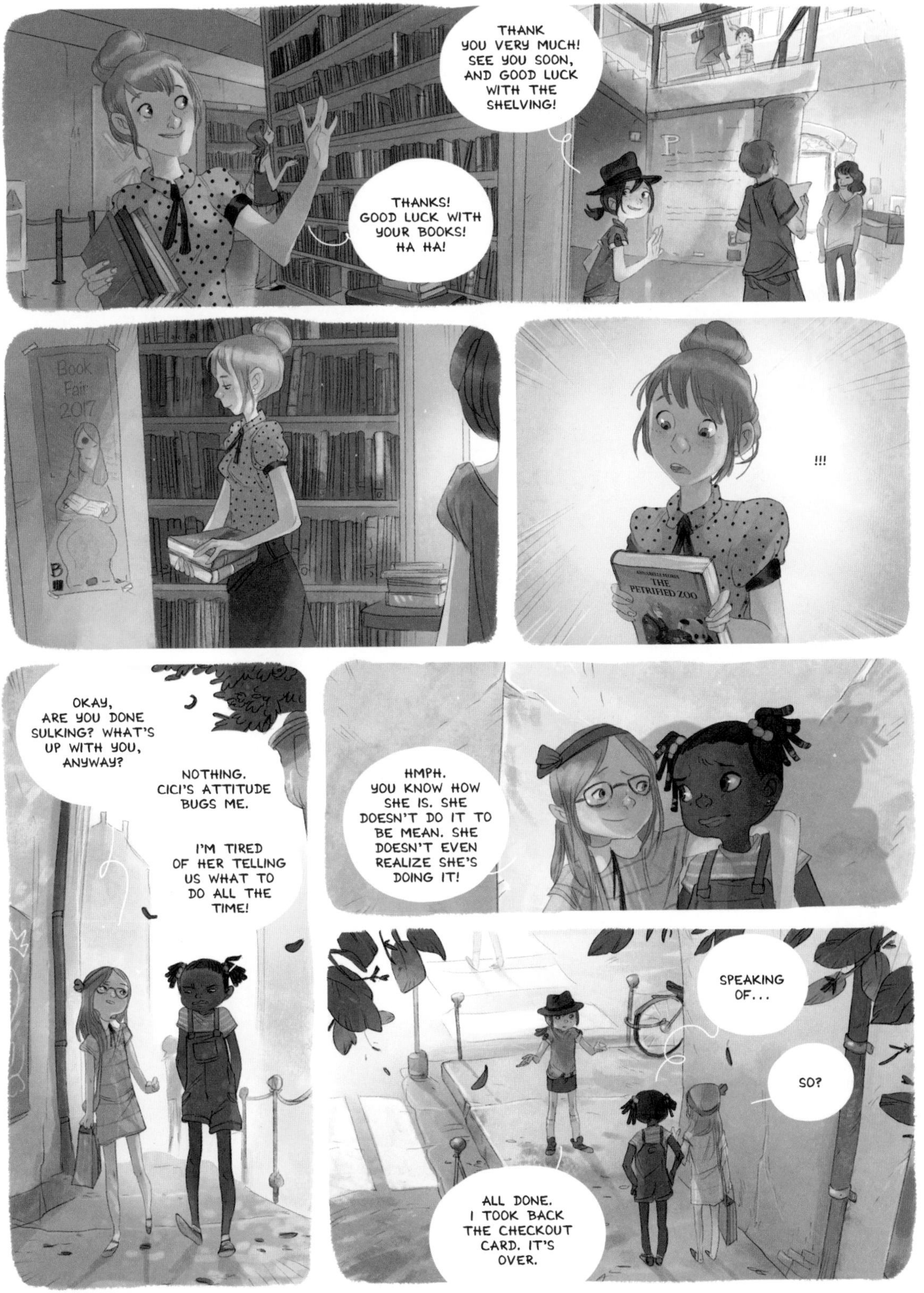
THANK YOU VERY MUCH! SEE YOU SOON, AND GOOD LUCK WITH THE SHELVING!
THANKS! GOOD LUCK WITH YOUR BOOKS! HA HA!
Book Fair 2017
!!!
THE PETRIFIED ZOO
OKAY, ARE YOU DONE SULKING? WHAT'S UP WITH YOU, ANYWAY?
NOTHING. CICI'S ATTITUDE BUGS ME.
I'M TIRED OF HER TELLING US WHAT TO DO ALL THE TIME!
HMPH. YOU KNOW HOW SHE IS. SHE DOESN'T DO IT TO BE MEAN. SHE DOESN'T EVEN REALIZE SHE'S DOING IT!
SPEAKING OF...
SO?
ALL DONE. I TOOK BACK THE CHECKOUT CARD. IT'S OVER.

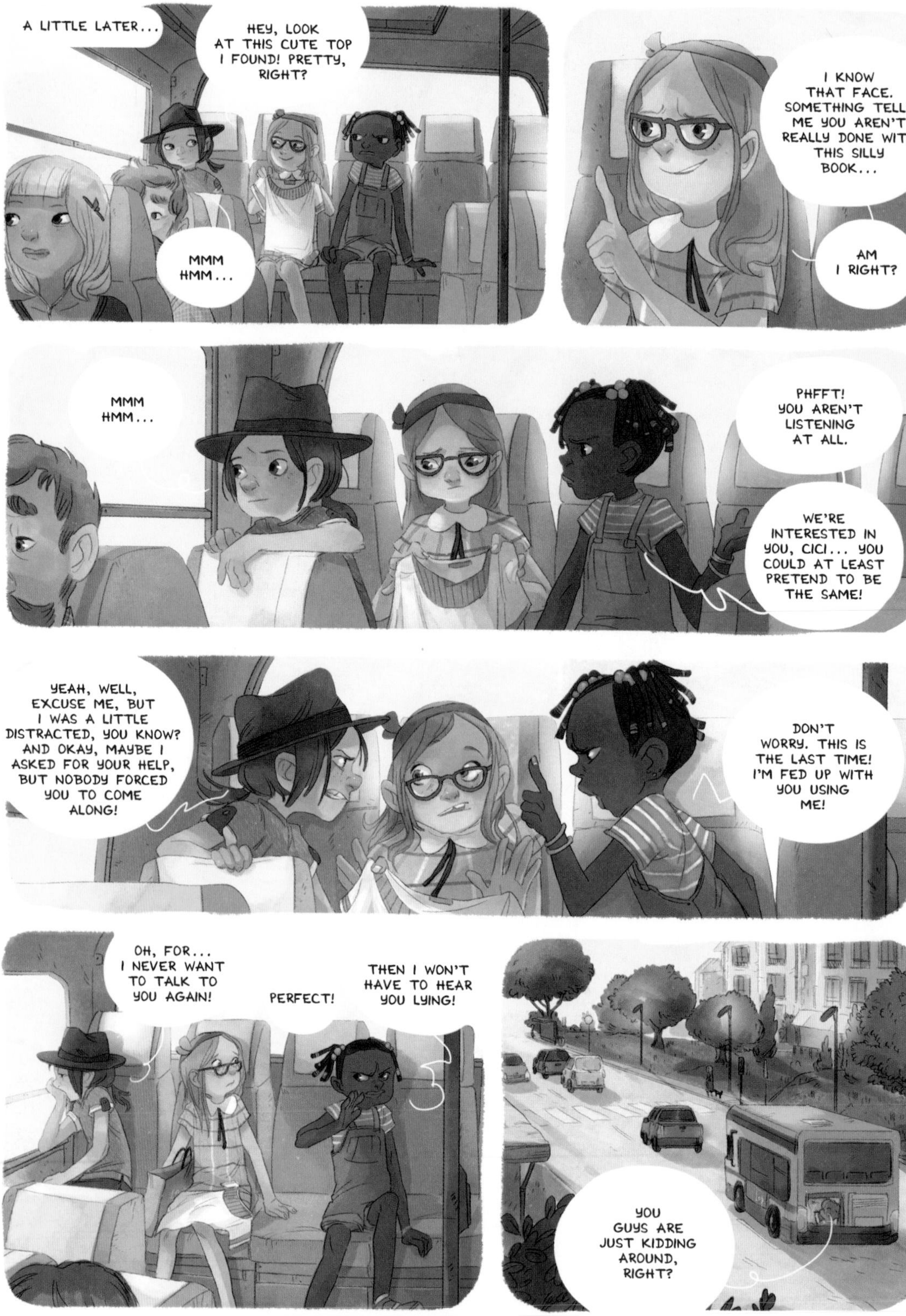
A LITTLE LATER...
HEY, LOOK AT THIS CUTE TOP I FOUND! PRETTY, RIGHT?
MMM HMM...
I KNOW THAT FACE. SOMETHING TELLS ME YOU AREN'T REALLY DONE WITH THIS SILLY BOOK...
AM I RIGHT?
MMM HMM...
PHFFT! YOU AREN'T LISTENING AT ALL.
WE'RE INTERESTED IN YOU, CICI... YOU COULD AT LEAST PRETEND TO BE THE SAME!
YEAH, WELL, EXCUSE ME, BUT I WAS A LITTLE DISTRACTED, YOU KNOW? AND OKAY, MAYBE I ASKED FOR YOUR HELP, BUT NOBODY FORCED YOU TO COME ALONG!
DON'T WORRY. THIS IS THE LAST TIME! I'M FED UP WITH YOU USING ME!
OH, FOR... I NEVER WANT TO TALK TO YOU AGAIN!
PERFECT!
THEN I WON'T HAVE TO HEAR YOU LYING!
YOU GUYS ARE JUST KIDDING AROUND, RIGHT?

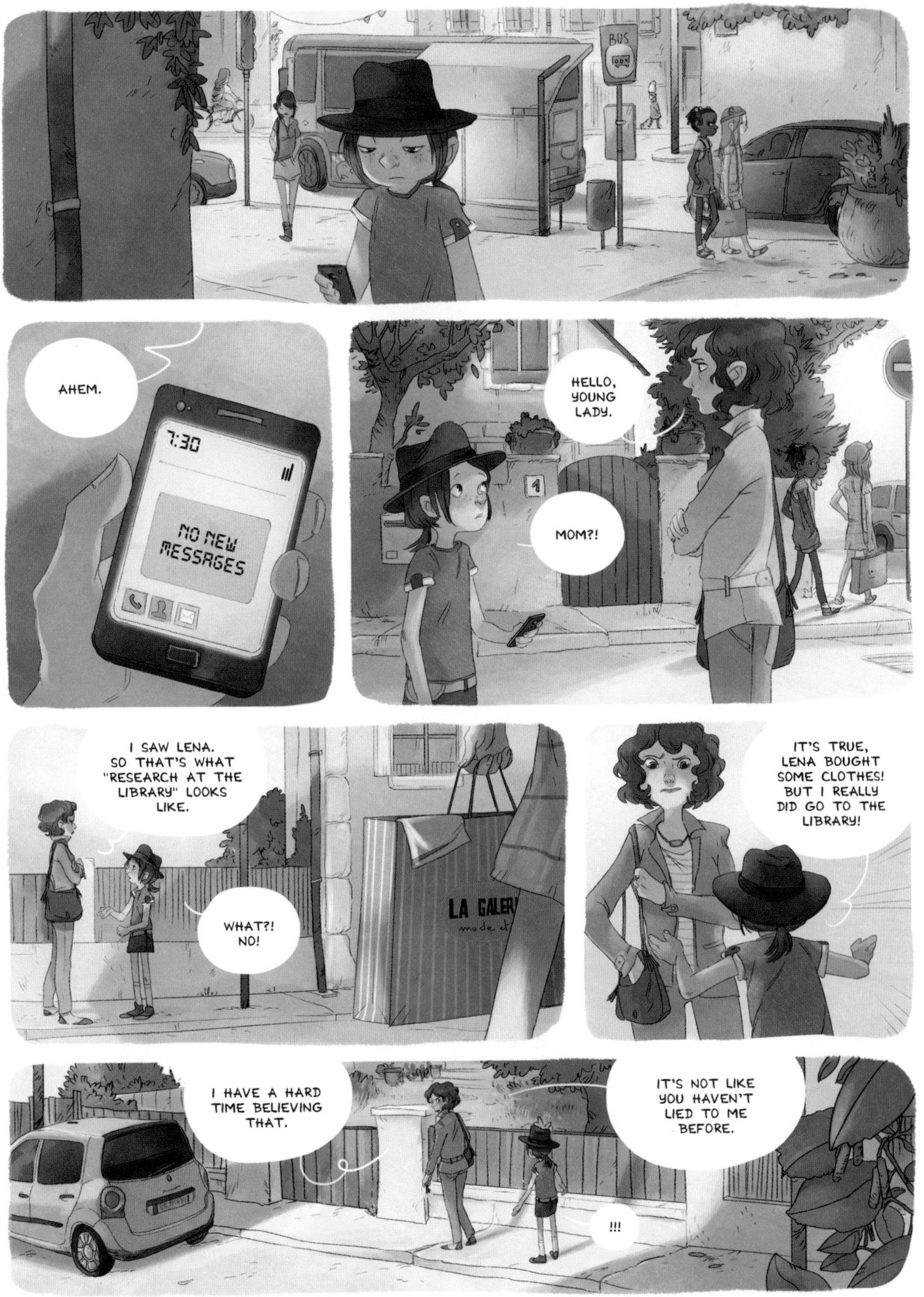

BUS
AHEM.
7:30
NO NEW MESSAGES
HELLO, YOUNG LADY.
MOM?!
I SAW LENA. SO THAT'S WHAT "RESEARCH AT THE LIBRARY" LOOKS LIKE.
WHAT?! NO!
LA GALER
IT'S TRUE, LENA BOUGHT SOME CLOTHES! BUT I REALLY DID GO TO THE LIBRARY!
I HAVE A HARD TIME BELIEVING THAT.
IT'S NOT LIKE YOU HAVEN'T LIED TO ME BEFORE.
!!!

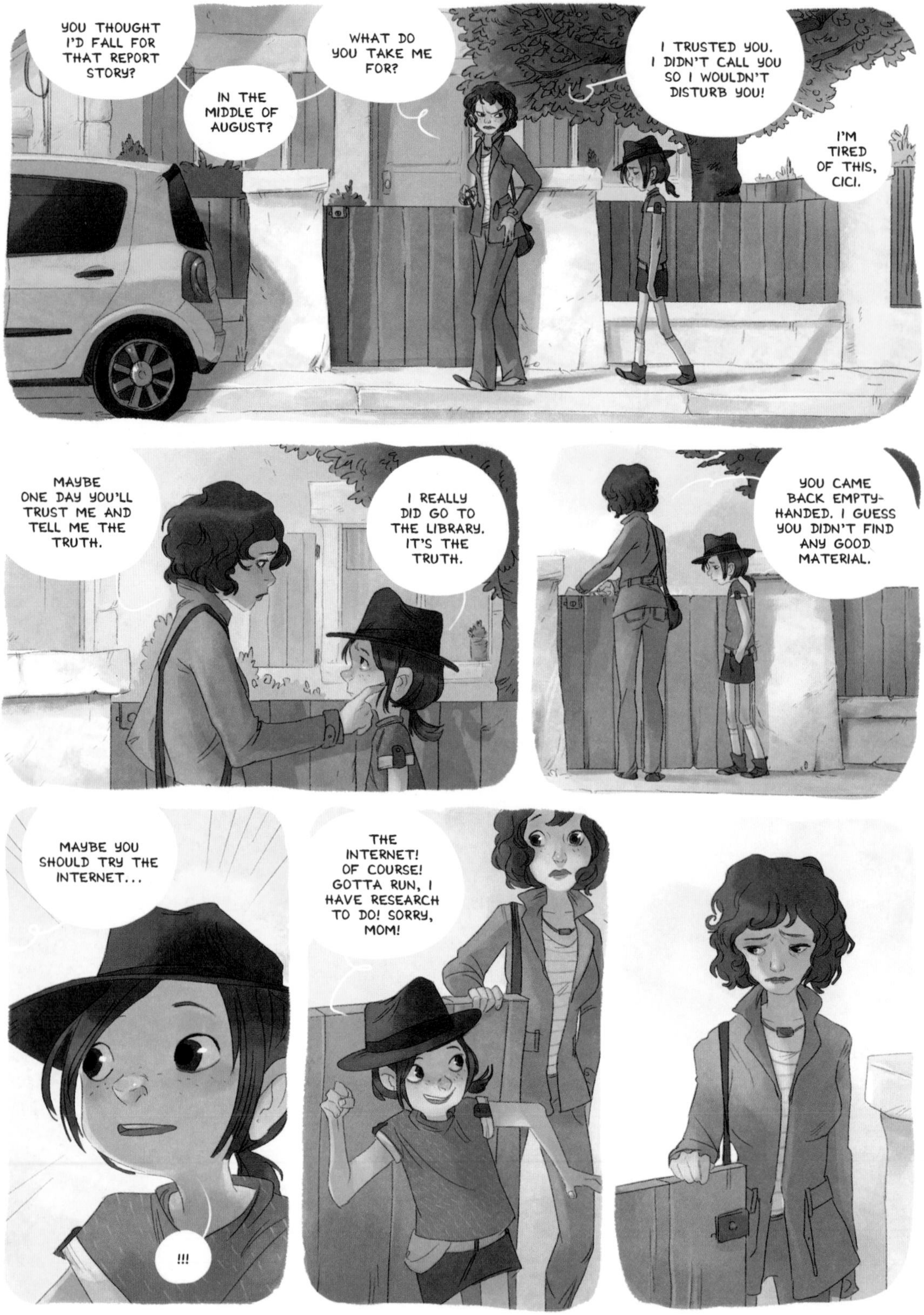
YOU THOUGHT I'D FALL FOR THAT REPORT STORY?
IN THE MIDDLE OF AUGUST?
WHAT DO YOU TAKE ME FOR?
I TRUSTED YOU. I DIDN'T CALL YOU SO I WOULDN'T DISTURB YOU!
I'M TIRED OF THIS, CICI.
MAYBE ONE DAY YOU'LL TRUST ME AND TELL ME THE TRUTH.
I REALLY DID GO TO THE LIBRARY. IT'S THE TRUTH.
YOU CAME BACK EMPTY-HANDED. I GUESS YOU DIDN'T FIND ANY GOOD MATERIAL.
MAYBE YOU SHOULD TRY THE INTERNET...
!!!
THE INTERNET! OF COURSE! GOTTA RUN, I HAVE RESEARCH TO DO! SORRY, MOM!

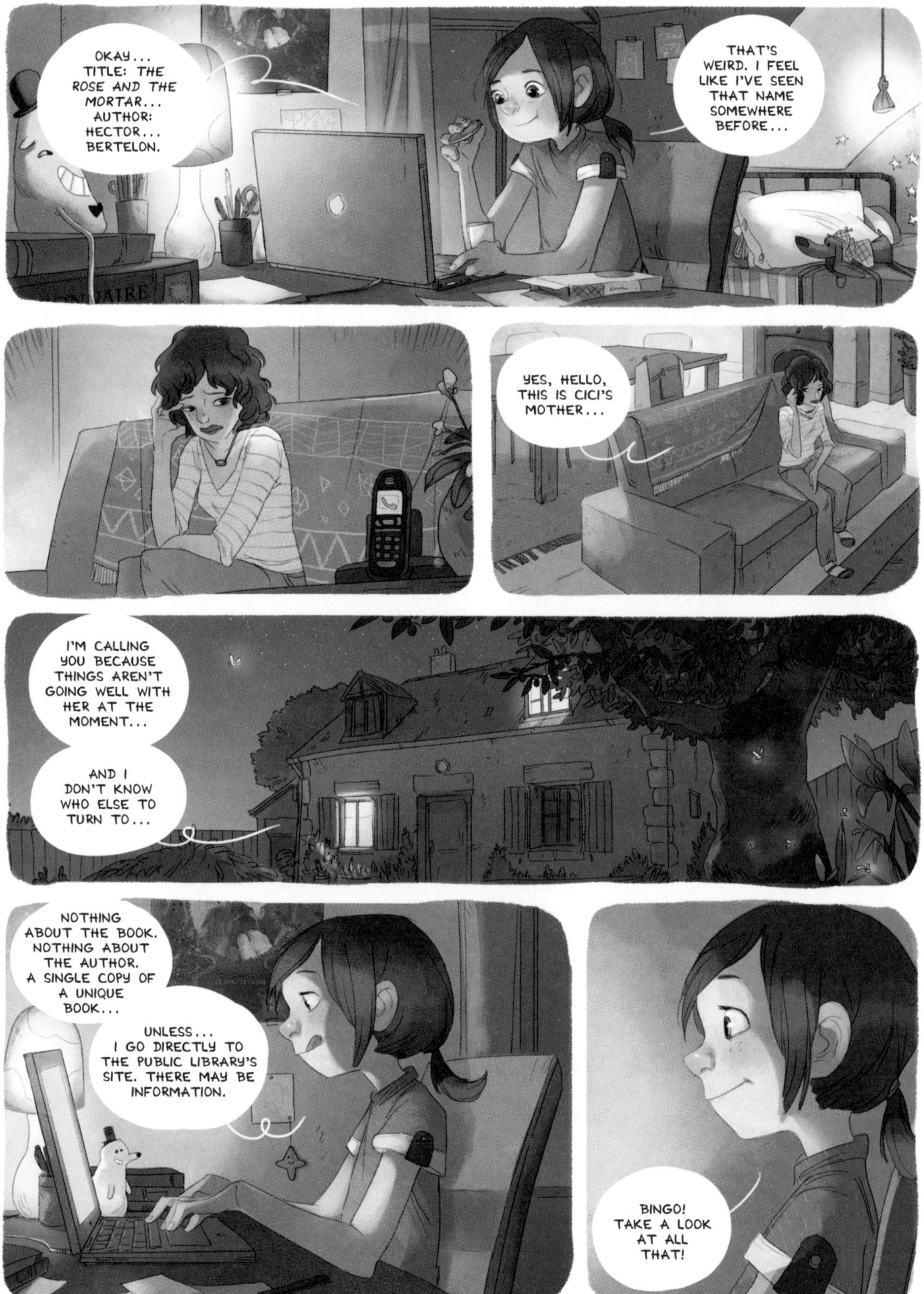
OKAY... TITLE: THE ROSE AND THE MORTAR... AUTHOR: HECTOR... BERTELON.
THAT'S WEIRD. I FEEL LIKE I'VE SEEN THAT NAME SOMEWHERE BEFORE...
YES, HELLO, THIS IS CICI'S MOTHER...
I'M CALLING YOU BECAUSE THINGS AREN'T GOING WELL WITH HER AT THE MOMENT...
AND I DON'T KNOW WHO ELSE TO TURN TO...
NOTHING ABOUT THE BOOK. NOTHING ABOUT THE AUTHOR. A SINGLE COPY OF A UNIQUE BOOK...
UNLESS... I GO DIRECTLY TO THE PUBLIC LIBRARY'S SITE. THERE MAY BE INFORMATION.
BINGO! TAKE A LOOK AT ALL THAT!

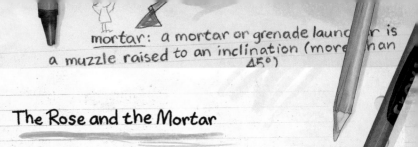

mortar: a mortar or grenade launcher is a muzzle raised to an inclination (more than 45°)

The Rose and the Mortar

HECTOR BERTELON

The Rose and the Mortar

HB

I've copied down everything I found!

The cover is great.

Maybe he designed it himself?

I'd really like to know more!

Bertelon
Bertelon
Bertelon
BERTELON
? ?

Description: A young writer sent to the front lines during World War II, Hector Bertelon delivers through these letters a new look at the horror of war. A gifted writer depicts life in "The Mortar"—a secret communications battalion. Discover who these men were and plunge into the daily experience of one unit of soldiers at the heart of conflict.

Bertelon

I knew I'd seen his name before!

Bertelon?
Bertelon

1: works by numerical classification (old classification) "The Rose and the Mortar." Work 86-R-43.

2: works, classified by genre (new classification) "The Rose and the Mortar," no reference...

??

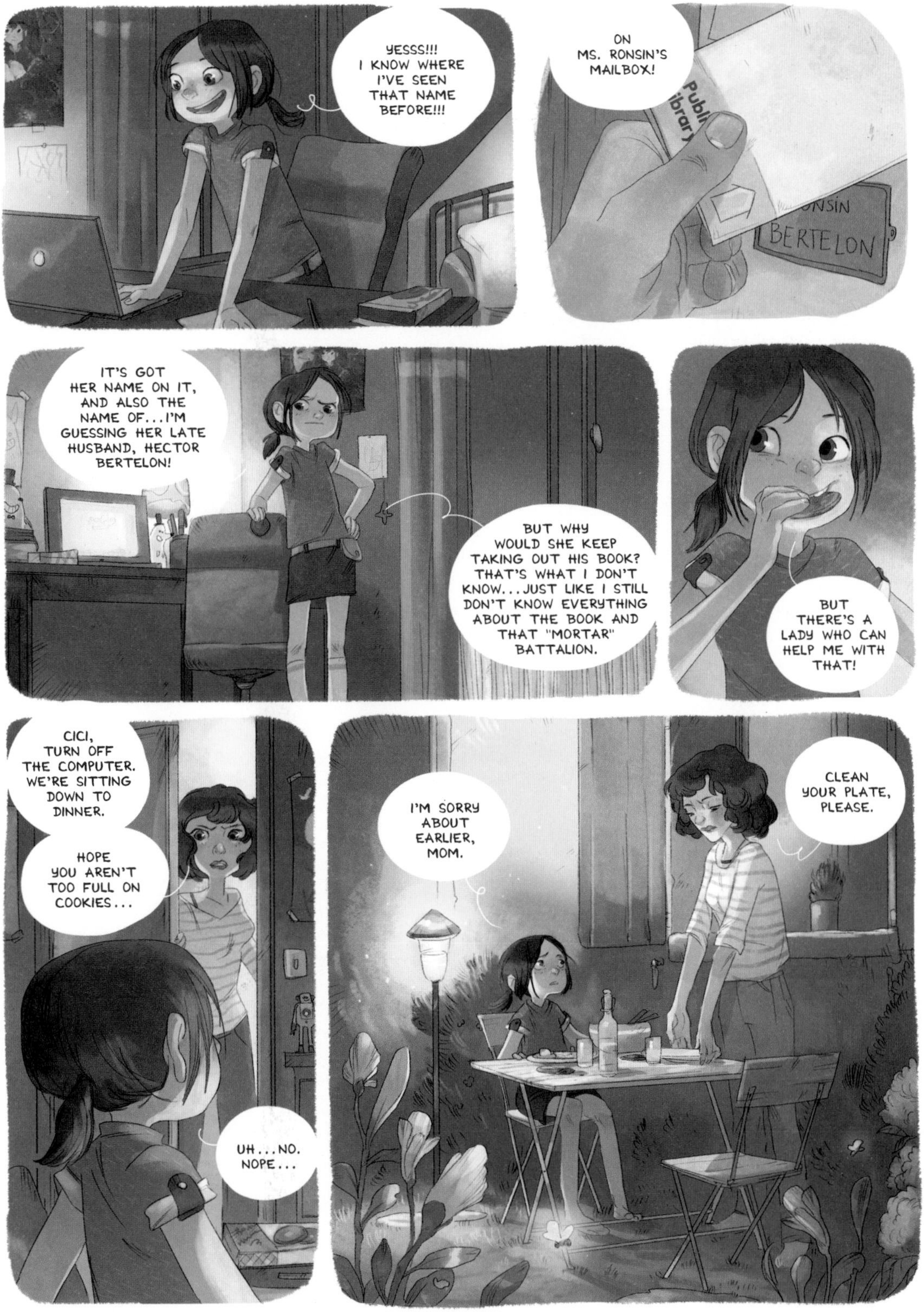
YESSS!!! I KNOW WHERE I'VE SEEN THAT NAME BEFORE!!!
ON MS. RONSIN'S MAILBOX!
Public library
RONSIN BERTELON
IT'S GOT HER NAME ON IT, AND ALSO THE NAME OF...I'M GUESSING HER LATE HUSBAND, HECTOR BERTELON!
BUT WHY WOULD SHE KEEP TAKING OUT HIS BOOK? THAT'S WHAT I DON'T KNOW...JUST LIKE I STILL DON'T KNOW EVERYTHING ABOUT THE BOOK AND THAT "MORTAR" BATTALION.
BUT THERE'S A LADY WHO CAN HELP ME WITH THAT!
CICI, TURN OFF THE COMPUTER. WE'RE SITTING DOWN TO DINNER.
HOPE YOU AREN'T TOO FULL ON COOKIES...
UH...NO. NOPE...
I'M SORRY ABOUT EARLIER, MOM.
CLEAN YOUR PLATE, PLEASE.

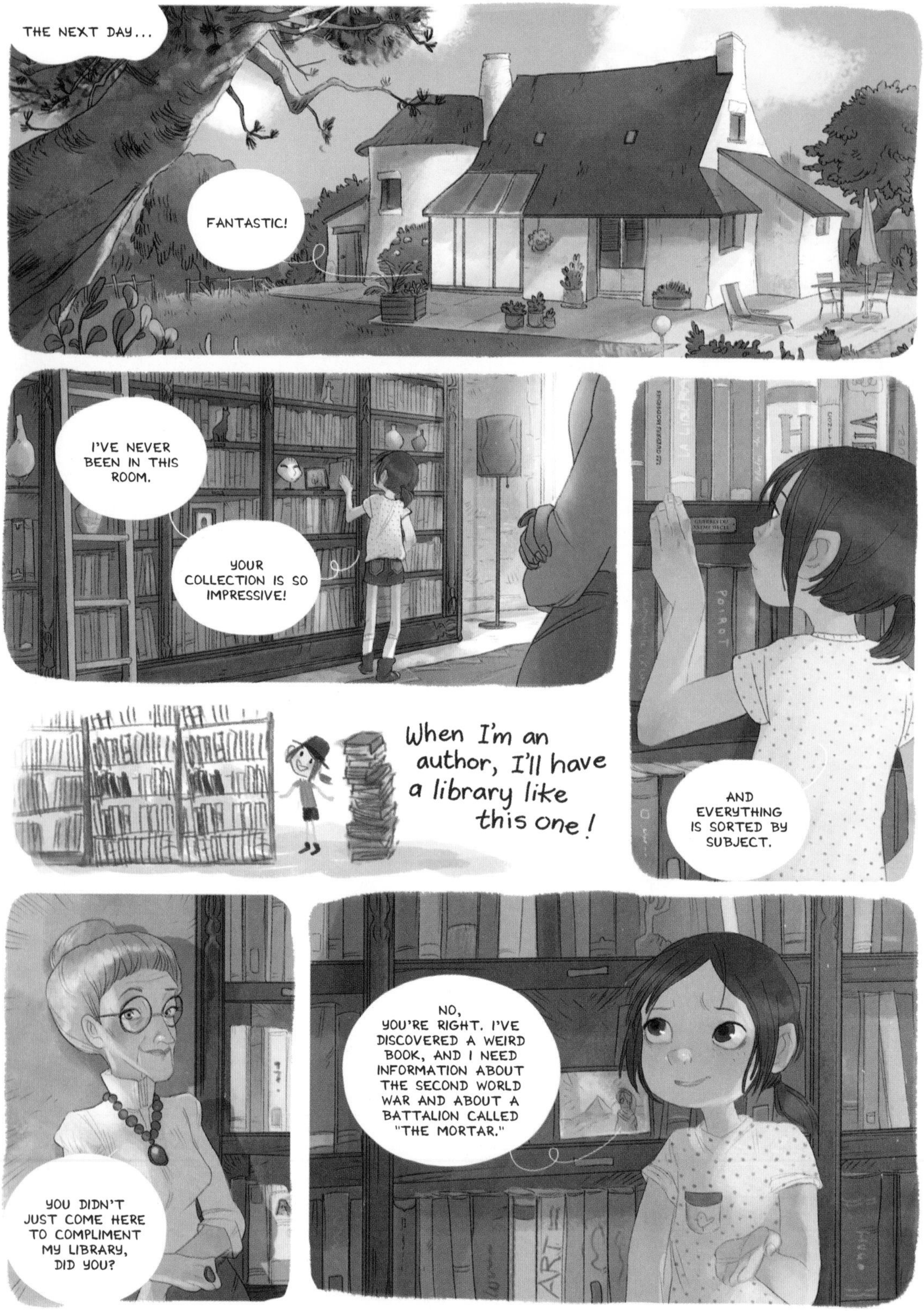
THE NEXT DAY...
FANTASTIC!
I'VE NEVER BEEN IN THIS ROOM.
YOUR COLLECTION IS SO IMPRESSIVE!
AND EVERYTHING IS SORTED BY SUBJECT.
When I'm an author, I'll have a library like this one!
YOU DIDN'T JUST COME HERE TO COMPLIMENT MY LIBRARY, DID YOU?
NO, YOU'RE RIGHT. I'VE DISCOVERED A WEIRD BOOK, AND I NEED INFORMATION ABOUT THE SECOND WORLD WAR AND ABOUT A BATTALION CALLED "THE MORTAR."
POIROT
ART

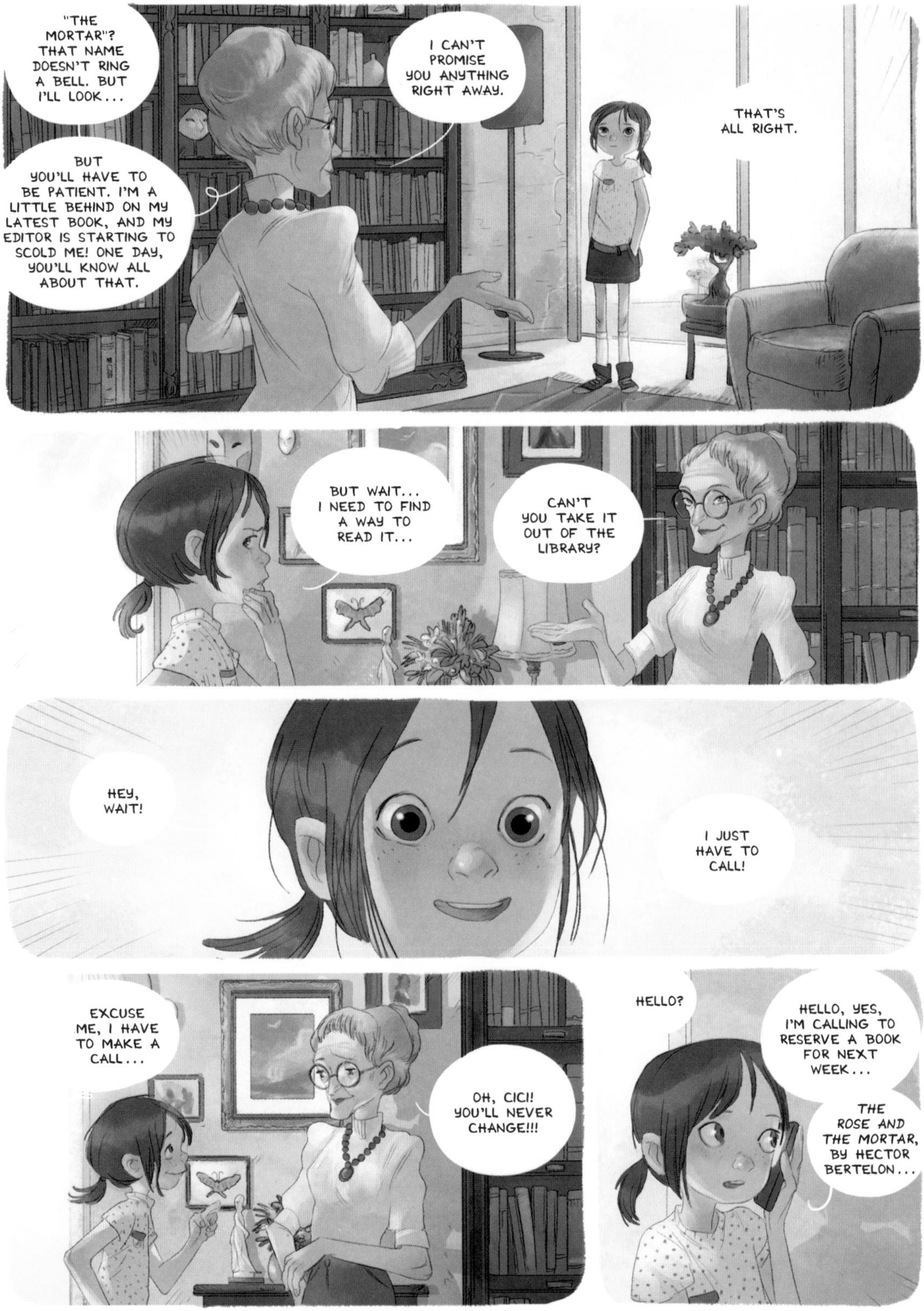
"THE MORTAR"? THAT NAME DOESN'T RING A BELL. BUT I'LL LOOK...
I CAN'T PROMISE YOU ANYTHING RIGHT AWAY.
BUT YOU'LL HAVE TO BE PATIENT. I'M A LITTLE BEHIND ON MY LATEST BOOK, AND MY EDITOR IS STARTING TO SCOLD ME! ONE DAY, YOU'LL KNOW ALL ABOUT THAT.
THAT'S ALL RIGHT.
BUT WAIT... I NEED TO FIND A WAY TO READ IT...
CAN'T YOU TAKE IT OUT OF THE LIBRARY?
HEY, WAIT!
I JUST HAVE TO CALL!
EXCUSE ME, I HAVE TO MAKE A CALL...
OH, CICI! YOU'LL NEVER CHANGE!!!
HELLO?
HELLO, YES, I'M CALLING TO RESERVE A BOOK FOR NEXT WEEK...
THE ROSE AND THE MORTAR, BY HECTOR BERTELON...

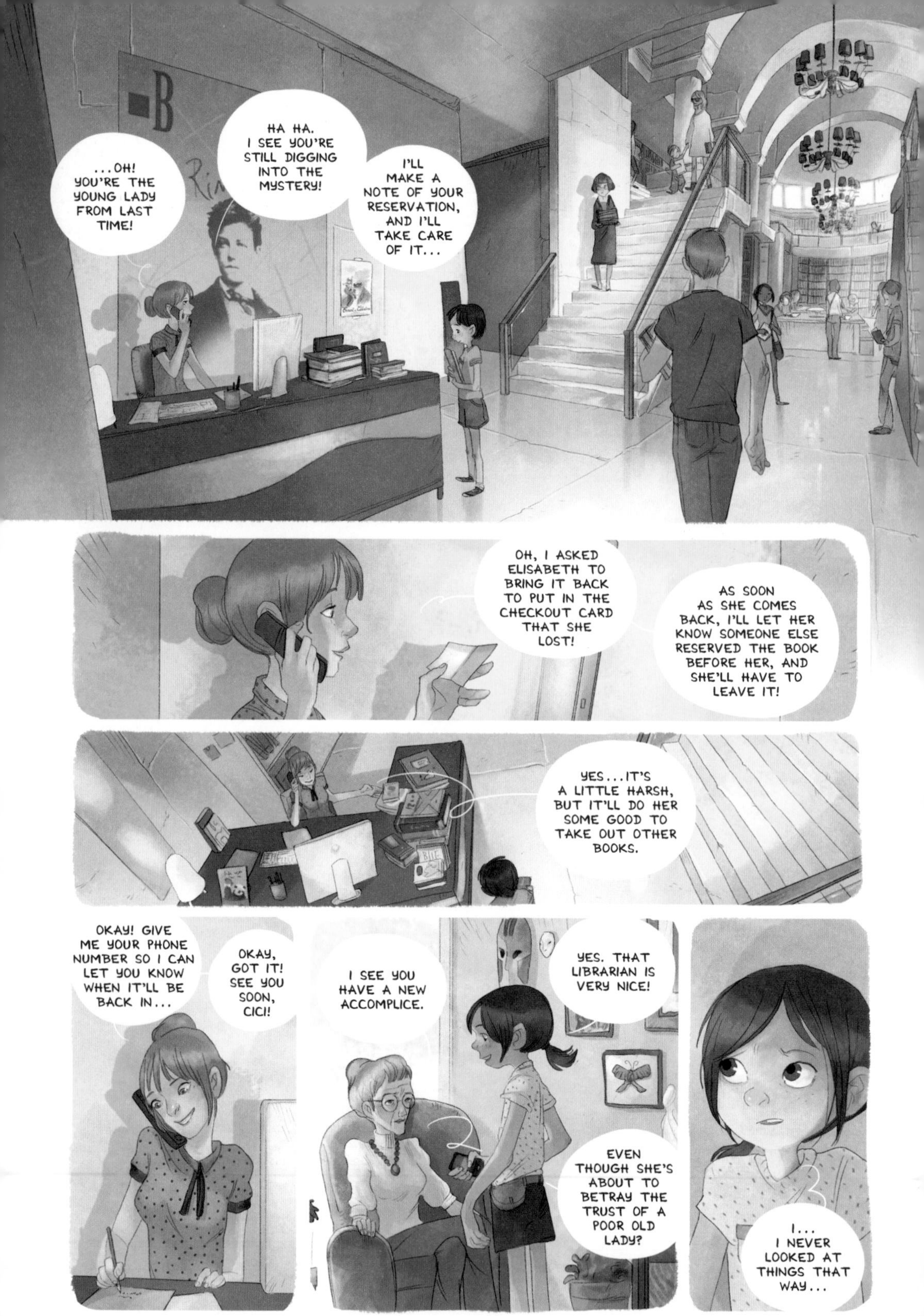
...OH! YOU'RE THE YOUNG LADY FROM LAST TIME!
HA HA. I SEE YOU'RE STILL DIGGING INTO THE MYSTERY!
I'LL MAKE A NOTE OF YOUR RESERVATION, AND I'LL TAKE CARE OF IT...
OH, I ASKED ELISABETH TO BRING IT BACK TO PUT IN THE CHECKOUT CARD THAT SHE LOST!
AS SOON AS SHE COMES BACK, I'LL LET HER KNOW SOMEONE ELSE RESERVED THE BOOK BEFORE HER, AND SHE'LL HAVE TO LEAVE IT!
YES...IT'S A LITTLE HARSH, BUT IT'LL DO HER SOME GOOD TO TAKE OUT OTHER BOOKS.
OKAY! GIVE ME YOUR PHONE NUMBER SO I CAN LET YOU KNOW WHEN IT'LL BE BACK IN...
OKAY, GOT IT! SEE YOU SOON, CICI!
I SEE YOU HAVE A NEW ACCOMPLICE.
YES. THAT LIBRARIAN IS VERY NICE!
EVEN THOUGH SHE'S ABOUT TO BETRAY THE TRUST OF A POOR OLD LADY?
I... I NEVER LOOKED AT THINGS THAT WAY...

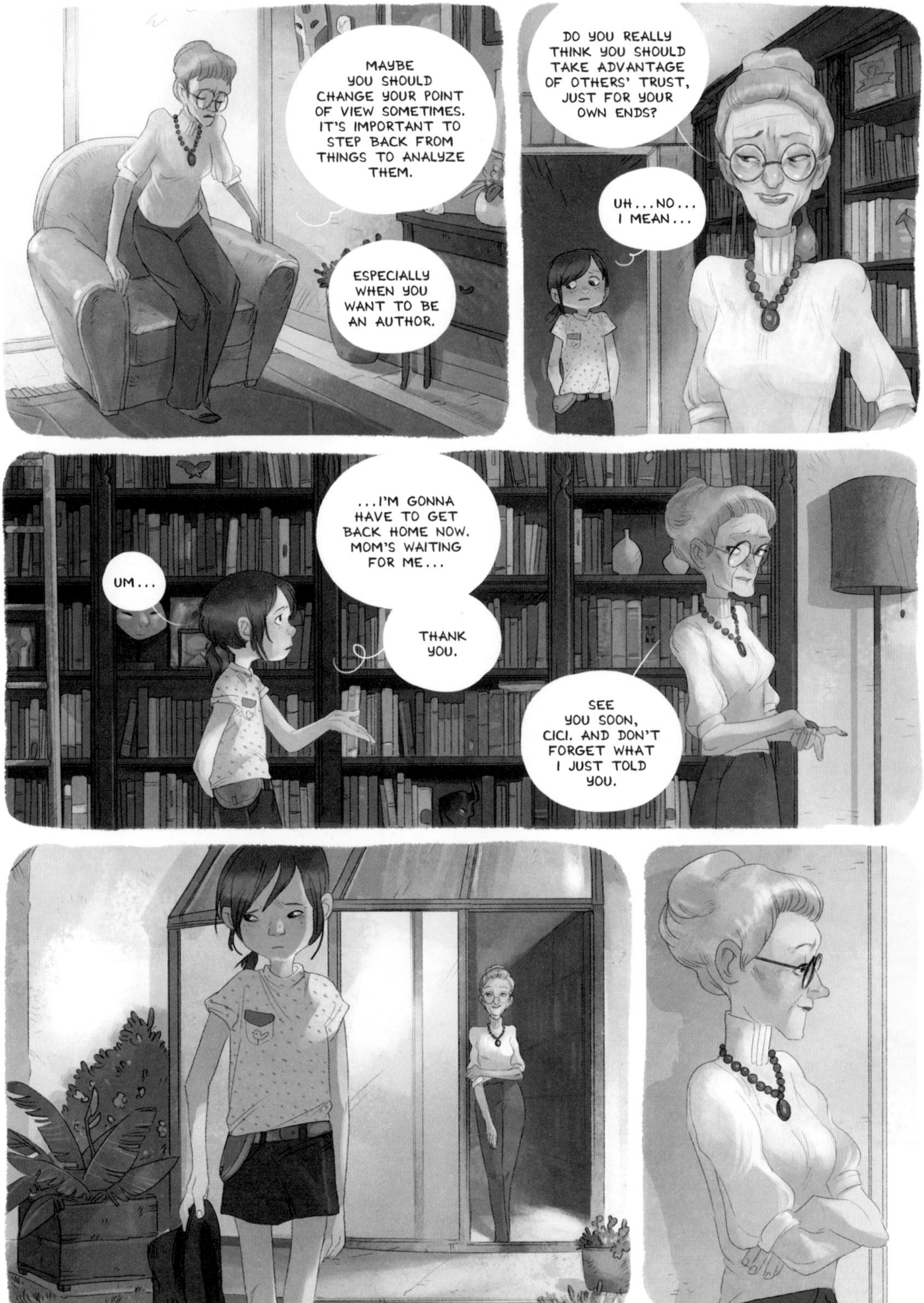
MAYBE YOU SHOULD CHANGE YOUR POINT OF VIEW SOMETIMES. IT'S IMPORTANT TO STEP BACK FROM THINGS TO ANALYZE THEM.
ESPECIALLY WHEN YOU WANT TO BE AN AUTHOR.
DO YOU REALLY THINK YOU SHOULD TAKE ADVANTAGE OF OTHERS' TRUST, JUST FOR YOUR OWN ENDS?
UH... NO... I MEAN...
UM...
...I'M GONNA HAVE TO GET BACK HOME NOW. MOM'S WAITING FOR ME...
THANK YOU.
SEE YOU SOON, CICI. AND DON'T FORGET WHAT I JUST TOLD YOU.

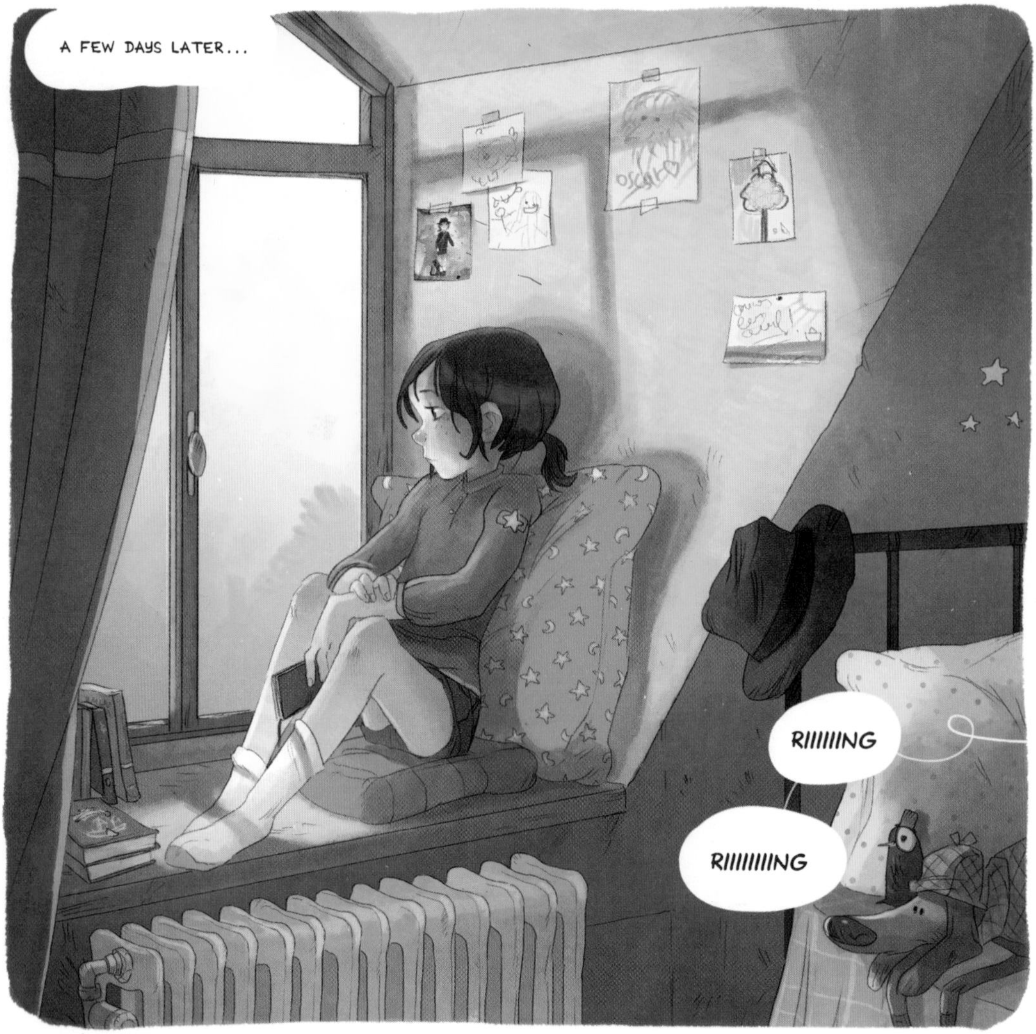
A FEW DAYS LATER...
RIIIIIING
RIIIIIIIING

Once when she was visiting, Mrs. Flores looked out this window during our writing exercise. A while later, she asked me: "If it was Cici who passed by your window, down below, what would you write about her?" I never knew what to tell her.

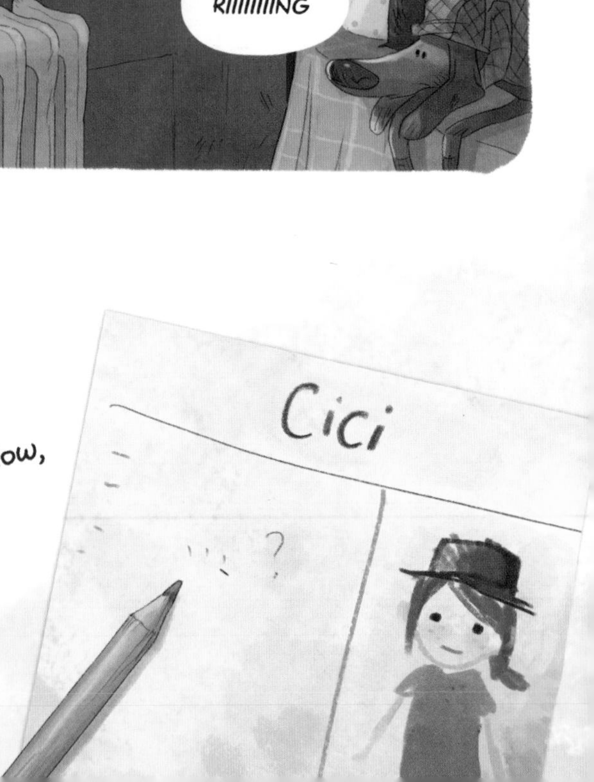
Cici

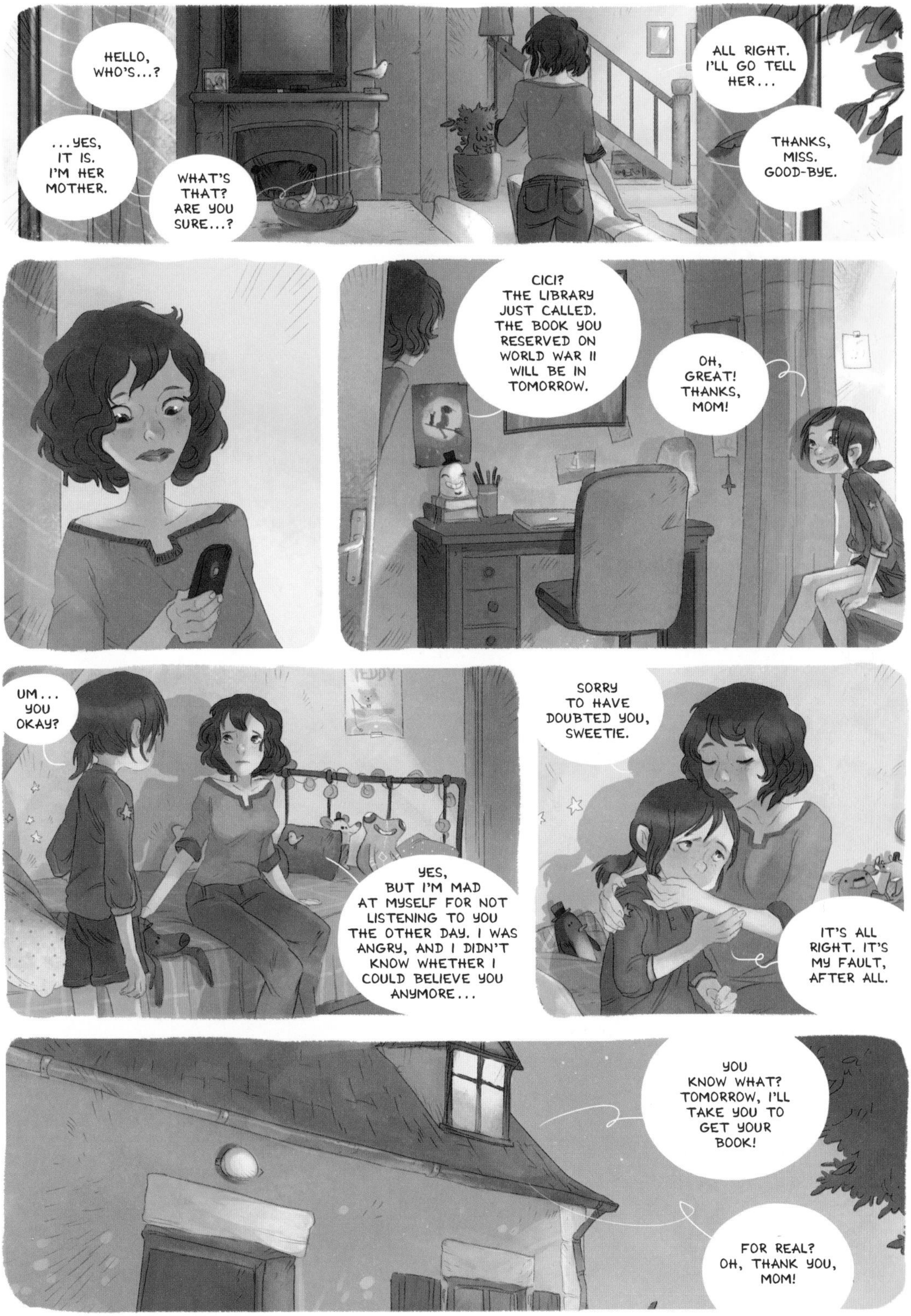
HELLO, WHO'S...?
...YES, IT IS. I'M HER MOTHER.
WHAT'S THAT? ARE YOU SURE...?
ALL RIGHT. I'LL GO TELL HER...
THANKS, MISS. GOOD-BYE.
CICI? THE LIBRARY JUST CALLED. THE BOOK YOU RESERVED ON WORLD WAR II WILL BE IN TOMORROW.
OH, GREAT! THANKS, MOM!
UM... YOU OKAY?
YES, BUT I'M MAD AT MYSELF FOR NOT LISTENING TO YOU THE OTHER DAY. I WAS ANGRY, AND I DIDN'T KNOW WHETHER I COULD BELIEVE YOU ANYMORE...
SORRY TO HAVE DOUBTED YOU, SWEETIE.
IT'S ALL RIGHT. IT'S MY FAULT, AFTER ALL.
YOU KNOW WHAT? TOMORROW, I'LL TAKE YOU TO GET YOUR BOOK!
FOR REAL? OH, THANK YOU, MOM!

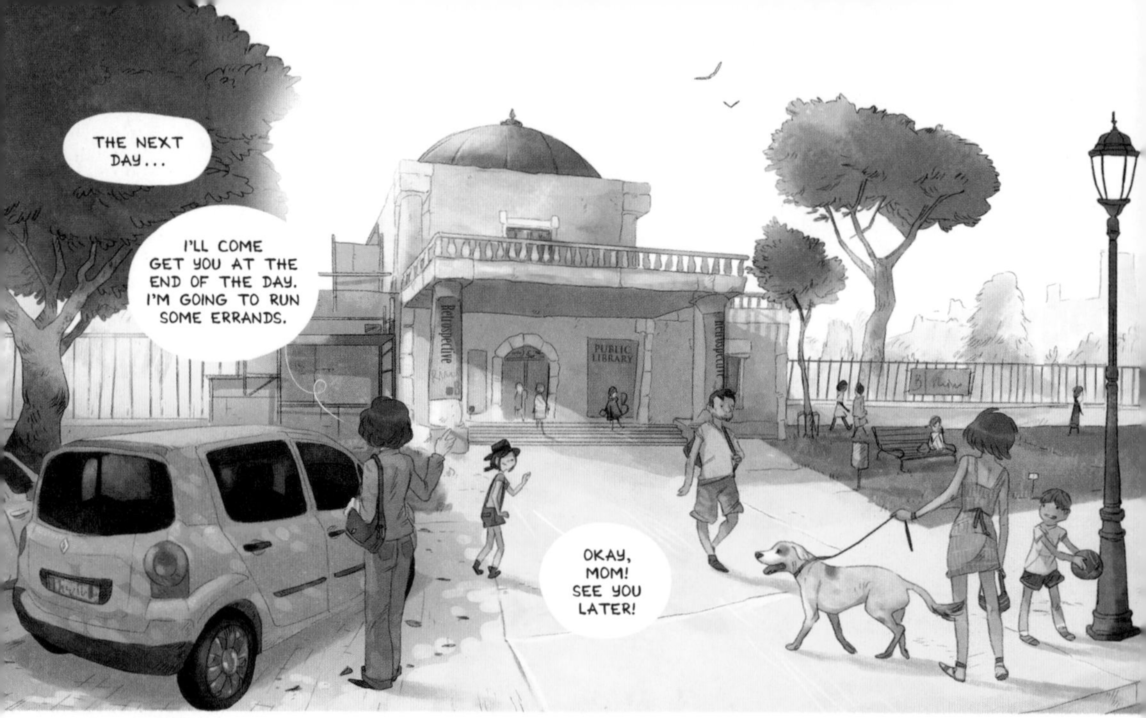
THE NEXT DAY...
I'LL COME GET YOU AT THE END OF THE DAY. I'M GOING TO RUN SOME ERRANDS.
PUBLIC LIBRARY
OKAY, MOM! SEE YOU LATER!

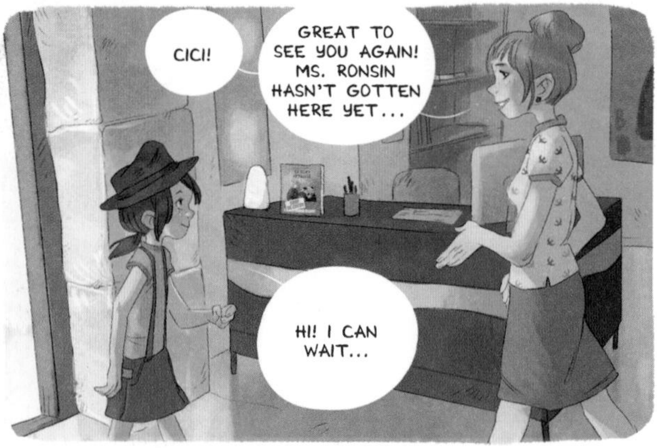
CICI!
GREAT TO SEE YOU AGAIN! MS. RONSIN HASN'T GOTTEN HERE YET...
HI! I CAN WAIT...

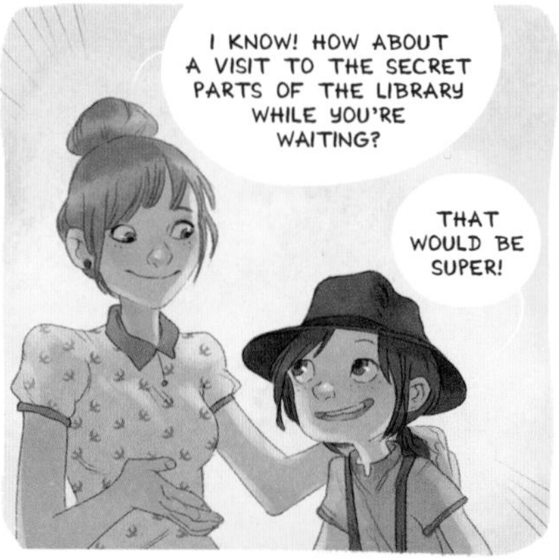
I KNOW! HOW ABOUT A VISIT TO THE SECRET PARTS OF THE LIBRARY WHILE YOU'RE WAITING?
THAT WOULD BE SUPER!

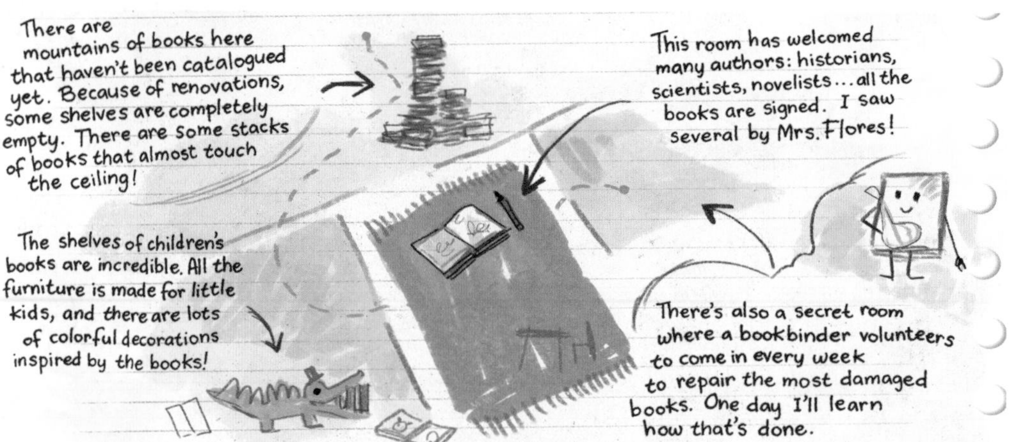
There are mountains of books here that haven't been catalogued yet. Because of renovations, some shelves are completely empty. There are some stacks of books that almost touch the ceiling!
This room has welcomed many authors: historians, scientists, novelists... all the books are signed. I saw several by Mrs. Flores!
The shelves of children's books are incredible. All the furniture is made for little kids, and there are lots of colorful decorations inspired by the books!
There's also a secret room where a bookbinder volunteers to come in every week to repair the most damaged books. One day I'll learn how that's done.

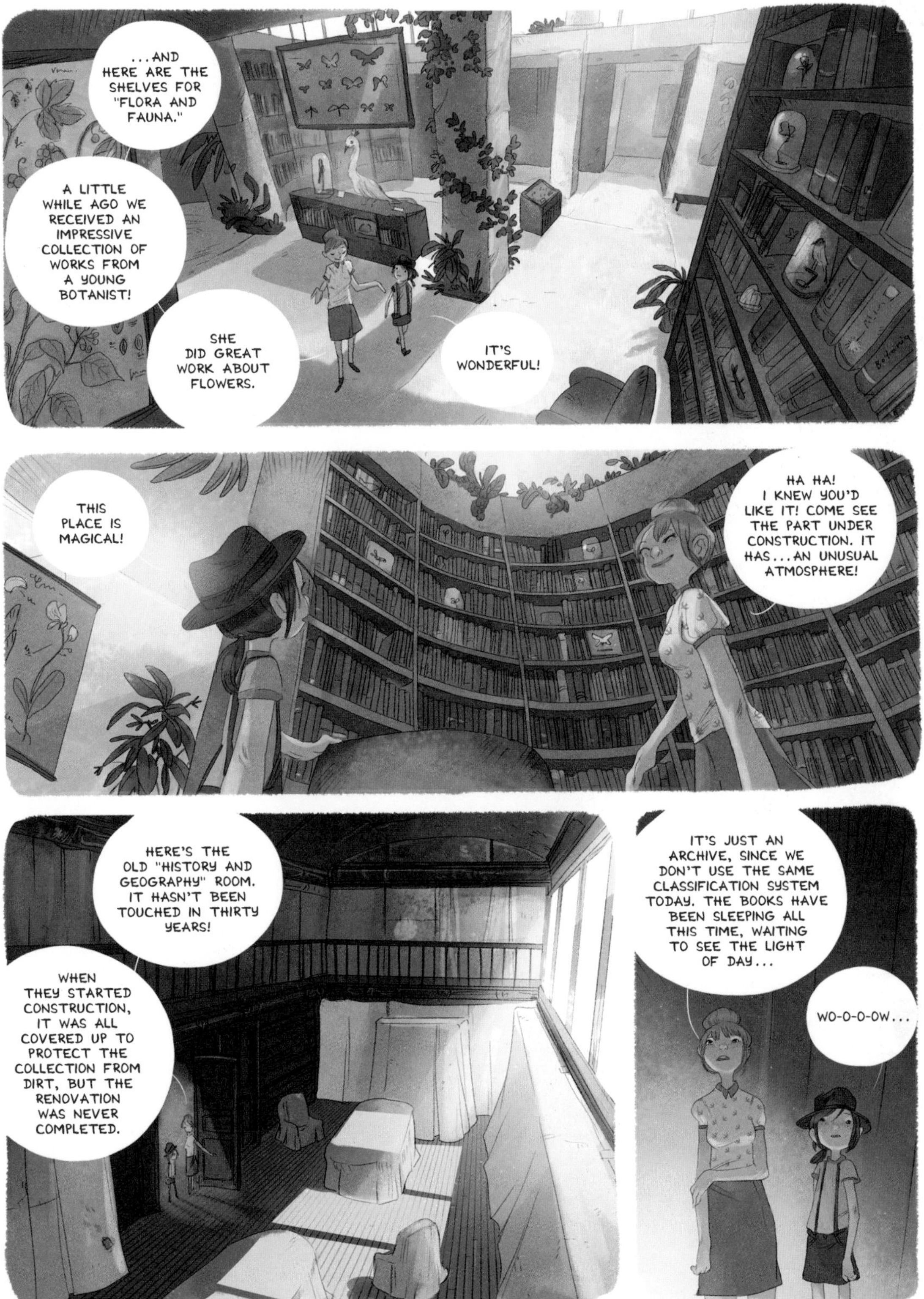
...AND HERE ARE THE SHELVES FOR "FLORA AND FAUNA."
A LITTLE WHILE AGO WE RECEIVED AN IMPRESSIVE COLLECTION OF WORKS FROM A YOUNG BOTANIST!
SHE DID GREAT WORK ABOUT FLOWERS.
IT'S WONDERFUL!
THIS PLACE IS MAGICAL!
HA HA! I KNEW YOU'D LIKE IT! COME SEE THE PART UNDER CONSTRUCTION. IT HAS...AN UNUSUAL ATMOSPHERE!
HERE'S THE OLD "HISTORY AND GEOGRAPHY" ROOM. IT HASN'T BEEN TOUCHED IN THIRTY YEARS!
WHEN THEY STARTED CONSTRUCTION, IT WAS ALL COVERED UP TO PROTECT THE COLLECTION FROM DIRT, BUT THE RENOVATION WAS NEVER COMPLETED.
IT'S JUST AN ARCHIVE, SINCE WE DON'T USE THE SAME CLASSIFICATION SYSTEM TODAY. THE BOOKS HAVE BEEN SLEEPING ALL THIS TIME, WAITING TO SEE THE LIGHT OF DAY...
WO-O-O-OW...

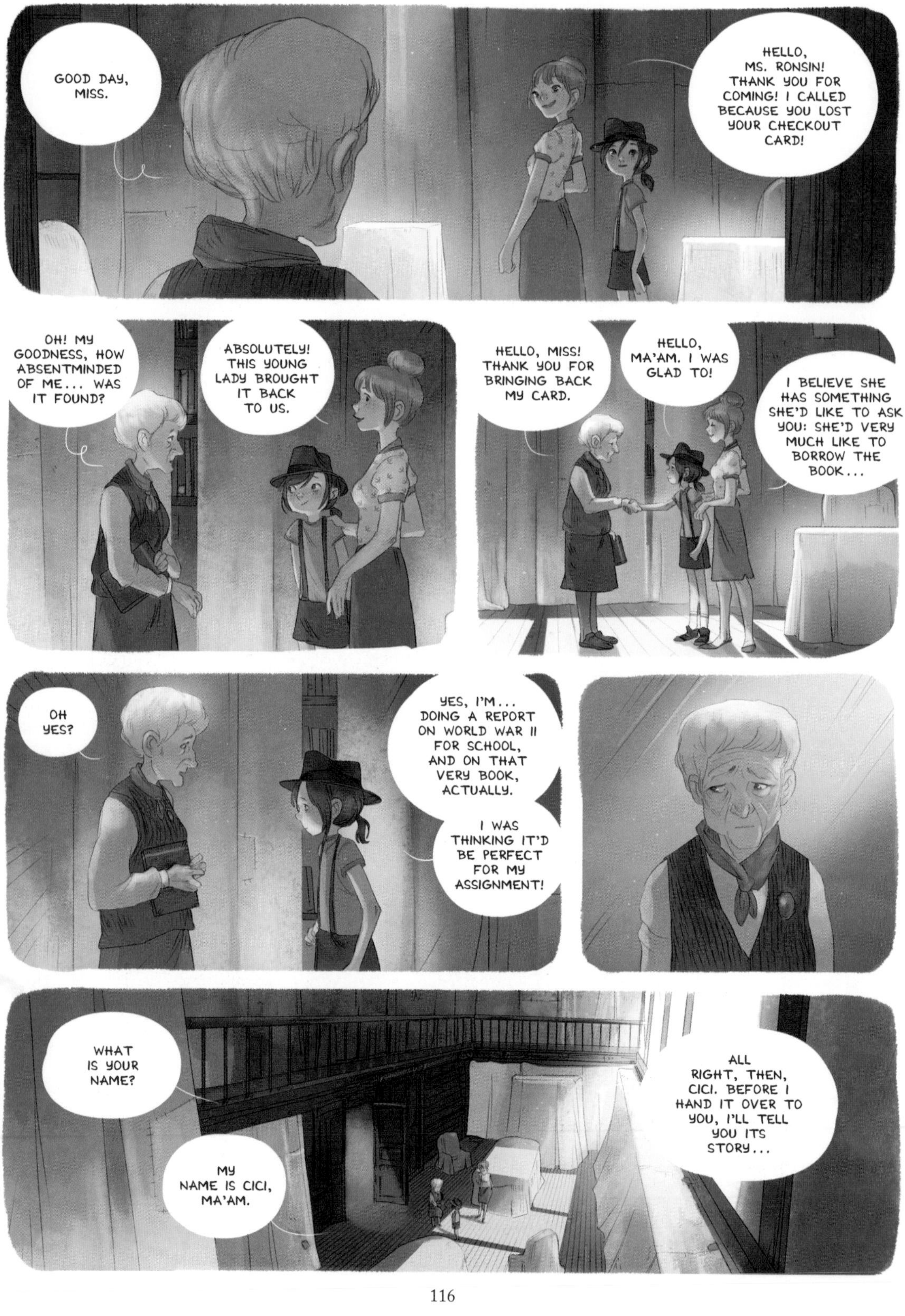
GOOD DAY, MISS.
HELLO, MS. RONSIN! THANK YOU FOR COMING! I CALLED BECAUSE YOU LOST YOUR CHECKOUT CARD!
OH! MY GOODNESS, HOW ABSENTMINDED OF ME... WAS IT FOUND?
ABSOLUTELY! THIS YOUNG LADY BROUGHT IT BACK TO US.
HELLO, MISS! THANK YOU FOR BRINGING BACK MY CARD.
HELLO, MA'AM. I WAS GLAD TO!
I BELIEVE SHE HAS SOMETHING SHE'D LIKE TO ASK YOU: SHE'D VERY MUCH LIKE TO BORROW THE BOOK...
OH YES?
YES, I'M... DOING A REPORT ON WORLD WAR II FOR SCHOOL, AND ON THAT VERY BOOK, ACTUALLY.
I WAS THINKING IT'D BE PERFECT FOR MY ASSIGNMENT!
WHAT IS YOUR NAME?
MY NAME IS CICI, MA'AM.
ALL RIGHT, THEN, CICI. BEFORE I HAND IT OVER TO YOU, I'LL TELL YOU ITS STORY...

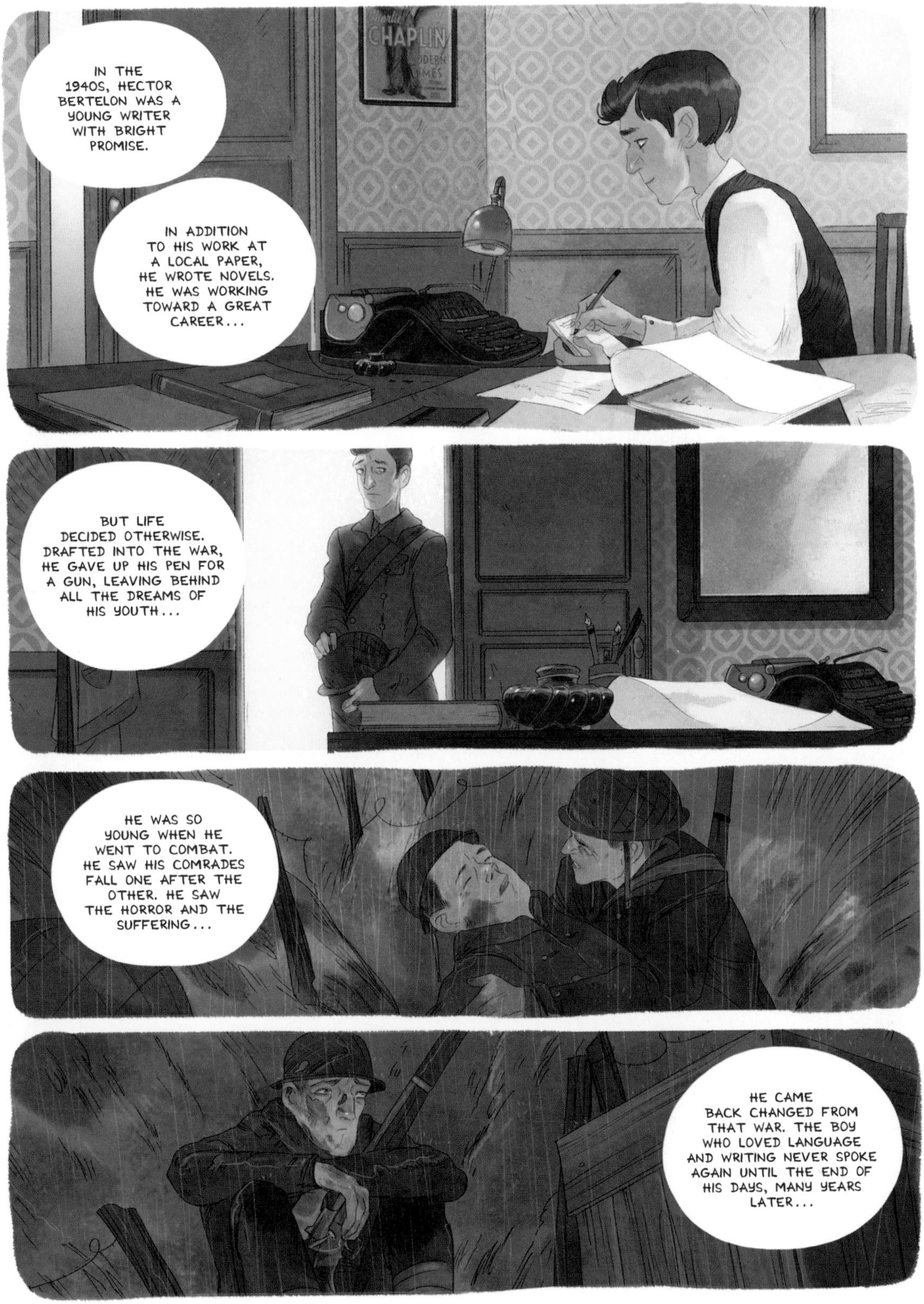
CHAPLIN
IN THE 1940S, HECTOR BERTELON WAS A YOUNG WRITER WITH BRIGHT PROMISE.
IN ADDITION TO HIS WORK AT A LOCAL PAPER, HE WROTE NOVELS. HE WAS WORKING TOWARD A GREAT CAREER...
BUT LIFE DECIDED OTHERWISE. DRAFTED INTO THE WAR, HE GAVE UP HIS PEN FOR A GUN, LEAVING BEHIND ALL THE DREAMS OF HIS YOUTH...
HE WAS SO YOUNG WHEN HE WENT TO COMBAT. HE SAW HIS COMRADES FALL ONE AFTER THE OTHER. HE SAW THE HORROR AND THE SUFFERING...
HE CAME BACK CHANGED FROM THAT WAR. THE BOY WHO LOVED LANGUAGE AND WRITING NEVER SPOKE AGAIN UNTIL THE END OF HIS DAYS, MANY YEARS LATER...

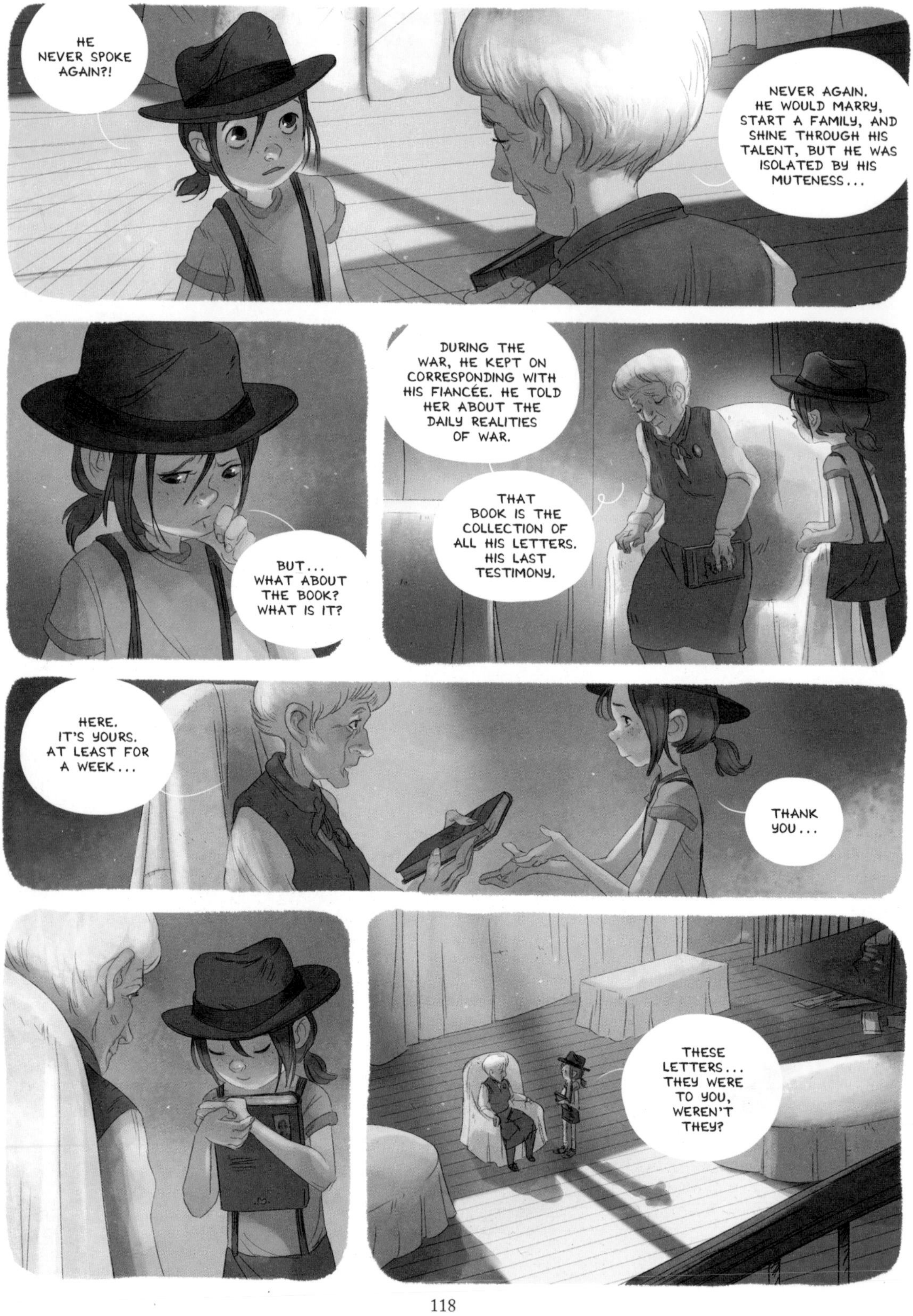
HE NEVER SPOKE AGAIN?!
NEVER AGAIN. HE WOULD MARRY, START A FAMILY, AND SHINE THROUGH HIS TALENT, BUT HE WAS ISOLATED BY HIS MUTENESS...
BUT... WHAT ABOUT THE BOOK? WHAT IS IT?
DURING THE WAR, HE KEPT ON CORRESPONDING WITH HIS FIANCÉE. HE TOLD HER ABOUT THE DAILY REALITIES OF WAR.
THAT BOOK IS THE COLLECTION OF ALL HIS LETTERS. HIS LAST TESTIMONY.
HERE. IT'S YOURS. AT LEAST FOR A WEEK...
THANK YOU...
THESE LETTERS... THEY WERE TO YOU, WEREN'T THEY?

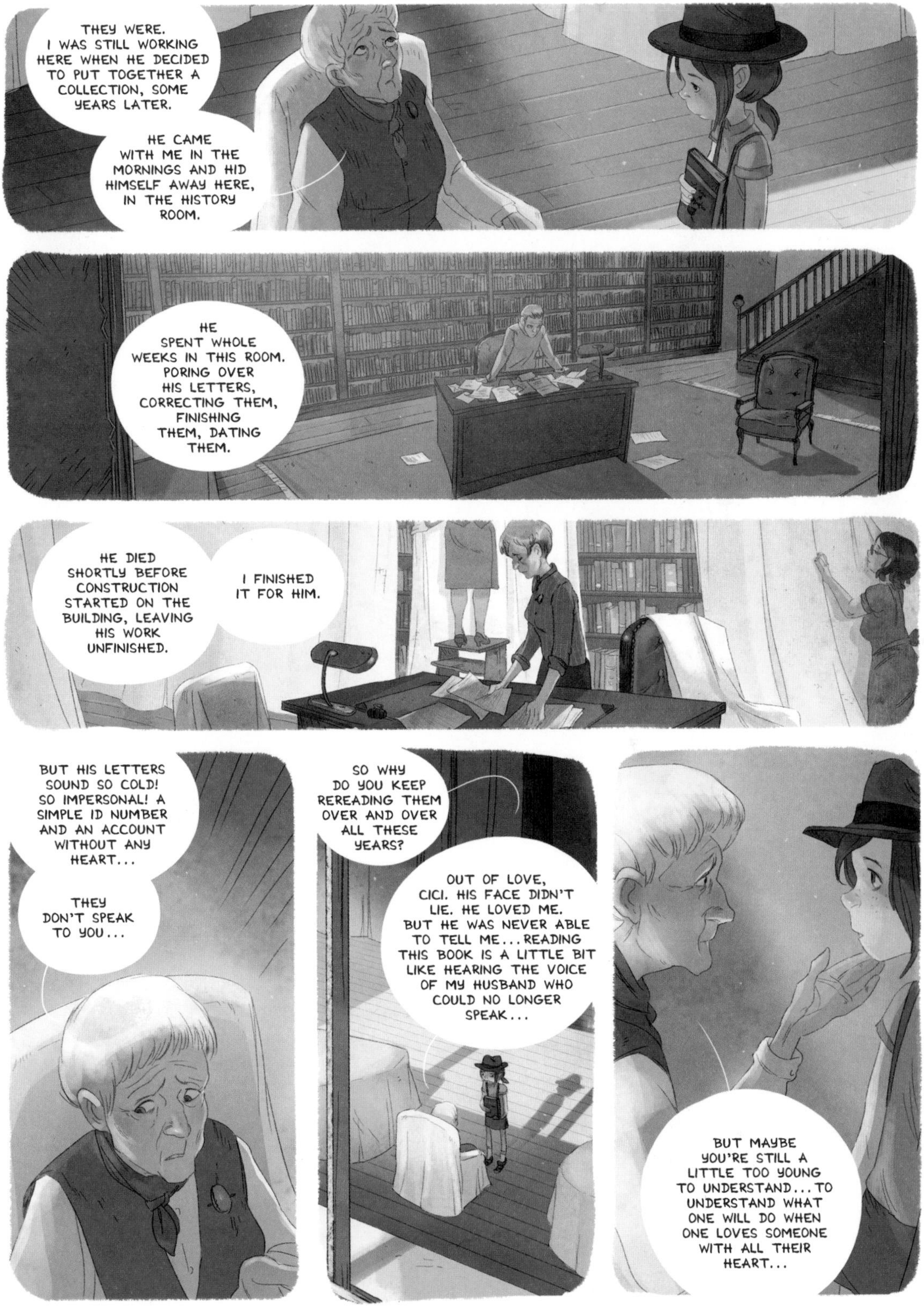
THEY WERE. I WAS STILL WORKING HERE WHEN HE DECIDED TO PUT TOGETHER A COLLECTION, SOME YEARS LATER.
HE CAME WITH ME IN THE MORNINGS AND HID HIMSELF AWAY HERE, IN THE HISTORY ROOM.
HE SPENT WHOLE WEEKS IN THIS ROOM. PORING OVER HIS LETTERS, CORRECTING THEM, FINISHING THEM, DATING THEM.
HE DIED SHORTLY BEFORE CONSTRUCTION STARTED ON THE BUILDING, LEAVING HIS WORK UNFINISHED.
I FINISHED IT FOR HIM.
BUT HIS LETTERS SOUND SO COLD! SO IMPERSONAL! A SIMPLE ID NUMBER AND AN ACCOUNT WITHOUT ANY HEART...
THEY DON'T SPEAK TO YOU...
SO WHY DO YOU KEEP REREADING THEM OVER AND OVER ALL THESE YEARS?
OUT OF LOVE, CICI. HIS FACE DIDN'T LIE. HE LOVED ME. BUT HE WAS NEVER ABLE TO TELL ME... READING THIS BOOK IS A LITTLE BIT LIKE HEARING THE VOICE OF MY HUSBAND WHO COULD NO LONGER SPEAK...
BUT MAYBE YOU'RE STILL A LITTLE TOO YOUNG TO UNDERSTAND... TO UNDERSTAND WHAT ONE WILL DO WHEN ONE LOVES SOMEONE WITH ALL THEIR HEART...

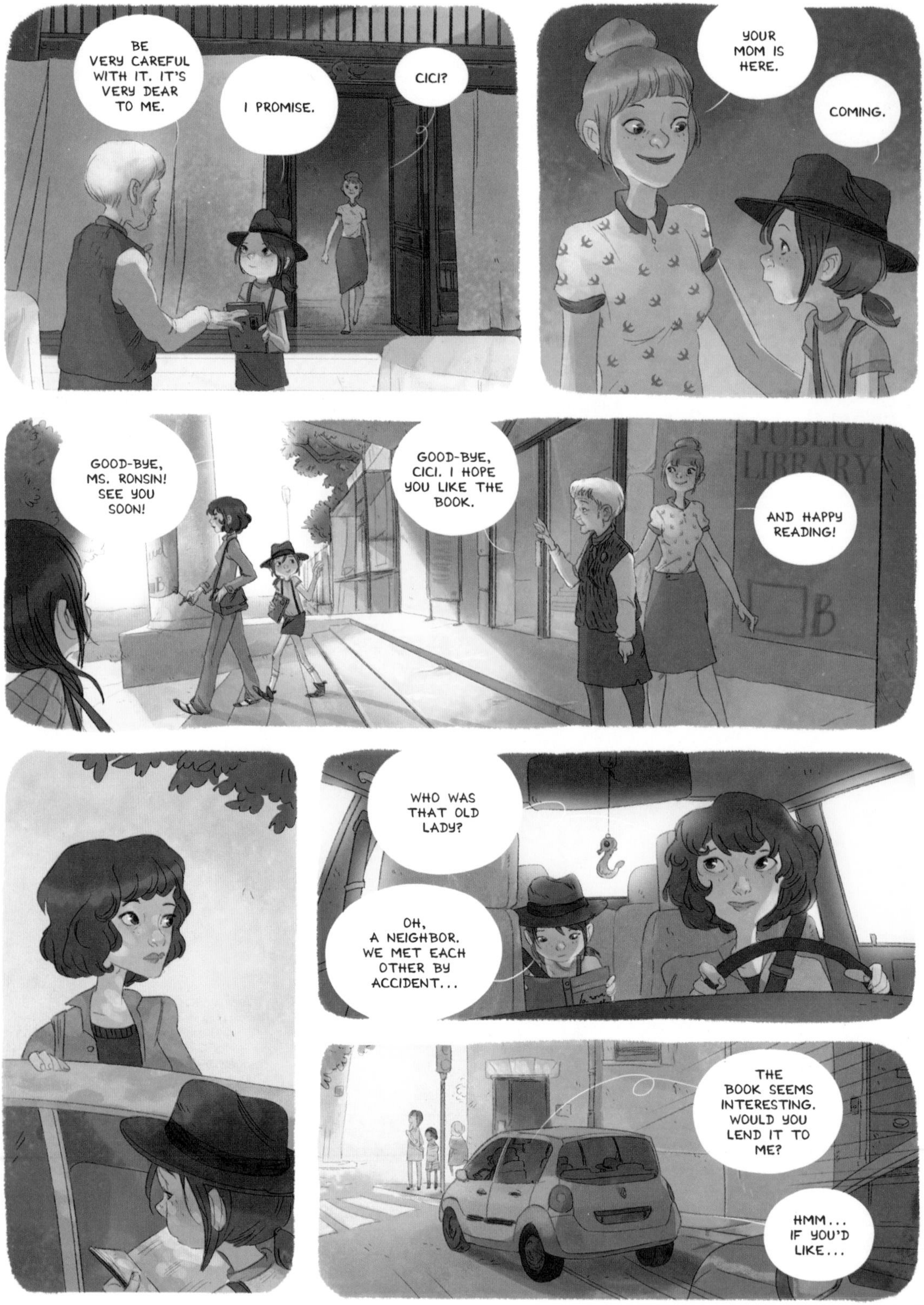
BE VERY CAREFUL WITH IT. IT'S VERY DEAR TO ME.
I PROMISE.
CICI?
YOUR MOM IS HERE.
COMING.
GOOD-BYE, MS. RONSIN! SEE YOU SOON!
GOOD-BYE, CICI. I HOPE YOU LIKE THE BOOK.
AND HAPPY READING!
PUBLIC LIBRARY
WHO WAS THAT OLD LADY?
OH, A NEIGHBOR. WE MET EACH OTHER BY ACCIDENT...
THE BOOK SEEMS INTERESTING. WOULD YOU LEND IT TO ME?
HMM... IF YOU'D LIKE...

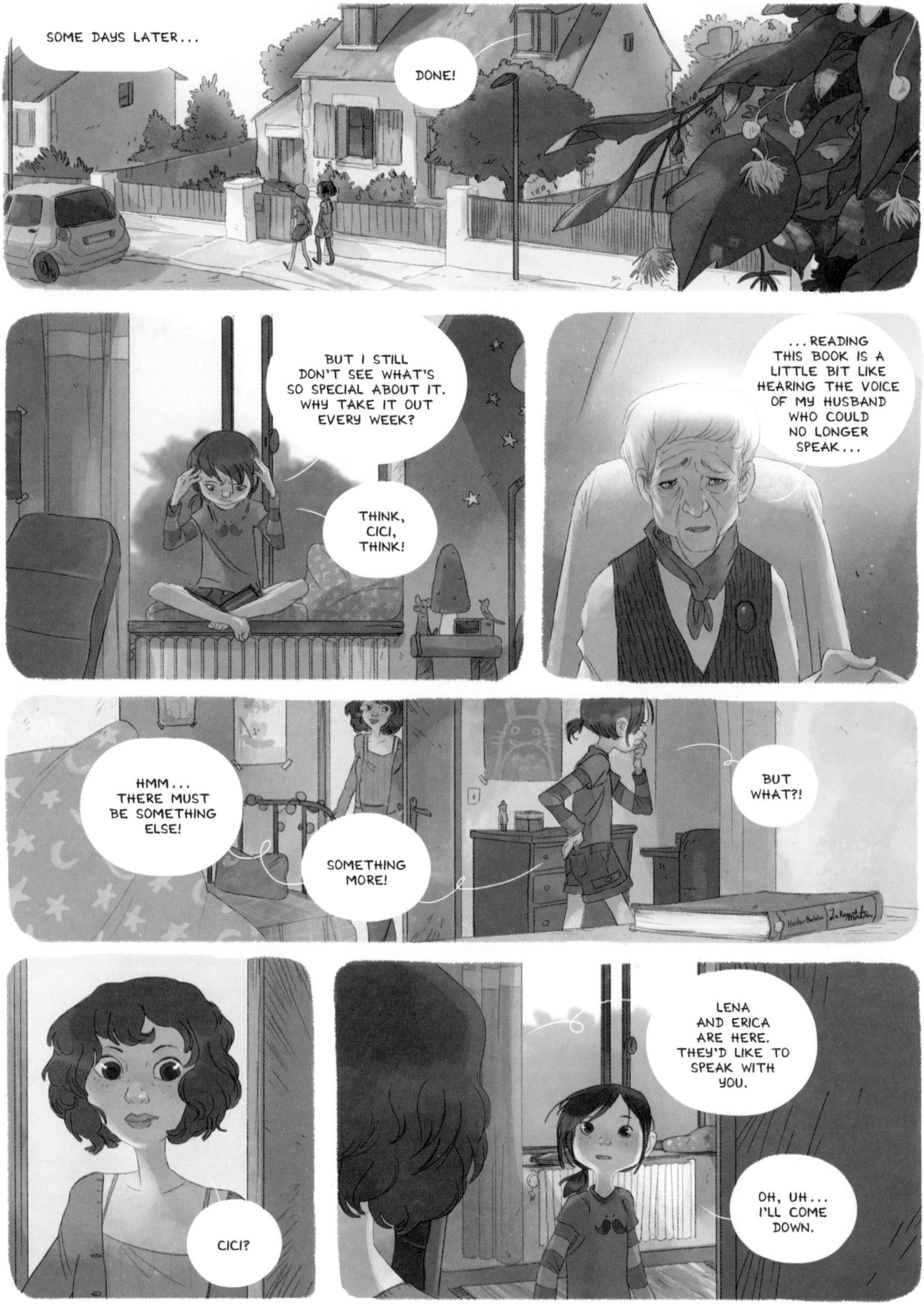
SOME DAYS LATER...
DONE!
BUT I STILL DON'T SEE WHAT'S SO SPECIAL ABOUT IT. WHY TAKE IT OUT EVERY WEEK?
THINK, CICI, THINK!
...READING THIS BOOK IS A LITTLE BIT LIKE HEARING THE VOICE OF MY HUSBAND WHO COULD NO LONGER SPEAK...
HMM... THERE MUST BE SOMETHING ELSE!
SOMETHING MORE!
BUT WHAT?!
CICI?
LENA AND ERICA ARE HERE. THEY'D LIKE TO SPEAK WITH YOU.
OH, UH... I'LL COME DOWN.

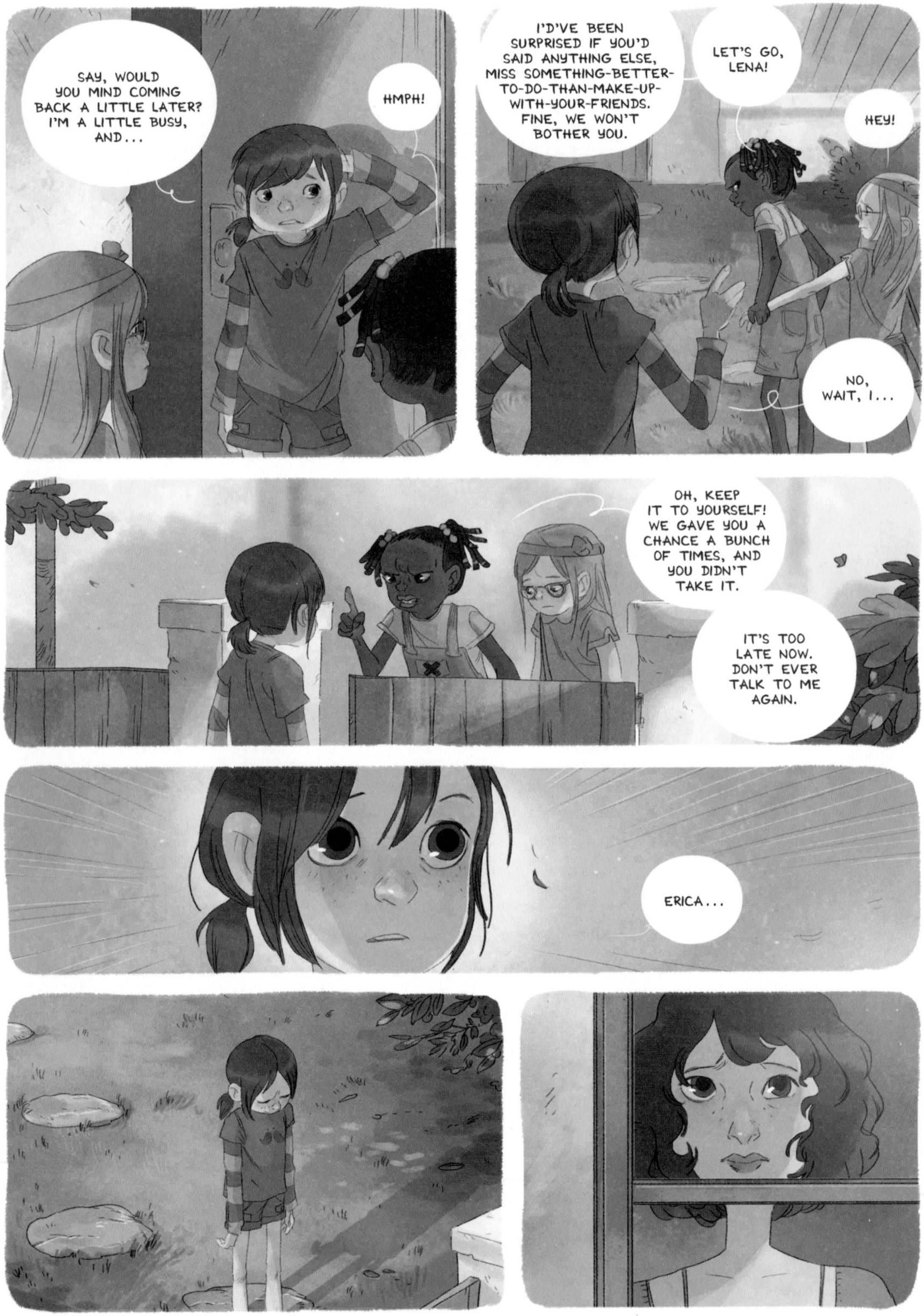
SAY, WOULD YOU MIND COMING BACK A LITTLE LATER? I'M A LITTLE BUSY, AND...
HMPH!
I'D'VE BEEN SURPRISED IF YOU'D SAID ANYTHING ELSE, MISS SOMETHING-BETTER-TO-DO-THAN-MAKE-UP-WITH-YOUR-FRIENDS. FINE, WE WON'T BOTHER YOU.
LET'S GO, LENA!
HEY!
NO, WAIT, I...
OH, KEEP IT TO YOURSELF! WE GAVE YOU A CHANCE A BUNCH OF TIMES, AND YOU DIDN'T TAKE IT.
IT'S TOO LATE NOW. DON'T EVER TALK TO ME AGAIN.
ERICA...

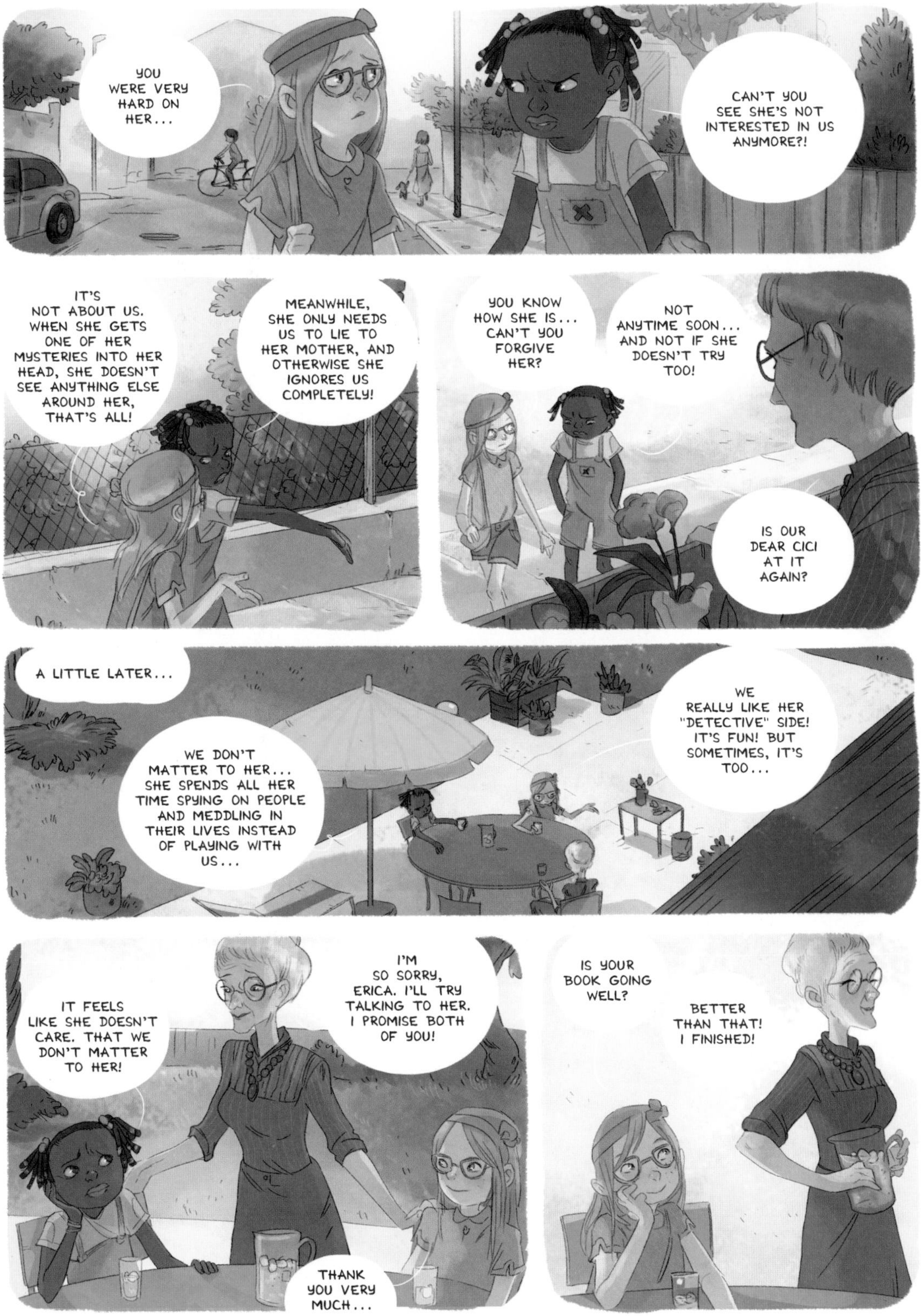
YOU WERE VERY HARD ON HER...
CAN'T YOU SEE SHE'S NOT INTERESTED IN US ANYMORE?!
IT'S NOT ABOUT US. WHEN SHE GETS ONE OF HER MYSTERIES INTO HER HEAD, SHE DOESN'T SEE ANYTHING ELSE AROUND HER, THAT'S ALL!
MEANWHILE, SHE ONLY NEEDS US TO LIE TO HER MOTHER, AND OTHERWISE SHE IGNORES US COMPLETELY!
YOU KNOW HOW SHE IS... CAN'T YOU FORGIVE HER?
NOT ANYTIME SOON... AND NOT IF SHE DOESN'T TRY TOO!
IS OUR DEAR CICI AT IT AGAIN?
A LITTLE LATER...
WE DON'T MATTER TO HER... SHE SPENDS ALL HER TIME SPYING ON PEOPLE AND MEDDLING IN THEIR LIVES INSTEAD OF PLAYING WITH US...
WE REALLY LIKE HER "DETECTIVE" SIDE! IT'S FUN! BUT SOMETIMES, IT'S TOO...
IT FEELS LIKE SHE DOESN'T CARE. THAT WE DON'T MATTER TO HER!
I'M SO SORRY, ERICA. I'LL TRY TALKING TO HER. I PROMISE BOTH OF YOU!
THANK YOU VERY MUCH...
IS YOUR BOOK GOING WELL?
BETTER THAN THAT! I FINISHED!

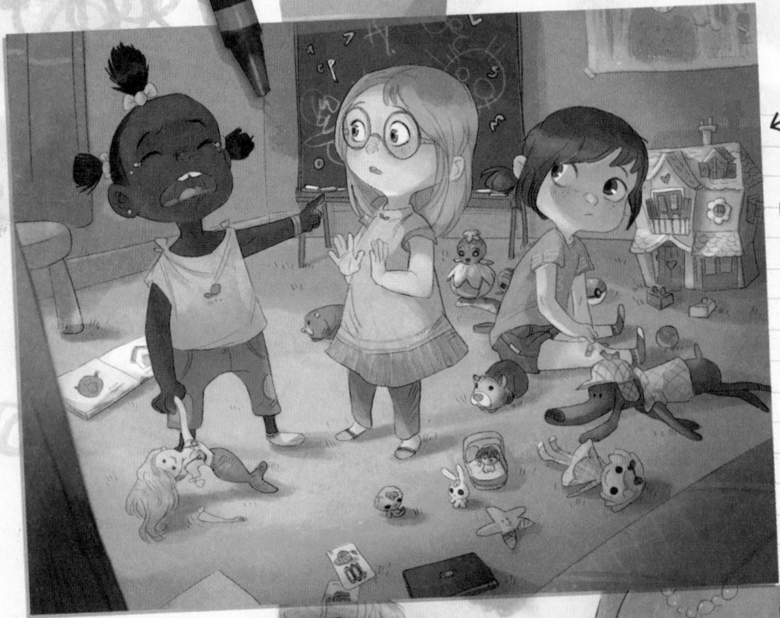

Even when she was little, Erica was already complaining!

Lena's first camera! She was so happy.

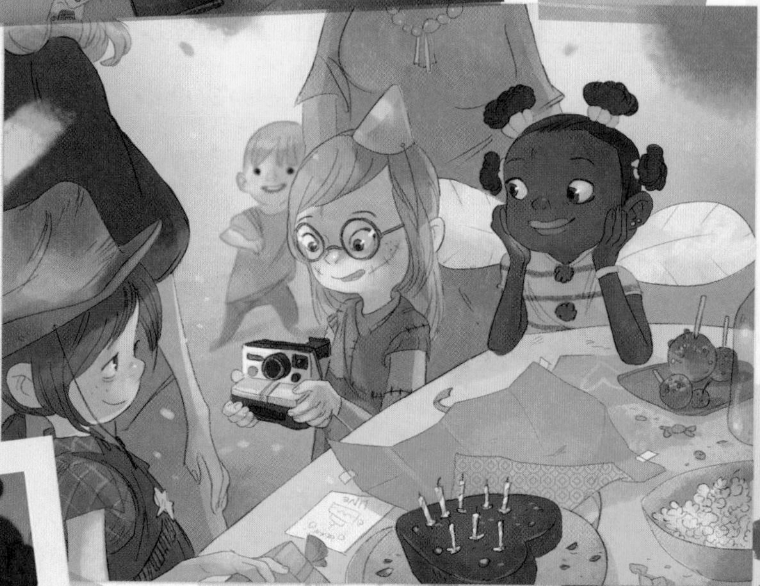

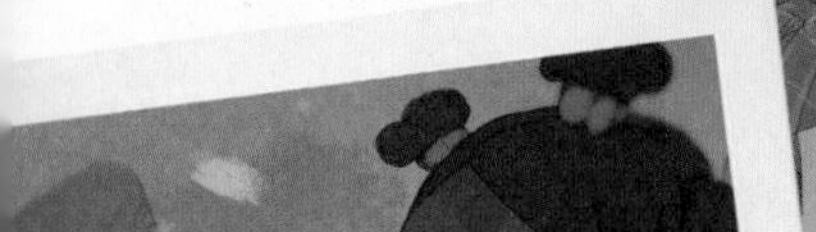

Lena's little brother told us: « When I grow up, I'm going to marry both of you! » ☺

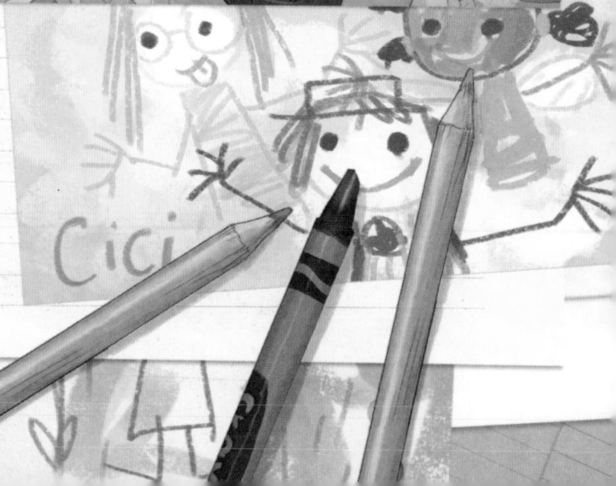

Cici

After the merry-go-round, there's nothing like a big cotton candy to put your stomach back in place!

Michael...
it's been a long time since I've gone to see him at the zoo. So many memories from those days of rebuilding!

Paint fight after finishing the front gate!!!

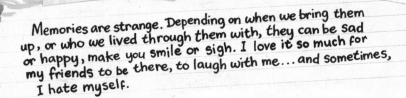

Memories are strange. Depending on when we bring them up, or who we lived through them with, they can be sad or happy, make you smile or sigh. I love it so much for my friends to be there, to laugh with me... and sometimes, I hate myself.

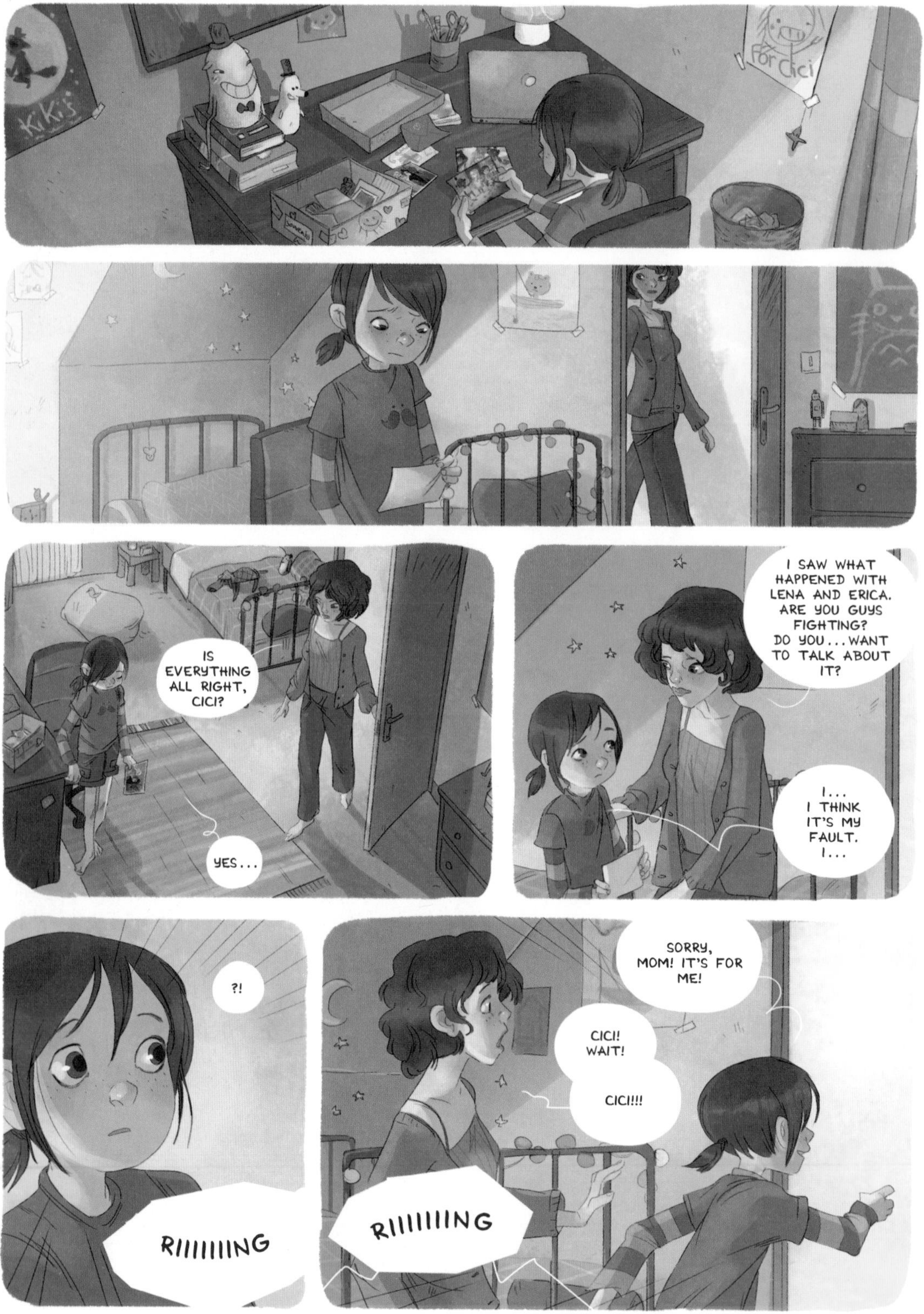

For Cici
IS EVERYTHING ALL RIGHT, CICI?
YES...
I SAW WHAT HAPPENED WITH LENA AND ERICA. ARE YOU GUYS FIGHTING? DO YOU...WANT TO TALK ABOUT IT?
I... I THINK IT'S MY FAULT. I...
?!
RIIIIIIING
RIIIIIIING
SORRY, MOM! IT'S FOR ME!
CICI! WAIT!
CICI!!!

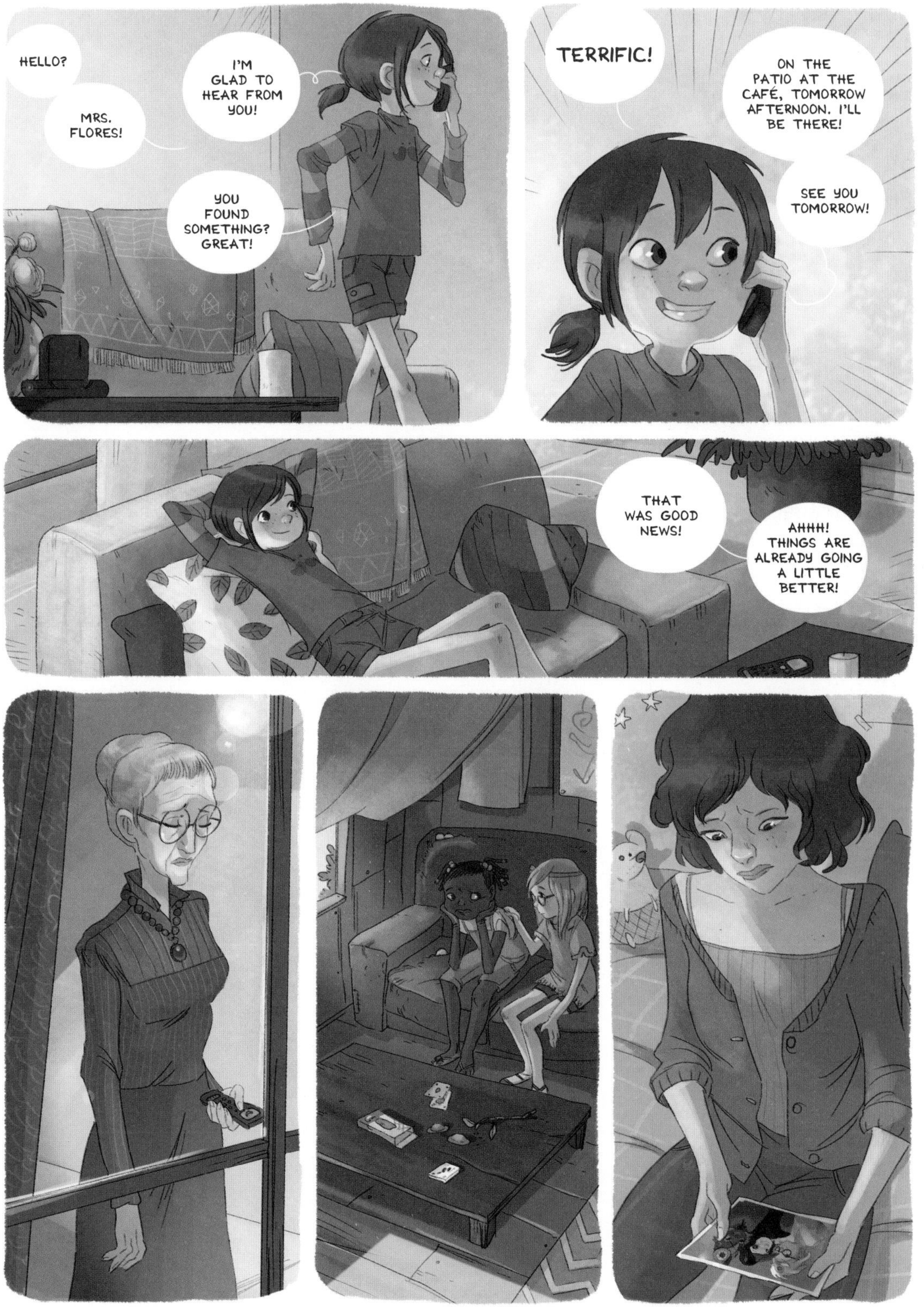
HELLO?
MRS. FLORES!
I'M GLAD TO HEAR FROM YOU!
YOU FOUND SOMETHING? GREAT!
TERRIFIC!
ON THE PATIO AT THE CAFÉ, TOMORROW AFTERNOON. I'LL BE THERE!
SEE YOU TOMORROW!
THAT WAS GOOD NEWS!
AHHH! THINGS ARE ALREADY GOING A LITTLE BETTER!

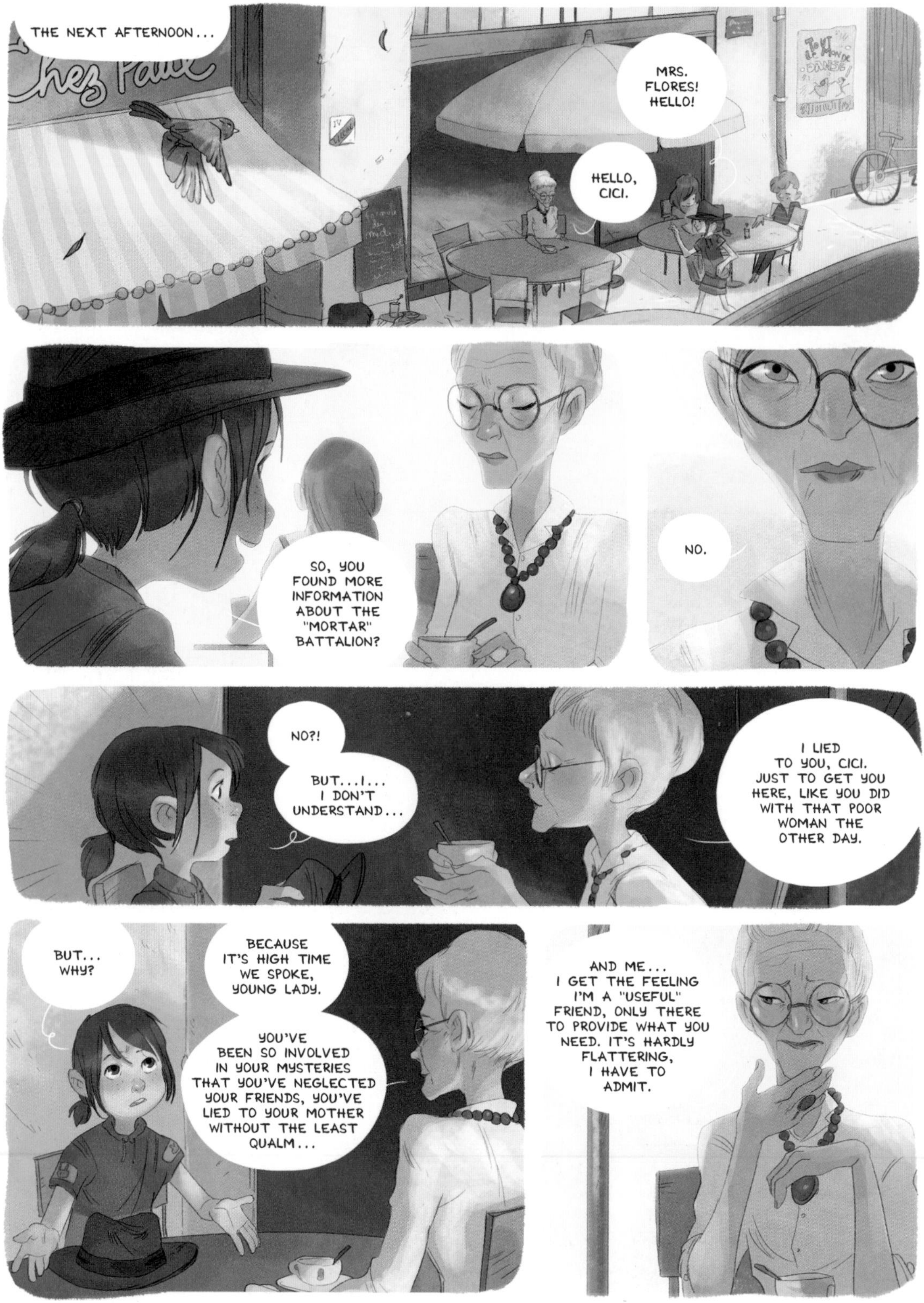
THE NEXT AFTERNOON...
Chez Paul
MRS. FLORES! HELLO!
HELLO, CICI.
SO, YOU FOUND MORE INFORMATION ABOUT THE "MORTAR" BATTALION?
NO.
NO?!
BUT...I... I DON'T UNDERSTAND...
I LIED TO YOU, CICI. JUST TO GET YOU HERE, LIKE YOU DID WITH THAT POOR WOMAN THE OTHER DAY.
BUT... WHY?
BECAUSE IT'S HIGH TIME WE SPOKE, YOUNG LADY.
YOU'VE BEEN SO INVOLVED IN YOUR MYSTERIES THAT YOU'VE NEGLECTED YOUR FRIENDS, YOU'VE LIED TO YOUR MOTHER WITHOUT THE LEAST QUALM...
AND ME... I GET THE FEELING I'M A "USEFUL" FRIEND, ONLY THERE TO PROVIDE WHAT YOU NEED. IT'S HARDLY FLATTERING, I HAVE TO ADMIT.

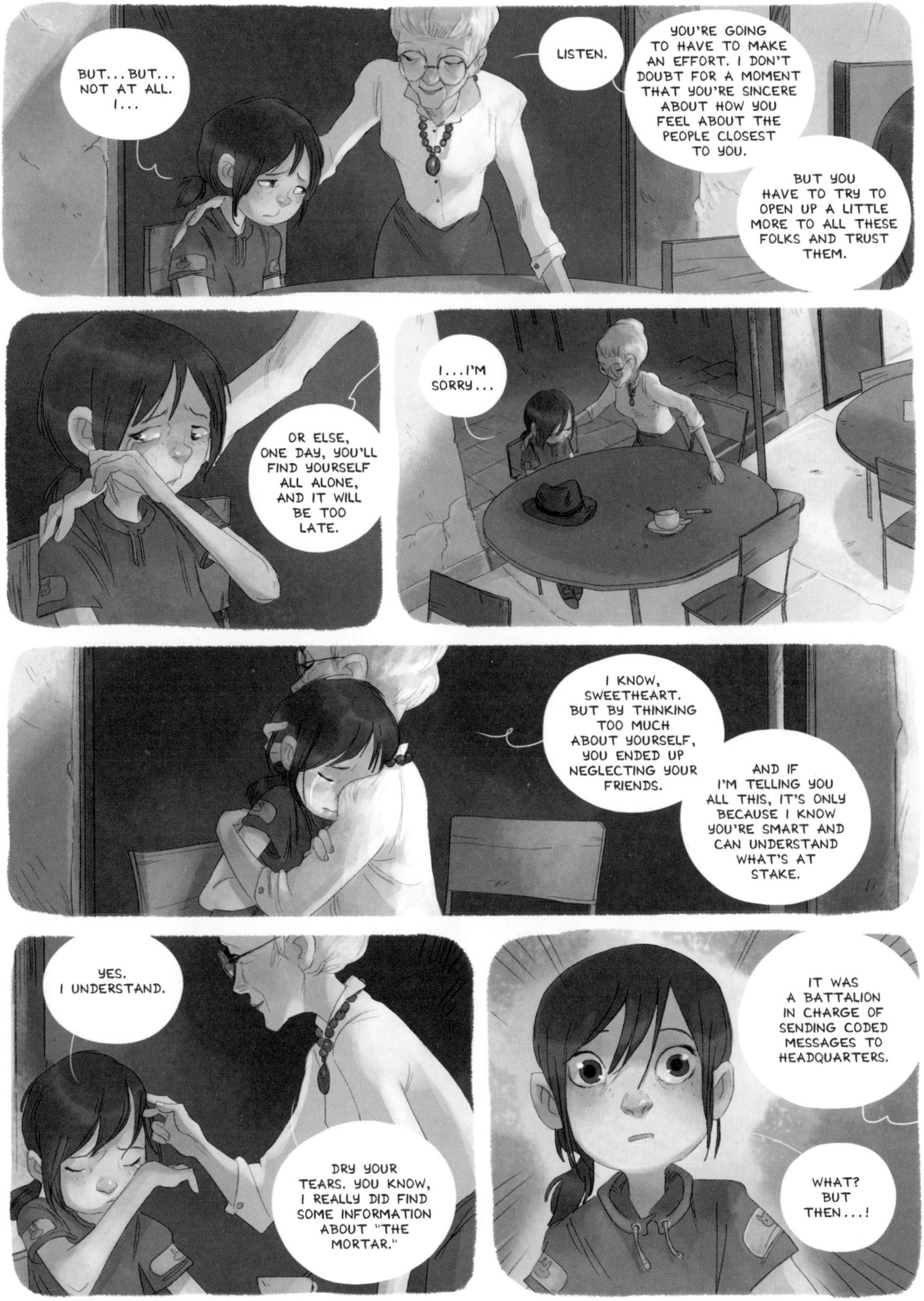
BUT... BUT... NOT AT ALL. I...
LISTEN.
YOU'RE GOING TO HAVE TO MAKE AN EFFORT. I DON'T DOUBT FOR A MOMENT THAT YOU'RE SINCERE ABOUT HOW YOU FEEL ABOUT THE PEOPLE CLOSEST TO YOU.
BUT YOU HAVE TO TRY TO OPEN UP A LITTLE MORE TO ALL THESE FOLKS AND TRUST THEM.
OR ELSE, ONE DAY, YOU'LL FIND YOURSELF ALL ALONE, AND IT WILL BE TOO LATE.
I...I'M SORRY...
I KNOW, SWEETHEART. BUT BY THINKING TOO MUCH ABOUT YOURSELF, YOU ENDED UP NEGLECTING YOUR FRIENDS.
AND IF I'M TELLING YOU ALL THIS, IT'S ONLY BECAUSE I KNOW YOU'RE SMART AND CAN UNDERSTAND WHAT'S AT STAKE.
YES. I UNDERSTAND.
DRY YOUR TEARS. YOU KNOW, I REALLY DID FIND SOME INFORMATION ABOUT "THE MORTAR."
IT WAS A BATTALION IN CHARGE OF SENDING CODED MESSAGES TO HEADQUARTERS.
WHAT? BUT THEN...!

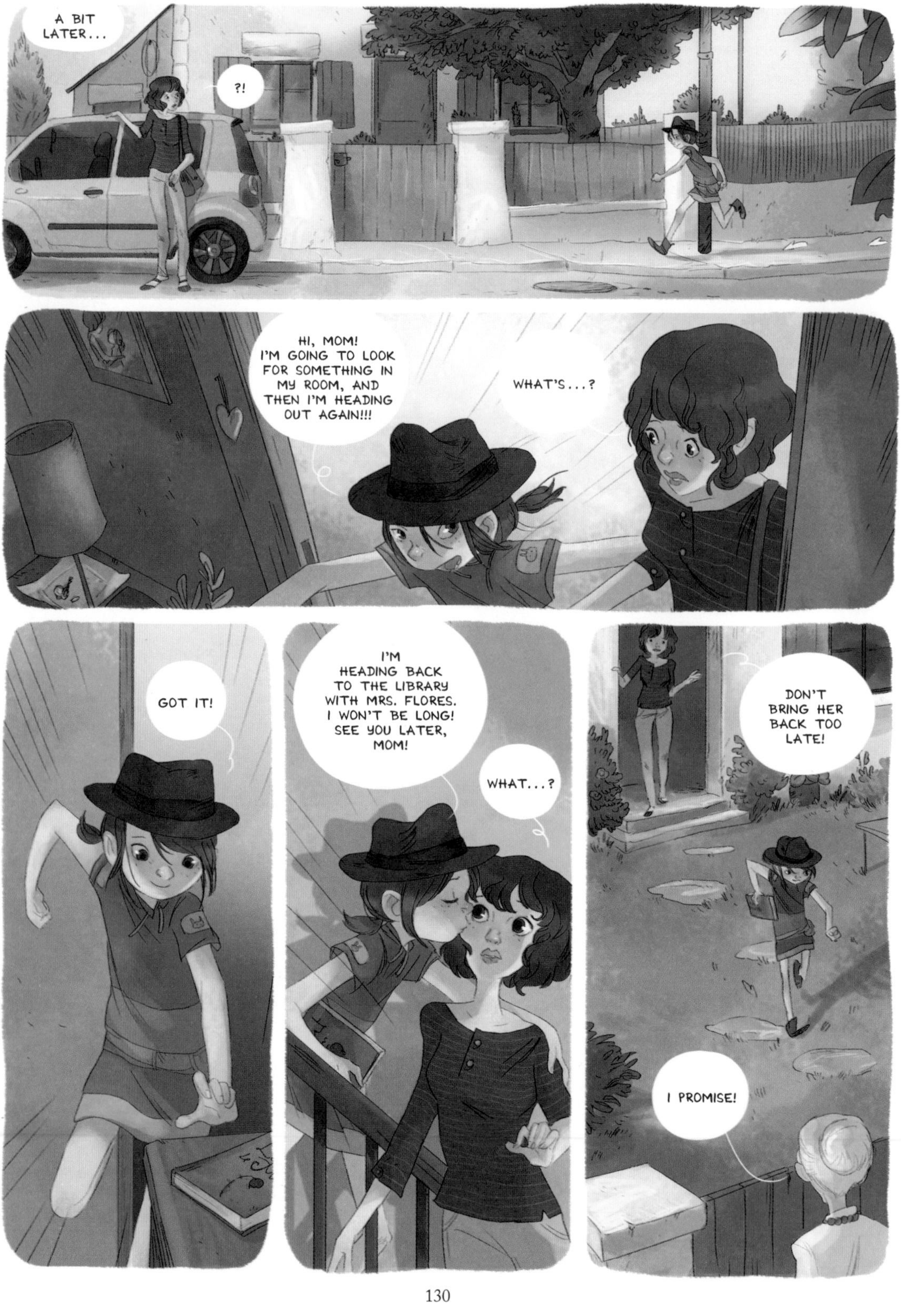
A BIT LATER...
?!
HI, MOM! I'M GOING TO LOOK FOR SOMETHING IN MY ROOM, AND THEN I'M HEADING OUT AGAIN!!!
WHAT'S...?
GOT IT!
I'M HEADING BACK TO THE LIBRARY WITH MRS. FLORES. I WON'T BE LONG! SEE YOU LATER, MOM!
WHAT...?
DON'T BRING HER BACK TOO LATE!
I PROMISE!

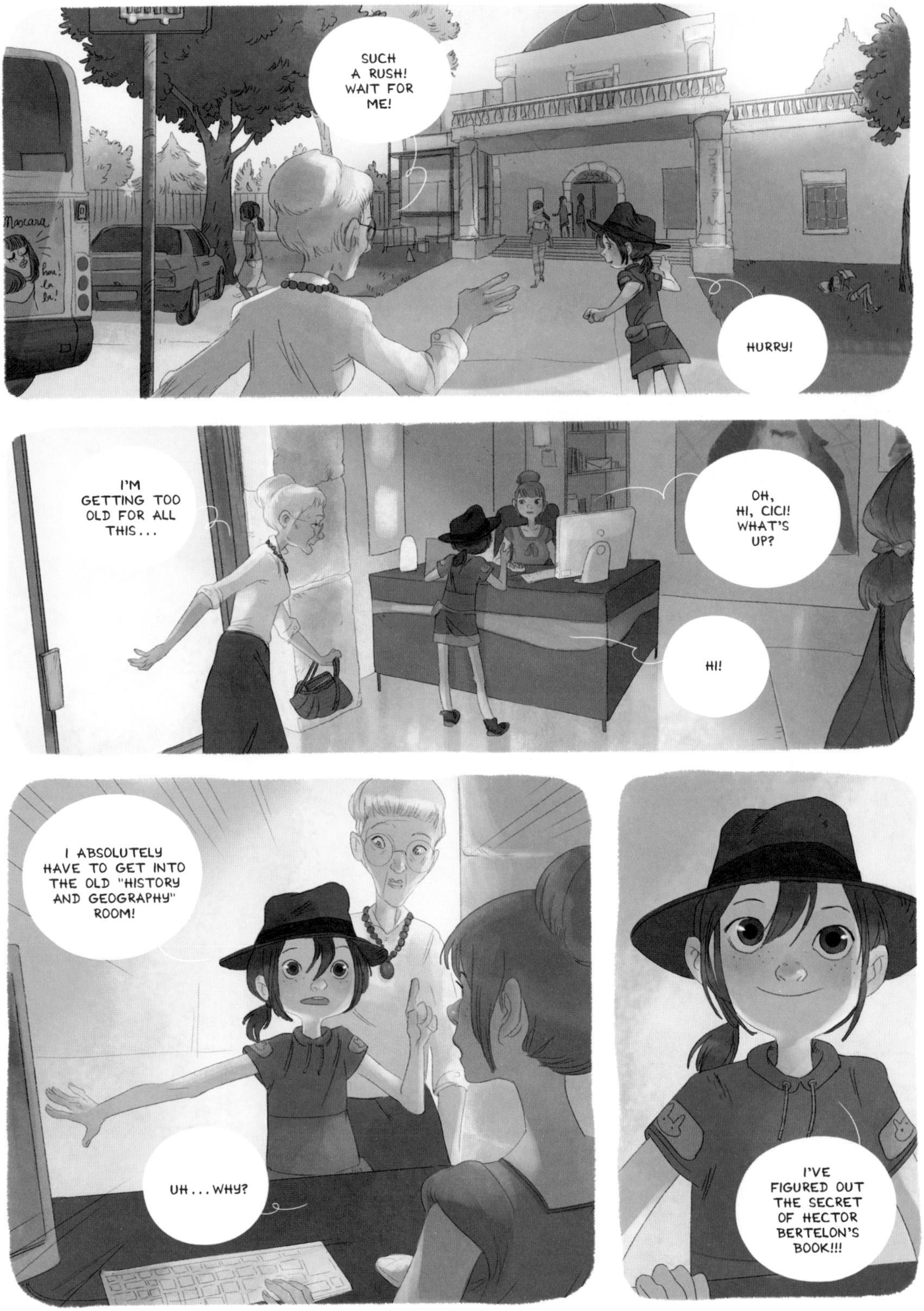
Mascara
SUCH A RUSH! WAIT FOR ME!
HURRY!
I'M GETTING TOO OLD FOR ALL THIS...
OH, HI, CICI! WHAT'S UP?
HI!
I ABSOLUTELY HAVE TO GET INTO THE OLD "HISTORY AND GEOGRAPHY" ROOM!
UH... WHY?
I'VE FIGURED OUT THE SECRET OF HECTOR BERTELON'S BOOK!!!

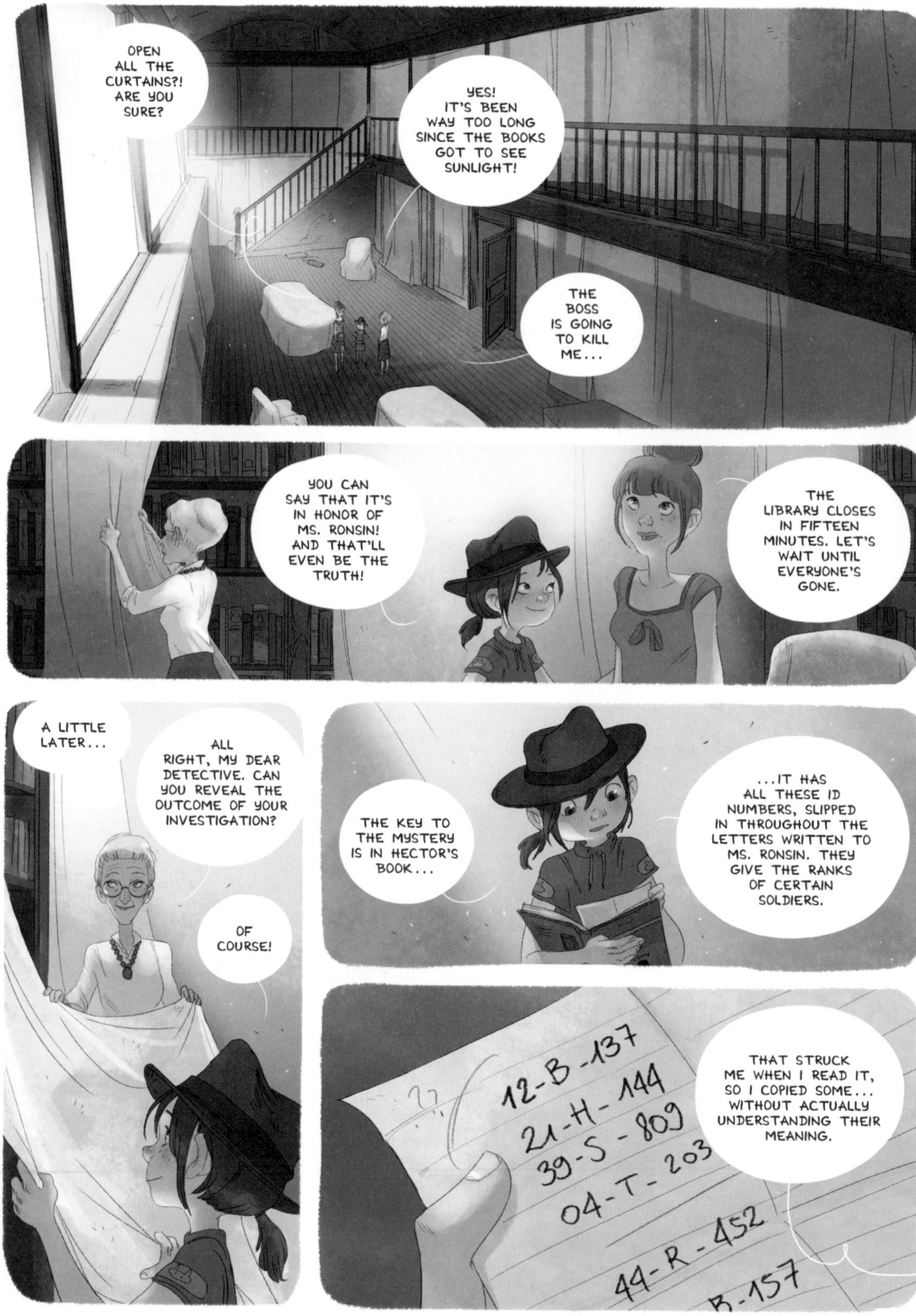
OPEN ALL THE CURTAINS?! ARE YOU SURE?
YES! IT'S BEEN WAY TOO LONG SINCE THE BOOKS GOT TO SEE SUNLIGHT!
THE BOSS IS GOING TO KILL ME...
YOU CAN SAY THAT IT'S IN HONOR OF MS. RONSIN! AND THAT'LL EVEN BE THE TRUTH!
THE LIBRARY CLOSES IN FIFTEEN MINUTES. LET'S WAIT UNTIL EVERYONE'S GONE.
A LITTLE LATER...
ALL RIGHT, MY DEAR DETECTIVE. CAN YOU REVEAL THE OUTCOME OF YOUR INVESTIGATION?
OF COURSE!
THE KEY TO THE MYSTERY IS IN HECTOR'S BOOK...
...IT HAS ALL THESE ID NUMBERS, SLIPPED IN THROUGHOUT THE LETTERS WRITTEN TO MS. RONSIN. THEY GIVE THE RANKS OF CERTAIN SOLDIERS.
12-B-137
21-H-144
39-S-809
04-T-203
44-R-452
THAT STRUCK ME WHEN I READ IT, SO I COPIED SOME... WITHOUT ACTUALLY UNDERSTANDING THEIR MEANING.

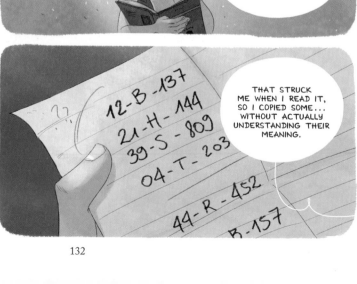

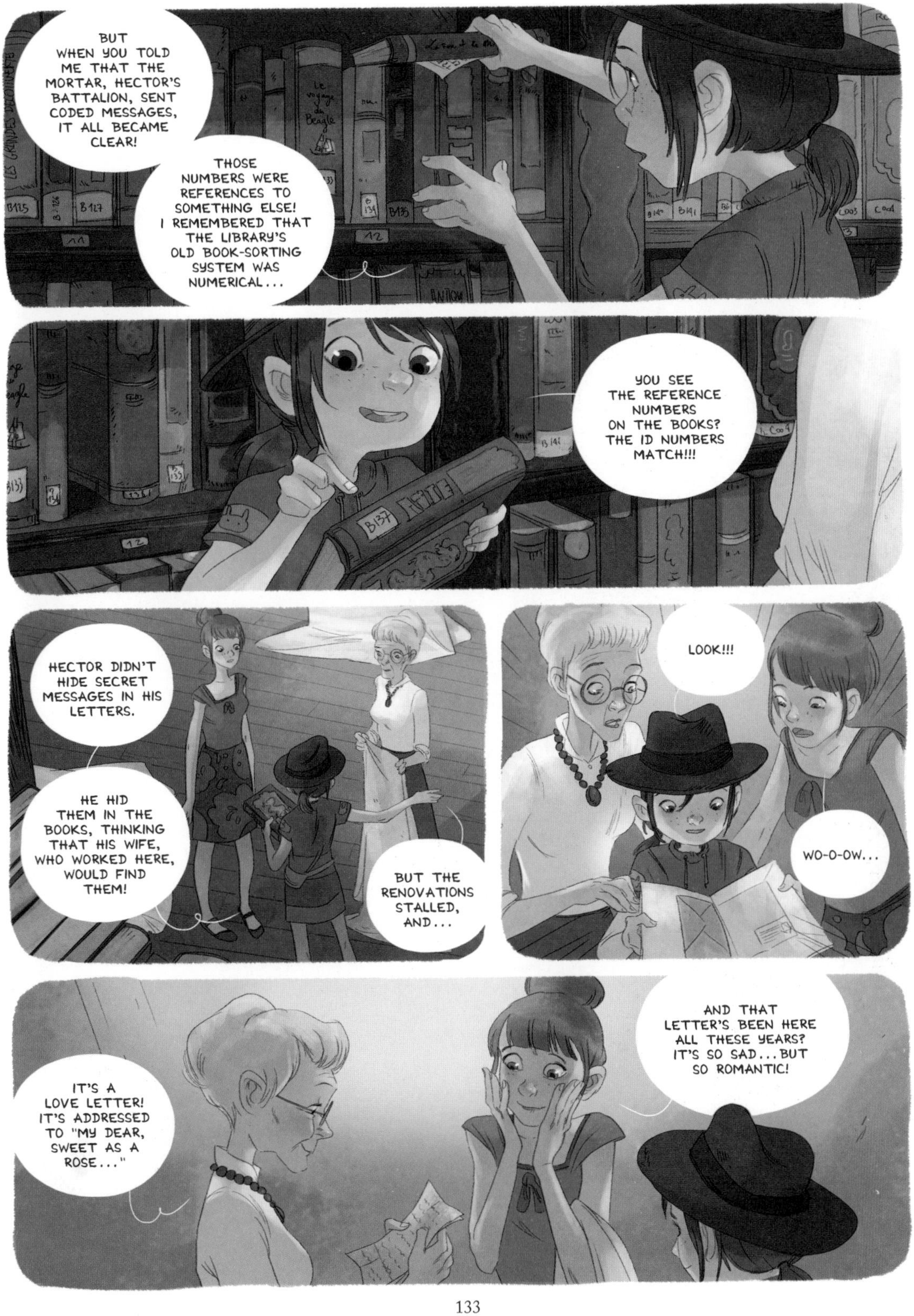
BUT WHEN YOU TOLD ME THAT THE MORTAR, HECTOR'S BATTALION, SENT CODED MESSAGES, IT ALL BECAME CLEAR!
THOSE NUMBERS WERE REFERENCES TO SOMETHING ELSE! I REMEMBERED THAT THE LIBRARY'S OLD BOOK-SORTING SYSTEM WAS NUMERICAL...
YOU SEE THE REFERENCE NUMBERS ON THE BOOKS? THE ID NUMBERS MATCH!!!
HECTOR DIDN'T HIDE SECRET MESSAGES IN HIS LETTERS.
HE HID THEM IN THE BOOKS, THINKING THAT HIS WIFE, WHO WORKED HERE, WOULD FIND THEM!
BUT THE RENOVATIONS STALLED, AND...
LOOK!!!
WO-O-OW...
IT'S A LOVE LETTER! IT'S ADDRESSED TO "MY DEAR, SWEET AS A ROSE..."
AND THAT LETTER'S BEEN HERE ALL THESE YEARS? IT'S SO SAD... BUT SO ROMANTIC!

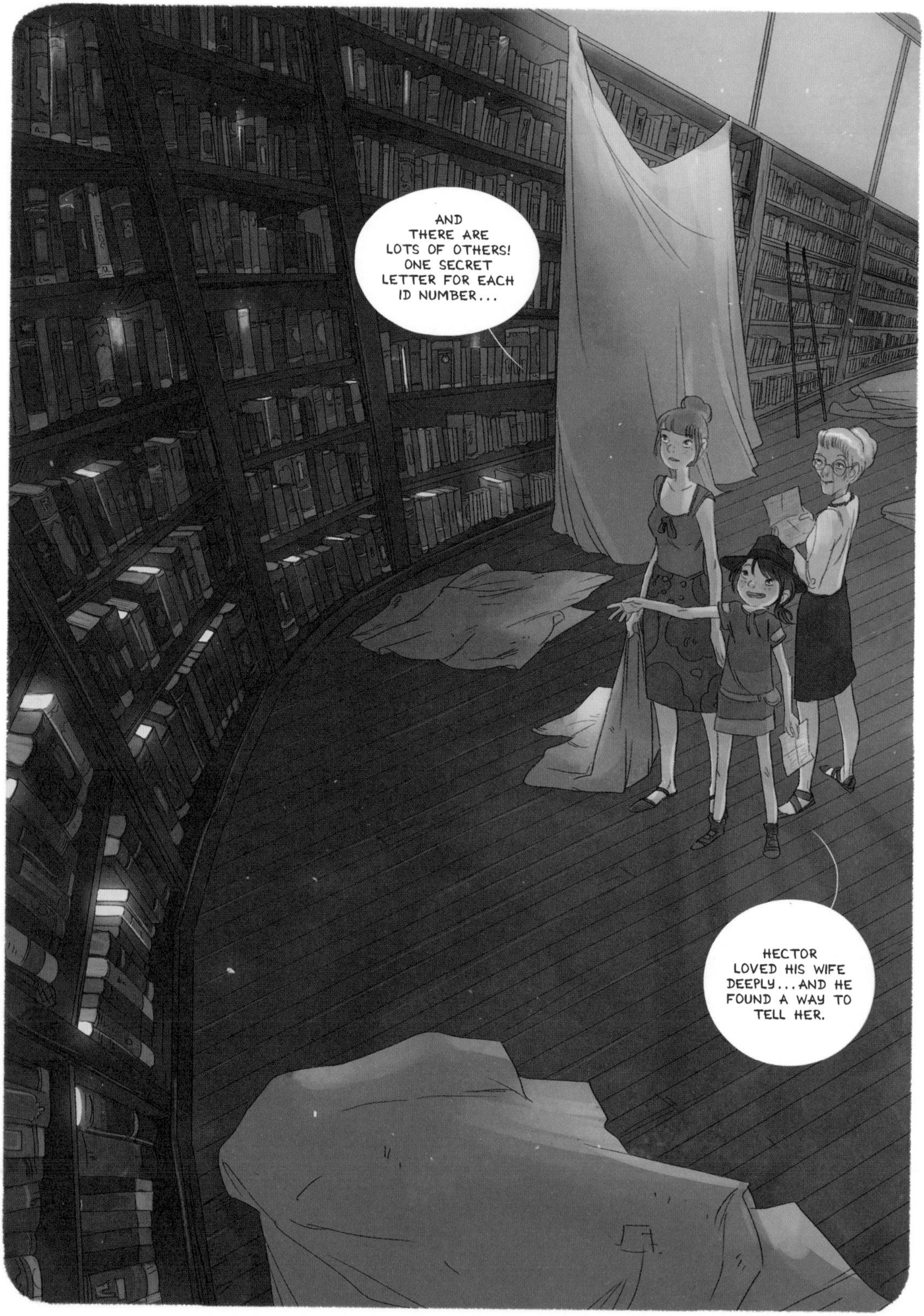
AND THERE ARE LOTS OF OTHERS! ONE SECRET LETTER FOR EACH ID NUMBER...
HECTOR LOVED HIS WIFE DEEPLY...AND HE FOUND A WAY TO TELL HER.

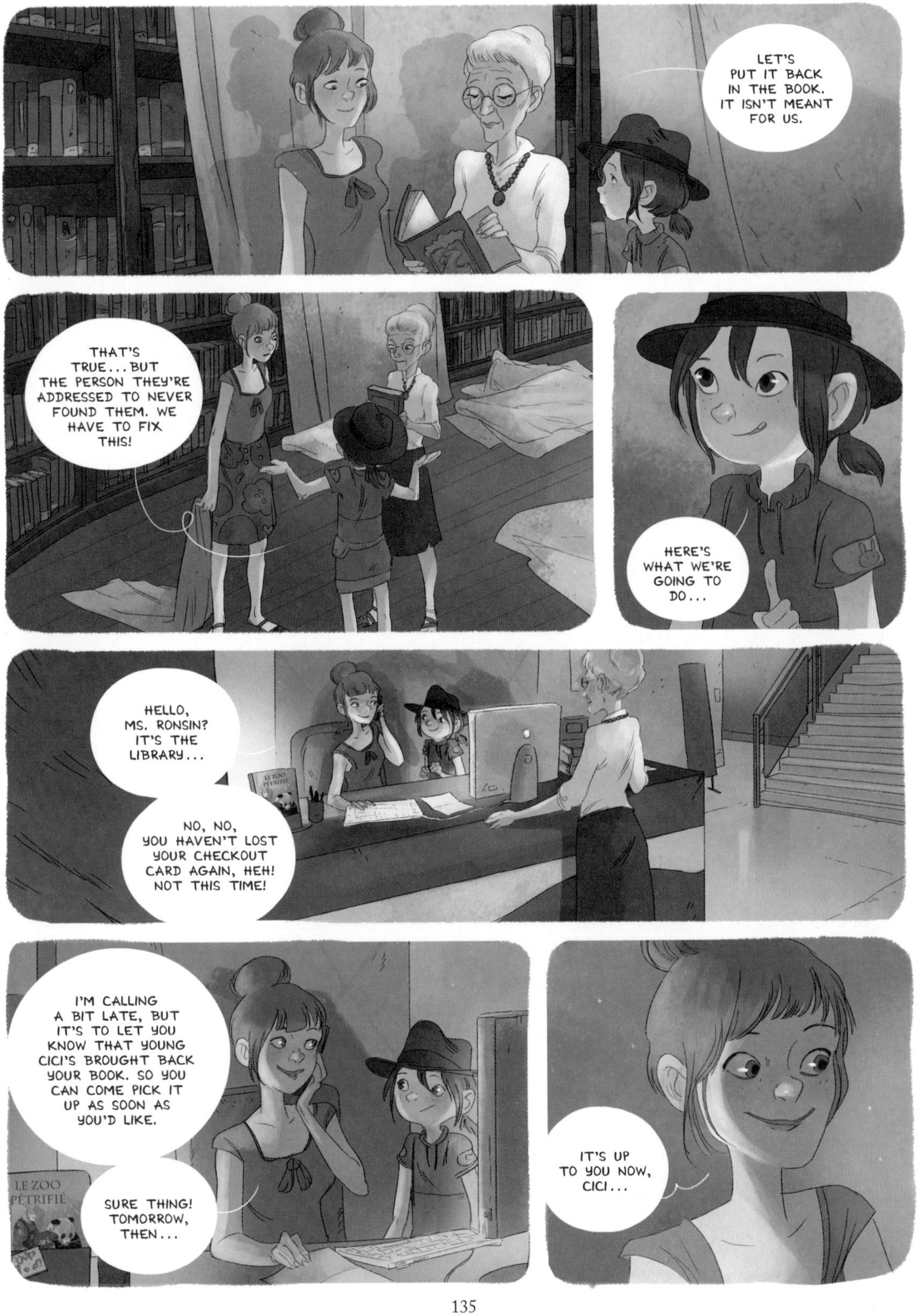
LET'S PUT IT BACK IN THE BOOK. IT ISN'T MEANT FOR US.
THAT'S TRUE... BUT THE PERSON THEY'RE ADDRESSED TO NEVER FOUND THEM. WE HAVE TO FIX THIS!
HERE'S WHAT WE'RE GOING TO DO...
HELLO, MS. RONSIN? IT'S THE LIBRARY...
LE ZOO PÉTRIFIÉ
NO, NO, YOU HAVEN'T LOST YOUR CHECKOUT CARD AGAIN, HEH! NOT THIS TIME!
I'M CALLING A BIT LATE, BUT IT'S TO LET YOU KNOW THAT YOUNG CICI'S BROUGHT BACK YOUR BOOK. SO YOU CAN COME PICK IT UP AS SOON AS YOU'D LIKE.
LE ZOO PÉTRIFIÉ
SURE THING! TOMORROW, THEN...
IT'S UP TO YOU NOW, CICI...

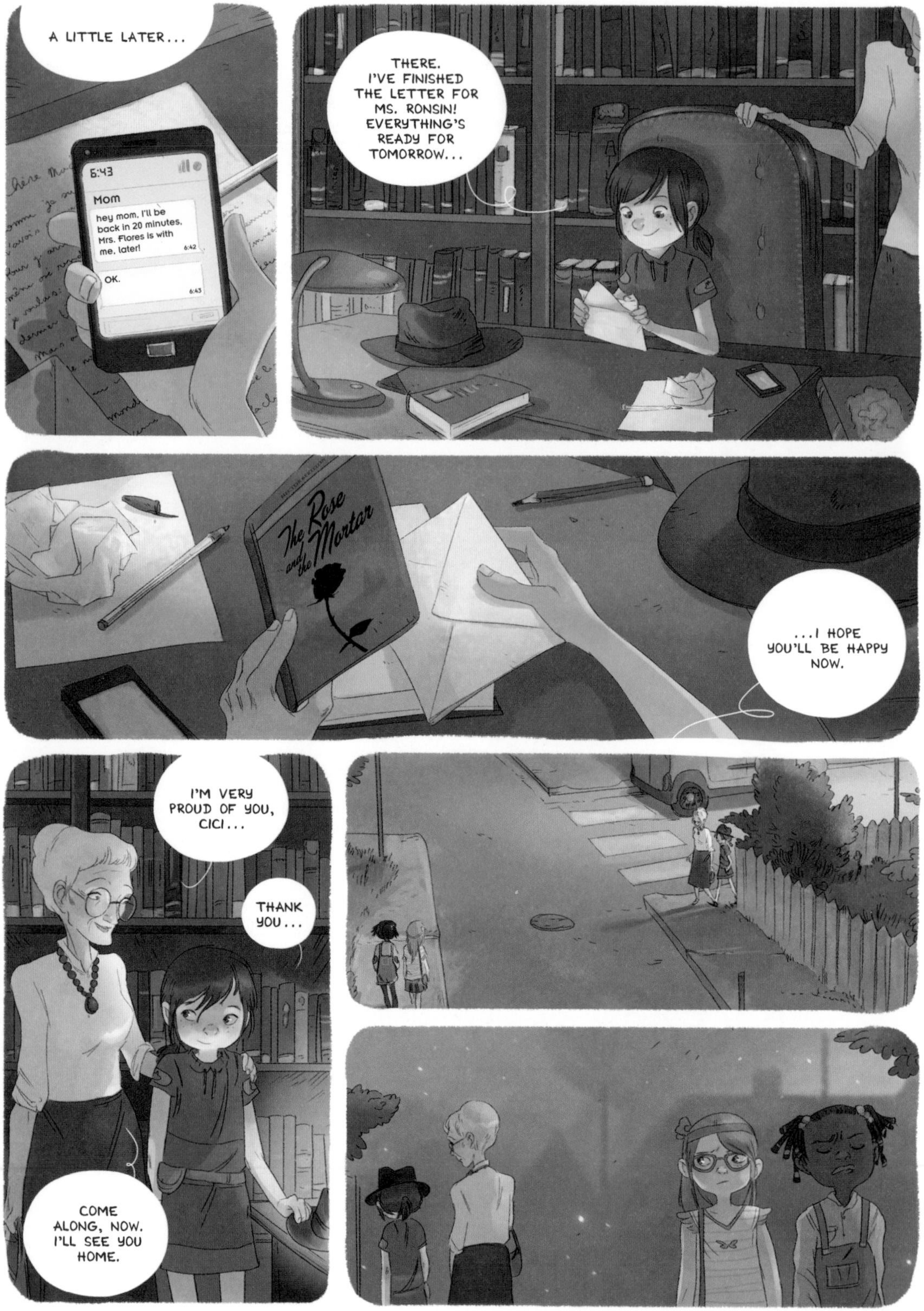
A LITTLE LATER...
6:43
Mom
hey mom, I'll be back in 20 minutes, Mrs. Flores is with me, later!
6:42
OK.
6:43
THERE. I'VE FINISHED THE LETTER FOR MS. RONSIN! EVERYTHING'S READY FOR TOMORROW...
The Rose and the Mortar
...I HOPE YOU'LL BE HAPPY NOW.
I'M VERY PROUD OF YOU, CICI...
THANK YOU...
COME ALONG, NOW. I'LL SEE YOU HOME.

Dear Ms. Ronsin,

Since I'm a very curious person, I wanted to know why you were always taking out the same book. I observed you for a few weeks, and I really wanted to find out your secret.

To do that, I put my mother's trust and the friendship of my three very best friends at risk. I'm giving your book back to you, but first, I need to tell you that I made a discovery. Some people have trouble saying what's in their hearts— I know a thing or two about that. But Hector found a way to break through his silence.

I wrote the ID numbers from the letters out on a sheet of paper. I didn't really understand what they were doing in there. Those numbers intrigued me. A friend's research turned up the fact that The Mortar was a secret battalion in charge of coded messages during World War II. So I realized that the book was a code! You remember how the classification system in the library was changed after the renovation? The numbers in your husband's letters weren't ID numbers, they were really references to books where he had hidden letters for you...

One secret letter for every number.

Cici

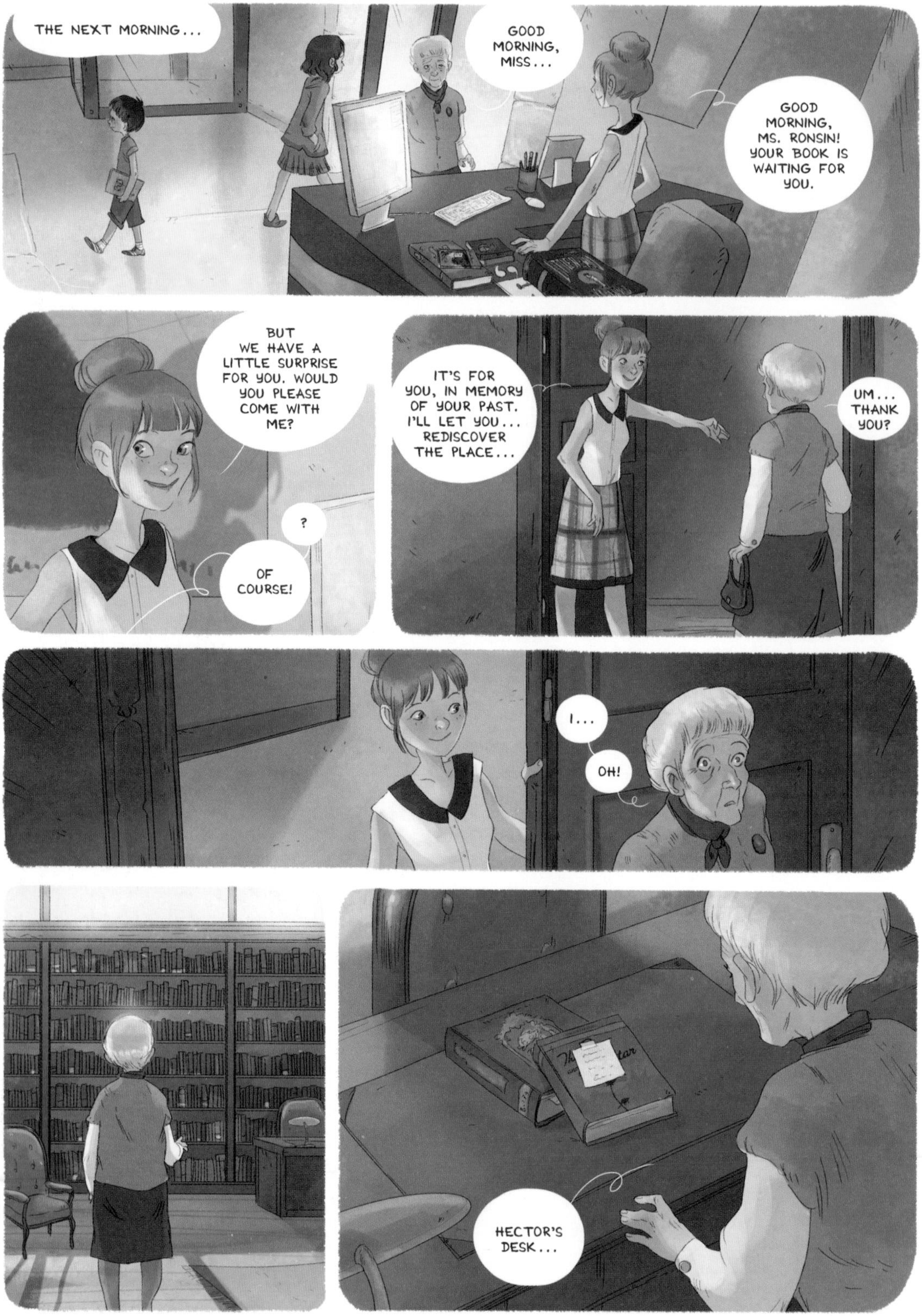
THE NEXT MORNING...
GOOD MORNING, MISS...
GOOD MORNING, MS. RONSIN! YOUR BOOK IS WAITING FOR YOU.
BUT WE HAVE A LITTLE SURPRISE FOR YOU. WOULD YOU PLEASE COME WITH ME?
?
OF COURSE!
IT'S FOR YOU, IN MEMORY OF YOUR PAST. I'LL LET YOU... REDISCOVER THE PLACE...
UM... THANK YOU?
I...
OH!
HECTOR'S DESK...

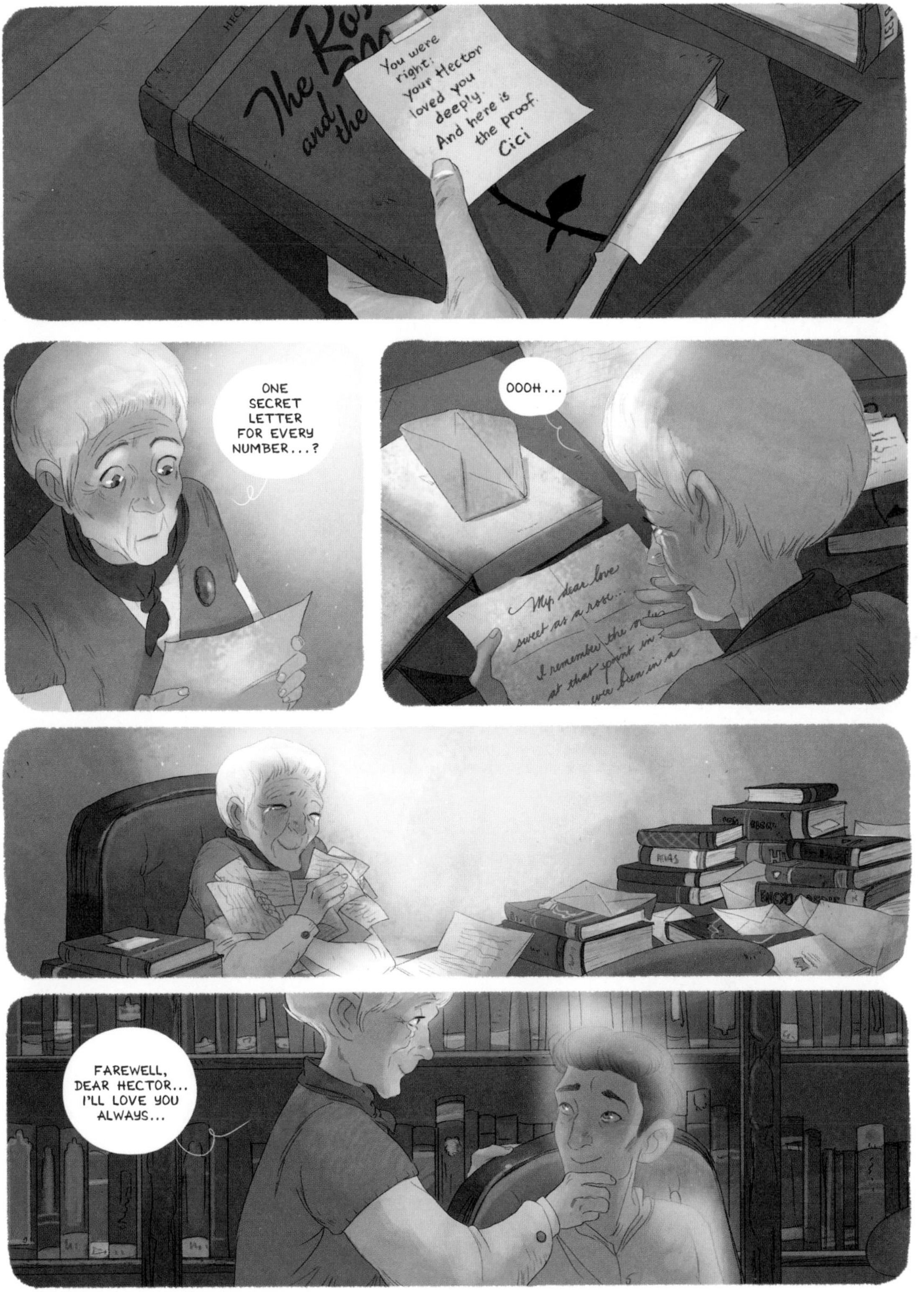
You were right: your Hector loved you deeply. And here is the proof. Cici
ONE SECRET LETTER FOR EVERY NUMBER...?
OOOH...
My dear love
sweet as a rose...
FAREWELL, DEAR HECTOR... I'LL LOVE YOU ALWAYS...

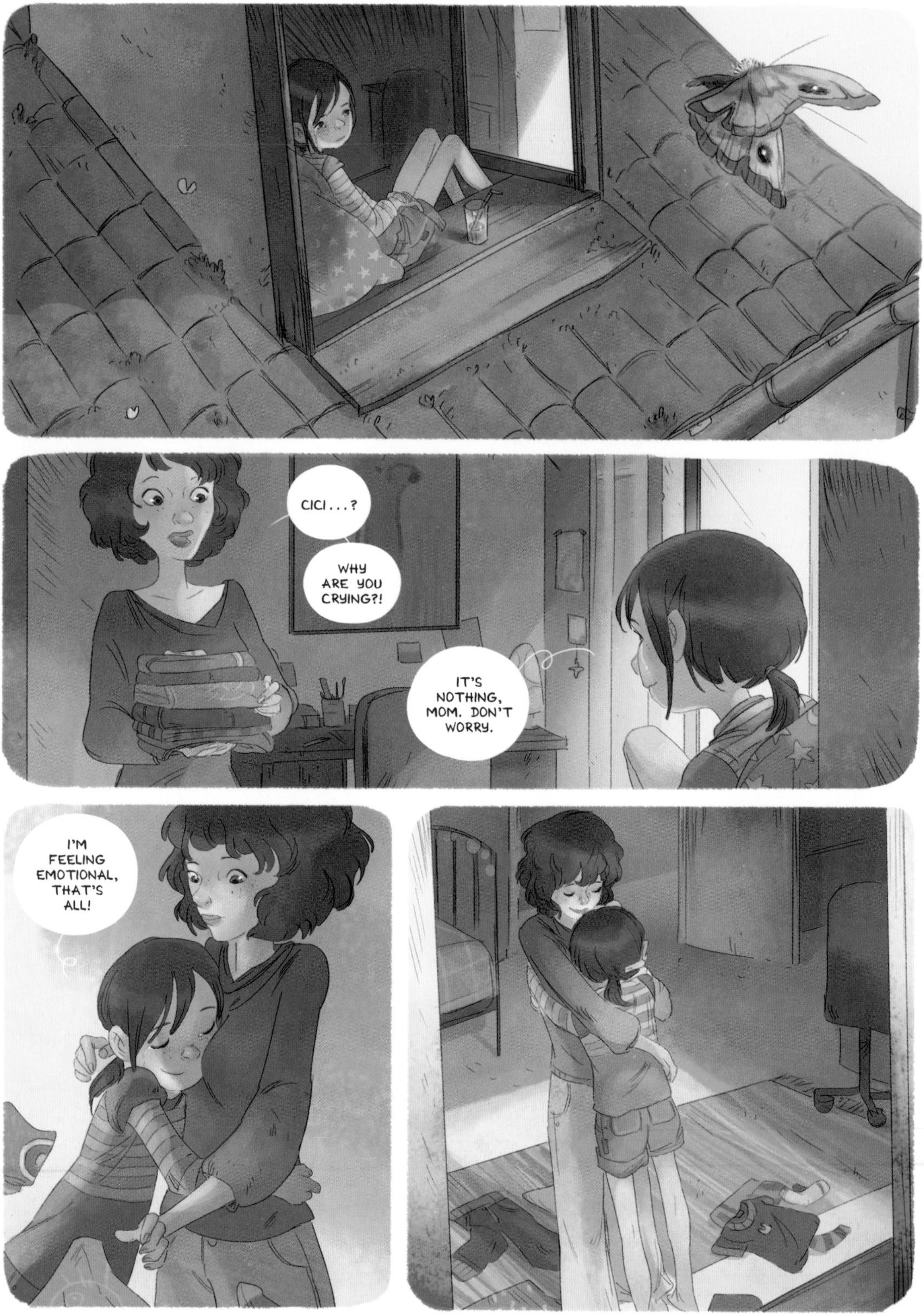
CICI . . . ?
WHY ARE YOU CRYING?!
IT'S NOTHING, MOM. DON'T WORRY.
I'M FEELING EMOTIONAL, THAT'S ALL!

Like I did with my first journal, where I solved the Michael mystery, I've tagged on an extra page. I wanted to go over Ms. Ronsin's life.

I went to her place to find out more. (Mom was surprised that I didn't want to go to the pool that day...)

- Elisabeth Ronsin worked at the library for 30 years, running programs to bring culture to the poorest families, to help kids in school, to create reading groups in hospitals, retirement homes, prisons...

- Her whole life was dedicated to helping others. I admire her for her courage and generosity. She's had a great career!

- She retired a few years after they started renovations on the library. She became an advisor for the new layout. The current librarian must not have known, but it was Ms. Ronsin who created the children's space and the meet-the-author forum!

- To thank me for what I did, she gave me this photo of her and Hector when they were young.

Before I left, Ms. Ronsin talked to me about the letter I wrote to her. She was overwhelmed by what I'd done to figure it all out, and she asked me to tell her about it. I gave her the embarrassing list:

- I was banished for life by the only two friends I've ever had. And it was all my fault, because I was so obsessed with the book and what it was hiding. I was so caught up in other people's lives, I ruined part of my own.

- I made the same mistake with Mrs. Flores, another friend who's very dear to me, by only using her to get stuff I wanted to know. I'm lucky she's smarter than I am and that she took the time to give me a little lesson and help me figure out some solutions. She didn't have to do that.

- With Mom, it's a little confusing. The truth became a lie, then the lie became true again. I think that something changed for the better anyway. But it's still hard to go to her and tell her all of this.

What a list!

Then Ms. Ronsin told me: "Don't make the same mistake Hector did, because when we keep what we're feeling locked inside, in the end we become the prisoner. Speak up. Don't be embarrassed by what you feel. Express your doubts, your fears. Tell the people you love that you have them in your heart. They'll always be grateful."

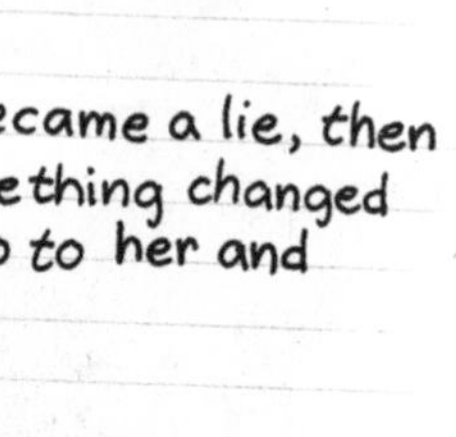
...

I'll see what I can do. I hope it's not already too late.

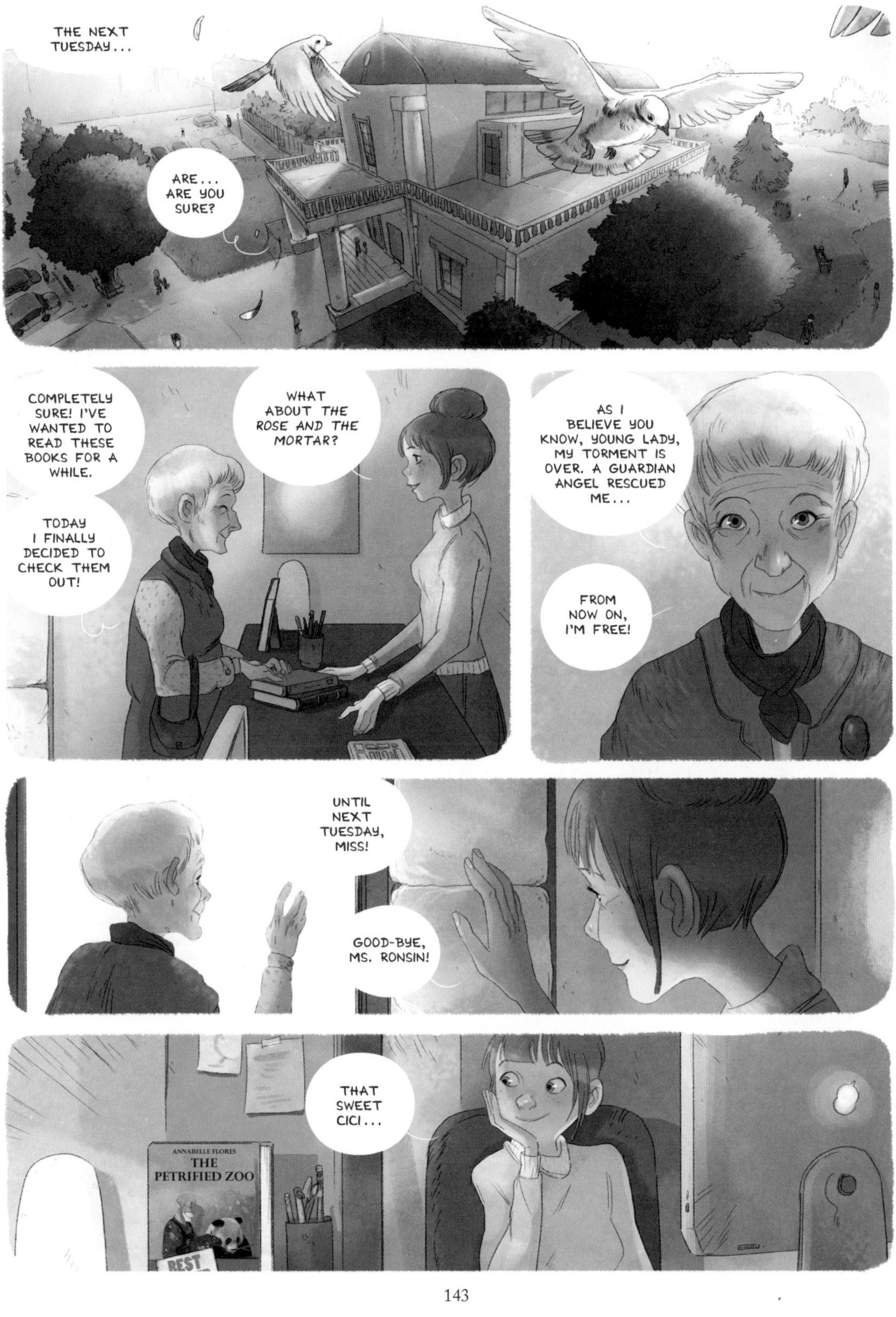
THE NEXT TUESDAY...
ARE... ARE YOU SURE?
COMPLETELY SURE! I'VE WANTED TO READ THESE BOOKS FOR A WHILE.
TODAY I FINALLY DECIDED TO CHECK THEM OUT!
WHAT ABOUT THE ROSE AND THE MORTAR?
AS I BELIEVE YOU KNOW, YOUNG LADY, MY TORMENT IS OVER. A GUARDIAN ANGEL RESCUED ME...
FROM NOW ON, I'M FREE!
UNTIL NEXT TUESDAY, MISS!
GOOD-BYE, MS. RONSIN!
THAT SWEET CICI...
ANNABELLE FLORES
THE PETRIFIED ZOO

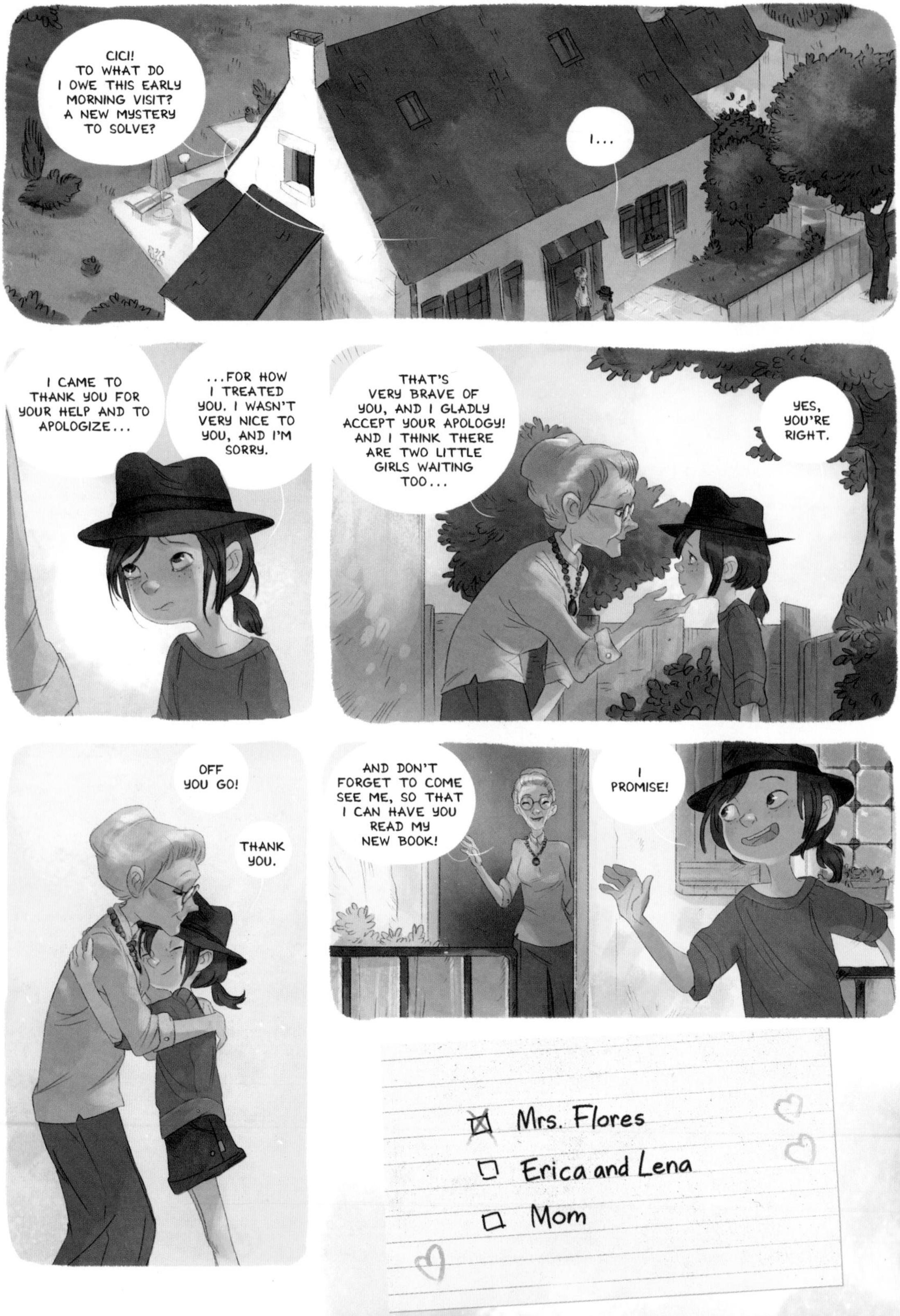
CICI! TO WHAT DO I OWE THIS EARLY MORNING VISIT? A NEW MYSTERY TO SOLVE?
I...
I CAME TO THANK YOU FOR YOUR HELP AND TO APOLOGIZE...
...FOR HOW I TREATED YOU. I WASN'T VERY NICE TO YOU, AND I'M SORRY.
THAT'S VERY BRAVE OF YOU, AND I GLADLY ACCEPT YOUR APOLOGY! AND I THINK THERE ARE TWO LITTLE GIRLS WAITING TOO...
YES, YOU'RE RIGHT.
OFF YOU GO!
THANK YOU.
AND DON'T FORGET TO COME SEE ME, SO THAT I CAN HAVE YOU READ MY NEW BOOK!
I PROMISE!
Mrs. Flores
Erica and Lena
Mom

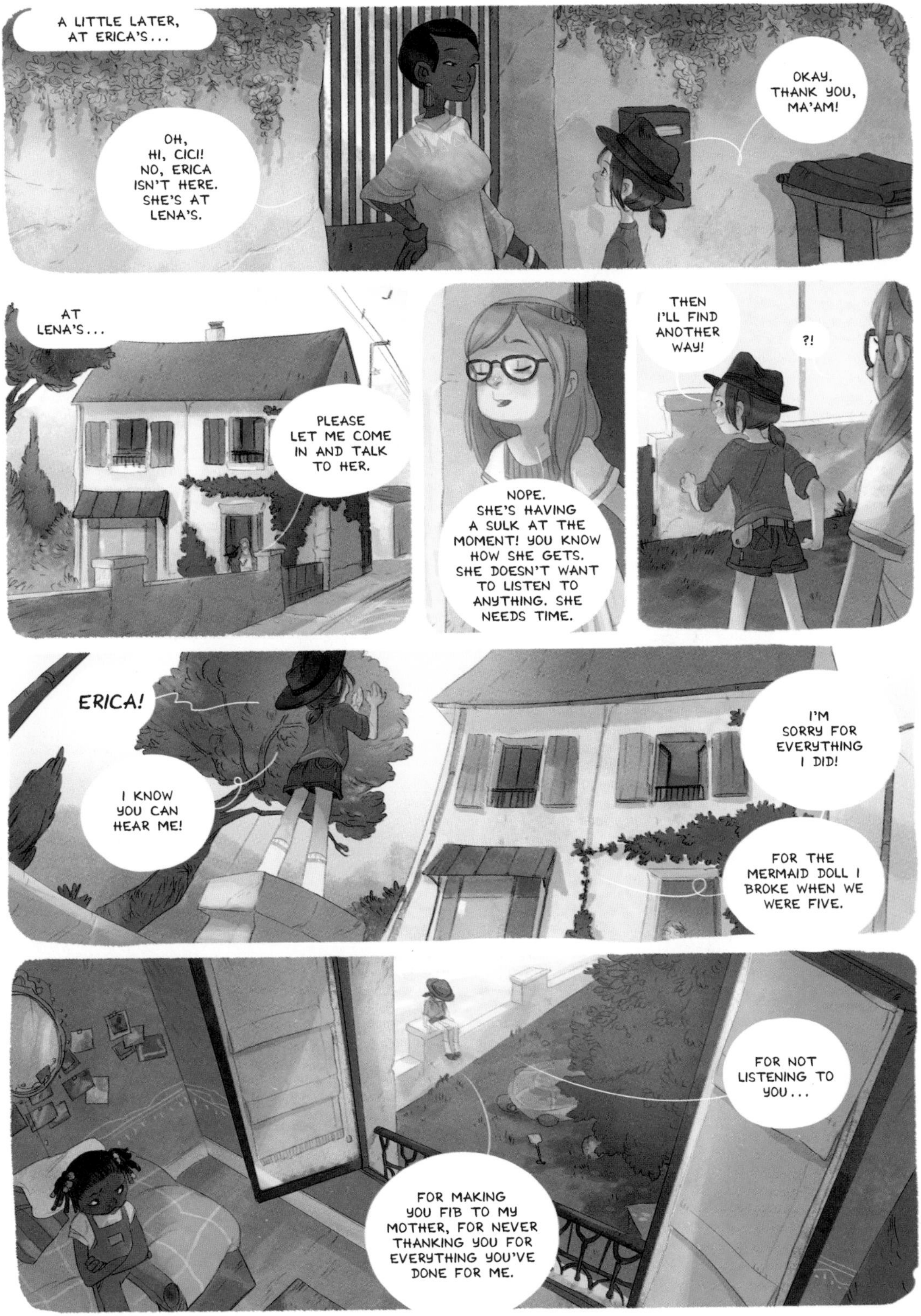
A LITTLE LATER, AT ERICA'S...
OH, HI, CICI! NO, ERICA ISN'T HERE. SHE'S AT LENA'S.
OKAY. THANK YOU, MA'AM!
AT LENA'S...
PLEASE LET ME COME IN AND TALK TO HER.
NOPE. SHE'S HAVING A SULK AT THE MOMENT! YOU KNOW HOW SHE GETS. SHE DOESN'T WANT TO LISTEN TO ANYTHING. SHE NEEDS TIME.
THEN I'LL FIND ANOTHER WAY!
?!
ERICA!
I KNOW YOU CAN HEAR ME!
I'M SORRY FOR EVERYTHING I DID!
FOR THE MERMAID DOLL I BROKE WHEN WE WERE FIVE.
FOR NOT LISTENING TO YOU...
FOR MAKING YOU FIB TO MY MOTHER, FOR NEVER THANKING YOU FOR EVERYTHING YOU'VE DONE FOR ME.

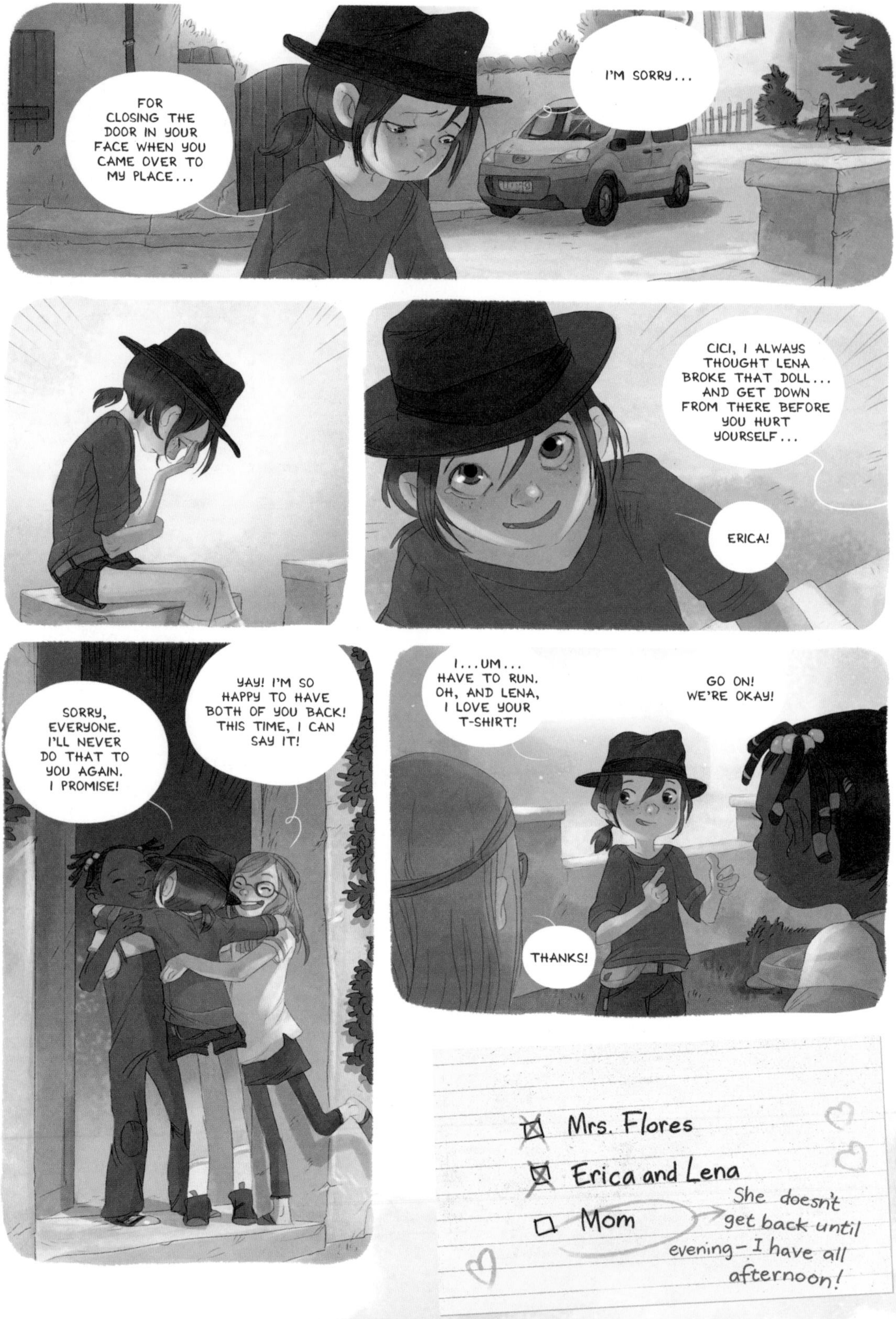
FOR CLOSING THE DOOR IN YOUR FACE WHEN YOU CAME OVER TO MY PLACE...
I'M SORRY...
CICI, I ALWAYS THOUGHT LENA BROKE THAT DOLL... AND GET DOWN FROM THERE BEFORE YOU HURT YOURSELF...
ERICA!
SORRY, EVERYONE. I'LL NEVER DO THAT TO YOU AGAIN. I PROMISE!
YAY! I'M SO HAPPY TO HAVE BOTH OF YOU BACK! THIS TIME, I CAN SAY IT!
I...UM... HAVE TO RUN. OH, AND LENA, I LOVE YOUR T-SHIRT!
GO ON! WE'RE OKAY!
THANKS!
Mrs. Flores
Erica and Lena
Mom
She doesn't get back until evening – I have all afternoon!

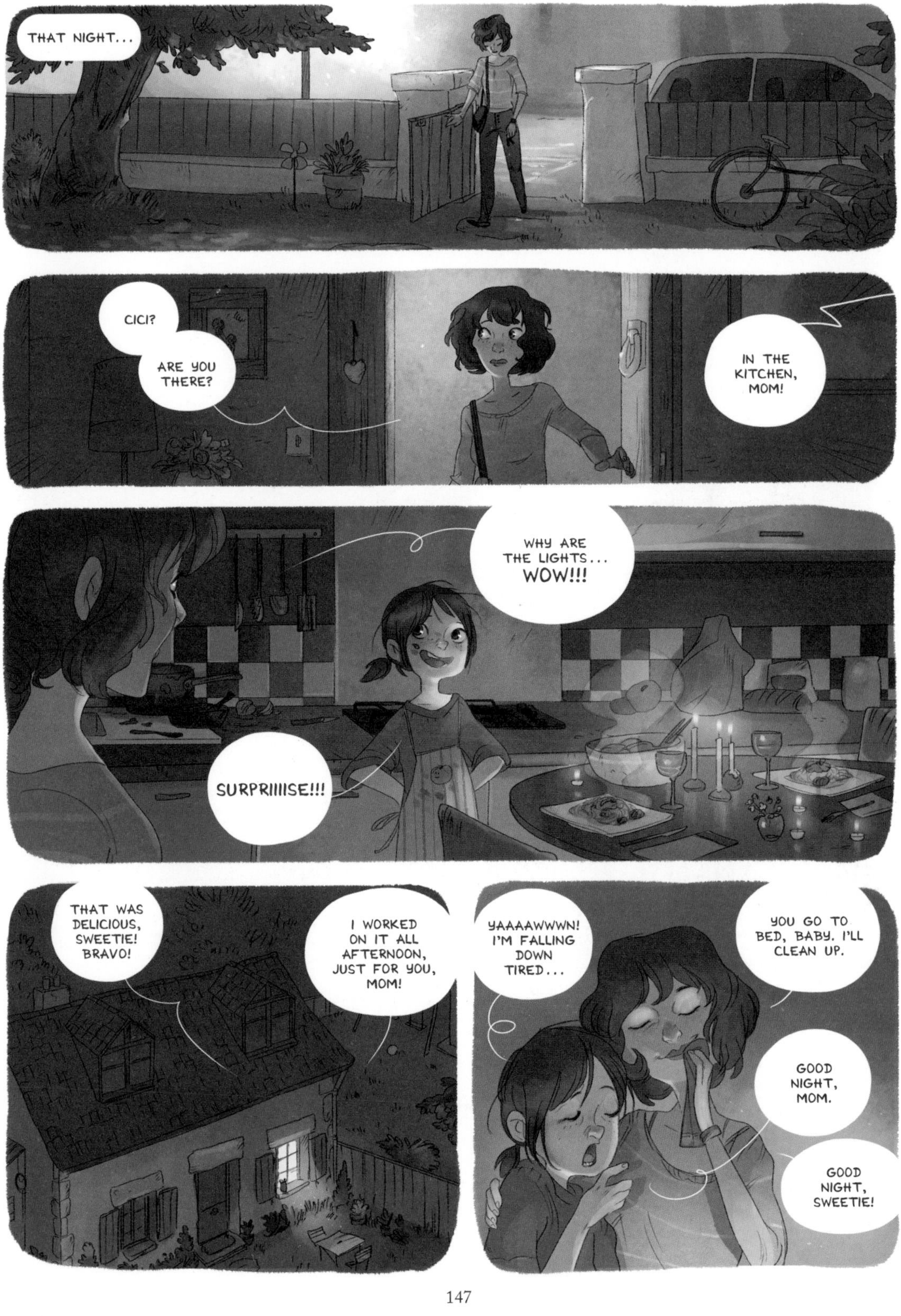
THAT NIGHT...
CICI?
ARE YOU THERE?
IN THE KITCHEN, MOM!
WHY ARE THE LIGHTS... WOW!!!
SURPRIIIISE!!!
THAT WAS DELICIOUS, SWEETIE! BRAVO!
I WORKED ON IT ALL AFTERNOON, JUST FOR YOU, MOM!
YAAAAWWWN! I'M FALLING DOWN TIRED...
YOU GO TO BED, BABY. I'LL CLEAN UP.
GOOD NIGHT, MOM.
GOOD NIGHT, SWEETIE!

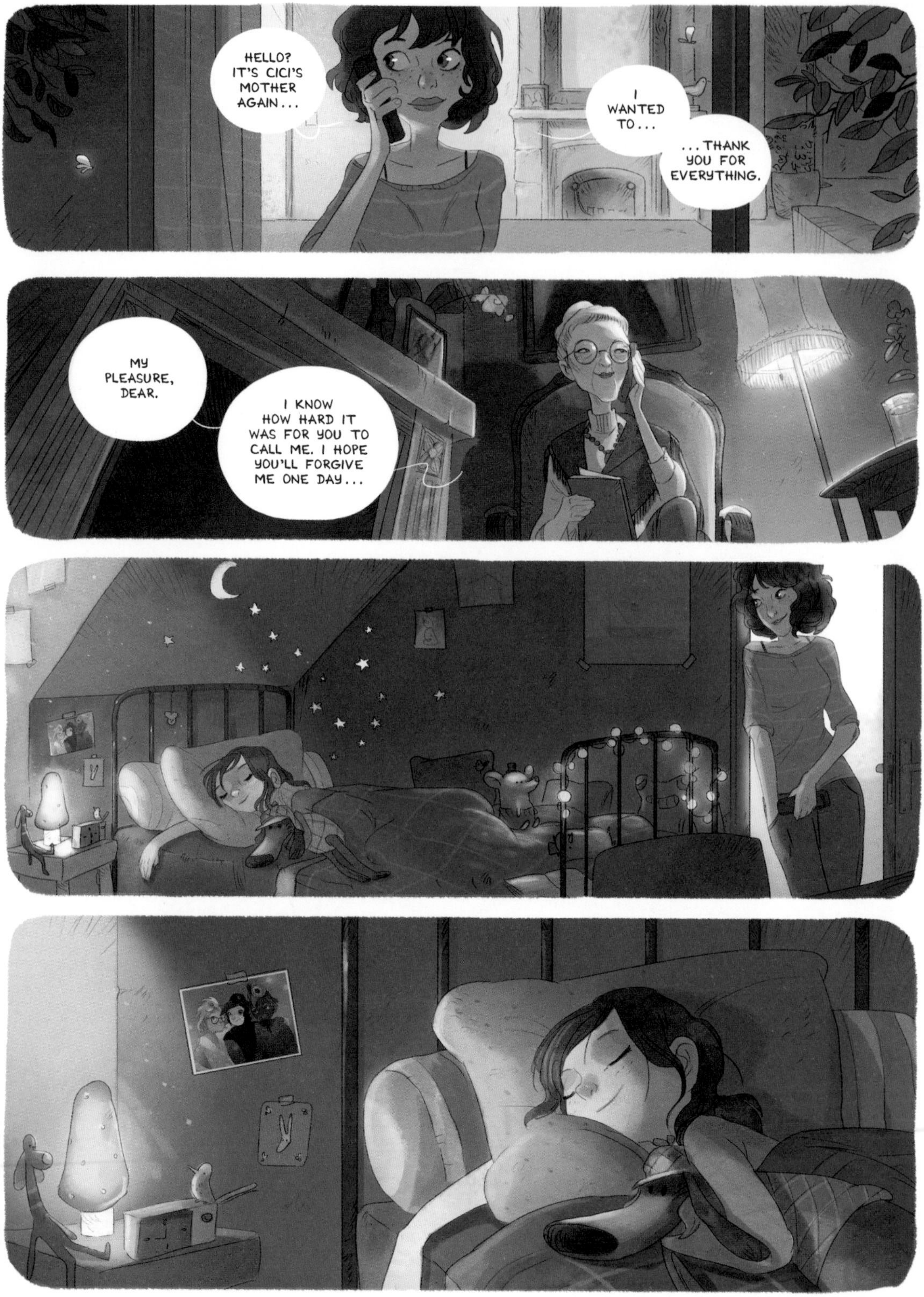
HELLO? IT'S CICI'S MOTHER AGAIN...
I WANTED TO...
...THANK YOU FOR EVERYTHING.
MY PLEASURE, DEAR.
I KNOW HOW HARD IT WAS FOR YOU TO CALL ME. I HOPE YOU'LL FORGIVE ME ONE DAY...

Ta-da! The new journal's filled up, and school is starting again. But this vacation will be carved into my memory forever.

Ms. Ronsin is volunteering a few days a week at the library. She does story time for the toddlers. I think she's gotten a taste for it again, and I'm really happy for her. I'm definitely going to attend some of her readings.

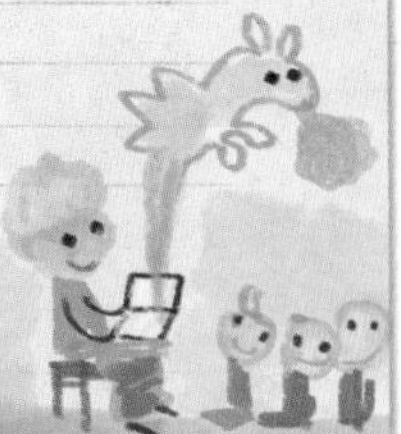

Lena picked out a million photos that she took of her nephew. Poor thing, he can still only see shapes and colors, but he's had lots of flashes in his eyes! But she hasn't forgotten her little brother, who wants her attention even more than before. He's not the littlest one in the family anymore!

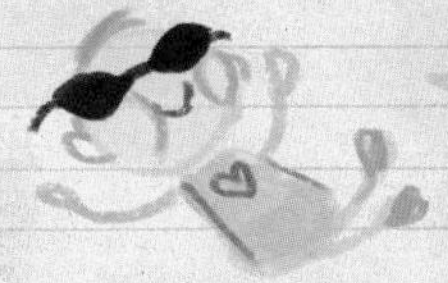

It turns out that everything's mixed up at Erica's house. Two of her brothers are moving out. They're grown-up, going to school, and getting jobs. They're reorganizing the house, and everything is different for her family. It's been making Erica extra cranky, but I think it's hardest on her mom. Erica and Lena and I will pitch in to make sure there's lots of noise in the house!

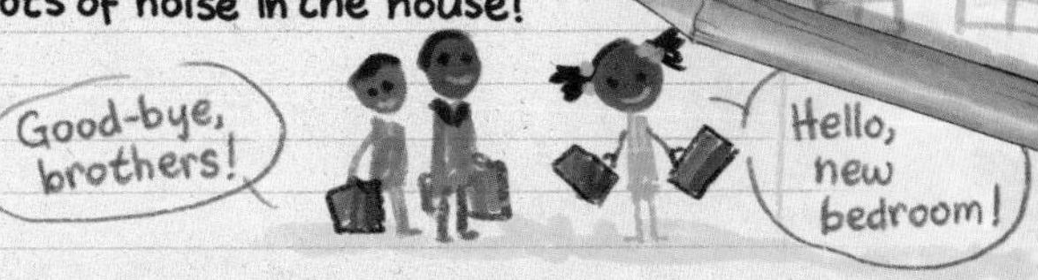
Good-bye, brothers!
Hello, new bedroom!

I went to see Mrs. Flores, to read her new book and to show her the character cards I found. That brought back memories. She was happy to hear I hadn't forgotten that game, but she was surprised that two of the character cards were still blank. So they're glued in at the end of my journal, to say: "I think it's time for these two characters to meet. I'm sure they'll have a lot of things to talk about..."

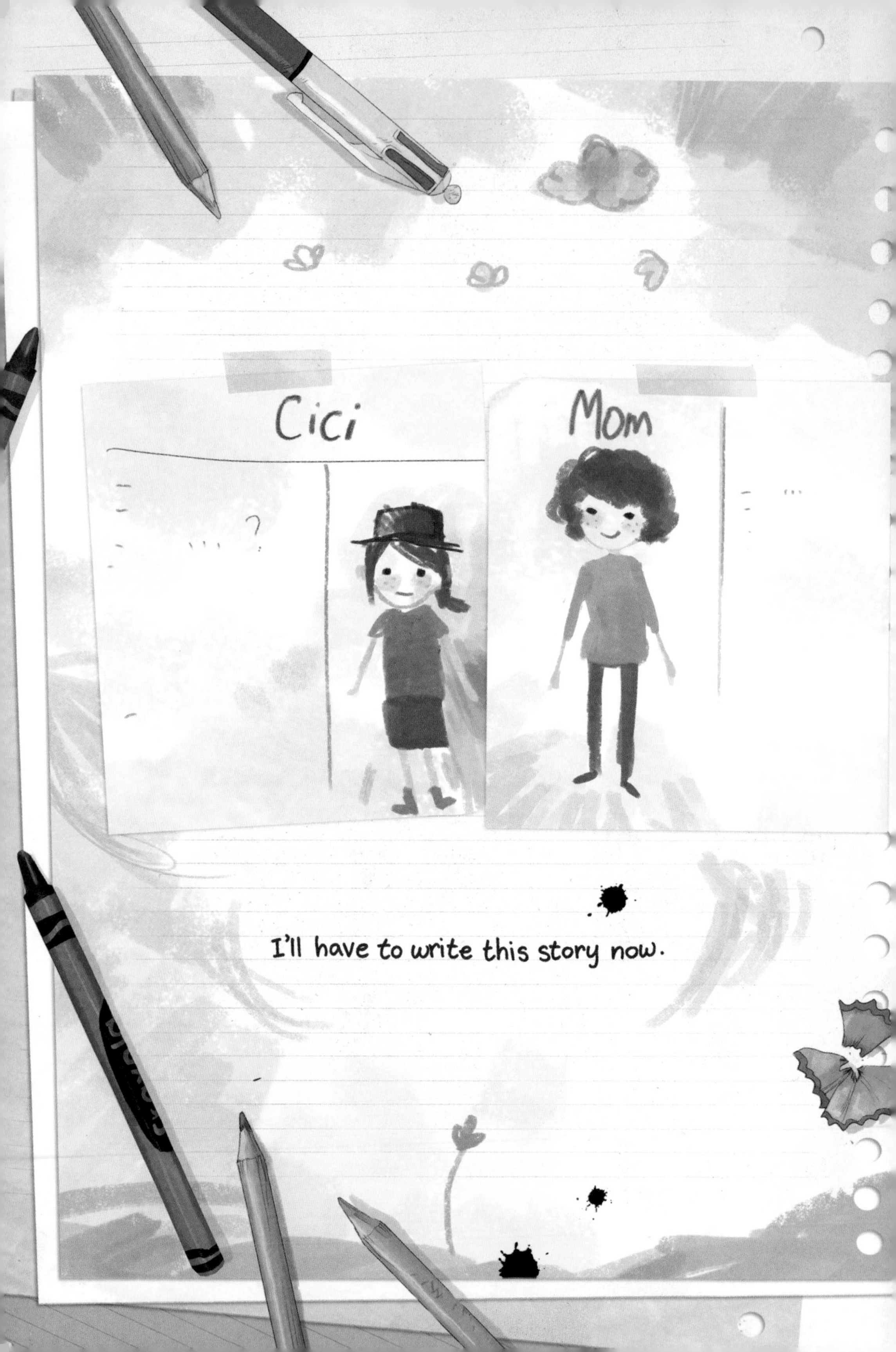
Cici
Mom

I'll have to write this story now.

It's not easy to write a letter to your best friends...
I'd love a little help!

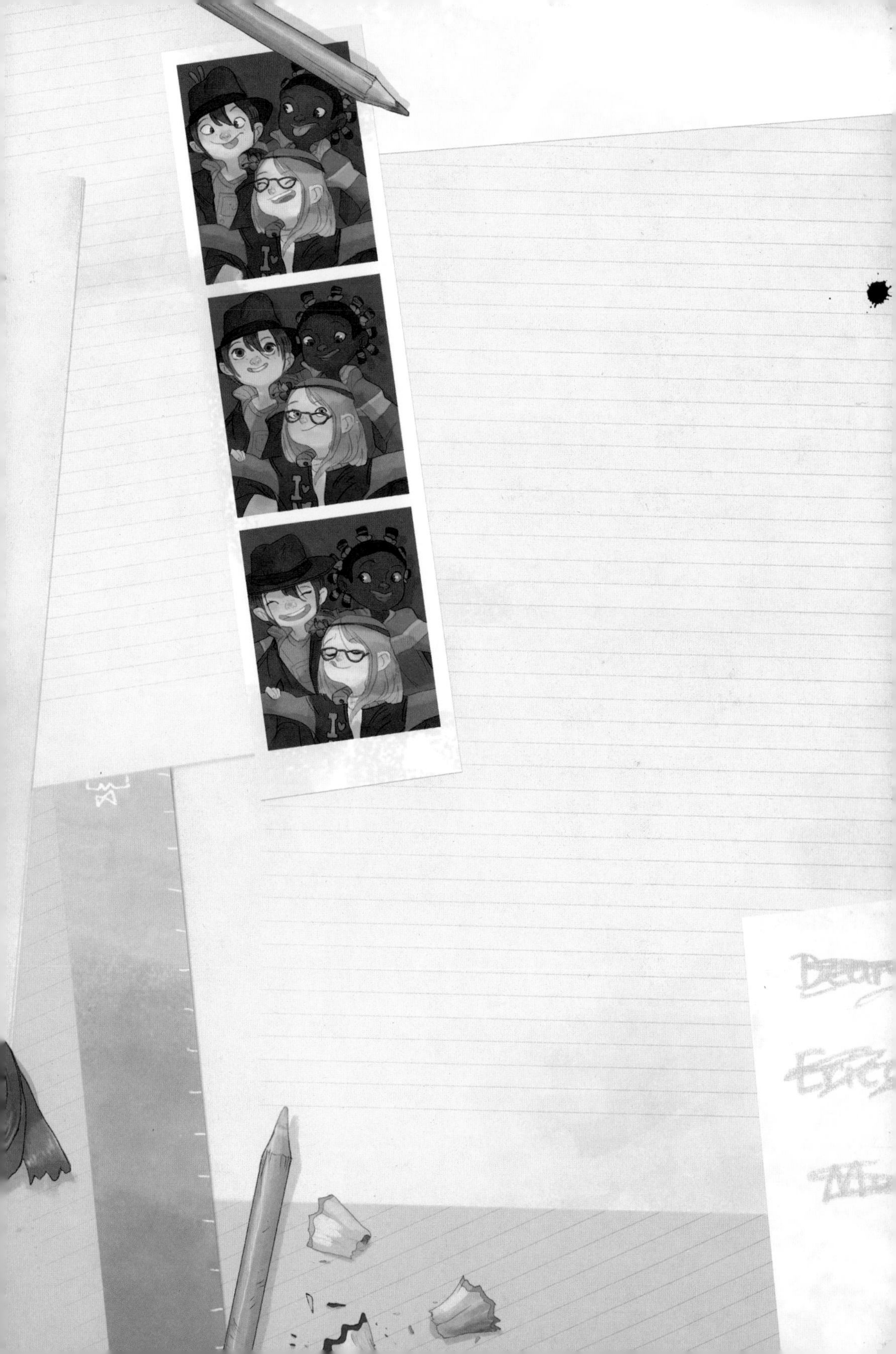

First Second

Published by First Second
First Second is an imprint of Roaring Brook Press,
a division of Holtzbrinck Publishing Holdings Limited Partnership
120 Broadway, New York, NY 10271
firstsecondbooks.com
mackids.com

Library of Congress Control Number: 2016961592

Our books may be purchased in bulk for promotional, educational, or business use. Please contact your local
bookseller or the Macmillan Corporate and Premium Sales Department at (800) 221-7945 ext. 5442 or by email at
MacmillanSpecialMarkets@macmillan.com.

Originally published in French in 2012 by Éditions Soleil, in the Metamorphose collection directed by Barbara Canepa
and Clotilde Vu, as *Les Carnets de Cerise, Tome 1: Le Zoo Pétrifiée* and in 2013 as *Carnets de Cerise, Tome 2: Le Livre d'Hector*
French edition © 2012, 2013 by Éditions Soleil/ Chamblain/ Neyret
First American edition, 2017
English translation by Carol Klio Burrell
Edited by Calista Brill
Cover design by Kirk Benshoff
Interior book design by Chris Dickey
Printed in China by RR Donnelley Asia Printing Solutions Ltd., Dongguan City, Guangdong Province

ISBN 978-1-62672-247-7 (paperback)
10 9 8 7 6 5 4 3 2 1

ISBN 978-1-62672-248-4 (hardcover)
10 9 8 7 6

Don't miss your next favorite book from First Second!
For the latest updates go to firstsecondnewsletter.com and sign up for our enewsletter.